Xantcha came to another door, the source of a fetid Phyrexian breeze. She hesitated. She had her armor, a boot knife and a handful of fuming coins, a passive defense and no offense worth mentioning. Wisdom said, this is foolish. Then she heard a sound behind her on the spiral stairs, and wisdom said, *hide!*

Three steps beyond the door, the corridor jogged sharply to the right and into utter darkness. Xantcha put one hand behind her back and finger-walked into the unknown. The loudest sound was the pulsing in her ears. She had a sense that she'd entered a larger chamber when the breeze died.

She had a sense, too, that she wasn't alone; she was right.

"Meatling."

Thirty-four hundred years, give or take a few decades, and Xantcha knew that voice instantly.

"Gix."

Artifacts Cycle

THE BROTHERS' WAR
Jeff Grubb

PLANESWALKER
Lynn Abby

TIME STREAMS
J. Robert King

BLOODLINES
Loren Coleman

Masquerade Cycle

MERCADIAN MASQUES
Francis Lebaron

NEMESIS
Paul B. Thompson

PROPHECY
Vance Moore

Invasion Cycle

THE THRAN (A PREQUEL)
J. Robert King

INVASION
J. Robert King

PLANESHIFT
J. Robert King

APOCALYPSE
J. Robert King

Anthologies

RATH AND STORM

THE COLORS OF MAGIC

THE MYTHS OF MAGIC

THE DRAGONS OF MAGIC

THE SECRETS OF MAGIC

PLANESWALKER

ARTIFACTS CYCLE • BOOK II

⚙ ⚙ ⚙ ⚙ ⚙ ⚙

Lynn Abbey

PLANESWALKER

©1998 Wizards of the Coast, Inc.

Distributed in the United States by Holtzbrinck Publishing. Distributed in Canada by Fenn Ltd.

Distributed to the hobby, toy, and comic trade in the United States and Canada by regional distributors.

Distributed worldwide by Wizards of the Coast, Inc. and regional distributors.

Cover art by r.k. post
First Printing: September 1998
Library of Congress Catalog Card Number: 97-062377

9 8 7 6 5 4 3 2

US ISBN: 0-7869-1182-4
620-08732-002-EN

U.S., CANADA,
ASIA, PACIFIC, & LATIN AMERICA
Wizards of the Coast, Inc.
P.O. Box 707
Renton, WA 98057-0707
+1-800-324-6496

EUROPEAN HEADQUARTERS
Wizards of the Coast, Belgium
P.B. 2031
2600 Berchem
Belgium
+32-70-23-32-77

Visit our web site at **www.wizards.com/magic**

With heartfelt thanks to the usual suspects;
you know who you are.
And special thanks to Peter Archer, Mary Kirchoff, Jess Lebow,
and Scott McGough, on the inside,
Jeff Grubb, Rob King, Jonathan Matson, and Brian Thomsen,
on the outside.

Digo, paciencia y barajar

Miguel de Cervantes

Don Quixote, chapter 23

MAGIC TIME LINE

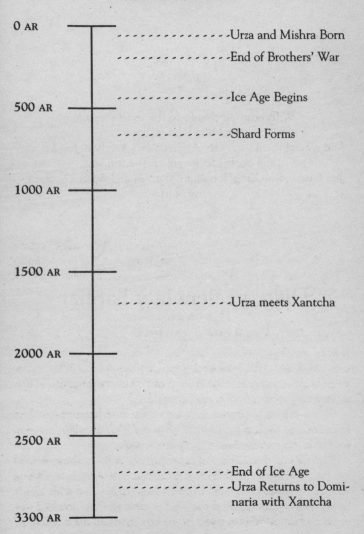

0 AR	Urza and Mishra Born
	End of Brothers' War
	Ice Age Begins
500 AR	Shard Forms
1000 AR	
1500 AR	
	Urza meets Xantcha
2000 AR	
2500 AR	
	End of Ice Age
	Urza Returns to Dominaria with Xantcha
3300 AR	

Chater 1

A man descended.

His journey had begun in the clouds, riding the winds in search of a place remembered but no longer known. He'd found the place, as he'd found it before, by following the ancient glyphs an ancient folk had carved into the land, glyphs that had endured millennia of neglect and the cataclysmic finale of the Brothers' War five years ago.

Much of Terisiare had vanished in the cataclysm, reduced to dust by fratricidal hatred. That dust still swirled overhead. Everyone coughed and harvests were sparse, but the sunsets and sunrises were magnificent luminous streaks of amber reaching across the sky, seeking escape from a ruined world.

The brothers in whose names the war had been fought had been reduced to curses: *By Urza's whim and Mishra's might, may you rot forever beneath the forests of sunken Argoth.*

Rumors said that Urza had caused the cataclysm when he used Lat Nam sorcery to fuel his final, most destructive, artifact. Others said that the cataclysm was Mishra's curse as he died with Urza's hands clasped around his throat. A few insisted that Urza had survived his crimes. Within a year of the cataclysm, all the rumors had

1

merged in an increasingly common curse: *If I met Urza on the road, I'd cripple him with my own two hands, as he and his brother crippled us, then I'd leave him for the rats and vultures as he left Mishra.*

Urza had survived. He'd heard the curse in its infinite variations. After nearly five years in self-chosen exile, the erstwhile Lord Protector of the Realm had spent another year walking amongst the folk of blasted Terisiare: the dregs of Yotia, the survivors of Argive, the tattered, the famished, the lame, the disheartened. No one had recognized him. Few had known him, even in the glory days. Urza had never been one to harangue his troops with rhetoric. He'd been an inventor, a scholar, an artificer such as the world had not seen since the Thran, and all he'd ever wanted was to study in peace. He'd had that peace once, near the beginning, and lost it, as he'd lost everything, to the man—the abomination—his brother had become.

A handful of Urza's students had survived the cataclysm. They'd denounced their master, and Urza hadn't troubled them with a visit. Urza's wife, Kayla Bin-Kroog had survived, too. She now dwelt in austere solitude with her grandson, writing an epic she called *The Antiquity Wars*. Urza hadn't visited her either. Kayla alone might have recognized him, and he had no words for her. As for her grandson, Jarsyl, black-haired and stocky, charming, amiable and quick-witted . . . Urza had glimpsed the young man just once, and that had been one time too many.

His descent continued.

Urza had not wanted to return to this place where the war had, in a very real sense, begun nearly fifty years earlier. He wasn't ashamed of what he'd done to end the war. Filling the bowl-shaped sylex with his memories had been an act of desperation; the sylex itself had been a sudden, suspect gift, and until that day he'd neither studied nor practiced sorcery. He hadn't known what using the sylex would do, but the war had had to be stopped. The *thing* his brother had become had to be stopped, else Terisiare's fate would have been worse.

Much worse.

No, Urza would not apologize, but he was not pleased by his own survival.

Urza should have died when the sylex emptied. He suspected that he had died, but the powerstones over which he and his brother had contended had preserved him. When Urza had awakened, the two Thran jewels had become his eyes. All Thran devices had been powered by such faceted stones, but his Mightstone and Mishra's Weakstone had been as different from ordinary powerstones as a candle to the sun.

Once rejoined within Urza's skull, the Thran jewels had restored him to his prime. He had no need for food or rest, though he continued to sleep because a man needed dreams even when he no longer needed rest. And his new eyes gave him vision that reached around dark corners into countless other worlds.

Urza believed that in time the battered realms of Terisiare would recover, even thrive, but he had not wished to watch that excruciatingly slow process, and so he'd walked away. For five years after the sylex-engendered cataclysm, Urza had explored the 'round-the-corner worlds his faceted eyes revealed.

In one such world he'd met another traveler, a woman named Meshuvel who'd confirmed what he'd already guessed: He'd lost his mortality the day he destroyed Mishra. The blast had slain him, and the Thran powerstones had brought him back to life because he was—had always been—a planeswalker, like Meshuvel herself.

Meshuvel explained to Urza that the worlds he'd visited were merely a handful of the infinite planes of the multiverse, any of which could be explored and exploited by an immortal planeswalker. She taught Urza to change his shape at will and to comprehend thought without the inconvenience of language or translation. But even among planeswalkers Urza was unique. For all her knowledge, Meshuvel couldn't see the multiverse as Urza saw it. Her eyes were an ordinary brown, and she'd never heard of the Thran. Meshuvel could tell Urza nothing about his eyes, except that she feared them; and feared them so much that she tried to snare him in a time pit. When that failed, she fled the plane where they'd been living.

Urza had thought about pursuing Meshuvel, more from curiosity than vengeance, but the plane she'd called Dominaria—the plane where he'd been born, the plane he'd nearly destroyed—kept its claws in his mind. Five years after the cataclysm, Dominaria had pulled him home.

Urza's descent ended on a wind-eroded plateau.

Clouds thickened, turned gray. Cold wind, sharp with ice and dust, plastered long strands of ash-blond hair across Urza's eyes. Winter had come earlier than Urza had expected, another unwelcome gift from the sylex. A few more days and the glyphs would have been buried until spring.

Four millennia ago, the Thran had transformed the plateau into a fortress, an isolated stronghold wherein they'd made their final stand. Presumably, it once had a name; perhaps the glyphs proclaimed it still, but no one had cracked that enigmatic code, and no one cracked it that afternoon. Urza's jeweled eyes gave him no insight into their makers' language. Fifty years ago, in his natural youth, Urza and his brother had named the great cavern within the plateau Koilos, and Koilos it remained.

Koilos had been ruins then. Now the ruins were themselves ruined, but not merely by the sylex. The brothers and their war had wrought this damage, plundering the hollow plateau for Thran secrets, Thran powerstones.

In truth, Urza had expected worse. Mishra had held this part of Terisiare for most of the war, and it it pleased Urza to believe that his brother's allies had been more destructive than his own allies had been. In a dusty corner of his heart, Urza knew that had he been able to ravage Koilos, even the shadows would have been stripped from the stones, but Mishra's minions had piled their rubble neatly, almost reverently. Their shredded tents still flapped in the rising wind. Looking closer, Urza realized they'd left suddenly and without their belongings, summoned, perhaps, to Argoth, as Urza had summoned his followers for that final battle five years earlier.

Urza paused on the carefully excavated path. He closed his eyes and shuddered as memories flooded his mind.

He and Mishra had fought from the beginning in a sunlit Argive nursery. How could they not, when he was the eldest by less than a year and Mishra was the brother everyone liked better?

4

Yet they'd been inseparable, so keenly aware of their differences that they'd come to rely on the other's strengths. Urza never learned the arts of friendship or affection because he'd had Mishra between him and the rest of the world.

And Mishra? What had he given Mishra? What had Mishra ever truly needed from him?

"How long?" Urza asked the wind in a whisper that was both rage and pain. "When did you first turn away from me?"

Urza reopened his eyes and resumed his trek. He left no footprints in the dust and snow. Nothing distracted him. The desiccated corpse propped against one tent pole wasn't worth a second glance, despite the metal plates rusting on its brow or the brass pincers replacing its left arm. Urza had seen what his brother had become; it wasn't surprising to him that Mishra's disciples were similarly grotesque.

His faceted eyes peered into darkness, seeing nothing.

Now, that was a surprise, and a disappointment. Urza had expected insight the way a child expects a present on New Year's morning. Disappoint Mishra and you'd have gotten a summer tantrum: loud, violent and quickly passed. Disappoint Urza and Urza got cold and quiet, like ice, until he'd thawed through the problem.

After four thousand years had they plundered the last Thran powerstone? Exposed the last artifact? Was there nothing left for his eyes to see?

A dull blue glint caught Urza's attention. He wrenched a palm-sized chunk of metal free from the rocks and rubble. Immediately it moved in his hand, curving back on itself. It was Thran, of course. An artificer of Urza's skill didn't need jeweled eyes to recognize that ancient craftsmanship. Only the Thran had known how to forge a sort of sentience between motes of metal.

But Urza saw the blue-gray metal more clearly than ever before. With time, the right tools, the right reagents, and a bit of luck, he might be able to decipher its secrets. Then, acting without deliberate thought, as he very rarely did, Urza drove his right thumbnail into the harder-than-steel surface. He thought of a groove, a very specific groove that matched his nail. When he lifted his thumb, the groove was in the metal and remained as he slowly counted to ten.

"I see it. Yes, I see it. So simple, once it can be seen."

Urza thought of Mishra, spoke to Mishra. No one else, not even his master-student, Tawnos, could have grasped the shifting symmetries his thoughts had imposed on the ancient metal.

"As if it had been your thumb," Urza conceded to the wind. Impulse, like friendship, had been Mishra's gift.

Urza could almost see him standing there, brash and brilliant and not a day over eighteen. An ice crystal died in Urza's lashes. He blinked and saw Mishra's face, slashed and tattered, hanging by flesh threads in the cogs of a glistening engine.

"Phyrexia!" he swore and hurled the shard into the storm.

It bounced twice, ringing like a bell, then vanished.

"Phyrexia!"

He'd learned that word five years ago, the very day of the cataclysm, when Tawnos had brought him the sylex. Tawnos had gotten the bowl from Ashnod and, for that reason alone, Urza would have cast it aside. But he'd fought Mishra once already that fateful day. For the first time, Urza had poured himself into his stone, the Mightstone, and if his brother had been a man, his brother would have died. But Mishra had no longer been a man; he hadn't died, and Urza needed whatever help fate offered.

In those chaotic moments, as their massed war engines turned on one another, there'd been no time to ask questions or consider implications. Urza believed Mishra had transformed himself into a living artifact, and that abominable act had justified the sylex. It was after, when there was no one left to ask, that the questions had surfaced.

Tawnos had mentioned a demon—a creature from Phyrexia—that had ambushed him and Ashnod. Never mind the circumstances that had brought Urza's only friend and his brother's treacherous lieutenant together on the Argoth battlefield. Tawnos and Ashnod had been lovers once, and love, other than an abstract devotion to inquiry or knowledge, meant very little to Urza. Ask instead, what was a Phyrexian doing in Argoth? Why had it usurped all the artifacts, his and Mishra's? Then, ask a final question, what had he or Mishra to do with Phyrexia that its demon had become their common enemy?

Some exotic force—some Phyrexian force—had conspired against them. Wandering, utterly alone across the ruins of Terisiare, there had seemed no other explanation.

In the end, in the forests of Argoth, only the sylex had prevented a Phyrexian victory.

Within a year of the cataclysm, Urza had tracked the sylex back through Ashnod's hands to a woman named Loran, whom he'd met in his youth. Though Loran had studied the Thran with him and Mishra under the tutelage of the archeologist Tocasia, she'd turned away from artifice and become a scholar in the ivory towers of Teresia City, a witness of the land-based power the sylex had unleashed.

The residents of Terisia City had sacrificed half their number to keep the bowl out of his or Mishra's hands. Half hadn't been enough. Loran had lost the sylex and the use of her right arm to Ashnod's infamous inquiries, but the rest of her had survived. Urza had approached Loran warily, disguised as a woman who'd lost her husband and both her sons in what he bitterly described as "the brothers' cursed folly."

Loran was a competent sage and a better person than Urza hoped to be, but she was no match for his jeweled eyes. As she'd heated water on a charcoal brazier, he'd stolen her memories.

The sylex, of course, was gone, consumed by the forces it had released, and Loran's memory of it was imperfect. That was Ashnod's handiwork. The torturer had taken no chances with her many victims. Loran recalled a copper bowl incised with Thran glyphs Urza had forgotten until he saw them again in Loran's memory. Some of the glyphs were sharp enough that he'd recognize them if he saw them again, but most were blurred.

He could have sharpened those memories, his eyes had that power, but Urza knew better than to make the suggestion. Loran would sooner die than help him, so they drank tea, watched a brilliant sunset, then went their separate ways.

Urza had learned enough. The Thran, the vanished race who'd inspired his every artifact, had made the sylex, and the sylex had saved Dominaria from Phyrexia. Although mysteries remained, there was symmetry, and Urza had hoped that symmetry would be enough to halt his dreams. He'd resumed his planeswalking. It had taken five years—Urza was nothing if not a determined, even stubborn, man—before he'd admitted to himself that his hopes were futile. A year ago, he'd returned to Dominaria, to Argoth itself, which he'd avoided since the war ended. He'd found the ruined hilltop where he'd unleashed the land's fury and pain. He'd found Tawnos's coffin.

Tawnos had spent five years sealed in stasis within the coffin. For him, it was as if the war hadn't yet ended and the cataclysm hadn't yet happened. The crisp images on the surface of Tawnos's awakened mind had been battlefield chaos, Ashnod's lurid hair, and the demon from Phyrexia.

" . . . if this thing is here . . ." Tawnos had recalled his erstwhile lover's, onetime torturer's words.

Ashnod's statement had implied, at least to Tawnos and from him to Urza, that she'd recognized the demon: a man-tall construction of strutted metal and writhing, segmented wires. Urza recognized it too—or parts of it. He'd seen similar wires uncoiled from his brother's flensed body, attaching Mishra to a dragon engine.

"This one is mine. . . ." More of Ashnod's sultry words lying fresh in Tawnos's mind.

Urza's only friend had wanted to argue with Ashnod, to die beside her. She wouldn't grant him that dubious honor. Instead she'd given him the sylex.

Tawnos's memories had clouded quickly as he'd absorbed the vastly changed landscape. While Tawnos had sorted his thoughts, Urza had looked westward, to the battlefield, now replaced by ocean.

Ashnod, as treacherous as she'd been beautiful, had betrayed everyone who fell into her power. Tawnos's back still bore the scars. Mishra had judged her so unreliable that he'd banished her, only to let her back for that last battle.

Or had he?

Had Mishra known Ashnod carried the sylex? Had the traitor himself been betrayed? Which was the puppet and which the master? Why had the demon stalked Ashnod across the battle-field? What was her connection to Phyrexia?

Urza had wrestled with such questions until Tawnos had asked his own. "Your brother?"

"Dead," Urza had replied as his questions converged on a single answer. "Long before I found him."

The words had satisfied Tawnos, who began at once to talk of other things, of rebuilding the land and restoring its vitality. Tawnos—dear friend Tawnos—had always been an optimist. Urza left him standing by the coffin, certain that they'd never meet again.

For Urza, the realization that he hadn't slain Mishra with the sylex had given him a sense of peace that had lasted almost a month, until a new, stronger wave of guilt had engulfed it. He was the elder brother, charged from birth with his younger sibling's care.

He'd failed.

When Mishra had need of an elder brother's help, that elder brother had been elsewhere. He'd failed Mishra and all of Dominaria. His brother had died alone, betrayed by Ashnod, transformed by a Phyrexian demon into a hideous amalgam of flesh and artifice.

Urza had returned to Argoth and Tawnos as the snows had begun, almost exactly one year ago. He'd denied himself sleep or shelter, kneeling in the snow, waiting for Mishra, or death; it hadn't mattered which. But Meshuvel had been correct: Urza had transcended death, and he'd found, to his enduring dismay, that he lacked the will for suicide. A late spring had freed him from his icy prison. He'd stood up, no weaker than he'd been when he'd knelt down.

The left side of his face had been raw where bitter tears had leaked from the Weakstone, but it had healed quickly, within a few moments. He'd walked away with no marks from his season-long penance.

In his youth, when his wife's realm of Yotia had still sparkled in the sun, a man named Rusko had told Urza that a man had many souls throughout his life, and that after death each soul was judged according to its deeds. Urza had outlived his souls. The sylex had blasted him out of judgment's hands. No penance would ever dull the ache of failure.

All that remained was vengeance.

Urza had spent the spring and summer assuring himself that Ashnod had not survived. He'd skipped through the planes, returning after each unreal stride to Dominaria in search of a woman who was too proud to change her appearance or her ways. When fall had arrived without a trace of her, Urza had turned his attention to Koilos, where he and Mishra had come to manhood pursuing relics of the Thran.

His immortal memory, he'd discovered, was fallible. Planeswalking couldn't easily take him to a place he didn't quite remember. In the end, searching for places that had faded from memory, he'd been reduced to surveying vast tracts of barren land from the air, as he and his brother had surveyed in their youth.

He'd have given his eyes and immortality to have back just one of those days he and Mishra had spent in Tocasia's camp.

Sleety wind shot up his sleeves. Urza wasn't immune to the discomforts of cold, merely to their effects. He thought of a felted cloak; it spread downward from his shoulders, thickening as he added a fur lining, then gloves, fleece-lined boots and a soft-brimmed hat that didn't move in the wind. He continued along the path Mishra's workers had left. As before, and despite his new boots, Urza left no footprints.

With each stride, pain ratcheted through his skull. This close to the place where they'd been joined for millennia, his jeweled eyes recalled another purpose. Hoping to dull the pain, Urza turned his back to the cavern. His throbbing eyes saw the snow-etched ruins as shadows painted on gauzy cloth; nothing like the too-real visions he'd suffered the day he'd acquired the Mightstone. Then, the shadows expanded and began to move. They were different from his earlier visions, but not entirely. Where before he had watched white-robed men constructing black-metal spiders, now he saw a battlefield swarming with artifacts, another Argoth but without the demonic disorder.

At first Urza couldn't distinguish the two forces, as an observer might not have been able to distinguish his army from Mishra's. But as he looked, the lines of battle became clear. One side had its back against the cavern and was fighting for the freedom of the plains beyond the hollow plateau. The other formed an arc as it emerged from the narrow defile that was the only way to those plains, meaning to crush its enemy against the cliffs. Blinding flashes and plumes of dense smoke erupted everywhere, testaments to the desperation with which both sides fought.

Urza strained his eyes. One force had to be the Thran, but which? And what power opposed them?

During the moments that Urza pondered, the defile force scored a victory. A swarm of their smaller artifacts stormed the behemoth that anchored the enemy's center. It went down in a whirlwind of flame that drove both forces back. The defile force regrouped quicker and took a bite from the cavern force's precious ground. A mid-guard cadre from the defile brought rays of white light to bear on the behemoth's smoldering hulk. Soot rained and the hulk glowed red.

Caught up in the vision, Urza began to count, "One . . . two . . ."

The hulk's flanks burst, and all-too-familiar segmented wires uncoiled. Tipped with scythes, the wires slashed through the defile cadre, winnowing it by half, but too late. The Thran powerstones completed the destruction of the Phyrexian behemoth.

Millennia after the battle's dust had settled, Urza clenched his jaws together in a grimly satisfied smile. Ebb and flow were obvious, now that he'd identified the Thran and their goal: to drive the Phyrexians into the cavern where, presumably, they could be annihilated.

It was, as the Argoth battle between him and Mishra had been, a final battle. Retreat was not an option for the Phyrexians, and the Thran offered no quarter. Urza lost interest in his own time as the shadow war continued. The Phyrexians assembled behind their last behemoth, charged the Thran line on its right flank and very nearly broke through. But the Thran held nothing back. As ants might swarm a fallen bit of fruit, they converged upon the Phyrexian bulge.

Again, it became impossible to distinguish one force from the other.

Urza counted to one hundred and ten, by which time there was no movement within the shadows. When he reached one-hundred and twelve, the shadows brightened to desert-noon brilliance. Reflexively, Urza shielded his eyes. When he lowered his hand, there was only snow. The pain in his skull was gone. He entered the cavern thoroughly sobered by what he had seen.

His eyes had recorded the final battle between the Thran and the Phyrexians. It seemed reasonable to assume that recording Phyrexian defeats was part of their function. From that assumption, it was easy to conclude that the Thran had intended the recording stones as a warning to all those who came after.

Urza had had a vision when he first touched what became his Mightstone. He recalled it as he entered the cavern. Despite his best efforts, the images were dreamlike yet they strengthened his newborn conviction: The Thran had vanished because they'd sacrificed themselves to defeat the Phyrexians.

Within the cavern, Urza gazed up at the rough ceiling. "We didn't know," he explained to any lingering Thran ghosts. "We didn't know your language. . . . We didn't guess what we couldn't understand."

He knew now. The artifact in which they'd found the single stone—the artifact that he and Mishra had destroyed utterly—had been the Thran legacy to Dominaria and the means through which they'd locked their enemy out of Dominaria.

"We didn't know. . . ."

When the stone had split into its opposing parts, the lock had been sprung and the Phyrexians had returned. The enemy had known better than to approach him, the bearer of the Mightstone, but they had—they must have—suborned, corrupted, and destroyed Mishra, who'd had only the Weakstone for protection. The stones were not, after all, truly equal. Might was naturally dominant over weakness, as Urza, the elder brother, should have been dominant over the younger.

But blinded by an elder brother's prejudice and—admit it!—jealousy, Urza had done nothing.

No, he'd done worse than nothing. He'd blamed Mishra, gone to war against Mishra, and undone the Thran sacrifice.

Guilt was a throbbing presence within Urza's skull. He closed his eyes and clapped his hands over his ears, but that only made everything worse.

Why hadn't he and Mishra talked?

Through their childhood and youth, he and Mishra had fought constantly and bitterly before repairing the damage with conversation. Then, after the stones had entered into their lives, they hadn't even tried.

Then insight and memory came to Urza. There had been one time, about forty-five years ago in what could be called the war's morning hours. They'd come together on the banks of the river Kor, where it tumbled out of the Kher mountains. The Yotian warlord, his wife's father, had come to parley with the qadir of the Fallaji. Urza hadn't seen or heard from his brother for years. He'd believed that Mishra was dead, and had been stunned to see him advising the qadir.

He, Urza—gods and ghosts take note—had suggested that they should talk, and Mishra had agreed. As Urza recalled the conversation, Mishra had been reluctant, but that was his brother's style, petulant and sulky whenever his confidence was shaken, as surely it would have been shaken with the Weakstone burden slung around his neck, and the Phyrexians eating at his conscience.

Surely Mishra would have confessed everything, if the warlord hadn't taken it into his head to assassinate the qadir as the parley began.

Urza recalled the carnage, the look on Mishra's face.

Back in Koilos, in the first snows of the fifth winter after the cataclysm, Urza staggered and eased himself to the ground. For a few moments the guilt was gone, replaced by a cold fury that reached across time to the warlord's neck. *It was YOUR fault! Your fault!* But the warlord shrugged him away. *He was your brother, not mine.*

If the Phyrexians had not taken Mishra's soul before that day on the banks of the Kor, they had surely had no difficulty afterward.

The blame, then, was Urza's, and there was nothing he could do to ease his conscience, except, as always, in vengeance against the Phyrexians. For once, Urza was in the right place. Koilos was where the Thran had stopped the Phyrexians once and where his own ignorance had given the enemy a second chance. If there was a way to Phyrexia, it was somewhere within Koilos.

Urza left tracks in the dust as he searched for a sign.

The sun had set. Koilos was tomb dark. Urza's eyes made their own light, revealing a path, less dusty than any other, that led deep into the cavern's heart. He found a chamber ringed with burnt-out powerstones. Two sooty lines were etched on the sandstone floor. Marks that might have been Thran glyphs showed faintly between the lines. Urza used his eyes to scour the spot, but the glyphs—if glyphs they were—remained illegible.

He cursed and knelt before the lines. This was the place, it had to be the very place, where the Phyrexians had entered Dominaria. There could be no doubt. Looking straight ahead, past the lines and the exhausted powerstones, there was a crystal reliquary atop a waist-high pyramid. The reliquary was broken and empty, but the pyramid presented an exquisitely painted scene to Urza's glowing eyes: the demon he had seen in Tawnos's memory.

Circling the pyramid, Urza saw two other demonic portraits and a picture of the chamber itself with a black disk rising between the etched lines. He tore the chamber apart, looking for the disk—either its substance or the switch that awakened it—and not for the first time in his life, Urza failed.

When Urza walked among the multiverse of planes, he began his journey wherever he happened to be and ended it with an act of will or memory. He realized that the Phyrexians had used another way, but it lay beyond his comprehension, as did the plane from which they'd sprung. The multiverse was vast beyond measure and filled with uncountable planes. With no trail or memory to guide him, Urza was a sailor on a becalmed sea, beneath a clouded sky. He had no notion which way to turn.

"I am immortal. I will wander the planes until I find their home, however long and hard the journey, and I will destroy them as they destroyed my brother."

Chapter 2

"*Nearly five years after Argoth was destroyed and the war between the brothers had ended, Tawnos came to my courtyard. He told me much that I had never known, much that I have written here. He told me that my husband was dead and that he'd died with my name on his lips. It is a pretty thought, and I would like to believe it, but I am not certain that Urza died and, if he did, he would have died calling to Mishra, not me.*"

Xantcha lightly brushed her fingertips over brittle vellum before closing her tooled-leather cover of *The Antiquity Wars*. It was the oldest among her copies of Kayla Bin-Kroog's epic history, and the scribe who'd copied and translated it nearly twelve hundred years earlier claimed he'd had Kayla's original manuscript in front of him. Xantcha had her doubts, if not about the scribe's honesty, then about his gullibility.

Not that either mattered. For a tale that had no heroes and a very bitter ending, *The Antiquity Wars* had been very carefully preserved for nearly three and a half millennia. It was as if everyone still heeded the warning in Kayla's opening lines: "Let this, the testament of Kayla Bin-Kroog, the last of Yotia, serve as memory, so that our mistakes will never be repeated."

15

Xantcha stared beyond the table. On a good night, the window would have been open and she could have lost her thoughts in the stars twinkling above the isolated cottage, but Dominaria hadn't completely recovered from the unnatural ice age had that followed the Brothers' War. Clear nights were rare on Xantcha's side of the Ohran Ridge, where the cottage was tucked into a crease of land, where the grass ended and the naked mountains began. Mostly the weather was cool or cold, damp or wet, or something in between. Tonight, gusty winds were propelling needle-sharp sleet against the shutters.

The room had cooled while she read. Her breath was mist and, with a shivering sigh, Xantcha made her way to the peat bin. There were no trees near the cottage. Her meager garden sprouted a new crop of stones every spring, and the crumbling clods that remained after she'd picked out the stones were better suited for the brazier than for nurturing grains and vegetables. She'd had to scrounge distant forests for her table and shutters. Even now that the cottage was finished, she spent much of her time scrounging the remains of Terisiare for food and rumors.

Shredding a double handful of peat into the brazier beneath the table, Xantcha found, as she often did, the squishy remains of an acorn: a reminder of just how much Urza and his brother had changed their world with their war. When whole, the acorn would have been as large as her fist, and the tree that had dropped it would have had a trunk as broad as the cottage was wide. She crumbed the acorn with the rest and stirred the coals until palpable heat radiated from the iron bucket.

Xantcha forgot the table and hit her head hard as she stood. She sat a moment, rubbing her scalp and muttering curses, until she remembered the candlestick. With a louder curse, she scrabbled to her feet. Waste not, want not, it hadn't toppled. Her book was safe.

She returned to her stool and opened to a random page. Kayla's portrait stared back at her: dusky, sloe-eyed, and seductive. Xantcha owned four illustrated copies of *The Antiquity Wars*. Each one depicted Kayla differently. Her favorite showed Urza's wife as a tall, graceful and voluptuous woman with long blond hair, but

Xantcha knew none of the portraits were accurate. Staring at the shutters, she tried to imagine the face of the woman who had known, and perhaps loved, Urza the Artificer while he was a mortal man.

One thing was certain, Xantcha didn't resemble Kayla Bin-Kroog. There were no extravagant curves in Xantcha's candlelit silhouette. She was short, not tall, and her hair was a very drab brown, which she cropped raggedly around a face that was more angular than attractive. Xantcha could, and usually did, pass herself off as a slight youth awaiting his full growth and first beard. Still, Xantcha thought, she and Kayla would have been friends. Life had forced many of the same hard lessons down their throats.

Kayla, however, wasn't the epic character who intrigued Xantcha most. That honor went to Urza's brother, Mishra. Three of Xantcha's illustrated volumes depicted Mishra as a whip-lean man with hard eyes. The fourth portrayed him as soft and lazy, like an overfed cat. Neither type matched Kayla's word picture. To Kayla, Mishra had been tall and powerful, with straight black hair worn wild and full. Mishra's smile, his sister-by-law had written, was warm and bright as the sun on Midsummer's day, and his eyes sparkled with wit—when they weren't flashing full of suspicion.

Not all *The Antiquity Wars* in Xantcha's collection included Kayla's almost indiscreet portrait of her husband's brother. Some scribes had openly seized an opportunity to take a moral stance, not only against Mishra, but other men of more recent vintage—as if a princess of ancient Yotia could have foreseen the vices of the Samisar of Evean or Ninkin the Bold! One scribe, writing in the year 2657 admitted that she'd omitted the Mishra section entirely, because it was inconsistent with Kayla's loyalty to her husband and, therefore, a likely fraud—and absolutely inappropriate for the education of the young prince, who was expected to learn his statecraft from her copy of the epic.

Xantcha wondered if that priggish scribe had seen the picture on her table. The Kayla Bin-Kroog of Xantcha's oldest copy wore a veil, three pearl ropes, and very little else. Few men could have resisted her allure. One of them had been her husband. Beyond doubt, Urza had neglected his wife. No woman had ever intrigued

Urza half as much as his artifacts. How many evenings might Kayla have gone to bed railing at the fates who'd sent the chaste Urza to her father's palace, rather than his charming brother?

Urza had never questioned his wife's fidelity. At least, Xantcha had never heard him raise that question. Then again, the man who lived and worked on the other side of the wall at Xantcha's back had never mentioned his son or grandson, either.

With a sigh and a yawn, Xantcha stowed the book in a chest that had no lock. They didn't need locks in the absolute middle of nowhere. Urza had the power to protect them from anything. The heavy lid served only to discourage the mice that would otherwise have devoured the vellum.

"Xantcha!" Urza's voice came through the wall; as she contemplated the precious library she'd accumulated over the last two and a half centuries

She leapt instantly to her feet. The lid fell with a bang. Urza had shut himself in his workroom while she'd been off scrounging, and she'd known better than to interrupt him when she'd returned. Sixteen days had passed since she'd heard his voice.

Their cottage had two rooms: hers, which had begun as a shed around an outdoor bread oven, and Urza's, which consumed everything under the original roof, a dugout cellar and a storage alcove—Urza traveled light but settled deep. Each room had a door to a common porch whose thatched roof provided some protection from the weather.

Wind-driven sleet pelted her as Xantcha darted down the porch. She shoved the door shut behind her, then, when Urza hadn't noticed the sound or draft, took his measure before approaching him.

Urza the great artificer sat at a high table on a stool identical to her own. By candlelight, Xantcha saw that he was dressed in the same tattered blue tunic he'd been wearing when she'd last seen him. His ash-blond hair spewed from the thong meant to confine it at the nape of his neck. It wasn't dirty—not the way her hair would have gotten foul if it went that long between washings. Urza didn't sweat or purge himself in any of the usual ways. He didn't breathe when he was rapt in his studies and never needed to eat, though he spoke in the mortal way and ate heartily sometimes, if she'd cooked something that appealed to him. He drank water, never caring where it came from or how long it had stood stagnant, but the slops bucket beside his door never needed emptying. Urza didn't get tired either, which was a more serious problem because he remained man enough to need sleep and dreams for the purging of his thoughts.

There were times when Xantcha believed that all Urza's thoughts needed purging; this was one of them.

Mountains rose from Urza's table. All too familiar mountains shaped from clay and crockery. Quicksilver streams overflowed the corners. As melting sleet trickled down her spine, Xantcha wondered if she could retreat and pretend she hadn't heard. She judged that she could have, but didn't.

"I've come," she announced in the language only she and Urza spoke, rooted in ancient Argivian with a leavening of Yotian and tidbits from a thousand other worlds.

Urza spun quickly on the stool, too quickly for her eyes to follow his movement. Indeed, he hadn't moved, he'd reshaped himself. It was never a good sign when Urza forgot his body. Meeting his eyes confirmed Xantcha's suspicions. They glowed with their own facet-rainbow light.

"You summoned me?"

He blinked and his eyes turned mortal, dark irises within white sclera. But that was the illusion; the other was real.

"Yes, yes! Come see, Xantcha. Look at what has been revealed."

She'd sooner have entered the ninth sphere of Phyrexia. Well, perhaps not the ninth sphere, but the seventh, certainly.

"Come. Come! It's not like the last time."

At least he remembered the last time when the mountains had exploded.

Xantcha crossed the narrows of the oblong room until she stood at arm's length from the table. Contrary to his assurance, it was like the last time, exactly like the last time and the time before that. He'd recreated the plain of the river Kor below the Kher Ridge and covered the plain with gnats. She kept her distance.

"I'm no judge, Urza, but to my poor eyes it looks . . . similar."

"You must get closer." He offered her a glass lens set in an ivory ring.

It might have been seething poison for the enthusiasm with which she took it. He offered her his stool. When that didn't entice her, he grabbed her arm and pulled. Xantcha clambered onto the stool and bent over the table with the glass between her and the gnats.

Despite reluctance and reservation, Xantcha let out an awed sigh; as an artificer, Urza was incomparable. What had appeared to be gnats were, as she had known they would be, tiny automata, each perfectly formed and unique. In addition to men and women, there were horses, their tails swishing in imperceptible breezes, harnessed to minuscule carts. She didn't doubt that each was surrounded by a cloud of flies that the glass could not resolve. Nothing on the table was alive. Urza was adamant that his artifacts remained within what he called "the supreme principle of the Thran." Artifacts were engines in service to life, never life itself, and never, ever, sentient.

Bright tents pimpled Urza's table landscape. There were even miniature reproductions of the artifacts he and his brother had brought to the place and time that Kayla had called "The Dawn of Fire."

Xantcha focused her attention on the automata. She found Mishra's shiny dragon engine, a ground-bound bumblebee among the gnats and Urza's delicate ornithopters. When Xantcha saw an ornithopter spread its wings and rise above the table, she was confident that she'd seen the reason for Urza's summons. Miniaturizing those early artifacts had been a greater challenge than creating the swarms of tiny men and women who milled around them.

"You've got them flying!"

Urza pushed her aside. His eyes required no polished glass assistance; he could most likely see the horseflies, the fleas, and the worms as well. Xantcha noticed that he was frowning.

"It's very good," she assured him, fearing that her initial response hadn't been sincere enough.

"No, no! You were looking in the wrong place, Xantcha. Look

here—" He positioned her hands above the largest tent. "What do you see now?"

"Blue cloth," she replied, knowing full well that within the tent, automata representing Urza and the major characters of Kayla's epic were midway through a scene she'd observed many times before. At first she'd been curious to see how Urza's script might differ from his wife's, but not any more.

Urza muttered something—it was probably just as well that Xantcha didn't quite catch it—and the blue cloth became a shadow through which the automata could be clearly seen. There was Urza, accurate down to the same blue shirt and threadbare trousers. His master-student, Tawnos, stood nearby, a half head taller than the rest. The Kroog warlord, the Fallaji qadir and a score of others, all moving as if they were alive and oblivious to the huge face hovering overhead. Mishra was in the shadowed tent too, but Urza was peculiar about his younger brother's gnat. While all the others had mortal features, Mishra was never more than wisps of metal at the qadir's side.

"Is it the second morning?" Xantcha asked. Urza was breathing down her neck, expecting conversation. She hoped he didn't intend to show her the assassinations. Suffering, even of automata, repelled her.

Another grumble from Urza, then, "Look for Ashnod!"

According to *The Antiquity Wars*, auburn-haired Ashnod wasn't at "The Dawn of Fire," but Urza always made a gnat in her image. He'd put it on the table, where it did nothing except get in the way of the others. To appease her hovering companion, Xantcha moved the glass slightly and found a red-capped dot in the shadow of another tent.

"You moved her there?"

"Never!" Urza roared. His eyes flashed, and the air within the cottage was very still. "I refine my understanding, I do not ever control them. Each time, I create new opportunities for the truth to emerge. Time, Xantcha, time is always the key. I call them motes of time—the tiny motes of time that replay the past, long after events have passed beyond memory. The more I refine my automata, the more of those motes I can attract. Truth attracts truth as time attracts time Xantcha, and the more motes of time I can attract, the more truth I learn about that day. And finally—finally—the truth clings to Ashnod, and she has been drawn out of her lies and deception. Watch as she reveals what I have always suspected!"

Urza snapped his fingers, and, equally fascinated and repelled, Xantcha watched Ashnod's gnat skulk from shadow to shadow until it was outside the parley tent, very near Mishra's back. Then the Ashnod-gnat knelt and manipulated something—the glass wasn't strong enough to unmask the object—and a tiny spark leaped from her hands. Mishra's wisps and filings glowed green.

The illusion of movement and free will was so seamless that Xantcha asked, "What did she do?" rather than *What did it do?*

"What do you think? Were your eyes open? Were you paying attention? Must I move them backward and do it again?" Urza replied.

Urza was less tolerant of free will in his companions. Xantcha marveled that Tawnos never left him, but perhaps, Urza had been less acid-tongued in his mortal days. "I don't know." She set the lens on a shelf slung beneath the table. "It has never been my place to think. Tell me, and I will stand enlightened."

Their eyes locked, and for a moment Xantcha stared into the ancient jewels through which Urza interpreted his life. Urza could reduce her to memory, but he blinked first.

"Proof. Proof at last. Ashnod's the one. I always suspected she was the first the Phyrexians suborned." Urza seized the lens and thrust it back into Xantcha's hands. "Now, look at the dragon engine. The Yotians have not begun to move against the qadir, but see . . . see? It has already awakened. Ashnod cast her spark upon my brother, and he called to it. It would only respond to him, you know."

Xantcha didn't peer through the lens. A blanket of light had fallen across the worktable, a hungry blanket that rose into Urza's glowing eyes rather than fell from them.

"Mishra! Mishra!" Urza whispered. "If only you could see me, hear me. I was not there for you then, but I am here for you now.

Cast your heart upward and I will open your eyes to the treachery around you!"

Xantcha didn't doubt Urza's ability, only his sanity, especially when he started talking to his gnat-brother. Urza believed that each moment of time contained every other moment, and that it was possible to not only recreate the past but to reach into it and affect it. Someday, as sure as the sun rose in the east, Urza would talk to the gnats on his table. He'd tell Mishra all the secrets of his heart, and Mishra would answer him. None of it would be the truth, but all of it would be real.

Xantcha dreaded that coming day. She set the lens down again and tried to distract Urza with a question. "So, your side—?"

Urza focused his eyes uncanny light on her face. "Not my side! I was not a party to anything that happened that day! I was ignorant of everything. They lied to me and deceived me. They knew I would never consent to their treachery. I would have stopped them. I would have warned my brother!"

Xantcha beat a tactical retreat. "Of course. But even if you had, the end would not have changed," she said in her most soothing tone. "If you've got it right, now, then the warlord's schemes were irrelevant. Through Ashnod, the Phyrexians had their own treachery—against the qadir and the warlord, against you and Mishra. None of you were meant to survive."

"Yes," Urza said on a caught breath. "Yes! Exactly! Neither the qadir nor the warlord were supposed to survive. It was a plot to capture me as they had already captured my brother. Thus he was willing, but also reluctant, to talk to me!" He turned back to the table. "I understand, Brother. I forgive! Be strong, Mishra—I will find a way to save you as I saved myself."

Xantcha repressed a shudder. There were inconsistencies among her copies of *The Antiquity Wars* but none on the scale Urza proposed. "Was your brother transformed then, or still flesh?"

Urza backed away from the table. His eyes were clouded, almost normal in appearance. "I will learn that next time, or the time after that. They have suborned him. See how he responds to Ashnod. She was their first creature. They must have known that if we talked privately, I would have sensed the change in him. . . .

I would have set him free. If there was still any part of him left that could have been freed. Or, I would have turned my wrath on them from that point forward. They knew I could not be suborned, Xantcha, because I possessed the Mightstone. The stones have equal power, Xantcha, but the power is different. The Weakstone is weakness, the Mightstone is strength, and the Phyrexians never dared my strength. Ah, the evil that day, Xantcha. If they had not driven us apart, there would have been no war, except against them. . . . You see that, Xantcha. You see that, don't you? My brother and I together would have driven them back to Koilos. They knew our power before we'd begun to guess it."

They and them. They and them. With Urza, it all came back to they and them: Phyrexians. Xantcha knew the Phyrexians for the enemies they were. She'd never argue that they hadn't played a pivotal role in Urza's wars. Perhaps they had suborned Mishra and Ashnod, too. But while Urza played with gnats on a tabletop, another wave of Phyrexians, real Phyrexians, had washed up on Dominaria's shores.

"It makes no difference," she protested. "Mishra's been dead for more than three thousand years! It hardly matters whether you failed him, or Ashnod destroyed him, or the Phyrexians suborned him, or whether it happened before "The Dawn of Fire" or after. Urza, you're creating a past that doesn't matter—"

"Doesn't matter! They took my brother from me, and made of him my greatest enemy. It matters, Xantcha. It will always matter more than anything else. I must learn what they did and how and when they did it." He breathed, a slow sigh. "I could have stopped them. I must not fail again." He held his hands above the table. Xantcha didn't need the lens to know that Mishra's gnat shone bright. "I won't, Mishra. I will never fail again. I have learned caution. I have learned deception. I will not be tricked, not even by you!"

Before Urza had brought Xantcha to Dominaria, she'd been more sympathetic to his guilt-driven obsessions. Now she said, "Not even you can change the past," and didn't care if he struck her down for impudence. "Are you going to stand by and play with toys while the Phyrexians steal your birthplace from you? They're back. I smelled them in Baszerat and Morvern. The Baszerati and the Morvernish are at war with each other, just as the Yotians and the Fallaji were, and the Phyrexians are on both sides. Sound familiar?"

Her neck ached from staring up at him and braving his gemstone stare. Xantcha had no arcane power to draw upon, but nose to nose, she was more stubborn. "Why are we here," she asked in the breathless silence, "if you're not going to take a stand against the Phyrexians? We could play games anywhere."

Urza retreated. He moistened his lips and made other merely mortal gestures. "Not games, Xantcha. I can afford no more mistakes. Dominaria has not forgotten or forgiven what happened last time. I must tread lightly. So many died, so much was destroyed, and all because I was blind and deaf. I did not see that my brother was not himself, that he was surrounded by enemies. I didn't hear his pleas for help."

"He never pled for help! That's why you didn't hear, and you can never know why he didn't, because you can never talk to him again. No matter what happens in this room, on that table, you can't bring him back! Now you've got Ashnod outside the tent. You've made her into another Phyrexian, pulling Mishra's strings. The Yotians were planning an ambush, the Phyrexians were planning an ambush, and you weren't wise to either plot. Waste not, want not, Urza—if the Phyrexians had Ashnod before "The Dawn of Fire," how did she manage, thirty years later, to send Tawnos to you with the sylex? Or was that part of a plot, too? A compleat Phyrexian doesn't have a conscience, Urza. A compleat Phyrexian doesn't feel remorse; it can't. Mishra never did."

"He couldn't. He'd been suborned," Urza shouted. "Usurped. Corrupted. Destroyed! He was no longer a man when I faced him in Argoth. They'd taken his will, flensed his flesh and stretched it over an abomination!"

"But they didn't take Ashnod's will? She sent the sylex. Was her will stronger than your brother's?"

Xantcha played a dangerous game herself and played it to the brink. Urza had frozen, no blinking or breathing, as if he'd become an artifact himself. Xantcha pressed her advantage.

"Was Ashnod stronger than you too? Strong enough to double-deal the Phyrexians and save Dominaria in the only way she could?"

"No," Urza whispered.

"No? No what, Urza? Once you start treating born men and women as Phyrexians, where do you stop? Ashnod skulking outside your tent before the Dawn of Fire, Ashnod sending Tawnos with the sylex? One time she's a Phyrexian puppet, the next she's not? Are you sure you know which is which? Or, maybe, she was the puppet both times, and what would that make you? You used the sylex."

Urza folded a fist. "Stop," he warned.

"The Phyrexians spent three thousand years trying to slay you, before they gave up. I think they gave up because they'd found a better way. Leave you alone on a mountainside playing with toys!"

He'd have been a powerful man if muscle and bone had been his strength's only source, but Urza had the power of the Thran through his eyes, and the power of a sorcerer standing on his native ground. His arm began to move. As long as she could see it moving, Xantcha believed she was safe.

The fist touched her hair and stopped. Xantcha held her breath. He'd never come that close, never actually touched her before. They couldn't go on like this, not if there was any hope for Dominaria.

"Urza?" she whispered when, at last, her lungs demanded air. "Urza, can you hear me? Do you see me?" Xantcha touched his arm. "Urza . . . Urza, talk to me."

He trembled and grabbed her shoulder for balance. He didn't know his strength; pain left her gasping. Her eyes were shut when he made the transition, temporary even at the best of times, back into the here and now. Something happened to Urza when he cast his power over the worktable, not the truth, but definitely real and definitely getting worse.

"Xantcha!" his hand sprang away from her as though she were made from red-hot metal. "Xantcha, what is this?" He stared at the crockery mountains as if he'd never seen them before—

though Xantcha had seen even that reaction more times than she cared to remember.

"You summoned me, Urza," she said flatly. "You had something new to show me."

"But this?" He gestured at his mountain-and-gnat covered table. "Where did this come from. Not—not me. Not again?"

She nodded.

"I was sitting on the porch as the sun set. It was quiet, peaceful. I thought of—I thought of the past, Xantcha, and it began again." He shrank within himself. "You weren't here."

"I was after food. You were inside when I returned. Urza, you've got to let go of the past. It's not . . . It's not healthy. Even for you, this is not healthy."

They stared at each other. This had happened so many times before that there was no longer a need for conversation. Even the moment when Urza swept everything off his table was entirely predictable.

"It's started, Urza, truly started. This time there's a war south of here," Xantcha said, while dust still rose from the crumbled mountains, quicksilver slithered across the packed dirt floor, and gnats by the hundreds scrambled for shelter.

"Phyrexians?"

"I kenned them on both sides. *Sleepers*. They take orders, they don't give them, but it's a Dominarian war with Phyrexian interference on both side."

He took the details directly from her mind: a painless process when she cooperated.

"Baszerat and Morvern. I do not know these names."

"They aren't mighty kingdoms with glorious histories. They're little more than walled cities, a few villages and, to keep the grudge going, a handful of gold mines in the hills between them; something for the Phyrexians to exploit. They're getting bolder. Baszerat and Morvern aren't the only places I've scented glistening oil in the wind, but this is the first war."

"You haven't interfered?"

His voice harshened and his eyes flashed. With Urza, madness was never more than a moment away.

"You said I mustn't, and I obey. You should look for yourself. Now is the time—"

"Perhaps. I dare not move too soon. The land remembers; there can be no mistakes. I must have cause. I must be very careful, Xantcha. If I reveal myself too soon, I foresee disaster. We must weigh our choices carefully."

Retorts swirled in Xantcha's mind. It was never truly *we* with Urza, but she'd made her choices long ago. "No one will suspect, even if you used your true name and shape. There've been a score of doom-saying Urzas on the road this year alone. You've become the stuff of legends. No one would believe you're you."

A rare smile lit up her companion's face. "That bad still?"

"Worse. But please, go to Baszerat and Morvern. A quarrel has become a war. So it began with the Fallaji and the Yotians. Who knows, there might be brothers. . . . You've been up here too long, Urza."

Urza reached into her mind again, gathering landmarks and languages, which she willingly surrendered. Then, in a blink's time, she was back into her own proper consciousness. Urza faded into the between-worlds, which was, among other things, the fastest way to travel across the surface of a single world.

"Good luck," she wished him, then knelt down.

Crashing crockery had crushed a good many of Urza's gnats. Quicksilver had dissolved uncounted others. Yet many swirled around in confusion on the floor. Xantcha labored until midnight, gathering them into a box no deeper than her finger, but far too steep for any of them to climb. When the dirt was motionless, she took the box into the alcove where Urza stored his raw materials.

The shelves were neat. Every casket and flask was clearly labeled, albeit in a language Xantcha couldn't read. She didn't need to read labels. The flask she wanted had a unique lambent glow. It was pure phloton, distilled from fire, starlight and mana, a recipe Urza had found on the world were he'd found Xantcha.

"Waste not, want not," she whispered over the seething box.

The gnats blazed like fireflies as they fell through the phloton, and then were gone.

Xantcha resealed the flask and replaced it on the shelf, exactly as she'd found it, before returning to her own room. She had a plan of her own, which she'd promised herself she'd implement when the time was right. That time had come when Urza touched her hair.

If Urza couldn't see the present Phyrexian threat because he was obsessed with the past . . . If he couldn't care about the folk of Baszerat or Morvern because he still cared too much about what had happened to Mishra, then Xantcha figured she had to bring the past and Mishra to Urza. She had it all worked out in her mind, as much as she ever worked anything out: find a young man who resembled Kayla's word picture, teach him the answers to Urza's guilty questions, then troll her trumped-up Mishra past Urza's eyes.

A new Mishra wouldn't cure his madness. Nothing could do that, not while those powerstone eyes were lodged in Urza's skull, but if a false Mishra could convince Urza to walk away from his worktable, that would be enough.

Chapter 3

Morning came to the Ohran Ridge, and found Xantcha sitting in the bottom of a transparent sphere as it drifted above spring-time mountain meadows. The sphere was as big around as Xantcha was tall and had been a gift from Urza. Or more accurately, the artifact that produced it had been Urza's gift. He'd devised the cyst to preserve her as she followed him from world to world. A deliberate yawn and a mnemonic rhyme drew a protective oil out of the cyst. Depending on the rhyme, the oil expanded into the buoyant sphere or ripened into a tough, flexible armor.

Urza had taught Xantcha the rhyme for the armor. The sphere was the result of Xantcha's curiosity and improvisations. Urza complained that she'd transformed his Thran-inspired artifact into a Phyrexian abomination. The complaint, though sincere, had always perplexed Xantcha. The Thran, as Urza described them, believed that sentience and artifice must always be separate. Xantcha's cyst wasn't remotely sentient, and she supposed she could have dug it out of her stomach, but it had become part of her, no different than her arms . . . or Urza's faceted eyes. Besides, if she hadn't discovered how to make her sphere, Urza would have had to provide her with food, clothing, and all the other things a flesh and blood person required, because Xantcha, though she was almost as old as Urza, was indisputably flesh and blood.

And just as indisputably Phyrexian.

Xantcha willed the sphere higher, seeking the swift wind-streams well above the mountains. She had a long journey planned, and needed strong winds if she wanted to finish it before Urza returned from the south. The sphere rose until the landscape resembled Urza's tabletop, and the sphere began to tumble.

Tumbling never bothered Xantcha. With or without the cyst, she had a strong stomach and an unshakable sense of direction. But tumbling wasted time and energy. Xantcha raised her arms level with her shoulders, one straight out in front of her, the other extended to the side; the tumbling stopped. Then she pointed both extended arms in the direction she wished to travel and rotated her hands so they were both palms up. She thought of rigging and sails, a firm hand on the tiller board, and the sphere began to move against the wind.

It was slow going at first, but before the sun had risen another two hand spans, Xantcha was scudding north faster than any horse could run. Xantcha couldn't explain how the sphere stayed aloft. It wasn't sorcery; she had no talent for calling upon the land. Urza swore it wasn't anything to do with him or his artifacts and refused to discuss the matter. Xantcha thought it was no different than running. The whys and wherefores weren't important so long as she found what she was looking for and got home safe.

But questions lurked where Xantcha's memories began. They crept forward once the sphere was moving smartly, and there was nothing to do but think and remember.

* * * * *

The beginning was liquid, thick and warm as blood, dark and safe. After the liquid came light and cold, emptiness and hard edges, a dim chamber in the Fane of Flesh, the first place she'd known, a soot-stained monolith of Phyrexia's Fourth Sphere. Her beginning wasn't birth, not as Urza had been born from his mother's body. There were no mothers or fathers in the decanting chamber only metal and leather priests tending stone-gouged vats.

The vat-priests of the Fane of Flesh were of no great status. Though compleat, their appliances were mere hooks and paddles and their senses were no better than the flesh they'd been decanted with. They took orders from above. In Phyrexia there was always above—or within, deeper and deeper through the eight spheres to the center where dwelt the Ineffable. He whose name was known but never spoken, lest he awaken from his blessed sleep.

Obey, the vat-priests said unnecessarily as she'd shivered and discovered her limbs. A small, warm stone fell from her hands. The vat-priests had said it was her heart and took it from her. There was a place, they said—in Phyrexia everything had a place, without place there was nothing—where hearts were kept. Her mistakes would be written on her heart, and if she made too many mistakes, the Ineffable who dwelt at Phyrexia's core would make her a part of his dreams, and that would be the end of her.

Obey and learn. Pay attention. Make no mistakes. Now, follow.

Later, when Xantcha had crossed more planes and visited more worlds than she could easily recount, she'd realize that there was no other place like Phyrexia. In no other world were full-grown newts, like her, decanted beside a sludge-vat. Only Phyrexian newts remembered the first opening of their eyes. Only Phyrexian newts remembered, and understood, the first words—threats— they heard. In her beginning, there was only the Fane of Flesh, and she obeyed without question, writhing across the stone floor because she hadn't the strength to walk.

Xantcha's bones hardened quickly. She learned to tend herself and perform such tasks as were suited to newts. When she had mastered those lessons, the vat-priests led her to the teacher-priests, who instructed the newts as they were transformed from useless flesh into compleat Phyrexians. The teacher-priests with their recording eyes and stinging-switch arms told her that she was Xantcha.

Xantcha wasn't a name, not as she later came to understood names. When Urza had asked, she had explained that Xantcha was the place where she stood when newts were assembled for instruction, the place where she received her food, and the box where she slept at night.

If days or nights had played a part in her early life.

Phyrexia was a world without sun, moon, or stars. Deep in the Fane of Flesh, priests called out the march of time: when she learned, when she ate, when she slept; there was no time for rest, no place for companionship. When she was returned to her box for sleeping, Xantcha dreamed of sunlight, grass and wind. She might have thought it strange that her mind held images of a place so clearly not Phyrexia, if she'd thought at all.

Even now, more than three millennia after her first awakenings, Xantcha didn't know if she'd been the only newt who'd dreamed of a green, sunlit world, or if the Ineffable had commanded the same dreams and longings for every newt that learned beside her.

You are newts, and newts you will remain, the teacher-priests had taught her. *You are destined to sleep in another place and prepare the way for those who will follow. Listen and obey.*

There were many other newts in the Fane of Flesh, organized into cadres and marched together through their educations. All newts began the same way, with meat and bones and blood-filled veins, then—according to their place in the Ineffable's design—tender-priests excised their flesh and reshaped their bodies with tough amalgams of metal and oil, until they were compleated. After each reshaping, the priests sent the excised flesh and blood to the renderers; eventually it was returned it to the vats. When the newt was fully reshaped, the tenders immersed it in the glistening oil; a Phyrexian's first time in the great fountain outside the Fane of Flesh. When it emerged, the newt was compleat and took its destined place in the Ineffable's grand plan for Phyrexia.

Xantcha remembered standing in her place on a Fane balcony, as fully reshaped newts were carried to the fountain. She remembered the cacophony as newly compleated Phyrexians emerged into the glare and glow of the Fourth Sphere furnaces. To the extent that any newt felt hope, it hoped for a good compleation, a privileged place. The knowledge that she would be forever bound in a newt's body was greater pain than any punishment the priests ever lashed across her back.

Hatred had no place in Phyrexia. Contempt replaced hatred and looked down on the special newts, whose destiny was to sleep in another place. Xantcha looked forward to the moments when she was alone in her box with her dreams.

Once she went to sleep, dreamed her dreams, as she'd always done, and awoke beneath the bald, gray sky of the First Sphere. There were different teacher-priests tending her cadre. The new priests were larger than those in the Fane of Flesh. More metal than leather, they had four feet and four arms. Their feet were clawed, and each of their arms ended in a different metal weapons. They were supposed to protect the newts from the dangers of the First Sphere. Newts had never dwelt on the First Sphere, but the four-armed teachers were not honored by their new responsibilities. They obeyed their orders without enthusiasm, until one of the newts made a mistake.

Newts you are, and newts you shall remain forever, they'd recite as they dealt out punishment with one hand after the other. *You are destined to sleep on another world. Now learn the ways of another world. Listen and obey.*

Xantcha wondered what would have happened if she'd failed to listen or obey. At the time, the notion simply didn't occur to her. Life on the First Sphere was hard enough without disobedience. The newts were taught farming, in preparation for the day when their destiny would be fulfilled, but the slippery dirt of the First Sphere resisted their every effort. The plows, sickles, hoes, and pitchforks that they were commanded to use left their muscles aching. The whiplike, razor-grass—the only plant they could grow—slashed them bloody, and the harsh light blistered their skin mercilessly.

Xantcha remembered another newt, Gi'anzha; whose place was near hers in the cadre. Gi'anzha had used a grass sheaf to hack off its arm, then shoved a pitchfork shaft into the bloody socket. Gi'anzha was meat by the time they found it, but Xantcha and the other newts understood why it had done what it had.

Newts were small and fragile compared to everything else that dwelt on the First Sphere. Their uncompleated bodies suffered injuries rather than malfunctions. They could not be repaired but were left to heal as best they could, which sometimes wasn't good enough. Failed newts—meat newts—were whisked back to the Fourth Sphere for rendering. Waste not, want not, nothing in Phyrexia was completely without use, though meat was reviled by the compleat, who'd transcended their flesh and were sustained by glistening oil.

As her cadre was reduced to meat, Xantcha's place within it changed. Another newt should have been Xantcha, she should have become G'xi'kzi or Kra'tzin, but too much time had passed since the vat-priests had organized the cadre. The patterns of their minds were as fixed as those of their soft, battered bodies. Xantcha she was, and Xantcha she remained, even when the cadre had shrunk so much that the priests alloyed it with another, similarly depleted group.

Xantcha found herself face-to-face with another Xantcha. For both of them, it was . . . confusion. The word scarcely existed in Phyrexia, except to describe the clots of slag and ash that accumulated beneath the great furnaces. Together they consulted the priests, as newts were trained to do. The priests judged that as a result of the recombination, neither of them truly stood in the spot of Xantcha. The alloyed cadre's Xantcha was a third newt, who thought of itself as Hoz'krin and wanted no part of this Xantcha confusion. Xantcha and Xantcha were each told to recognize new places within the alloyed cadre or face the lash.

Lash or no, the priests' judgment was not acceptable. Places had become names that could not be surrendered, even under the threat of punishment. The Xantchas stayed awake when they should have slept in their boxes. They slipped away from the priests and spoke to each other privately. Meeting in private with another newt was something neither had done before. They negotiated and they compromised, though there were no Phyrexian words for either process. They agreed to make themselves unique. Xantcha broke off a blade of the razor-sharp grass and hacked off the hair growing on the left side of her skull. The other Xantcha soaked its hair in an acid stream until it turned orange.

They had rebelled—a word as forbidden as the Ineffable's true name and almost as feared. Only the tender-priests could change a newt's shape and only according to the Ineffable's plan. When the Xantchas returned to the place where their cadre gathered for food and sleep, the other newts gaped and turned away, as the teacher-priests came rumbling and clanking from the perimeter.

Xantcha had taken the other newt's flesh-fingered hand. Thirty-three hundred Dominarian years afterward, Xantcha knew that the touch of flesh was a language unto itself, a language that Phyrexia had forgotten. At the time, the gesture had confused the priests utterly and left them spinning in their tracks.

Not long after, the bald, gray sky had brightened painfully.

Xantcha had recalled her heart and the vat-priests' threat: too many mistakes and the Ineffable would seize her heart. Until the other Xantcha had tumbled into her life, she'd made less than her share of the cadre's mistakes, but perhaps one mistake, if it were great enough, was enough to rouse the Ineffable.

She'd thought the shining creature who'd descended from the too-bright sky was the Ineffable. He was nothing like the priests she'd seen and nothing at all like a newt. His eyes were intensely red, and an abundance of teeth filled his protruding jaw. And she'd known, perhaps because of that jaw filled with teeth, that it was he, as the Ineffable was he and not it in the way of newts and priests.

"You can call me Gix," he'd said, using his toothsome jaw to shape the words in an almost newtish way, though he didn't have the soft-flesh lips that were useful for eating but got in the way of proper Phyrexian pronunciation.

Gix was a name, the first true name Xantcha had ever heard, because it couldn't be interpreted as a place within a cadre. Gix was a demon, a Phyrexian who'd looked upon the Ineffable face with his own eyes and who, while the Ineffable slept, controlled Phyrexia. From a newt's lowly perspective, a demon's name might just as well be ineffable.

Gix offered his hand. The only sound Xantcha heard was a slight whirring as his arm extended and extended to at least twice his height. As Gix's hand unfurled, black talons sprang from each elegantly articulated finger. He touched the other Xantcha lightly beneath its chin. Xantcha felt trembling terror in the other newt's hand. The demon's talons looked as if they could pierce a priest's leather carapace or go straight through a newt's skull. A blue-green spark leapt from the demon to the other Xantcha, whose hand immediately warmed, relaxed, and slipped away.

Deep-pitched rumbling came out of the demon's throat. He lowered his hand, his head swiveled slightly, and Xantcha felt a cold, green light take her measure. Gix didn't touch her as he'd touched the other Xantcha. His arm retreated, each segment clicking sharply into the one behind it, then more whirring as his jaw assumed a sickle smile.

"Xantcha."

All remaining doubts about the difference between names and places vanished. Xantcha had become a true name, and confronted with *him*, Xantcha became *her*. The notions for male and female, dominance and submission, were already in Xantcha's mind, rooted in her dreams of soft, green grass and yellow sun.

"You will be ready," the demon said. "I made you. No simple rendering for you, Xantcha. Fresh meat. Fresh blood. Brought here from the place where you will go, where you will conquer. You have their cunning, their boldness, and their unpredictability, Xantcha, but your heart is mine. You are mine forever."

The demon meant to frighten her, and he did; he meant to distract her, too, while a blue-green spark formed on his shiny brass brow. In that, he was less successful. Xantcha saw the spark race toward her, felt it strike the ridge between her eyes and bury itself in the bone. The demon had inserted himself in her mind.

He made himself glorious before her. At least, that's what he tried to do. Xantcha felt the urge to worship him in awe and obedience, to feed him with the mind-storm turbulence no compleat Phyrexian could experience, except by proxy. Gix made promises in Xantcha's mind: privilege, power, and passion, all of them irresistible, or meant to be irresistible, but Xantcha resisted. She made a new place for herself, within herself. It wasn't terribly difficult. If there could be two Xantcha's within the cadre, there could be two within her mind, a Xantcha who belonged to Gix and a Xantcha who did not.

She filled the part that belonged to Gix with images from her dreams: blue skies, green grass, and gentle breezes. The demon drank them down, then spat them out. The light went out of his eyes. He turned away from her, to others in her cadre and found them more entertaining. For her part, Xantcha stood very still. She had denied the demon, rejected him before he could reject her. She expected instant annihilation, but the Ineffable did not seize her. Whatever else she had done, it was not a mistake great enough to destroy her heart.

After sating himself on newtish thoughts and passions, Gix departed. The teacher-priests sought to reclaim their place above the cadre, but after the elegance and horror of a demon, they seemed puny. In time, they became afraid of their charges and kept their distance as the newts began to talk more freely among themselves, planning for their glorious futures on other worlds.

Xantcha maintained her place, eating, sleeping, laboring, and taking part in the discussions, but she was no longer like the other newts. That moment when she'd created two Xantchas in her mind had transformed her, as surely as the tender-priests reshaped newts in the Fane of Flesh. She was aware of herself as no one else—except Gix—seemed to be. She stumbled into loneliness, and, seeking relief from that singular ache, she sought out the Xantcha whose hand she'd once held.

"I am without," she'd said, because at the time she hadn't known a better word. "I need to touch you."

She'd offered both hands, but the other Xantcha had reeled backward, screaming as if it were in terrible pain. The rest of the cadre swarmed between them, and Xantcha was lucky to survive.

Xantcha remembered the newt that had sawed off its arm with the razor grass, but what she wanted was an end to her isolation, not an end of existence. She considered running away. The First Sphere was vast. A newt could easily lose herself beyond the shimmering horizon, but if she placed herself beyond her cadre and its priests, Xantcha would slowly starve, because despite their constant efforts with hoes and plows and sickles, nothing edible grew in First Sphere's soil. Except for the meaty sludge brought up from Fane of Flesh, there was nothing on Phyrexia's First Sphere that a newt could eat.

When the cadre closed ranks to keep her from the simmering cauldrons the priests brought from the Fane, Xantcha picked up a sickle and cleared a path to her place. Five newts went down with the cauldron for rendering; one priest, too. Xantcha went to sleep with a full stomach and the sense that she'd never reopen her eyes. But neither Gix nor the Ineffable came to claim her. Once again, it seemed that she hadn't made a mistake.

Others did . . . newts began to disappear, a few at a time while they slept. Xantcha contrived to make a tiny hole in her box. She kept watch when she should have been asleep, but the Ineffable wasn't consuming newts. Instead, priests picked up a box here, a box there, and took them away. Speaker-equipped priests could spew words faster than soft-lipped newts; sometimes they forgot that newts heard faster than they spoke. Xantcha hid in a place on the edge and listened to chittering, metallic conversations.

The moment she and the others had been promised since their decanting had arrived. Newts were leaving Phyrexia. They were sleeping on another world. One of the priests had gone through the portal. It didn't like what it had found. Its coils had corroded and its joints had clogged because water, not oil, flowed everywhere: in fountains, across the land and in blinding torrents from the sky that was sometimes blue, sometimes black, sometimes speckled and sometimes streaked with fire. A worthless place, the priest said, rust and dust, fit only for newts.

Xantcha held her breath, as she'd held it before Gix. Although she'd never seen or felt it, she remembered water and knew in her bones that a place where water fell from the sky would be a place where a newt could get lost without necessarily starving. She began to make herself more useful, more visible, to the others, in hopes that the priests would pick her box, but though the disappearances continued, the priests didn't take her.

The cadre withered. Xantcha was certain she'd be taken away. There simply weren't that many left. Then the taking stopped. The newts slept and worked, slept and worked. Xantcha wasn't the only one who listened to the priests. None of them liked what they heard. There were problems in the other world. Newts had been exposed and destroyed.

Thirty centuries after the fact, when she and Urza returned to Dominaria, Xantcha had pieced together what might have happened. Appended to some of the oldest chronicles in her collection were accounts of strangers, undersized and eerily identical, who'd appeared suddenly and throughout what was left of Terisiare, some twenty years after the Brothers' War had ended. The Dominarians hadn't guessed what the strangers suddenly tromping through their fields were or where they'd come from, but ignorance hadn't kept them from exterminating the nearly defenseless newts.

But at the time, in Phyrexia, there'd been only whispers of disaster, thwarted destiny, and newts transformed to meat in a place where not even the Ineffable could find them.

The whispers reached Xantcha's cadre along with orders that they were to move. New cadres were coming, fresh from the Fane of Flesh. Xantcha caught sight of them as she dragged her box through the sharp, oily grass. The replacement cadres were composed of newts who were bigger than her. No two of the larger newts were quite the same and every one was obviously male or female.

Xantcha had lost her destiny. She and the rest of her depleted cadre became redundant. Even the tools with which they'd turned the sterile Phyrexian soil were taken away, and the food cauldrons, which had always arrived promptly between periods of work and sleep, sleep and work, appeared only before sleep . . . if the cadre was lucky.

Luck. A word that went with despair. Denied their promised place, some newts crawled into their boxes and never came out again. Not Xantcha. As regarded luck, Gix was lucky that she didn't know where to find him or how to destroy him. It took time to grow a newt in the vats, and more time to teach it the most basic tasks, and transform it into a Phyrexian. So much time that the male and female newts she'd glimpsed farming her cadre's old place must have been already growing in the vats when the demon had planted his blue-green spark in her skull.

Gix had lied to her. It was a small thing compared to the other hardships she endured, now that her cadre was redundant, but it sustained her for a long time until another wave of rumors swept across the First Sphere. A knife had sliced through the passage that connected Phyrexia with the other world; it had broken and was beyond repair. Half of the larger newts were trapped on the wrong side; the rest were as redundant as she had become.

Without warning, as was usually the case in her Phyrexian life, all the redundant newts, including Xantcha, were summoned to the Fourth Sphere to witness the excoriation of the demon Gix. The Ineffable's plan for Phyrexian glory had been thwarted by the Knife and someone had to be punished. Gix's lustrous carapace was corroded and burnt before he was consigned to the Seventh Sphere for torment. It was a magnificent spectacle. Gix fought like the hellspawn he was, taking four fellow demons into the reeking fumarole with him. Their shrieks were momentarily louder than the roar of the crowds and furnaces, though they faded quickly.

For a while, Xantcha remained in the Fourth Sphere. She had no place, no assignment. In a place as tightly organized as Phyrexia, a place-less newt should have been noticeable, but Xantcha wasn't. She dwelt among the gremlins. Even in Phyrexia, time spent in gremlin town couldn't be called living, but gremlins were flesh. They had to eat, and Xantcha ate with them, as she learned things about flesh no compleat priest could teach her.

Chapter 4

Chaotic air currents rising above a patchwork of cultivated fields seized Xantcha's sphere. For several panicked heartbeats, as she battled the provisions bouncing around inside the sphere, Xantcha didn't know where she was or why. After more than three thousand years, she needed that long to climb out of her memories.

The disorientation had passed before disaster could begin. Xantcha was in control before the sphere brushed the bank of a tree-shadowed stream. It collapsed around her, a warm, moist film that evaporated quickly, as it had countless times before, but thoughts of what might have happened left her gasping for air.

Xantcha hadn't intended to lose herself in her memories. The past, when there was so much of it crammed into a single mind, was a kind of madness. She dropped to her knees and wiped the film from her face before it had a chance to dry. Between coughs, Xantcha took her bearing from the horizons: sun sinking to the west, mountains to the south, and gentle hills elsewhere. She'd come to her senses over inner Efuan Pincar, precisely the place she'd wanted to be. Luck, Xantcha told herself, and succumbed to another round of coughing.

Xantcha never liked to rely on luck, but just then, thoughts of luck were preferable to the alternatives. She'd been thinking of her beginnings, as she rarely did. Worse, she'd been thinking of Gix. She'd never forgotten that blue-green spark. Despite everything, she worried that the demon's mark might still be lurking somewhere within her skull.

She made herself think about Urza and all that they'd survived together. He could look inside her and destroy her if she became untrustworthy. So long as he didn't, Xantcha believed she could trust herself. But thoughts of Gix were no reason to fear Gix. Nothing escaped the excoriations of Phyrexia's Seventh Sphere. Even if the blue-green spark remained, the demon who'd drilled it into her was gone.

Urza insisted that she steer clear of Phyrexians, once she scented them. He didn't want his enemies to know where he was or that he'd returned to the land of his birth. They both knew that if she ever fell back into Phyrexian hands, they'd strip her memories before they consigned her to the Seventh Sphere, and she knew too many of Urza's secrets to justify the risk.

The Phyrexian presence on Dominaria had been growing over the past fifty years. Morvern and Baszerat were only two among a score of places where Xantcha had once scrounged regularly, but were—or soon would be—off limits. Efuan Pincar was not, however, among them. The little realm on the wrong side of the great island of Gulmany was so isolated and unimportant, that the rest of what had once been Terisiare scarcely acknowledged its existence. It was the last place Xantcha expected to scent a Phyrexian. If she'd succumbed to thoughts of Gix while soaring over Efuan Pincar, it wasn't because a Phyrexian had tickled her mind, but because she'd begun to doubt Urza.

True, he'd go to the places where she'd scented *sleepers*, and he'd find them, but he wouldn't do anything about them. Newts disguised as born-folk weren't enough to goad Urza into action. Xantcha thought it would take death for that. She'd been perversely pleased when she'd found a war in Baszerat and Morvern. She thought for sure that would overcome Urza's obsession with the past, and perhaps it had; he'd never come so close to striking her.

Kayla Bin-Kroog hadn't mentioned Efuan Pincar in her epic. Efuand chroniclers explained that omission by proclaiming that their land had been empty until three hundred years ago, when a handful of boats had brought a band of refugees to Gulmany's back side. Xantcha doubted that there'd ever been enough boats in Terisiare to account for all the living Efuands, but scribes lied, she knew that from her *Antiquity Wars* collection. What mattered to Xantcha was that among any ten men of Efuan Pincar, at least one matched Kayla's word picture of Mishra, and another had his impulsive temperament. To find better odds she'd have to soar across the Sea of Laments, something she'd done just once, by mistake, and had sworn she'd never try again.

Xantcha knew her plan to bring Urza face to face with a dark, edgy youth who might remind him of his long-dead brother, wasn't the most imaginative strategy, but she was Phyrexian, and as Urza never ceased telling her, Phyrexians lacked imagination. Urza himself was a genius, a man of great power and limitless imagination, when he chose to exercise it. Once she had him face-to-face with her false Mishra, Xantcha expected Urza's imagination would repair any defects in her clumsy Phyrexian strategy.

Then Xantcha caught herself thinking about other notoriously failed strategies: Gix and thousands of identical sexless newts.

"What if I'm wrong?" she asked the setting sun; the same question that Urza asked whenever she tried to prod him into action.

The sun didn't answer, so Xantcha gave herself the same answer she gave Urza, "Dominaria's doomed if Urza does nothing. If he thinks his brother's come back to him, he might do something, and something—anything—is better than nothing."

Xantcha watched the last fiery sliver of sunlight vanish in the west. Her sphere had dried into a fine white powder that disappeared in the breeze. By her best guess, she'd been aloft without food, water, or restful sleep for two and a half days. There was water in the stream and more than enough food in her shoulder sack, but sleep proved elusive. Wrapped in her cloak, Xantcha saw

Gix's toothsome face each time she closed her eyes. After watching the stars slide across the sky, she yawned out another sphere as the eastern horizon began to brighten.

* * * * *

Xantcha hadn't thought she'd find her Mishra in the first village she visited. Though experience on other worlds had convinced her that every village harbored at least one youth with more ambition than sense, it had stood to reason that she might need to visit several villages before she found the right combination of temperament and appearance. But temperament and appearance weren't her problems.

In the twenty years since her last visit, war and famine had come to Efuan Pincar. The cultivated field in which she'd spent her first sleepless night had proved the exception to the new rules. The first village that Xantcha approached was still smoldering. The second had trees growing from abandoned hearths. Those villages that remained intact did so behind palisades of stone, brick, and sharpened stakes.

She approached the closed gates warily, regretting that she'd disguised herself as a cocky and aristocratic youth. It was an easy charade, one that matched her temperament and appearance, but throughout their wandering, she and Urza had come across very few wars that couldn't be blamed on aristocratic greed or pride.

The war in Efuan Pincar, however, proved to one of the rare exceptions. The gates swung open before she announced herself. The whole village greeted her with pleading eyes. They'd made assumptions: She was a young man who'd lost his horse and companions to the enemy. She needed their help. But most of all, they assumed she'd come to help them. Outnumbered and curious, Xantcha made her own assumption. She'd learn more if she let them believe what they wanted to believe.

"You will go to Pincar City and tell Tabarna what is happening?" the village spokesman asked, once he had offered her food and drink. "We are all too old to make the journey."

"Tabarna does not know," another elder said, and all the villagers bobbed their heads in agreement.

"He cannot know. If Tabarna knew, he would come to us. If he knew, he would help us. He would not let us suffer." A multitude of voices, all saying the same thing.

A man named Tabarna had governed Efuan Pincar twenty years ago. Part priest, part prince, he'd been an able ruler. If the villagers' Tabarna were still the man Xantcha remembered, though, he'd be well past his prime, and beloved or not, someone would be taking advantage of him. Usually, that someone would be a man dressed as she was dressed, in fine clothes and with a good steel sword slung below his hip. Xantcha couldn't ask too many questions, not without compromising her disguise, but she promised to deliver the villagers' message. Red-Stripes and Shratta were terrorizing the countryside.

The village offered to give her a swaybacked horse for her journey. Xantcha bought it instead with a worn silver coin and left the next day, before her debts grew any higher. The elders apologized that they couldn't offer the escort a young nobleman deserved, but all their young men were gone, swept up by one side or the other.

As she rode away, Xantcha couldn't guess how the Shratta had gotten involved in a war. Twenty years ago, the Shratta had been a harmless sect of ascetics and fools. They preached that anyone who did not live by the two hundred and fifty-six rules in Avohir's holy book was damned, but no one had taken them seriously. She had no idea who or what the Red-Stripes were until she'd visited a few more villages. The Red-Stripes had begun as royal mercenaries, charged with the protection of the palaces and temples that the suddenly militant Shratta had begun threatening, some fifteen years ago.

Oddly enough, in none of the tales Xantcha listened to did she hear of the two groups confronting each other. Instead, they roamed the countryside, searching out each others' partisans, making accusations when nothing could be proved, then killing the accused and burning their homes.

"The Shratta," a weary villager explained, "tell us they are the wrath of Avohir and they punish us if we do not live closely by Avohir's holy book. Then, after the Shratta have finished with us, the Red-Stripes come. They see that the Shratta didn't take everything, so they take what's left."

"Every spring, it begins again," one of the old women added. "Soon there will be nothing left."

"Twice we sent men to Tabarna, twice they did not come back. We have no men left."

Then, as in the other villages, the survivors asked Xantcha to carry their despair to Tabarna's ear. She nodded, accepted their food, and left on her swaybacked horse, knowing that there was nothing she could do. Her path would not take her to Pincar City, Tabarna's north coast capital. She'd begun to doubt that it would take her to a suitable Mishra either. With or without pitched battles, Efuan Pincar had been at war for nearly a decade, and young men were in short supply.

Xantcha's path—a rutted dirt trail because her sphere wouldn't accommodate a horse—took her toward Medran, a market town. A brace of gate guards greeted her with hands on their sword hilts and contempt in their eyes: Where had she been? How did a noble lad with fine boots and a sword come to be riding a swaybacked nag?

Xantcha noticed that their tunics were hemmed with a stripe of bright red wool. She told them how she'd ridden into the countryside with older, more experienced relatives. They'd been beset by the Shratta, and she was the sole survivor, headed back to Pincar City.

"On a better horse, if there's one to be found."

Xantcha sniffed loudly; when it came to contempt, she'd learned all the tricks before the first boatload of refugees struck the Efuan Pincar shore. She'd also yawned out her armor before she'd ridden up to the gate. The Red-Stripes were in for a surprise if they drew their swords against her.

Good sense prevailed. They let her pass, though Xantcha figured to keep an eye for her back. Even with a sword, a slight, beardless youth in too-fine clothes was a tempting target, especially when the nearest protectors were also the likeliest predators.

Xantcha followed the widening streets until they brought her to a plaza, where artisans and farmers hawked produce from wagons. She gave the horse to the farmer with the largest wagon in exchange for black bread and dried fruit. He asked how an unbearded swordsman came to be peddling a nag in Medrantown. Xantcha recited her made-up tale. The farmer wasn't surprised that Shratta would have slain her purported companions.

"The more wealth a man has, the less the Shratta believe him when he says he abides by the book. Strange, though, that they'd risk a party as large as the one your uncle had assembled. Were me, I'd suspect the men he'd hired weren't what they'd said they were."

Xantcha shrugged cautiously. "I'm sure my uncle thought the same . . . before they killed him." Then, because the farmer seemed more world-wise than the villagers, she tempted him with a thought that had nagged her from the beginning. "He'd hired Red-Stripes. Thought it would keep us safe. Shratta never attack men with Red Stripes on their tunics."

The farmer took her bait, but not quite the way she expected. "The Red-Stripes don't bother the Shratta where they live, and the Shratta usually return the favor. But where there's wealth to be taken, every man's a target, especially to the . . ." He fingered the hem of his own tunic. "I won't speak ill of your dead, but it's a fool who trusts in stripes or colors."

Xantcha walked away from the wagon, thinking that it might be better to get out of Medran immediately. She was headed toward a different gate than the one she'd entered when she spotted a knot of men and women, huddled in the shade of a tavern. With a second glance Xantcha saw the bonds at their necks, wrists, and ankles. Prisoners, she thought, then corrected herself, slaves.

She hadn't seen slaves the last time she visited Efuan Pincar, nor had she seen any in the beleaguered villages, but it was a rare realm, a rarer world that didn't cultivate slavery in one of its many forms. Xantcha took a breath and kept walking. She could see that a swaybacked horse found a good home, but there was nothing she could do for the slaves.

disguised as a young and presumably curious man.

"A cousin," Xantcha repeated, showing more anxiety than she felt. Let the slaver laugh and think what she wanted. Xantcha had the other woman's attention, and she'd have the slave, too. "For ransom." She unslung her purse and fished out a gold coin as big as her nose.

"Five of those," the slaver said, smashing her open hand between Xantcha's shoulder blades. "For ransom!"

If she were truly in the market for a slave, Xantcha would have protested that no one was worth five golden *nari*, but she'd been prepared to split twelve of the heavy Morvern coins between a likely youth and his family. She dug out another four and handed them over to the slaver, who bit each one. Xantcha knew the coins were true but was relieved when they passed the slaver's test.

"Which one's your cousin?"

Xantcha pointed to the dark-haired youth, who didn't blink under scrutiny. The slaver, whose eyebrows remained resolutely skeptical, shook her head.

"Pick another relative, boy. That one will eat you alive."

"Blood's blood," Xantcha insisted, "and ours is the same. I won't leave with another."

"Garve!" the slaver shouted the eunuch to her side. She held out her hand, and Garve surrendered a slender black rod. The slaver took it and turned back to Xantcha. "Another *nari*. You're going to need this."

Would ancient Ashnod be pleased by the all the improvements Dominarian slavers and torturers had brought to her pain-inflicting artifacts in the centuries since her death? Xantcha bought the thing, if only to keep the slaver or Garve from ever using it again.

"Cut him out," the slaver told Garve and added, while Garve walked among the slaves, "Have fun, boy."

"I intend to," Xantcha assured her, then watched as Garve seized the leather band around the youth's neck and jerked him roughly to his feet.

Garve gave the band a vicious twist, so it choked the youth and kept him quiet while the eunuch snapped the rivets that bound

Xantcha's new slave to the others. The youth's face became red. His eyes rolled.

"I want him alive," Xantcha warned in a low voice, that promised her threats were as good as her gold.

Her new slave dropped to one knee when Garve suddenly released him. Hacking spittle, he got himself upright before the eunuch touched him again. Riveted leather manacles bound his wrists close behind his back; he couldn't clean his lightly bearded chin. A short iron chain ran between his ankles. He could walk, barely, but not run. As he came closer, watching his feet, Xantcha counted the sores and bruises she hadn't noticed while he was staring.

Xantcha hadn't been comfortable owning a horse; she didn't know what she'd do with a slave. The thought of grabbing the arm's length of leather hanging from the band around his neck repelled her, though that was what everyone, including the youth, expected her to do.

"You're too tall," she said at last, though he wasn't as tall as Urza. She hoped that wasn't going to be a problem further along in her plan. "You'll walk beside me until I can arrange something more. . . ." Xantcha paused. Phyrexians might not have imagination, but born-folk certainly did, and there was nothing like silence to inspire the use of it. "Something more appropriate."

She smiled broadly, and her slave walked politely beside her, his chain clanking on the plaza's cobblestones. Xantcha's thoughts were focused on the how she'd get them both out of Medran without attracting trouble from the Red-Stripes. She wasn't expecting any other sort of trouble until the youth staggered against her.

Muttering curses no Efuand had ever heard before, Xantcha got an arm around his waist and shoved him upright. It wasn't a hard shove, but he groaned and made no attempt to start walking again. Sick sweat bloomed on his face. He'd burned through his bravery.

"Do you see that curb beside the fountain?"

A slight nod and a catch in his muscles; he was dizzy and on the verge of fainting.

"Get that far and you can sit, rest, drink some water."

"Water," he repeated, a hoarse, painful-sounding whisper.

Xantcha hoped his problems weren't serious. If Garve had damaged him, Garve wouldn't live to see the sun set. Her slave shoved one foot forward; she helped him with his balance. In five steps, Xantcha learned to hate that treacherous chain between his ankles. He fell one stride short of the fountain curb. Xantcha looked the other way while he dragged himself onto it. Then she drew a knife from the seam of her boot.

The blade was tempered steel from another world, and it made fast work of the wrist manacles. Xantcha gasped when she saw rings of weeping sores. Without a second thought she hurled the slashed leather across the cobblestones. Her slave was already washing his face and slurping water from the fountain. Xantcha thought it was a good sign, but wasn't surprised when her next question, "Are you hungry?" won her nothing more than another cold, piercing stare.

She retrieved a loaf of black bread, tore off a chunk, and offered it to him. He reached past her offering toward the loaf in her other hand.

"You're bold for a slave."

"You're small for a master," he countered and closed his hand over the bread he wanted.

Xantcha dropped the smaller piece and seized his arm. She didn't like the feel of open sores beneath her fingers, and she had every intention of giving him the whole loaf eventually, but points had to be made. She tightened her grip. Appearances, her still nameless slave needed to learn, could be deceiving. In Phyrexia, newts were soft, useless creatures, but on most other worlds, Xantcha was as strong as a well-muscled man half again her size. With a groan, the slave let go of the larger portion, and when she'd released him, picked up the smaller portion from the ground.

"Slowly," Xantcha chided him, though she knew it would be impossible for him to obey. "Swallow, breathe, take a sip of water."

His hand shot out, while Xantcha wondered what she should do next. He captured the unguarded bread and held it tight. Only his eyes moved from Xantcha's face to the black prod she'd tucked through her belt.

"Ask first," she suggested but made no move for her belt.

Even if, by some miracle of carelessness, he stole the prod and struck her with it, Urza's armor would protect her.

"Master, may I eat?"

For a man still short of his final growth, Xantcha's slave had a mature grasp of sarcasm. He definitely had Mishra's attitude in addition to Mishra's appearance.

"I didn't buy you to starve you."

"Why did you, then?" he asked through a mouthful of bread.

"I have need of a man like you."

He gave Xantcha the same look the slaver and Garve had given her, and she began to think she'd gotten herself into the position of a fisherman who'd hooked a fish larger than his boat. Only time would tell if she'd bring him aboard or he'd drown her.

"Your name will be Mishra. You will answer to it when you hear it."

Mishra laughed, a short, snorting sound. "Oh, yes, Master Urza."

Despite what she'd told Urza, the details of Kayla Bin-Kroog's *Antiquity Wars* weren't that widely spread across what remained of Terisiare. Xantcha hadn't expected her slave to recognize his new name; nor was she prepared for his aggressive insolence. I've made a mistake, she told herself. I've done a terrible thing. Then Mishra started choking. He tugged on the tight leather band around his throat and managed to gulp down his mouthful of bread. His fingers came away stained with blood and pus.

Xantcha looked at her own feet. She might have made a mistake, but she hadn't done anything terrible.

"You may call me Xantcha. And when you meet him, Urza is just Urza. He would not like to be called Master, especially not by his brother."

"Xantcha? What kind of name is that? If I'm Mishra and you work for Urza, shouldn't your name be Tawnos? You're a little bit small for the part. Grow out your hair and you could play Kayla—

an ugly Kayla. By the love of Avohir, I was better off with Tucktah and Garve."

"You know *The Antiquity Wars?*"

"Surprised? I can read and write, too, and count without using my fingers." He held up his hand but saw something—the stains, perhaps, that she'd already noticed—that cracked his insolence. "I wasn't born a slave," he concluded softly, staring across the plaza at his memories. "I had a life . . . a name."

"What name?"

"Rat."

"What?" she thought she'd misunderstood.

"Rat. Short for Ratepe. I grew into it." Another snorted laugh—or maybe a strangled sob. Either way, it ended when the neck leather brought on another choking spell.

"Hold still," Xantcha told him and drew out her knife again. "I don't want to cut you."

There wasn't even a flicker of trust in Rat's eyes as she laid the blade against his neck. He winced as she slid it beneath the leather. She had to saw through the sweat-hardened leather and pricked his skin a handful of times before she was done. The tip was bloody when it emerged on the other side, but he didn't make a grab for her or the weapon.

"I'm sorry," she said when she was finished.

Xantcha raised her arm to hurl the collar away as she'd hurled the manacles. Rat caught the trailing leash. The leather fell into his lap.

"I'll keep it."

Xantcha knew that in the usual order of such things, slaves didn't have personal property, but she wasn't about to take the filthy collar away from him. "I have a task for you," she said as he worried the collar between his hands. "I would have offered you the gold, if you'd been free. You will be free, I swear it, when you've done what I need you to do."

"And if I don't?"

While Xantcha wrestled with an answer for that question, a noisy claque of Red-Stripes entered the plaza from the east, the direction through which Xantcha had hoped to leave. She and

Rat were far from alone on the cobblestones, and she reasonably hoped that despite their mismatched appearance—him in rags and weeping sores, her with her boots and sword—they wouldn't draw too much attention. Rat saw the Red-Stripes as well. He snapped the leather against his thigh like a whip.

Red-Stripes, Xantcha guessed, had something to do with his transformation from free to slave. Considering his apparent education and remembering the farmer's gesture, she wondered if he'd once worn the sort of garments she was wearing.

"Hold it in," she advised him. "You've got a chain. . . ." She left the thought incomplete as a gentle breeze brought her the last scent she ever wanted to smell: glistening oil.

One of the Red-Stripes was a *sleeper*, a newt like her, but different, too. Newts of this new invasion had born-folk ways and didn't clump together in cadres. In truth, they didn't seem to know they were Phyrexian. Xantcha didn't care to test her theory. She hunched on her knees as she sat, catching her breath in her hands, hiding the exhalations that might reveal her glistening scent. She couldn't relax or be too careful.

Beside Xantcha, Rat beat a counterpoint of curses and leather. There was a chance that the Red-Stripe *sleeper* could hear every word.

"Quiet!" Xantcha hissed a command as she clamped her hand over Rat's. "Quiet!" She squeezed until she felt the sores and sinews pop.

"Afraid of the Red-Stripes?"

She took a deep breath and admitted, "They're not my friends. Quiet!"

Rat bent over to match her posture, blocking her view as well. He wouldn't stop talking. "And who are your friends—the Shratta? You keep strange company: Urza, Mishra, the Shratta. You're asking for trouble."

Xantcha ignored him. She hunched lower until she could see beneath Rat's arms. The Red-Stripes were heading into the same tavern where the slaver drank. "We've got to leave. Can you walk?"

"Why? I'm not afraid of the Red-Stripes. I'd join them right now, if they'd have me."

The elders in the first village had warned Xantcha that the young men had chosen sides, one way or another. It figured that her Mishra would have Phyrexian inclinations. She didn't have time to persuade him, so she'd have to out-bluff him. "Want to hobble over and try? You'd better hurry. Or do you think the eunuch's saved you a seat?"

"I'm not that stupid. I lost my chance the moment I got sapped and sold."

"Then stand up and start walking."

"Yes, Master."

Chapter 5

Bread, water, and the absence of tight leather around his neck worked swift wonders for Rat's stamina. He didn't need Xantcha's help as they walked away from the fountain, but his natural pride clashed with the chain between his ankles and guaranteed the sort of attention Xantcha preferred not to attract. They'd never get through the gate without an incident, so once they were clear of the plaza, she chose the narrowest street at each crossing until they came to a long-abandoned courtyard.

"Good choice, Xantcha. The windows are mortared, the doors, too—except for the one we came in." Rat kicked at the rubble and picked up a bone that might have been a child's leg. "Been here before? Is this where you meet Urza?"

Xantcha let the comment slide. "Put your foot up here." She pointed to an overturned pedestal. "I've got to get rid of that chain."

"With what?" Rat approached the pedestal but kept both feet on the ground. "Garve's got the key."

Xantcha hefted a chunk of granite. "I'll break it."

"Not with that, you won't. I'll take my chances with Urza."

She shook her head. "We've got four days' traveling before

then. Waste not, want not, Rat—you can't run. You're helpless."

He didn't argue and didn't put his foot on the pedestal, either.

"Do you prefer being chained and hobbled like an animal?"

"I'm your slave. You bought me. Better keep me hobbled and helpless, if you want to keep me at all."

"I need a man who can play Mishra's part with Urza. I give you my word, play the part and you'll be free in a year." Free to tell Urza's secrets to the Red-Stripes? Never. But that was a worry for the future. For the present, "Give me your word."

"The word of a slave," Rat interrupted. "Remember that." He put his foot on the pedestal. "And be careful."

Xantcha brought the stone down with a crash that was louder than she'd expected, less effective, too. Perhaps it would be better to wait. Unfettering a youth who looked like Mishra might be all that Urza needed to free himself from the past.

And maybe they'd have to run from the Red-Stripes.

Xantcha understood how Urza must have felt when they traveled, worried about a companion who couldn't take care of herself; angry and bitter, too. She smashed the granite against the chain. Sparks flew, but the links didn't. Gritting her teeth, Xantcha pounded rapidly but to no greater success. When she paused for breath, Rat seized her wrists.

"Don't act the fool."

She could have dropped the stone on his foot and used both hands to throttle his insolence, and Xantcha might have, if she hadn't been so astonished to feel his warm, living flesh against hers. She and Urza touched each other, casually, but infrequently, and never with particular passion. Rat's hands shook as he held her, probably because slavery had weakened him, but there was something more, something elusive and unnerving. Xantcha was relieved that he released her the instant their eyes met.

"I'm trying to help you," she said acidly.

"You're not helping, you're just making noise. Noise is bad, if you're trying to hide. For that matter, why are we hiding? It's not as if Tucktah's going to tell the Red-Stripes I'm not your ransomed cousin."

"Just trying to keep you out of trouble."

Rat laughed. "You're too late for that, Xantcha. Now, why don't we stop playing child's games and go to your father's house? If Tabarna's laws still mean anything in this forsaken town, it's illegal for one Efuand to own another. You're the one who's in trouble for wasting your father's gold. You paid way too much to ransom me. Is your father a tyrant or can he be reasoned with?"

Given her disguise, Rat's presumptions weren't unreasonable. "I don't have a father. I don't live in this town. I live with Urza and we've got a long—" she considered telling him about the sphere and decided not to, "journey and since I have your word . . ." She brought the stone down on the metal.

"You'll be at that all afternoon and halfway through the night."

Xantcha shrugged. They couldn't leave before then, not if she were going to use the sphere to get them over the walls. She smashed the stone again. A flake of granite drew blood from Rat's shin; the link was unharmed.

Rat rubbed the wound and lowered his leg. "All right. I don't believe you, but if you're determined to play your game to its end, there's an easier way to get out of this town. Do you have any money left?" Xantcha didn't answer, but Rat had seen her purse and presumably knew it wasn't empty. "Look, go back to the plaza and pay some farmer to load me in his wagon . . . or, better, find a smith with a decent hammer and chisel. Get these damn things off the same way they got put on."

With *sleepers* in the town, Xantcha didn't want to go looking for strangers, but there was one farmer in the plaza market who wasn't a stranger.

"I gave my horse to a farmer with a wagon—"

"You had a horse!?"

"I had no further need of it, so I gave it to a man who did and promised to care for it."

"Avohir's mercy, you had no need of a horse, so you gave it away. You didn't even bargain with Tucktah." He swore again. "I've been sold by a beast to a madman! No, a mad child. Doesn't you father usually keep you locked up?"

"I could sell you back," Xantcha said coldly. "I imagine you had a long and pleasant life ahead of you."

She started to retrace their route. Rat followed as quietly as he could with the chain dragging on the ground. Once they were back in the plaza, Xantcha told him to wait in the shadows while she negotiated with the farmer. He agreed, but measured every wall with his eyes and twisted each battered link, in the obvious hope that she'd weakened it, as soon as he thought she couldn't see him.

Well, he'd warned her what his word was worth.

When Xantcha pointed him out to the farmer, he wanted no part of her plan.

"I'll give you your horse back."

"A horse is no use to a slave with a chain between his ankles."

"Imagine if you set the slave free, he'd be willing to travel with you," the farmer countered, still skeptical.

"I forgot to buy the key to his chains."

The farmer hesitated. The slaver and her coffle had moved on, but the farmer had glanced toward the tavern when Xantcha had mentioned slaves. Likely he'd watched the whole scene with her, the slaver, Garve, and Rat.

"Have him come over, and I'll speak to him myself. Alone."

Moments later, Xantcha told Rat, "It's your choice. He wants to know if you're worth the risk."

Rat gave Xantcha a look that said liar, and got to his feet. Xantcha blocked his path.

"Look, I didn't tell him the truth about Urza or Mishra or anything like that, just that we were cousins. And before, when I gave him the horse, I told him that I was alone because I'd been traveling with my uncle. We'd been ambushed by Shratta and everybody but me had been killed. It was good enough at the time, before I'd spotted you, but it's going to make things more difficult now."

Rat frowned and shook his head. "If I was as dumb as you, I'd've died before I learned to walk. What names did you give him?"

"None," Xantcha replied. "He didn't ask."

"You need a keeper, Xantcha," Rat muttered as he walked away from her. "You haven't got the sense Avohir gives to ants and worms."

Rat could have run, or tried to, but chose to get out of the town instead. The farmer waved for Xantcha to join them.

"Not saying I believe you, either of you," he said, offering Xantcha his plain woven cloak to wear instead of her fancier one. "Climb in quickly now. These are strange times . . . bad times. A man doesn't put his trust in words; I put mine in Avohir. I'll get you out of Medran, and Avohir be my judge if I'm wrong."

Xantcha considered stowing her sword in the wagon bed where Rat rode, with straw and empty baskets piled all around him to hide the chain. But her slave had a flair for storytelling. His imagination made her nervous.

"You're not wrong, good man," Rat said cheerfully as he rearranged the baskets. "Not about my cousin and me, not about the times, either. Two months ago, I had everything. Then one night I went carousing with friends who weren't friends and lost it all. Woke up in chains. I told them who I was: Ratepe, eldest son of Mideah from Pincar City, and said my father would ransom me; got a swift kick and a broken rib. I'd given up hope months ago, but I hadn't reckoned on my cousin, Arnuwan."

Xantcha jumped when Rat slapped her between the shoulders. Arnuwan was probably a less conspicuously foreign name than Xantcha, and the moment Rat introduced it, the farmer relaxed and offered his.

"Assor," he said and embraced Rat, not her.

Xantcha was used to following someone else. She'd followed Urza for over three thousand years, but Rat was different. Rat smiled and told Assor easy tales of pranks he and Arnuwan had pulled on their elders. He was very persuasive. She would have believed him herself, if she hadn't known that she was supposed to be Arnuwan. Of course, maybe there was an Arnuwan, and maybe Rat's only lie was that he didn't look at her while he was spinning out his tales. Maybe he was harmless, but Xantcha, who was nowhere near as harmless as she pretended to be, hadn't survived Phyrexia, Urza, and countless other perils, by assuming that anything was harmless.

She kept her sword close and palmed a few black-metal coins that hadn't come from any king or prince's mint. Then, as Assor called *home* to his harnessed horse, she settled in for the ride.

Silence hung thick among them. Ordinary folk going about their late-afternoon affairs looked up as they passed. Xantcha could think of nothing to say except that she longed to be in the air, headed back to the cottage, neither of which were safe subjects for conversation.

Then Rat asked the farmer, "Do you keep sheep in your fallows, or do you grow peas?" He followed that question with another and another until he'd lured the farmer into an animated discussion about the proper way to plow a field. The farmer favored straight furrows. Rat said a sunwise spiral toward the center was better. They were in mid-argument when the Red-Stripes waved the wagon through the gate.

As they cleared the first rise beyond the town walls, even Assor realized what Rat had done and while Xantcha willed away her armor he asked:

"Where are you from, lad? The truth . . . no more of your lies. You're no one's cousin, and I'll wager you're no farmer either, despite your talk. You're too clever by half to be village-bred."

Rat grinned and told a different story. "I read, once, how Hatusan the Blind, had escaped from a besieged city by talking about the weather. It seemed worth trying."

"Read about it, eh?" Assor asked before Xantcha could say that she'd never heard of Hatusan the Blind. "Then, for certain, you're no farmer. I've never seen a book but Avohir's holy book and I listen 'stead of read. Is your name truly Ratepe, eldest son of Mideah?"

Xantcha was watching Rat closely from the corner of her eye. She caught him flinching as Assor sounded out his name. His rogue's grin vanished, replaced by an empty stare that looked at nothing and gave nothing away.

"It is," he answered with a voice that was both deeper and younger than she'd heard from him before. "And Mideah, my father, was a farmer when he died—a good farmer who plowed his fields sunwise every spring and fall. But he was a lector of philosophy at Tabarna's school in Pincar City before the Shratta burnt it down. . . ."

If Rat's second recounting of his life was more accurate than his first, he'd had a comfortable childhood and loving parents. But his cozy world had been overturned ten years ago when the Shratta swarmed the royal city, preaching that any knowledge that couldn't be read in Avohir's book wasn't knowledge at all. They had no use for libraries or schools, so they set them ablaze. Rat's father had been one of many who'd appealed to Tabarna for protection against the Shratta mobs, and to Tabarna's son, Catal, who funded the Red-Stripes to protect them. Then Catal died, poisoned by the Shratta, or so said the Red-Stripes, who'd avenged his death. The city dissolved into carnage and riot.

"We tried. Father grew a beard, Mother made jellies and sold them in the market. I stayed out of trouble—tried to stay out of trouble. But it wasn't any use. The Shratta knew our names. They caught my uncle—I called him my uncle, but he was only a friend, my father's closest friend. They drew his guts out through a hole in his belly, then they set fire to his house—after they'd locked his family inside. Our neighbors came to set our house ablaze, too. Father said that they were afraid of everything, ready to believe anything. He said it wasn't their fault, but that didn't stop the flames. We got away through a hole in the garden wall."

Xantcha wanted to believe her slave. She'd been to Pincar City where simple houses, each with a tidy garden, packed the narrow streets. She could almost see a frightened family running through moonlight, though Rat hadn't said whether they'd left by day or night. That seemed to be Rat's charm, Rat's near-magic. When he took a deep breath and started talking, everything he said rang true.

Mishra never stooped to flattery, Kayla Bin-Kroog had written nearly thirty-four hundred years earlier. *He didn't have to. He had the gift of sincerity, and he was the most dangerous man I ever met.*

"We fled to Avular, where my mother had kin. From Avular, we went to Gam."

Assor grunted; he'd heard of the place. "Good land for flocks and herding, not so good for grain-growing."

"Not so good for city-bred boys, either," Rat added. "But the Shratta didn't bother us. At least they didn't bother us any more than they bothered everyone else. We paid their tithes and lived by the book and thought we were lucky."

Xantcha clenched her teeth. In all the multiverse, there was no curse to compare with feeling lucky.

"I'd taken two sheep to the next village, to a man who didn't need sheep, but he had a daughter. . . ." Rat almost smiled before his face hardened. "I missed the Shratta as I left, and it was over when I returned. All Gam was dead: butchered, the men with their throats slit, the women strangled with their skirts, the children with their skulls smashed against the walls. . . ." Rat's voice had flattened, as if he were reciting from a dull text, yet that lack of expression served to make his words all the more believable. "I found my father, my mother, my brother and sister. I shouldn't have looked. It would have been better not to know. Then I ran to the next village, but I was too late there as well. Everybody I knew was dead. I wanted to join them. I wanted to die, or join the Red-Stripes, if I could get to Avular. I knew the way, but the slavers found me the second night."

Either Rat told the painful truth or he was a stone-cold liar. The farmer had no doubts. He cursed the Shratta, then the Red-Stripes, and having already heard Xantcha's false tale earlier in the day, invited them both into his family.

Xantcha declined. "We have family awaiting us in the south." The wagon was rolling west. "It's time for us to take our leave. Past time . . . we should have taken the last crossroads."

Both Xantcha and the farmer looked to Rat, who hesitated before shucking off the straw and baskets that had concealed his fetters.

"Good work," Xantcha whispered while the farmer scuttled about, filling one of the baskets with food.

"He's a good man," said Rat.

The farmer presented them with the basket before Xantcha could challenge her companion's resolve. Xantcha returned the homespun cloak.

"Walk fast," he said, then remembered Rat's fetters. "Try. There's been no trouble this close to Medran, but we all lay close after sundown. The moon's waxed; there'll be light on the road.

When you get south to Stezine, ask for Korde. He's the smith there. Tell him you rode with me, with Assor, his wife's brother-by-marriage. He'll break that chain on his anvil. Luck to you."

Xantcha hoisted the basket and started walking, glancing back over her shoulder after every few steps.

"He didn't believe you," Rat chided.

"He didn't believe either of us."

"He believed me because I told the truth."

"So did I," Xantcha countered.

Rat shook his head. "Not to me, you haven't. Urza, Mishra, dead uncles, and ransomed cousins. You're a lousy liar, Xantcha."

She let the provocations pass. They walked until the wagon had rolled from sight, and then Xantcha stopped. She set down the basket and faced Rat with her fists on her hips.

"I saved your life, Ratepe, that's no lie. All I've asked in return is that you help me with Urza. It doesn't matter if you believe me, so long as I can trust you."

"You bought me. You can make me do what you ask, but I'll fight you, I swear it, every step of the way. That's what you can trust."

"I ransomed you."

"Ransom? Avohir's mercy, you said I was your cousin—do you think Tucktah believed that? You're a bold liar, Xantcha. That's not the same as a good one. Tucktah sold me, you bought me. I'm still a slave. Don't bother being kind. I won't love you, and I will escape."

Xantcha sighed and rolled her eyes dramatically. Rat accepted the invitation by lunging for her throat. If it had been a fair fight, Xantcha would have gone down and stayed down. Rat's reach was half an arm longer than hers, and he weighed nearly twice as much. But Rat hadn't been fed enough to maintain the muscles on his long bones, and Xantcha was a Phyrexian newt. Urza said she was built like a cat or a serpent, slippery and supple, impossible to pin down or keep unbalanced.

Rat had her on her back for a heartbeat before she threw him aside. While he rose slowly to his knees, Xantcha sprang to her feet. She snapped her fingers.

"There . . . you're free. As simple as that. You're no longer a slave. I ask you to honor what I have given you, and help me with Urza. When you've done that, in a year, I'll return you to this place. I give you my word."

"You're a moon cow, Xantcha. Your parts don't fit together: fine clothes, a sword, gold *nari* from Morvern, and this Urza of yours. Avohir's mercy—what do you take me for?"

Rat tried to side step around her, but his fetters insured that his strides were shorter than hers. After a few more failed evasions, Xantcha seized his wrists.

"You were going to die, Ratepe."

"Maybe, maybe not—" Rat had the reach, the leverage to free himself, and as soon as he had an opportunity, he grabbed for the slave goad tucked in Xantcha's belt.

"Throw it down," Xantcha warned. "I don't want to hurt you."

Rat laughed and played his fingers over the rod's smooth black surface. A shimmering, yellow web sprang from its tip. "You can't hurt me. You can save yourself from getting hurt by dropping your purse and your sword on the ground, turning around, and following that wagon."

Xantcha eyed the web. She could feel its power where she stood, but it had belonged to Garve. Tucktah wouldn't have given her dim assistant a goad that could seriously damage the merchandise. With a frustrated sigh, she gave Rat one last chance. "You owe me your life. Make peace with me and be done with it."

Rat rushed her, raising his arm for a mighty blow that Xantcha easily eluded. She stomped one foot on his chain, then put her fist in his gut. He tried to move with the punch but lost his balance when the chain tightened. He fell hard, leading with his forehead and losing his grip on the slave goad. Xantcha grabbed the goad and broke it. Despite the numbing, yellow light that oozed over her arms, she hurled both pieces far into the brush beyond the road. She retrieved the farmer's basket.

Rat had levered himself onto one elbow and was trying to rise further, when she shoved him onto his back again. She put the food basket on his stomach then knelt on his breastbone.

"All right, you win. You're a slave, and you'll do what I tell you to do because I can make you."

Xantcha inhaled deeply. She ran through her mnemonic rhyme, then she yawned. The sphere was invisible but not imperceptible. Rat screamed as it flowed around him.

"Don't even think about trying to escape," Xantcha warned.

Weight wasn't a problem. Xantcha could have carried a barrel of iron or lead back to the cottage. Size was another matter. The sphere grew until it was wide as her outstretched arms. Then it stiffened and began to rise. Rat panicked. The sphere lurched and shot up like an arrow, throwing them against each other, the basket, and the scabbard slung at Xantcha's side.

There were too many things competing for Xantcha's attention. She eliminated the largest distraction by punching it in the gut. They were less than a man's height over the ground when she got everything steadied. Rat breathed noisily through his wide-open mouth, even after they'd begun to soar gently westward. He'd pressed himself against the bubble. His arms were sprawled, and his palms were flat against the sphere's inner curve. Nothing moved except his fingers, which clawed silently, compulsively: a cat steadying itself on glass.

Xantcha tried to sort out the tangle of legs, cloak, and overturned basket at the bottom of the sphere, but her least move pushed her companion toward panic. A nearly full moon showed faintly above the eastern horizon; she'd planned to soar through well into the night. That would have been unspeakably cruel, and though she was tempted—her forearms ached where the slavegoad's sorcery had surrounded them—she resisted the temptation.

The sphere swung like a falling leaf in the cooling night air— a pleasant, even relaxing movement for Xantcha, but sheer torture for Rat, who'd begun to pray between gasps. Xantcha guided them slowly to the ground near a twisting line of trees.

She warned him, "Put your hands over your face now. The sphere's skin will collapse against you when it touches the ground. It vanishes more quickly than cobwebs in a flame, but for that moment when it covers your mouth and nose, you'll think you're suffocating."

Rat moaned, which Xantcha took as a sign that he'd heard and understood, but he didn't take her advice. He clawed himself as he'd clawed the sphere. There were bloody streaks across his face before he calmed down.

"There's a stream through the trees. Wash yourself. Drink. You'll feel better afterward." Xantcha stood over him, offering an arm up, which, predictably, he refused. She gave him a clear path to the stream and another warning: "Don't think about running."

He was gone a long time. Xantcha might have worried that he'd thrown himself in if she hadn't been able to hear him heaving his guts out. She'd kindled a small fire before he returned— not something she usually did, but born-folk often found solace in the random patterns of flames against darkness. Rat was shivering and damp from the waist up when he returned.

"You need clothes. Tomorrow, I'll keep an eye out for another town. Until then—" she offered her cloak.

It might have been poison or sorcery by the way Rat stared at it, and he shrank a little when he finally took it.

"Can you eat? You should try to eat. It's been a hard day for you. The bread's good and this other stuff—" she held up a long, hollow tube. "Looks like parchment, tastes like apricots."

Another hesitation, but by the way he tore off and chewed through a finger's length of the tube, Xantcha guessed the sticky stuff might once have been one of his favorite treats.

"There's more," she assured him, hoping food might be a bridge to peace between them.

Rat set the apricot leather aside. "Who are you? What are you? The truth this time—like Assor said. Why me? Why did you buy me?" He took a deep breath. "Not that it matters. I've been as good as dead since the Shratta came."

"I must be a lousy liar, Rat, because I haven't lied to you. I'm Xantcha. I need you because Urza needs to talk to his brother, and when I saw you among the other slaves outside the tavern, I saw Mishra."

Rat stared at the flames. "Urza. Urza. You keep saying Urza. Do you mean the Urza? Urza the Artificer? The one who was born three thousand, four hundred and thirty-seven years ago? Avohir's sweet mercy, Xantcha, Urza's a legend. Even if he survived the sylex, he's been dead for thousands of years."

"Maybe Urza is a legend, but he's certainly not dead. The sylex turned the Weakstone and the Mightstone into his eyes; don't look too closely at them when you meet him."

"Thanks, I guess, for the warning, but I can't believe you. And if I could, it would only make it worse. If there were an Urza still alive he'd kill me once for reminding him of his brother and again because I'm not Mishra. I'm no great artificer, no great sorcerer, no great warrior. Sweet Avohir, I can't even fight you. The way you overpowered me and broke Tucktah's goad . . . and that sphere. That I don't understand at all. What are you, anyway? I mean, there are still artificers—not as good as Urza was supposed to have been, and not in Efuan Pincar, but Xantcha, that's not an Efuand name. Are you an artifact?"

Of all the questions Rat might have asked, his last was one for which Xantcha had no ready answer. "I was neither made nor born. Urza found me, and I have stayed with him because he is . . ." She couldn't finish that thought but offered another instead: "Urza blames himself for his brother's death, the guilt still eats at his heart. He won't fight you, Rat."

They both shivered, though the air was calm and warm around the little fire.

Rat spoke first, softly. "I'd always thought the one good thing that came out of that war was that the brothers finally killed each other. If they hadn't, it never would have ended."

"It was the wrong war, Rat. They shouldn't have fought each other. There was another enemy, the Phyrexians—"

"Phyrexians? I've heard of them. Living artifacts or some such. Nasty beasts, but slow and stupid, too. Jarsyl wrote about them, after the war."

Rat knew his history, as much of it as had been written down, errors and all. "They were there at the end of the war, maybe at the beginning—that's what Urza believes. They killed Mishra and turned him into one of their own; what Urza fought was a Phyrexian. He thinks if he'd known soon enough, he could have saved his brother and together they could have fought the Phyrexians."

"So the man you call Urza thinks that he could have stopped the war." Rat stared at Xantcha across the fire. "What do you think?"

He had Mishra's quick wit and perception.

"The Phyrexians are back, Rat, and they're not slow or stupid. They're right here in Efuan Pincar. I could smell them in Medran. Urza's got the power to fight them, but he won't do anything until he's settled his guilt with Mishra."

Rat swore and stared at the stars. "These Phyrexians . . . Tucktah and Garve?"

"No, not them. They were with the Red-Stripes. I smelled them."

He swore a second time. "I'd've been better off staying where I was."

Chapter 6

They didn't talk much after that. Xantcha let the fire burn down, and Rat made no attempt to revive it, choosing instead to pull his borrowed cloak tight around his shoulders. As little as he seemed to want to talk, Rat seemed reluctant to give his body the rest it needed. Three times Xantcha watched him slump sideways only to jolt himself upright. Exhaustion won the fourth battle. His chin touched his chest, and his whole body curled forward. He'd find himself in a world of pain when he woke up.

Xantcha touched Rat's arm gently and when that failed to rouse him, eased him to the ground, which was dry and no worse than wherever he might have slept last. He pulled his arms tight against his chest. Xantcha tried to straighten them but met resistance. His fists and jaw remained clenched even in sleep.

She'd thought that kind of tension was unique to Urza, to Urza's madness, but perhaps Rat's conscience was equally guilt-wracked. Whatever lies he'd told her and Assor, he'd been through hard times. His stained and aromatic clothes had once been sturdy garments, cut and sewn so carefully that their seams still held. Not slave's clothing, no more than his shoes were a slave's shoes. They were missing their buckles and had been shredded where the fetters rubbed against them.

If Xantcha were wiser in the ways of mortal misfortune, she might have read Rat's true history in the moonlight. Xantcha knew more about the unusual aspects of a hundred out-of-the-way worlds than she knew about ordinary life anywhere. The two and a half centuries she and Urza had spent in Dominaria was the most time she'd spent in any single place, and though she'd taught herself to read and traveled at every opportunity, all she'd really learned was the extent of her ignorance.

Xantcha's day hadn't been so exhausting as Rat's. She could have stayed awake all night and perhaps tomorrow night, if there'd been any need. But the night was calm, and although Rat's plight proved that there were slavers loose in Efuan Pincar, tonight they were in empty country, far from towns or villages. Xantcha heard owls and other night birds. Earlier she'd heard a wild cat yowling, but nothing large, nothing to keep her from settling down near Rat's feet, one arm touching his chain so she'd know if he moved unwisely during the night.

Were their positions reversed, Xantcha wouldn't have tried to escape. In her long experience, the unknown had never proven more hospitable than the known. She hadn't thought of escape in all the time she was a newt among Phyrexians, although that, she supposed, had been different. A better comparison might be her first encounter with Urza. . . .

* * * * *

After Gix's excoriation, Xantcha had hidden among the Fourth Sphere gremlins, but they'd eventually betrayed her to the Fane of Flesh. The teacher-priests caught her and punished her and then sent her to the furnaces. Xantcha worked beside metal-sheathed stokers. The hot, acrid air had burned her lungs. She'd staggered under the impossible burdens they piled on her back. It was no secret, the remains of Gix's newts were to be used up as quickly as possible, but when Xantcha's strength gave out, it was a burnished stoker who stumbled over her fallen body and plunged into a crucible of molten brass.

The fire-priests wouldn't have her after that, so the Fane sent Xantcha to the arena, where Phyrexian warriors honed their skills against engines and artifacts made in Phyrexia or creatures imported from other worlds. She was assigned tasks no warrior would have dared: feeding the creatures, repairing damaged engines, and destroying those artifacts the warriors had merely damaged. Her death had been expected, even anticipated, but when the fearsome wyverns with their fiery eyes and razor claws went on a rampage that reduced a hundred priests and warriors to oil-caked rubble, Xantcha the newt had survived without a scratch.

Since she wouldn't die and they'd failed to kill her, the planner-priests decided that Xantcha had the makings of a dodger.

Before he'd closed his eyes in sleep, the Ineffable had decreed that Phyrexia must be relentless in its exploration of other worlds and in the exploitation of whatever useful materials, methods and artifacts that exploration uncovered. Exploration was the easy part. A compleat Phyrexian, sheathed in metal and bathed in glistening oil, was thorough and precise. It was incapable of boredom and, when ordered to examine everything, it did exactly that, as accurate at the end as it had been in the beginning.

But confronted with something they'd never seen before, lesser Phyrexians often became confused, and through their rough bumbling they frequently destroyed not only themselves but whatever they'd been examining as well. It was an intolerable situation and necessitated an unpleasant solution. Whole colonies of gremlins were endured, even nurtured, for their canniness and spontaneity, but no gremlin was cannier than the remnants of Gix's newts; the ones that refused to die.

There were twenty of them summoned to the fountain, as identical as ever. They couldn't drink the glistening oil, so they were bathed in it while rows and ranks of compleat Phyrexians watched in silence. A mobile planner-priest described their new destiny:

Go forth with the diggers and the bearers. Gaze upon the creations of born minds. Decipher their secrets so that they may be exploited safely for the glory and dominion of Phyrexia.

There'd been more. Compleat Phyrexians never suffered from fatigue during an endless oration. They had no tongues to turn thick or pasty from overuse. And, of course, they lacked imagination. Never mind that Urza ridiculed Xantcha's imagination; she had more than the rest of Phyrexia rolled together. Standing beside the fountain, slick with glistening oil, Xantcha had imagined a wondrous future.

Her future began on a world whose name she had never known. Perhaps the searcher-priests had known its name when they came to investigate it, but once they discovered something useful to Phyrexia, the name of the place where they'd found it was of little importance to the team of diggers, bearers, and dodgers sent to exploit the discovery.

Once the ambulator portals were configured, it didn't matter where a world truly lay. Just one step forward into the glassy black disk the searcher-priests unrolled across the ground and whoosh, the team was where it needed to be. When the team finished its work—usually an excavation and extraction—they'd pack everything up, stride into the ambulator's nether end (identical to the prime end, except that it lacked the small configuration panel) and whoosh, they were back where they started, waiting for the next assignment.

The ambulators were horrible artifacts: suffocating, freezing, and endless, and a dodger's work was worse than cleaning up after the warriors. The chief digger would lead a newt, and a gremlin or two to whatever artifact had roused the searcher-priests' attention, then sit back at a safe distance while dodgers did the dangerous work. Much of what the teams excavated was abandoned weapons, frequently still primed and hair-triggered; the rest, while not intended as weapons, still had a tendency to explode.

Xantcha quickly realized that gremlins weren't any more imaginative than Phyrexians. They were simply more expendable. That very first time outside the nether end of an ambulator, when she saw blue-gray gremlin hands reaching for the shiniest lever in sight, Xantcha had decided she'd work alone and thrust her knife through the gremlin's throat before his imagination got her killed. The diggers hadn't cared. They only cared that she found and disconnected the tiny wires between that lever and a throbbing crimson crystal deep within the artifact.

After the bearers got the inert crystal back to Phyrexia, a herald had conducted Xantcha to one of the great obsidian Fanes of the First Sphere, where the planner-priests—second only to the demons in Phyrexia's complex hierarchy—interrogated her about the excavation and the insights that had inspired her as she disconnected the wires. They demanded that she attach the crystal to the immense body of one of the planners. Which Xantcha did, having no other alternative to obedience. No one was more surprised than Xantcha herself when both she and the planner survived.

The herald gave her a cloak of golden mesh and a featureless mask before conducting her back to the Fourth Sphere. For the first time, Xantcha looked like a compleat Phyrexian—provided she stood still.

Diggers and bearers had been compleated with scrap: bits of brass, copper, and tin. Their leather-patched joints leaked oil with every move. They were not pleased to have a gold-clad newt in their midst. Her life had never been gentle, but everything Xantcha had endured until then had derived from indifference. It wasn't until she'd been rewarded by the planners that she experienced personal hatred and cruelty.

* * * * *

Beneath Xantcha's arm, the iron chain shifted slightly. Her fingers clamped over the shifting links before her eyes were open, but the movement was merely Rat shifting in his sleep. A blanket of clouds had unfurled between them and the moon. The land had gone quiet; Xantcha sniffed for storms or worse and found the air as empty as before. She loosened her grip on the chain without releasing it completely.

Rat would run. Though he remained fettered and had no hope of survival in the open country, he'd try to run as long as he believed freedom lay somewhere else.

There was no word for freedom in Phyrexian. The only freedom a Phyrexian knew was the effortless movement of metal against metal when each piece was cushioned in glistening oil, and even that freedom was inaccessible to a flesh-bound newt. Battered and starved by the diggers who depended on her for their own survival, Xantcha had taken refuge in endurance. Though none of the worlds she'd visited matched the moist, green world of her dreams—in truth, Dominaria itself didn't match those dreams—the worst of them had been more hospitable than Phyrexia.

And if perversity were a proper measure of accomplishment, then Xantcha took perverse pride in surmounting the challenge she found at the nether end of each ambulator portal. Once an artifact lay exposed in front of her, she'd forget the diggers' prejudice, the bearers' brutality. Every artifact was different, yet they were all the same, too, and if Xantcha studied them long enough—whether they'd been made by Urza, Phyrexia, or some nameless artificer on a nameless world—she'd eventually unravel their secrets.

Xantcha would never be truly compleat, but she had achieved usefulness. She'd become a dodger, the fifth dodger, by virtue of the crimson sphere, which began a revolution in the way Phyrexia powered its largest non-sentient artifacts. A few more finds and she'd become the second dodger, Orman'huzra, though in her thoughts she remained Xantcha. The teacher-priests were right about some things: Gix's newts were too old, too set to change.

There was no Phyrexian word for happiness, and contentment meant glistening oil, yet as Orman'huzra, Xantcha found a measure of both. The others might despise her, but with her gold-mesh cloak she was untouchable. And they needed her. Within their carapaces, Phyrexians were alive; they understood death and feared it more than a newt did because without flesh, compleat Phyrexians could not heal themselves, and scrap-made Phyrexians were almost as expendable as newts.

The next turning point in Xantcha's life came in the windswept mountains of a world with three small moons. The artifact was huge and ringed by the rotting flesh of the born-folk who'd died defending it. Countless hollow crystals, no two exactly alike, pierced its dark, convoluted surface. Flexible wires had sprouted among the crystals, each supporting a concave mirror.

When the mirrors moved, sound and sometimes light emerged from the hollow crystals.

The searcher-priests had been certain it was a weapon of unparalleled power.

Disable it, the searcher had told her. *Prepare it for bearing back to Phyrexia. Do not attempt to dismantle it. The born-folk fought hard. They could not defeat us, yet they did not retreat. They died to keep us from this artifact. Therefore we must have it, and quickly.*

Xantcha didn't need reasons. The artifact—any artifact—was sufficient. Solving each artifact's mystery was all that mattered to her. What the priests did with her discoveries didn't concern her. From a newt's vulnerable perspective, a new weapon meant nothing. Everything in Phyrexia was already deadly.

Ignoring the corpses, she'd approached the artifact as she'd approached all the others.

But the wind-crystal, as she named it, wasn't a weapon. Its crystals and mirrors had no power except what they borrowed from the sun, moons, wind, and rain; then they gave it back as patterns of light and sound. The artifact reached deep into Xantcha's dreams, where it awakened the notions of beauty that couldn't be expressed in Phyrexian words.

Xantcha refused to prepare the artifact as the searcher-priests had demanded. She told the diggers and bearers, *It has no secrets, nothing that Phyrexia can use. It simply is, and it belongs here.* She was Orman'huzra, and the immobile planner-priests of the First Sphere had given her a golden cloak. She'd thought her words would have weight with the scrappy diggers and bearers; and they had, in ways Xantcha hadn't imagined. They stripped away her golden cloak and beat her bloody. They destroyed the artifact, every crystal, every mirror. Then they told the searchers that Orman'huzra was to blame for the loss of a weapon that could reduce whole worlds to dust.

Battered and scarcely conscious, Xantcha had been dragged to the brink of the very same fumarole where Gix had fallen to the Seventh Sphere. One push and life would have ended for her, but Xantcha was made of flesh and the planner-priests had believed that flesh could be punished until it transformed itself. From the fumarole Xantcha was taken to a cramped cell, where she dwelt in darkness for some small portion of eternity, sustained by memories of dancing light and music. When the priests thought she had suffered enough, they dragged her out again. The searchers had found another inscrutable artifact on another nameless world.

Xantcha was Orman'huzra. She was still useful and she had the wit—the deceit—to grovel before the various priests, begging for her life on any terms they offered. They sent her back to work never guessing that a lowly newt, mourning the loss of beauty, had declared war on Phyrexia.

The diggers suspected, but the great priests paid no more attention to diggers than they did to newts, and suspicion notwithstanding, diggers who worked with Orman'huzra lasted longer than those who didn't. As soon as she finished with one extraction, she'd find herself assigned to another team.

Thirty artifacts and twenty-two worlds after being dragged out of her cell, Xantcha's war was going well. She hadn't destroyed every artifact they sent her to unravel, but she'd lost several and rigged several more so that the next Phyrexian who touched it never touched anything again. She grew quite pleased with herself.

The diggers were already in place when Xantcha arrived, alone and nauseous from the ambulator trek, on her twenty-third world. A rattling digger made of metal and leather, all of it slick with oil that stank rather than glistened, led her into a humid cave where rows of smoky meat-fat lanterns marked the excavation.

"They might be Phyrexian," the digger said as they approached the main trench. At least, that's what Xantcha thought it had said. Its voice box worked no better than the rest of it.

Xantcha peered into the trenches, into a pair of fire-faceted eyes, each larger than her skull. She sat on her ankles, slowly absorbing what the searchers had found this time.

"They might be Phyrexian," the digger repeated.

Whatever the artifact was, it wasn't Phyrexian and neither were the ranks and rows of partially excavated specimens behind it. Phyrexians were useful. Tender-priests compleated newt-flesh according to its place in the Ineffable's plan, and then they stopped. Function was everything. These artifacts had no apparent function. They seemed, at first and second glance, to be statues: metal reproductions of the crawling insects that, like rats and buzzards, flourished everywhere, including Phyrexia. And though Xantcha had no liking for things that buzzed or stung, what she saw reminded her more of the long-destroyed wind-crystal than the digger beside her.

"I am told to ask, what will you need to secure them for bearing?"

Xantcha shook her head. Mostly the searcher-priests looked for sources of metal and oil because Phyrexia had none of its own; artifacts were a bonus, but the gems and precious metals that compleated the higher priests came to Phyrexia in the form of plunder.

It didn't take Orman'huzra to secure plunder.

There had to be more, and to find it Xantcha seized a lantern and leapt into the trench where the stronger but far less agile digger couldn't follow. At arm's length she realized that the insects were fully articulated. Whoever made them had meant them to move. She touched a golden plate; it was as warm as her own flesh and vibrated faintly.

Forgetting the digger on the trench-rim, Xantcha ran to one of the second-rank artifacts. It, too, was warm and vibrating, but unlike the first artifact, it had a steel-toothed mouth and steel claws—as nasty as any warrior's pincers—in addition to its golden carapace. On impulse, Xantcha tried to bend the raised edge of a golden plate.

A long, segmented antenna whipped around Xantcha's arm and hurled her against the trench wall, but not before she had the answer she wanted. The plate hadn't bent. It looked like gold, but it was made from something much stronger. Xantcha had another, less wanted, answer too. The artifacts were aware, possibly sentient and at least partially powered.

"Move! Move!" the rattletrap digger shrieked from the rim, less warning or concern for a damaged companion than a reaction to the unexpected.

Sure enough a reeking handful of diggers and bearers came clattering, some through the trenches and others along the rim.

One digger, in better repair than the rest, assumed command, demanding quiet from his peers and an explanation from Orman'huzra.

"Simple enough. It moved and I didn't dodge."

A cacophony of squeaks and trills echoed through the cave, as the diggers and bearers succumbed to laughter.

The better-made digger whistled for silence. "They have not moved. They do not move."

Xantcha displayed her welted arm. Sometimes, there was no arguing with flesh. Diggers did not have articulated faces, yet the chief digger contrived a worried look.

"You will secure them," it said, a command, not a request.

"I will need wire—" Xantcha began, then hesitated as half-formed plots competed in her head.

The searchers must have known that the shiny insects were more than plunder but the diggers and bearers, despite their trench excavations, hadn't known the artifacts could move. She stared at the huge, faceted eyes, fiery in reflected lantern light. The insects weren't Phyrexian; perhaps they could be enlisted in her private war against Phyrexia, if she could get them through intact and without getting herself killed in the process.

"Strong wire," she amended. "And cloth . . . thick, heavy cloth. And food . . . something to eat and not reeking oil."

"Cloths?" the digger whirled its mouth parts in confusion. Only newts, gremlins and the highest strata of priests draped their bodies in cloth.

"Unmade clothes," Xantcha suggested. "Or soft leather. Something . . . anything so I can cover their eyes."

The digger chattered to itself. The tender-priests could replace a newt's eyes, if its destiny called for a different sort of vision, but diggers had flesh-eyes within their immobile faces. This one had pale blue eyes that widened slowly with comprehension.

"Diggers will find," it said, then spun its head around and issued commands to its peers in the rapid, compleat Phyrexian way that Xantcha could understand but never duplicate. Fully half of them rumbled immediately toward the cave's mouth. The chief digger turned back to Xantcha. "Orman'huzra, begin."

And she did, walking the trenches, examining the insect arti-facts already excavated. Xantcha counted the golden, humming creatures that were visible. She climbed out of the trenches and measured the rest of the dig site with her eyes. The cave could easily contain an army. Xantcha hadn't been on this world long enough to know the measure of its day, but it seemed safe to think that she'd need at least a local season, maybe a local year, to get her warriors ready for their war.

Xantcha approached the golden swarm cautiously, starting with those she judged least likely to sever an arm or neck if she made a mistake—which she did several times before she learned what awakened them and what didn't. An isolated touch was more dangerous than a solid thwack to an armored underbelly, and they were much more sensitive to her flesh than to the dig-gers' shovel-hands.

She foresaw problems inciting her army to fight back in Phyrexia and studied the artifacts by herself, whenever rain drove all but a few diggers and bearers to the shelter beside the ambula-tor. Rain, especially a cold, penetrating rain, was a poorly-compleated Phyrexian's greatest enemy. The bearers would retreat all the way to Phyrexia once a storm started. Xantcha could have won her private war with just a few of the mud-swirling, gully-washing deluges that threatened the artifact cave as the world's seasons progressed.

Cold rain and mud weren't Xantcha's favorite conditions either. She commandeered pieces of the digger-scrounged cloth, which was, in fact, clothing for folk generally taller and broader than Xantcha herself. The garments were torn, often slashed, and always bloodstained. They rotted quickly in the wretched weather and when they grew too offensive, Xantcha would throw the cloth on her fire and find something fresh in the scrounge piles. Her need for Phyrexian vengeance hadn't led to any empathy for born-folk.

She successfully dismantled one of the smaller insect-artifacts and learned enough of its secrets to feel confident that they would awaken, as soon as they emerged from the Phyrexian prime end of the ambulator. After that, it was simply a matter of folding their legs and antennae, binding them with cloth and wire, and ordering the bearers to stack them in pyramid layers near the nether end for eventual transfer to Phyrexia.

It never occurred to her that the bearers would act on their own to carry the artifacts with them when they next escaped the rain, and by the time she realized that they had, it was already too late. There was a searcher-priest towering above the diggers and bearers.

"Orman'huzra," the searcher-priest called in that menacing tone only high-ranking Phyrexians could achieve. "You were told to secure these artifacts for Phyrexia. You were warned that inefficiency would not be tolerated. You have failed in both regards. The artifacts you subverted were dismantled before they could cause any damage."

The many-eyed searcher was between Xantcha and the cave mouth. There'd be no getting past it or getting through the massed diggers and bearers, if she'd been tempted to run, which she wasn't. Xantcha might dream of lush, green worlds, but she was Phyrexian, and though she'd learned how to declare war against her own kind, she hadn't learned how to disobey. When the priest called her forward, she threw down her tools and climbed out of the trench.

Diggers and bearers formed a ring around her and the searcher-priest. They chittered among themselves. This time Orman'huzra had gone too far and would not survive the searcher-priest's wrath.

"Dig," the searcher-priest commanded, and she understood what they intended for her.

Xantcha dug the damp ground until she'd scratched out a shallow hole as wide as her shoulders and as long as she was tall. There was nothing worse than a too short, too narrow prison. Her fingers were numb and bloodied, but she clawed the ground until the searcher-priest grew impatient and ordered a digger to finish the job. When it was done, the hole tapered from shallow to waist-deep along its length and was exactly the length and width Xantcha had laid out.

She'd been through this before and, with a sigh, jumped into the hole, her feet landing in the deeper end, ready to be buried alive.

"Not yet," the searcher-priest said as a length of segmented wire unwound from its arm.

Xantcha recognized it as the antenna from one of her insect warriors. She climbed out of the hole prepared for pain, prepared for death, because she was certain that the searcher-priest had lied. Only a few of her warriors had gotten to Phyrexia, and undoubtedly all of them had fallen by now, but at least one had done damage before it fell.

That was victory enough, as Xantcha's wrists were bound by a length of wire slung over a tree limb to keep her upright during the coming ordeal. It had to be enough, as the first lash stroke of the antenna cut through her ragged clothing, and the second cut deep into her flesh.

The diggers and bearers counted the strokes; lesser Phyrexians were very good at counting. Xantcha heard them count to twenty. After that, everything was blurred. She thought she heard the cry of forty and fifty, but that might have been a dream. She hoped it was a dream. Then it seemed that there was a stroke that didn't land on her and wasn't counted by the diggers and bearers. That, too, might have been a dream, except there were no strokes after that, and no one pushing her into what would almost certainly have been a permanent grave.

Instead there was bright light and great noise.

A storm, Xantcha thought slowly. Rain. Driving the diggers, bearers and even the searcher-priest to shelter. Her wounds had begun to hurt. Drowning would be a better, easier way to die.

Without the diggers and bearers to do the counting, there was no way to measure the time she slumped beneath the tree limb, unable to stand or fall. In retrospect, it could not have been very long before she heard a voice speaking the language of her dreams, the language that had given her the words for beauty.

Xantcha did notice that she didn't fall when her arms did and that the rain never fell.

The voice filled her head with comforting sounds. Then a hand, that was both warm and soft like her own, touched her face and closed her eyes.

When she awoke next, she was in a grave of pain and fire, but the voice was in her head telling her that fear was unnecessary, even harmful to her healing. She remembered her eyes and, opening them, looked upon a flaming specter with many-colored eyes. Xantcha thought of Gix, and for the first time in her life she fainted.

The next time Xantcha awoke the pain and fire were gone. She was weak, but whole, and lying on softness such as she had not felt since leaving the vats. A man hovered beside her, staring into the distance. She had the strength for one word and chose it carefully.

"Why?"

His face, worried as he stared, turned grim when he looked down.

"I thought the Phyrexians would kill you."

Beyond doubt, he spoke the language of Xantcha's dreams, the language of the place where she had been destined to sleep. He knew the name of her place, too, and had correctly guessed that the Phyrexians meant to kill her, but he hadn't seemed to recognize that she was also Phyrexian. Waves of caution washed through Xantcha's weakened flesh. She fought to hide her shivering.

A piece of cloth covered her. He pulled it back, revealing her naked flesh. His frown deepened.

"I thought they'd captured you. I thought they would change you, as they changed my brother. But I was too late. You bled. There is no metal or oil beneath your skin, but they'd already made you one of them. Do you remember who you were, child? Why did they take you? Did you belong to a prominent family? Where were you born?"

She took a deep breath. Honesty, under the present circumstances seemed the best course, as it had been with Gix, for surely this man was a demon. And, just as surely, he was already at war with Phyrexia. "I was not born, I have no family and I was never a child. I am the Orman'huzra who calls herself Xantcha. I am Phyrexian; I belong to Phyrexia."

He made white-knuckled fists above Xantcha's face. She closed her eyes, lacking the strength for any other defense, but the blows didn't fall.

"Listen to me closely, Xantcha. You belong to me, now. After what was done to you, for whatever reason it was done, you have no cause for love or loyalty to Phyrexia, and if you're clever, you'll tell me everything you know, starting with how you and the others planned to get home."

Xantcha was clever. Gix himself had conceded that. She was clever enough to realize that this yellow-haired man was both more and less than he seemed. She measured her words carefully. "There is a shelter at the bottom of the hill. Take me there. I will show you the way to Phyrexia."

Chapter 7

"Wake up!"

Words and jostling ended Xantcha's sleep so thoroughly that for a heartbeat she neither knew where she was nor what she'd been dreaming. In short order she recognized Rat and the streamside grove where she'd fallen asleep, both awash in morning light, but the dreams remained lost. She hadn't intended to fall deeply asleep and was angry with herself for that error and surprised to find Rat clinging to her forearm.

He retreated when she glowered.

"You had a nightmare."

Images shook out of Xantcha's memory: the damp world of insect artifacts, her last beating at Phyrexian hands, Urza hurling fire and sorcery to rescue her. Those were moments of her life that Xantcha would rather not dream about. Between them and anger, she was in a sour mood.

"You didn't take advantage?" she demanded.

Rat answered, "I considered it," without hesitation. "All night I considered it, but I'm a long way from anywhere, I've got a chain between my feet, and even though you may be stronger than me and have that thing that makes us fly, you're still a boy. You need someone to take care of you."

"Me? I need someone to take care of me?" Of all the reasons she could think of to find herself in possession of a slave, that was the last she'd expected. "What about your word?"

He shrugged. "I've had a night to think about it. When I woke up . . . at first I thought you were pretending to be asleep, waiting for me to run. But if I were going to run—walk—" Rat rattled the chain. "I'd have to make sure you couldn't catch me again."

"What were you going to do? Strangle me? Bash my head?"

Another shrug. "I didn't get that far. You started having your nightmare. It looked like a bad one, so I woke you—you don't believe that Shratta nonsense about dreams and your soul?"

"No." Xantcha knew little about the Shratta's beliefs, except that they were violently intolerant of everyone else's. Besides, Urza had said she'd lost her soul in the vats.

"Then why are you so cross-grained? I'm still here, and you're not dreaming a miserable dream."

Xantcha stretched herself upright. Assor's basket was where she'd left it, exactly as she left it, not a crumb unaccounted for. She separated another meal and tossed Rat a warning along with his bread.

"I don't need anyone taking care of me. Don't want it either. When we get to the cottage, your name becomes Mishra, and Urza's the one who needs your help."

Rat grunted. Xantcha expected something more, but it seemed that he'd discovered the virtues of silence and obedience, at least until she told him to sit beside her.

"There's no other way?" he asked, turning pale. "Can't we walk? Even with the chain, I'd rather walk."

Xantcha shook her head and Rat bolted for the bushes. After trying unsuccessfully to turn himself inside out and wasting his breakfast, Rat crawled back to her side.

"I'm ready now."

"I've never fallen from the sky, Rat. Never come close. You're safer than you'd be in a wagon or walking on your own two feet."

"Can't help it—" Rat began then froze completely as Xantcha yawned and the sphere spread from her open mouth.

He started for the bushes again. Knowing that his gut was empty and that she'd be the one who'd be vomiting if she had to bite off the sphere before it was finished, Xantcha grabbed the back of Rat's neck and held his head in her lap until the sphere was rising.

"The worst is over. Sit up. Don't think so much. There's always something to see. Watch the clouds, the ground."

Ground was the wrong word. Cursing feebly, Rat clung to her for dear life. If he couldn't relax, it was going to be a painful journey for both of them. Xantcha tried sympathy.

"Talk to me, Rat. Tell me why you're so afraid. Put your fears into words."

But he couldn't be reassured, so Xantcha tried a less gentle approach. Freeing one arm, she set the sphere tumbling, then yelled louder than his moans:

"I said, talk to me, Rat. You're giving in to fear, Rat." She thought of her feet touching ground, and the sphere plummeted; she thought of playing among the clouds and the sphere rebounded at a truly dizzying speed. "You haven't begun to know fear. Now, talk to me! Why are you afraid?"

Rat screamed, "It's wrong! It's all wrong. I can feel the sky watching me, waiting. Waiting for a chance to throw me down!"

He was sobbing, but his death grip loosened as soon as the words were out of his mouth.

Xantcha thumped Rat soundly between the shoulders. "I won't let the sky have you."

"Doesn't matter. It knows I'm here. Knows I don't belong. It's waiting."

She thumped him again. Rat's complaint was too much like her own in the early days, when Urza would drag her between-worlds. Urza had the planeswalker spark; the fathomless stuff between the multiverse's countless world-planes bent to his will. Xantcha had been, and remained, an unwelcome interloper. The instant the between-worlds furled around her, she could hear the vast multiverse sucking its breath, preparing to spit her out.

The planeswalker spark was something a mind either had, or didn't have. Xantcha didn't have it; Urza couldn't share his. The cyst was the only stopgap that he'd been able to devise. It didn't leave Xantcha feeling any less like an interloper, but it did give promise that she'd be alive when the multiverse spat her out. She'd ask Urza to implant a cyst in Rat's belly—in Mishra's belly—but until then, there was nothing she could do except keep him talking.

The sky above Efuan Pincar wasn't nearly as hostile as the between-worlds. There was a chance he'd talk himself out of his fears. She nudged him into another telling of his life story. The details differed from the second tale he'd told in Assor's wagon, but the overall spirit hadn't changed. When he came to the part where he'd found religious denunciations written in blood on the walls of his family's home, the intensity of his feelings forced Rat to sit straight and speak in a firm, steady voice.

"If the Shratta are men of Avohir, then I spit on Avohir. Better to be damned than live in the Shratta's fist."

That was the sort of fatal, futile sentiment that Xantcha understood, but she was less pleased to hear Rat declare, "When your Urza's done with me, I'll make my way to Pincar City and join the Red-Stripes. They've got the right idea: kill the Shratta. There's no other way. They'd sooner die than admit they're wrong, so let them die."

"There are Phyrexians among the Red-Stripes," Xantcha warned. "They're a much worse enemy than any Shratta."

"They're not my enemy, not if they're fighting the Shratta."

"Mishra may have thought the same thing, but it is not so simple. Flesh cannot trust them, because Phyrexia will never see flesh as anything but a mistake to be erased."

Rat watched her quietly.

"Flesh. We're flesh, you and I," Xantcha pinched the skin on her arm, "but Phyrexians aren't. They're artifacts. Like Urza's, during the Brothers' War . . . only, Phyrexians aren't artifacts. Their flesh has been replaced with other things, mostly metal, according to the Ineffable's plan. Their blood's been replaced with glistening oil. So it should be. Blood cannot trust Phyrexians because blood is a mistake."

His eyes had narrowed. They studied a place far beyond

Xantcha's shoulder. Urza talked about thinking, but he rarely did it. Urza either solved his problems instantly, without thinking, or he sank in the mire of obsession. Rat was changing his mind while he thought. Xantcha found the process unnerving to watch.

She spoke quickly, to conceal her own discomfort. "Flesh, blood, meat—what does it matter? Phyrexia is your enemy, Rat. The Brothers' War was just the beginning of what Phyrexia will do to all of Dominaria, if it can. There are Phyrexians in the Red-Stripes, and you'd be wiser, far wiser, to join the Shratta in the fight against them."

"It's just . . ." Rat was thinking even as he talked. His mind changed again and he met Xantcha's eyes with an almost physical force. "You said you smelled Phyrexians among the Red-Stripes. My nose is as good as my eyes, and I didn't smell anything at all. You said 'flesh cannot trust them,' but everybody was flesh, even Tucktah and Garve. On top of all, your talk about me pretending to be Mishra, for someone you call Urza. Something's not true, here."

"Do you think I'm lying?" Xantcha was genuinely curious.

"Whatever you smelled back in Medran, it scared you, because it was Phyrexian, not because it was Red-Stripe. So, I guess you're telling the truth, just not all of it. Maybe we're both flesh, Xantcha, but, Avohir's truth, you're not my sort of flesh."

"I bleed," Xantcha asserted, and to prove the point drew the knife from her boot and slashed a fingertip.

It was a deep cut, deeper than she'd intended. Bright blood flowed in a steady stream from finger to palm, from palm over wrist, where it began to stain her sleeve.

Rat grimaced. "That wasn't necessary," he said, pointedly looking beyond the sphere; the first time he'd done that. Eventually a person would face his fears, provided the alternatives were worse. "You'd know where to cut yourself."

Xantcha held the knife hilt where Rat would see it. He turned further away.

"You were thinking murder not long ago," she reminded him. "Bashing me so you could escape."

Rat shook his head. "Not even close. When my family left

Pincar City . . . My father learned to slaughter and butcher meat each fall, but I never could. I always ran away, even last year."

He shrank a little, as if he'd lost a bit of himself by the admission. Xantcha returned the knife to her boot.

"You believe me?" she asked before sticking her bloody finger in her mouth.

"I can't believe you, even if you're telling the truth. Urza the Artificer. Mishra. Smelling Phyrexians. This . . . this thing—" He flung his hand to the side, struck the sphere, and recoiled. "You're too strange. You look like a boy, but you talk . . . You don't talk like anyone I've ever heard before, Xantcha. It's not that you sound foreign, but you're not Efuand. You say you're not an artifact and not Phyrexian. I don't know what to believe. Whose side are you on?"

"Urza's side . . . against Phyrexia." Her finger hadn't stopped bleeding; she put it back in her mouth.

"Urza's no hero, not to me. What he did thirty-four hundred years ago, his gods should still be punishing him for that. You throw a lot of choices in front of me, all of them bad, one way or another. I don't know what to think."

"You think too much."

"Yeah, I hear that all the time. . . ." Rat's voice trailed off. Whoever had chided him last had probably been killed by the Shratta. *All the time* had become history for him, history and grief.

Xantcha left him alone. Her finger was pale and wrinkled. At least it had stopped bleeding. They'd been soaring due west in the grasp of a gentle, drifting wind. Clouds were forming to the north. So far the clouds were scattered, fluffy and white, but north of Efuan Pincar was the Endless Sea where huge storms were common and sudden. Xantcha used her hands to put the sphere on a southwesterly course and set it rising in search of stronger winds.

Belatedly, she realized she had Rat's undivided attention.

"How do you do that?" he asked. "Magic? Are you a sorcerer? Would that explain everything?"

"No."

"No?"

"No, I don't know how I do it. I don't know how I walk, either, or how the food I eat keeps me alive, but it does. One day, Urza handed me something. He said it was a cyst, and he said, swallow it. Since it came from Urza, it was probably an artifact. I don't know for sure because I never asked. I know how to use it. I don't need to know more, and neither will you."

"Sorry I asked. I'm just trying to think my way through this."

"You think too much."

She hadn't meant to repeat the comment that had jabbed his memory, but before she could berate herself, Rat shot back:

"I'm supposed to be Mishra, aren't I?"

He'd changed his mind again. It was possible that a man, a true flesh-and-blood man, not like Urza, couldn't think too much.

The sphere found the stronger winds and slewed sideways. Xantcha needed full concentration to stop the tumbling. Rat curled up against her with his head between his knees. To the north, clouds billowed as she watched. It was unlikely that they could outrun the brewing storm, but they could cover a lot of territory before she had to get them to shelter. There would, however, be a price.

"It's going to be fast and a little bumpy while we run the windstream. You ready?"

Taking Rat's groan for assent, Xantcha angled her hand west of southwest, and the sphere leapt as if it had been shot from a giant's bow. If she'd been alone, Xantcha would have pressed both hands against the sphere's inner curve and let the wind roar past her face. She figured Rat wasn't ready for such exhilaration and kept her guiding hand sheltered in her lap. The northern horizon became a white mountain range whose highest peaks were beginning to spread and flatten against an invisible ceiling.

"Somebody's going to get wild weather tonight," Xantcha said to her unresponsive companion. "Maybe not us, but someone's going to be begging Avohir's mercy."

She guided the sphere higher. Beneath them, the ground resembled one of Urza's tabletops, though flatter and emptier: a few roads, like rusty wire through spring-green fields, a palisaded village of about ten homesteads tucked in a stream bend. Xantcha considered her promise to replace Rat's rags and, implicitly, to have his fetters removed.

If she set the sphere down, the storm might keep them down until tomorrow. If she kept the sphere scudding, they'd cut a half-day or more off the journey. And by the amount of smoke rising from the village, the inhabitants were burning their fields—hardly a good time for strangers to show up asking favors. Xantcha swiveled her hand south of southwest, and the sphere bounced onto the new tack.

"Wait!" Rat shook Xantcha's ankle. "Wait! That village. Can't you see? It's on fire."

She looked again. Rat was right, fields weren't burning, roofs were. All the more reason to stay on the south by southwest course away from trouble.

"Xantcha! It's the Shratta. It's got to be. Red-Stripes come looking for bribes but don't destroy the villages. We can't just leave—You can't! People are dying down there!"

"I'm not a sorcerer, Rat. I'm not Urza. There's nothing I can do except get myself—and you—killed."

"We can't turn our backs. We're no better than the Shratta, no better than the Phyrexians, if we do that."

Rat had a real knack for getting under Xantcha's skin, a dangerous mixture of arrogance and charm, just like the real Mishra. Xantcha was about to disillusion her companion with the revelation that she was Phyrexian when he heaved himself toward the burning village. The sphere wasn't Rat's to command. It held to Xantcha's chosen course—as he must have known it would. Rat didn't seem the sort who'd sacrifice himself to prove a point, but he set the sphere tumbling. Everything was knees, elbows, food, and a sword before Xantcha got them sorted out.

"Don't you ever do that again!"

Rat accepted the challenge. This time Xantcha split his upper lip and planted her knee in his groin before she steadied the sphere.

"We're going home . . . to Urza. He's got the power to settle this."

"Too damn late! People are dying down there!"

Rat flung himself, but Xantcha was ready this time and the sphere scarcely bounced.

"I'll drop you if you don't settle yourself."

"Then drop me."

"You'll die."

"I'd rather be dead on the ground than alive up here."

Rat grabbed the scabbarded sword and, with his full weight behind the hilt, plunged it through the sphere. Xantcha reeled from the impact. She hadn't known damage to the sphere meant sharp pain radiating from the cyst in her gut. She could have lived another three thousand years without that particular bit of knowledge. She cocked her fist for a punch that would shatter Rat's jaw.

"Go ahead," he snarled defiantly. "Tell your precious Urza that you killed his brother a second time."

Xantcha lowered her hand. Maybe she was wrong about his willingness to sacrifice himself. By then they were drifting away from the village and nothing but Xantcha's will put them on a course for the flames. The closer they got, the clearer it was that Rat had been right. The north wind brought screams of pain and terror. Born-folk were dying.

When they were still several hundred paces from the wooden palisade, a young woman ran through the broken gate, her hair and hems billowing behind her, a sword-wielding thug in pursuit. Woman and thug both stopped short when they saw two strangers hovering in midair.

"Waste not, want not!" Xantcha muttered.

She thought *Collision* and *Now!* The cyst in her stomach grew fiery spikes, but the sphere plunged like a stooping hawk. It collapsed the instant it touched the gape-mouthed thug, leaving Xantcha to strike with sufficient force to knock him unconscious. She bounded to her feet and crushed the now-defenseless man's skull with her boot heel, deliberately splattering Rat with gore.

If he wanted death; she'd show him death.

The village woman screamed and kept running.

Xantcha seized the sword from the tangle of bodies and spilled baskets. "All right!" She thrust the hilt toward Rat. When he didn't take it up, she poked him hard. "This is what you wanted! Go ahead. Go in there. Save them!"

"I—I can't use a sword. I don't know how. . . . I thought—"

"You thought!" Xantcha angled the sword, prepared to clout him with the hilt. "You think too much!"

Rat got to his feet, stumbling over his chain. He stared at the iron links as if he hadn't seen them before. Whatever nonsense he'd been thinking, he hadn't remembered his fetters.

"I can't . . . You'll have to—"

She shook her head slowly. "I told you, I'm no damn sorcerer, no damn warrior. This is your idiot's idea, your fight. So, you choose: them or me."

It was the same ominous, otherworldly tone Xantcha had used with Garve and Tucktah. She cocked the sword a second time, and Rat grabbed the hilt. He couldn't run, so he skipped and hopped toward the gate.

"Lose the scabbard!" Xantcha shouted after him then muttered Phyrexian curses as Rat stumbled through the gate brandishing a scabbarded sword.

Rat was a fool, and fools deserved whatever harm befell them, but Xantcha's anger faded as soon as her nemesis was out of sight. She reached into her belt-pouch and finger-sorted a few of the smallest, blackest coins. Then, with them clutched loosely in her hand, she yawned out Urza's armor and followed Rat into the besieged village. Not being a sorcerer wasn't quite the same as not having any sorcerous tricks in her arsenal, and not being a warrior was a statement of preference, not experience. There weren't many weapons Xantcha didn't know how to use or evade. On other worlds she'd routinely carried several of them.

But not on Dominaria. She'd given her word.

"I know your temper," Urza had said after they arrived. "But this is home—my home. My traveling years are over. I'm never leaving Dominaria, and I don't want you starting brawls and drawing attention to yourself . . . or me. Promise me you'll stay out of trouble. Promise me that you'll walk away rather than start a fight."

"Waste not, want not—I did not start this, Urza. Truly, I did not."

A gutted corpse lay one step within the gate, but it wasn't Rat's. Xantcha leapt over it. A man bearing a bloody knife ran out of a burning cottage on her left. She slipped a coin into her throwing hand, then stayed her arm as a second, similarly armed, man burst out of the cottage.

Villagers or Shratta thugs? Was one chasing the other? Were they both fleeing? Or looking for more victims?

Xantcha couldn't tell by their clothes or manner. Few things were more frustrating or dangerous than barging into a brawl among strangers. After cursing Rat to the Seventh Sphere of Phyrexia, she entered the cottage the men had abandoned.

The one-room dwelling was filled with smoke. Xantcha called Rat's name and got no answer. Back on the village's single street, she headed for the largest building she could see and had taken about ten strides when an arrow struck her shoulder. Urza's armor was as good as granite when it came to arrows. The shaft splintered, and the arrowhead slid harmlessly down her back.

In one smooth movement, Xantcha spun around and hurled a small, black coin at a fleeing archer. The coin began to glow as soon as it left her hand. It was white-hot by the time it struck the archer's neck. He was dead before he hit the ground, with thick, greenish-black fumes rising from the fatal wound.

A swordsman attacked Xantcha next. He knocked her down with his first attack but was unnerved when she sprang up, unbloodied. Xantcha parried his next strike with her forearm as she closed in to kick him once in the stomach and a second time, as he crumbled, to the jaw. She paused to pick up the sword, then continued down the street shouting Rat's name, attracting attention.

Two more men appeared in front of her. They knew each other and the warrior's trade, giving each other room, exchanging gestures and cryptic commands as they approached. The strategy might have worked if Xantcha had been unarmored or if the sword had been her only weapon. Her aim with the coins wasn't as good with her off-weapon hand. Only one struck its target, but that was enough. The other two exploded when they hit the ground, leaving goat-sized craters in the packed dirt.

Her surviving enemy rushed forward, more intent on getting

out of the village than fighting. Xantcha swung, but he parried well and had momentum on his side. Xantcha slammed backward into the nearest wall when he shoved her aside. Elsewhere in the village, someone blew three rapid notes on a horn, and a weaponed quartet at the other end of the village street dashed for the gate. For religious fanatics, the Shratta were better disciplined than most armies. Dark suspicion led Xantcha to inhale deeply, but beyond the smoke and the blood, there was nothing Phyrexian in the air.

A straggler ran past. Xantcha let him go. This was Rat's fight, not hers, and she didn't yet know if he'd survived.

"Ra-te-pe!" She used all three syllables of his name. "Ra-te-pe, son of Mideah, get yourself out here!"

A face appeared in the darkened doorway of the barn that had been her destination. It belonged to an older man, armed with a pitchfork. He stepped unsteadily over the doorsill.

"No one here owns that name."

"There'd better be. He's meat if he ran."

Two more villagers emerged from the barn: a woman clutching her bloody arm against her side and a stone-faced toddler who clung to her skirt.

"Who are you?" the elder asked, giving the pitchfork a shake, reminding Xantcha that she held a bare and bloody sword.

"Xantcha. Rat and I were . . . nearby." She threw the sword into the dirt beside the last man she'd killed. "He saw the roofs burning."

They still were. The survivors made no effort to extinguish the blazes. A village like this probably had one well and only a handful of buckets. The cottages were partly stone; they could be rebuilt after the fires burnt out.

The elder shook his head. Plainly he didn't believe that anyone had simply been nearby. But Xantcha had laid down her weapon. He shouted an all's well that lured a few more mute survivors from their hiding places.

Still no Rat.

Xantcha turned, intending to investigate the other end of the village. The woman who'd fled—the one who'd seen them descend in the sphere—was on the street behind her. Her reappearance, alive and unharmed, broke the villagers' shock. Another woman let out a cry that could have been either joy or grief.

The returning woman replied, "Mother," but her eyes were locked on Xantcha and her hands were knotted in ward-signs against evil.

Time to find Rat and get moving. Xantcha walked quickly to the other end of the village where a whitewashed temple held the place of honor. The door was held open by a corpse.

Given who was fighting in Efuan Pincar, Xantcha supposed she shouldn't have been surprised that the temple had become a charnel house. She counted ten men, each with his hands bound and his throat slit, lying in a common, bloody pool. There were more corpses, similarly bound, sprawled closer to the altar, but she'd spotted Rat staring at a wall before she'd counted them.

"We've got to leave."

He didn't twitch. The scabbard was gone; the sword blade was dark and glistening in the temple's gloomy light. Rat had probably never held a sword before Xantcha made him more afraid of her than death. Odds were he'd become a killer, if not a fighter, in the past hour. A man could crack under that kind of strain. Xantcha approached him cautiously.

"Rat? Ratepe?"

The wall was covered with bloody words. Xantcha could read a score of Dominarian languages, most of them long-extinct, none of them Efuand.

"What does it say?"

"'Those who defile the Shratta will be cleansed in their own blood. Blessed be Avohir, in whose name this has been done.'"

Xantcha placed her hand over his sword-gripping hand. Without a word, Rat released the hilt.

"If there are gods," she said softly, "then thugs like the Shratta don't speak for them."

She tried to guide Rat toward the door; he resisted, quietly but completely. Mortals, men who were born and who grew old, saw death in ways no Phyrexian newt could imagine, in ways Urza had forgotten. Xantcha had exhausted her meager store of platitudes.

"You knew the Shratta were here, Rat. You must have known what you'd find."

"No."

"I stopped at other villages before I got to Medran. You weren't the first to tell me about the Shratta. This is their handiwork."

"It's not!" Rat shrugged free.

"It's time to leave." Xantcha grasped his arm again.

Rat struck like a serpent but did no harm only because Xantcha was a hair's breath faster in jumping away. She recognized madness on his tear-streaked face.

"All right. Tell me. Talk to me. Why isn't this Shratta handiwork?"

"Him."

Rat pointed at an isolated corpse slumped in the corner between the written-on wall and the wall behind the altar. The man had died because his gut had been slashed open, but he had other wounds, many other wounds, none of which had bled appreciably. Xantcha, who'd fought and sometimes succumbed to her own blind rages, knew at once that this was the man—probably the only man—that Rat had killed.

"All right, what about him?"

"Look at him! He's not Shratta!"

"How do you know?" Xantcha asked, willing to believe him, if he had a good answer.

"Look at his hands!"

She nudged them with her foot. The light was bad, but they seemed ordinary enough to her. "What? I see nothing unordinary."

"The Hands of God. The Shratta are Avohir's Avengers. They tattoo their hands with Shratta-verses from Avohir's holy book."

"Maybe he was a new recruit?"

Rat shook his head vigorously. "It's more than his hands. He's clean-shaven. The Shratta never cut their beards."

Xantcha ran through her memory. Since she'd arrived in Efuan Pincar the only clean-shaven men she'd seen had been in Medran, wearing Red-Stripe tunics, and here where the men she'd fought and the man Rat had killed were beardless.

"So, it's not the Shratta after all? It's Red-Stripes pretending to be Shratta?" she asked.

And knowing that the Phyrexians had invaded the Red-Stripe cadres, Xantcha asked another, silent, question: Had the Phyrexians created their own enemy to bring war and suffering to an obscure corner of Dominaria? If so, they'd learned considerable subtlety since Gix destined her to sleep on another world.

Rat's head continued to shake. "I've seen the Shratta cut through a family like ripe cheese. I saw them draw my uncle's guts out through a hole in his gut: they'd said he'd spilled dog's blood on the book. I know the Shratta, Xantcha, and this is what they'd do, except, this man isn't—and can't be—Shratta."

Keeping her voice calm, Xantcha said, "You said you were gone when the Shratta came through your village. You didn't see anything. It could have been the Red-Stripes."

"Could've," Rat agreed easily. "But I saw my uncle get killed, and I saw it before we left Pincar City, and it was the Shratta. By the book, by the true book, Xantcha. Why would Red-Stripes do this? No one but the Shratta support the Shratta. The people here . . . at home, what was home . . . the Shratta would come, real Shratta, and they'd tell us what to do, which was mostly give them everything we had and then some; and they would kill if they didn't get what they wanted." Rat shuddered. "My family were strangers, driven out of Pincar City, but everyone hated the Shratta as much as we did. We'd pray . . . we'd all pray, Xantcha, to Avohir to send us red-striped warriors from the cities. The Red-Stripes were our protectors."

"Be careful what you pray for, I guess. It sounds like the Red-Stripes may have been doing the Shratta's dirty work, and leaving behind no witnesses to reveal the truth."

Rat had reached a similar conclusion. "And if that's true, they're not finished with this place. They're waiting outside. They won't have gone away. Everyone here is dead, you and me, too, unless we can kill them all."

"It's worse than that, Rat. Somebody's gone. Somebody's running a report back somewhere." To a Phyrexian *sleeper*, saying he'd seen a dark-haired youth hovering in a sphere? No, she'd killed the thug who'd seen them in the sphere. But she'd shaken off an arrow. Phyrexians might lack imagination, but they had excellent memories. Somebody might remember Gix's identical newts, especially since Dominaria was the world Phyrexia coveted above all others, the world of her earliest dreams. Urza was right, as usual. She'd lost her temper, and the price could be very high. "We've got to leave."

"Everyone will die!"

"No deader than they'd be if we'd never set foot here."

"But their blood will be on our hands—on my hands, since you don't seem to have a conscience. I'm not leaving."

"There's no point in staying."

"The Red-Stripes will come back. We'll kill them, then we can leave."

"I told you, there's no point. They'll have sent a runner. This village is doomed."

Rat paced noisily. "All right, it's doomed. So after we kill the Red-Stripes that are still outside the village, you take these people, one by one, to other villages, where they can spread the truth and disappear. By the time the runner leads more Red-Stripes here, this place will be empty. It can be done."

"You can't be serious."

But Rat was, and Xantcha had a conscience. It could be done. First came a long, violent night roaming the fields outside the village with her armor and a sharp knife, followed by three days of burying the dead and another five of ferrying frightened survivors to places where they could "spread the truth about the Shratta and the Red-Stripes then disappear." But it was done, and on the morning of the tenth day, after leaving Rat's fetters draped across the defiled altar, they resumed their journey out of Efuan Pincar.

Chapter 8

Xantcha guided the sphere with a rigid hand. The Glimmer Moon hung low in the night sky, painfully bright yet providing little illumination for the land below. A dark ridge loomed to the south. On the other side of that ridge there was a familiar cottage with two front doors and the bed in which she expected to be sleeping before midnight.

It was a clear night reminiscent of winter. The air was dead-calm and freezing within the sphere. Her feet had been quietly numb since sundown. Beside her, Rat hadn't said a word since the first stars appeared. She hoped he was asleep.

And perhaps he was, but he awoke when the sphere pitched forward and plummeted toward a black-mirror lake Xantcha hadn't noticed. He'd had nearly two weeks to learn when to tuck his head and keep his terror to himself, but in the dark, with food and whatnot tumbling around them, Xantcha didn't begrudge Rat a moment of panic. In truth, she scarcely noticed his shouts; the plunge caught her unprepared. It was several moments before she heard anything other than her own heart's pounding.

By then Rat had reclaimed his perch atop the sacks. "You could set us down for the night," he suggested.

"We're almost there."

"You said that at noon."

"It was true then, and it's truer now. We're almost to the cottage."

Rat made an unhappy noise in the back of his throat. Xantcha gave him a sidelong glance. Through the dim light she could see that he'd hunched down in his cloak and pulled the cowl up so it formed a funnel around his face. She'd collected Rat's new clothes as she'd ferried Red-Stripe survivors to other Efuand villages. They were nothing like the clothes Mishra would have worn— nothing like the travel-worn silks and suedes Xantcha herself wore—but they were the best she'd been able to find, and Rat had seemed genuinely grateful for them.

He'd cleaned up better than Xantcha had dared hope. Their first full day in the ruined village, while she'd been talking relocation with the elders, Rat had persuaded one of the women to trim his hair. He'd procured a handful of pumice the same way and spent that afternoon scrubbing himself—and being scrubbed—in the stream-fed pool where the women did laundry.

"You didn't have to bother the villagers." Xantcha had told him when she'd seen him next, all pink and raw, especially on the chin. "I could have loaned you my knife."

He'd looked down at her, shaking his head and half-smiling. "When you're old enough to grow whiskers, Xantcha, you'll realize a man doesn't have to cut his own hair."

Xantcha had started to say that with or without whiskers Rat would never be as old as she was, but that half-smile had confused her. Even now, when she couldn't see through the dark or the cowl, she suspected he was half-smiling again, and she didn't know what to say. Once washed and dressed in clothes that didn't reek, he'd proved attractive, at least to the extent that Xantcha understood mortal handsomeness. Rat didn't resemble any of Xantcha's *Antiquity Wars* portraits, and there was a generosity to him that softened the otherwise hard lines of his face.

Rat had healed almost as fast as a newt. His bruises were shadows now, and the sores around his neck, wrists, and ankles shrank daily. Every morning had seen a bit more flesh on his bones, a bit more swagger in his stride. He'd become Mishra: charming, passionate, unpredictable, and vaguely dangerous. Kayla Bin-Kroog would have known what to say—Kayla had known what to say to Urza's brother—but Xantcha wasn't Urza's wife, and, anyway, Rat thought of her as a boy, a deception that, all other things considered, Xantcha thought she might continue after they returned to the cottage . . . if Urza cooperated.

She touched his shoulder gingerly. "Don't worry, we'll be there tonight."

Rat shrugged her hand away. The cowl fell, and she could see his face faintly in the moonlight. He wasn't smiling. "Tonight or tomorrow morning, what difference can it make?"

"Urza's waiting. It's been more a month since I left. I've never been gone this long."

"You'll be gone forever if you don't stop pushing yourself. Even if he were the real Urza, he'd tell you to rest before you hurt yourself."

Rat didn't know Urza. Urza was inexhaustible, indestructible; he assumed Xantcha was too, and so, usually, did she.

"We're almost there. I'm not tired, and I don't need to rest."

The words were no sooner said than the sphere caught another downdraft, not as precipitous as the first one, but enough to fling them against each other.

"You're making mistakes."

"You know nothing about this!" Xantcha shot back. She tilted her hand too far, overcorrected, and wound up in Rat's lap.

He pushed her away. "What more do I need to know? Put it down."

"I didn't argue with you when you said those villagers needed to be rescued."

"I'm not arguing with you. I know you want me to meet Urza. You think there's not a moment to lose against the Phyrexians, but not like this, Xantcha. This is foolish, as foolish as buying me in the first place, only I can't help you keep this damn thing in the air."

"Right—you can't help, so be quiet."

And he was, as quiet as he'd been that first night out of Medran. Xantcha hadn't believed it was possible, but Rat's silence was worse than Urza's, because Rat wasn't ignoring her. He wasn't frightened, either; just sitting beside her, a cold, blank wall even when she pushed the sphere against the wind. There were moments when she could believe that Rat was Urza's real brother.

"You don't have to be Mishra, not yet."

Another of Rat's annoyed, annoying noises. "I'm not being Mishra. Mishra wouldn't care if you killed yourself getting him to Urza and, if you asked me, the real Urza wouldn't either. The real Urza didn't care about anything except what he wanted. The way you're acting, I'm starting to think you believe what you've been telling me. It's all over your face, Xantcha. You're the one who's worried because you're afraid. More afraid of the man you call Urza, I think, than of any Phyrexian."

It was Xantcha's turn to stare at the black ridge on the southern horizon and convince herself that Rat was wrong. The ridge was beneath them before she broke the silence.

"You don't believe anything I've told you."

"It's pretty far-fetched."

"But you've come all this way with me. There were so many times, when I was ferrying the villagers about, that you could have run away, but you didn't. I thought you'd decided I was telling you the truth. Why did you stop trying to run away, if you didn't believe anything I said?"

"Because six months ago I would've sworn on my life that I'd never leave Efuan Pincar, not with some half-wit boy whose got a thing in his belly. I'd've sworn a lot of things six months ago, and I'd've been wrong about all of them. I'm getting used to being wrong and I did give you my word, freely, when you agreed to get those villagers to safety, that I'd play your game. You weren't paying attention, but I was. You saved them because I asked you to, and that makes you my friend, at least for now."

"You've got to believe, Rat. If you don't believe, Urza won't, and I don't know what he'll do—to either of us—if he thinks I've tried to deceive him."

"I'll worry about Urza the Artificer," Rat said wearily.

He was patronizing her, despite everything she'd told him. All the lessons in language and history she'd given to him after dark in the village, Rat didn't believe.

He continued, "You worry about that shadow coming up. I think it's another lake, and I think we're going to go rump over elbows again if you don't wriggle your hand around it."

Rat was right about the lake. Xantcha wove her hand to one side, and another unpleasant moment was averted. It had taken her decades to learn the tricks that air could play on her sphere. Rat was quicker, cleverer than she'd ever been. There was a chance he was right about Urza, too, especially when she saw eldritch light leaking through the cottage windows after the sphere cleared the ridge.

"He's locked himself in," she muttered, unable to keep disappointment out of her voice.

"You didn't think he'd be waiting by the door, not in the middle of the night? A locked door isn't a bad idea, if you're alone and you've got the sorcery to make it stick. A man gets tired," said Rat.

"Not Urza," Xantcha said softly as the sphere touched down and collapsed.

Without the sphere's skin to support them, their supplies rearranged themselves across the ground. It was quicker than the chaos they endured when the sphere tumbled through the air, but quite a bit more painful on the hard ground; a wooden box corner came down squarely on Xantcha's cold ankle.

She was still cursing when the eldritch locks vanished. Urza appeared in the open doorway.

"Xantcha! Where have—?"

He'd noticed Rat. His eyes began to glow. Xantcha hadn't considered the possibility that Urza might simply kill any stranger who appeared outside his door.

"No!" Xantcha wanted to get herself between the two men, but her feet wouldn't cooperate. "Urza! Listen to me!"

She'd no sooner gotten Urza's attention than Rat wrested it away again with a single, soft-spoken word:

"Brother . . ."

Every night in the village Xantcha had sat up with Rat telling him about Urza and Jrza's obsessions. She'd warned him about Urza's uncanny eyes and the tabletop where his gnats recreated—

refined—the scenes from Kayla's epic. She'd taught him the rudiments of the polyglot language she and Urza spoke when they were alone because it was rich in the words he'd shared with Mishra, when they were both men. She'd taught him the word for *brother* and insisted he practice it until he got it right, but the word he'd said was pure Efuand dialect.

For a moment the space between them was as dark as the space between the stars overhead, then the golden light that had been in the cottage flowed from Urza toward Rat, who didn't flinch as it surrounded him.

"You wished to see me, Brother," he continued in Efuand. "It's been a long, hard journey, but I've come back."

Urza could absorb a new language as easily as a plowed field absorbed the spring rains. Most of the time, he didn't notice the switch, but Xantcha had thought Urza might pay attention to Mishra's language, to the language that anyone pretending to be Mishra spoke during the critical first moments of their encounter. She was ready to kill Rat with her own hands, if Urza didn't do it for her. His eyes hadn't stopped glowing, and she'd seen those jewels obliterate creatures vastly more powerful than an overconfident slave from Efuan Pincar.

"Speak to me, Urza. It's been so long. We never finished our last conversation, never truly began it."

"Where?" Urza asked, a whisper on a cold, cold wind. At least he'd spoken Efuand.

"Before the blood-red tent of the warlord of Kroog. We stood as far apart as we stand now. You said we should remember that we were brothers."

"The tent was not red, and I said no such thing."

"Do you call me a liar, Brother? I remember less, Brother, but I remember very clearly. I have been here all the time, waiting for you; it would have been easier if your memory were not flawed."

Urza's eyes took on the painful brilliance of the Glimmer Moon. Xantcha was certain that Rat would sizzle like raindrops in a bonfire, yet the light didn't harm him, and after a few ribthumping heartbeats she began to perceive Rat's unexpected brilliance. The real Mishra had been supremely confident and never, even in the best of times, willing to concede a point to his elder brother. Between Urza and Mishra, attitude was more important than language, and Rat had the right attitude.

"It is possible," Urza conceded as his eyes dimmed to a mortal color. "Each time I refine my automata, I learn what I had forgotten. It is a short step between forgotten and misremembered."

Raising his hand, Urza took a hesitant stride toward Rat—toward Mishra. He stopped short of touching his putative brother's flesh.

"I dreamed that in time, through time, I'd find a way to talk to you, to warn you of the dangers neither of us saw when we were alive together. I never dreamed that you would find me. You. It is you, Mishra?"

Urza moved without moving, placing his open hand across Rat's cheek. Even Xantcha, who knew Urza could change his shape faster than muscle could move bone, was stunned. As for Rat himself—Rat, who'd refused to believe her warnings that her Urza was the Urza who'd become more like a god than a man—he went deathly pale beneath Urza's long, elegant and essentially lifeless fingers. His eyes rolled, and his body slackened: he'd fainted, but Urza's curiosity kept him upright.

"They took your skin, Mishra, and stretched it over one of their abominations. Do you remember? Do you remember them coming for you? Do you remember dying?"

Rat's limp arms and legs began to tremble. Xantcha's breath caught in her throat. She'd never believed that Urza was cruel, merely careless. He'd lived so long in his own mad isolation that he'd forgotten the frailties of ordinary flesh, especially of flesh more ordinary than that of a Phyrexian newt. She was certain that once Urza noticed what was he was doing, he'd relent. He could heal as readily as he harmed.

But Urza didn't notice what he was doing to the youth she'd brought from Efuan Pincar. Rat writhed like a stuck serpent. Blood seeped from his nose. Xantcha threw herself into the golden light.

"Stop!" Xantcha seized Urza's outstretched arm. She might

have been a fly on a mountain top for the effect she had. "You're killing him."

Suddenly, Urza's arm hung at his side again. Xantcha reeled backward, fighting for balance while Rat collapsed.

"There is nothing in his mind. I sought the answers that have eluded me: when did the Phyrexians come for him? Did he fight? Did he surrender willingly? Did he call my name? He has no answers, Xantcha. He has nothing at all. My brother's mind is as empty as yours. I do not understand. I found you too late; the damage had already been done. But how and why has Mishra come back to me if he is not himself, if his mind is not alive with the thoughts I know should be there."

Xantcha knew her mind was empty. She was Phyrexian, a newt engendered in a vat of turgid slime. She had no imagination, no great thoughts or ambitions, not even a heart that could be crushed by humiliation, whether that humiliation came from Urza or Gix.

Rat was another matter. He lay face-down in a heap of awkwardly bent limbs. "He's a man," Xantcha snarled. She'd caught her balance, but kept her distance. Another step closer and she'd be a child looking up to meet Urza's eyes. She was too angry for that. "His mind is his own. It's not a book for you to read and cast aside!"

Xantcha couldn't guess whether Rat was still alive, even when Urza put his foot against the youth's flank to shove him onto his back.

"This is only the first. There will be others. The first is never final; there must always be refinements. If I have learned nothing else, I have learned that. I was working in the wrong direction—thinking that I'd have to reach back through time to find Mishra and the truth. And because I was not looking for Mishra, he could not find me, not as he must find me. But his truth will come to me once I have refined the path. I can see them, Xantcha: a line of Mishras, each bearing a piece of the truth. They will come and come until one of them bears it all." Urza headed to his open door. "There is no time." He stopped and laughed aloud. "Time, Xantcha . . . think of it! I have finally found the way to negate time. I will start again. Do not disturb me."

He was mad, Xantcha reminded herself, and she'd been a fool to think she could outwit him. Unlike Rat, Urza never changed his mind. He interpreted everything through the prism of his obsessions. Urza couldn't be held responsible for what had happened.

That burden fell on her.

Xantcha had never kept count of those she'd slain or watched die. Surely there were hundreds . . . thousands, if she included Phyrexians, but she'd never betrayed anyone as she'd betrayed Ratepe, son of Mideah. She knelt beside him, straightening his corpse, starting with his legs. Ratepe hadn't begun to stiffen; his skin was still warm.

"There will be no others!"

Urza turned around. "What did you say?"

"I said, this was a man, Urza. He was a man, born and living until you killed him. He wasn't an artifact on your table that you could sweep onto the floor when you were finished with him. You didn't make him—" She hesitated. Burdened with guilt, she saw that her clever plan to have Ratepe pose as Mishra required confession. "That tabletop didn't reach through the past. I went looking for a man who resembled your brother, I found him, and I brought him here.

"I won't do it again, so there won't—"

"You, Xantcha? Don't speak nonsense. This was my brother— the first shadow of my brother. You could not have found him without me."

"I'm not speaking nonsense! You had nothing to do with this, Urza. This was my idea, my bad idea. His name was never Mishra. His name was Ratepe, son of Mideah. I bought him from a slaver in Efuan Pincar."

Urza appeared thunderstruck. Xantcha leaned forward to straighten Ratepe's other leg. Efuands buried their dead in grass-lined graves that faced the sunrise. She'd helped dig several of them. There was a suitable spot not far from her window where she'd see it easily and lament her folly each time she did.

Unless she left . . . soared back to Efuan Pincar to do battle with the Phyrexians in Ratepe's name. If the cyst would still respond to her whims. If Urza didn't destroy her when his thoughts finally made their way back to the world of life and death.

She reached for Ratepe's crooked arm.

"A slaver? You sought my brother's avatar in a slaver's pens?"

Avatar—a spirit captured in flesh. Xantcha recognized the word but had never consciously used it; it was the right word, though, for what she'd wanted Ratepe to become. "Yes." She straightened Ratepe's elbow. "Mishra was a Fallaji slave."

"Mishra was advisor to the qadir."

"Mishra was a slave. The Fallaji captured him before you got to Yotia; they never freed him—not formally. It's in *The Antiquity Wars*. He told Kayla, and she wrote down his words."

Xantcha had never told Urza about her chest filled with copies of his wife's epic. He hadn't asked, hadn't volunteered any sense of his past here in his home, except what arose from his tabletop artifacts. He didn't appear pleased to hear Kayla's name falling off her tongue. Xantcha sensed she was living dangerously, very dangerously.

She took Ratepe's hand. It was stiff; rigor had begun. Gently, she uncurled his fingers.

They resisted, tightened, squeezed.

Before she could think, Xantcha jerked her hand away—or tried to. Ratepe didn't let go, and she stayed where she was, kneeling beside him, breathless with shock. She looked down. He winked, then kept both eyes shut.

"Waste not, want not," she whispered and cast her glance quickly in Urza's direction but Urza was elsewhere.

"I did not tell you to read that story." His voice came from a cold place, far from his heart. "Kayla Bin-Kroog never knew the truth and did not write it, either. She chose to live in a mist, with neither light nor shadow to guide her. You cannot believe anything in *The Antiquity Wars*, Xantcha, especially about Mishra. My wife saw her world through a veil of emotions. She saw people, not patterns, and when she saw my brother . . ." He didn't finish his thought, but offered another: "She didn't mean to betray me. I'm sure she thought she could be the bridge between us; it was too late. I honored Harbin, but after that, it was all lies between us. I couldn't trust her. You can't either."

Before Xantcha could say that Kayla's version of the war made more sense, Ratepe sat bolt upright.

"I've heard it said that there's no way a man can be absolutely certain that his wife's child is his and only one way he can be certain that it's not. Kayla Bin-Kroog was an attractive woman, Urza, and wiser than you'll know. She did try to become a bridge, but not with her body. She was tempted. I made certain she was tempted, but she never succumbed, which, my Brother, begs one almighty question: How and why are you so certain Harbin was not your son?"

Suddenly, they were all in darkness as Urza's golden light vanished.

"You've done it now," Xantcha said softly and with more than a little admiration. She'd never gotten the better of Urza that way. "He's gone 'walking."

But Urza hadn't 'walked away, and when the light returned it flowed from an Urza that Xantcha had never seen before: a youthful Urza, dressed in a dirt-laborer's dusty clothes and smiling as he reached out to take Ratepe's hands.

"I have missed you, Brother. I've had no one to talk to. Stand up, stand up! Come with me! Let me show you what I've learned while you were gone. It was Ashnod, you know—"

Ratepe proved he was as consistent as he was reckless. He folded his arms across his chest and stayed where he was. "You've had Xantcha. He's not 'no one.' "

"Xantcha!"

While Urza laughed, Xantcha got to her feet.

"Xantcha! I rescued Xantcha a thousand years ago—no, longer than that, more than three thousand years ago. Don't be fooled by appearances, as I was. She's Phyrexian—cooked up in one of their vats. A mistake. A failure. A slave. They were getting ready to bury her when I came along; thought she was Argivian at first. She's loyal . . . to me. She's got her own reasons for turning on Phyrexia. But her mind is limited. You can talk to her, but only a fool would listen."

Xantcha couldn't meet Ratepe's eyes. When they were alone and Urza belittled her, she could blame it on his madness. Now there were three of them standing outside the cottage. Urza wasn't talking to her, he was talking about her, and there were no excuses. All their centuries together, all the experiences no one else had shared, and he'd never conquered his distrust, his disdain.

"I think—" Ratepe began, and Xantcha forced herself to catch his attention.

She mouthed the single word, *Don't*. It didn't matter what Urza thought of her, so long as he stopped playing with his tabletop gnats. Xantcha mouthed a second word, *Phyrexia*, and made a fist where Ratepe could see it. She hoped she'd told him what mattered, and that it wasn't her.

Ratepe cleared his throat. He said, "I think it is not the time to argue, Urza," and made the words sound sincere. "We have always done too much of that. I always did too much of that. There, I've admitted it, and the world did not end. Not yet; not again. You think we made our fatal mistake on the Plains of Kor. I think we made it earlier. After so long, it doesn't matter, does it? It was the same mistake either way. We couldn't talk, we could only compete. And you won. I see the Weakstone in your left eye. Have you ever heard it singing to you, Urza?"

Sing?

Anyone who'd read *The Antiquity Wars* would know that Urza's eyes had once been his Mightstone and his brother's Weakstone. Tawnos had brought that scrap back to Kayla. Ratepe claimed he'd read Kayla's epic several times, and between two stones and two eyes, he could have made a lucky guess. The Weakstone had, indeed, become Urza's left eye. But sing? Urza had never mentioned singing.

Xantcha couldn't guess what had fired Ratepe's all-too-mortal imagination, but as Urza frowned and stared at the stars, she guessed it had propelled him too far.

Then Urza began to speak. "I hear it now, faintly, without word, but a song of sadness. Your song?"

Xantcha was stunned.

Urza continued: "The stone we found—the single stone—was

a weapon, you know: The final defense of the Thran, their last sacrifice. They blocked the portal to Phyrexia. You and I, when we sundered the stone, we opened the portal. We let them back into Dominaria. I never asked you what you saw that day."

Ratepe grinned. "Didn't I say that we made our mistake much earlier?"

Urza clapped his hands together and laughed heartily. "You did! Yes, you did! We've got a second chance, brother. This time, we'll talk." He opened his arms, gesturing toward the open doorway. "Come, let me show you what I've learned while you were gone. Let me show you the wonders of artifice, pure artifice, Brother—none of those Phyrexian abominations. And Ashnod! Wait until I show you Ashnod: a viper at your breast, Brother. She was their first conquest, your biggest mistake."

"Show me everything," Ratepe said, walking into Urza's embrace. "Then we'll talk."

Arm in arm, they walked toward the cottage. A few steps short of the threshold, Ratepe shot a glance over his shoulder. He seemed to expect some gesture from her, but Xantcha, unable to guess what it should be, simply stood with her arms limp at her sides.

"And when we're done talking, Urza, we'll listen to Xantcha."

The door shut without a sound. The light was gone, and Xantcha was left with only moonlight to help her haul the food supplies.

Chapter 9

Cold fog rolled down from the mountains. Xantcha's fingers stiffened, and the rest of her grew clumsy. When she wasn't tripping over her feet, she dropped bundles and cursed loudly, not caring if she disturbed the two men on the other side of the wall.

She didn't disturb them. Urza had a new audience for his tabletop. He wouldn't notice the world if it ended. And Ratepe? Ratepe was playing the dangerous game Xantcha had told him to play and playing it better than she'd dared hope. She'd all but told him not to pay any attention to her; she could hardly begrudge obedience—or fail to notice that Urza's door was unwarded. She could have left the sacks where the sphere had scattered them.

Ratepe—Rat—Mishra—would have defended her right to join them. Xantcha was tempted to walk through the door, if only to hear what the young Efuand would say, which, considering all that hung in the balance was a selfish temptation. She resisted it until the last of the supplies was stowed in the pantry and the fog had matured into an ice-needle rain.

Inside her room, with the shutters bolted against the chill, Xantcha found herself too tired to sleep. Eyes open and empty, she lay on her bed able to hear the sounds of conversation beyond the wall without catching any of the words. She piled pillows atop her face, pulled the blankets tight, then threw everything aside. Before long, Xantcha had wedged herself into the corner at the foot of the bed. With her knees tucked beneath her chin and a blanket draped over her head, Xantcha tried to think of other things. . . .

Of her first conversation with Urza . . .

"There is a shelter at the bottom of the hill. Take me there. I'll show you the way to Phyrexia."

* * * * *

Urza frowned. Xantcha had rarely seen a face creased with displeasure. She expected his jaw to fall to the ground. But her rescuer was flexible—a newt like herself, or one of born-folk, about whom she knew very little. When his frown had sunk as much as it could, it rebounded and became a bitter laugh.

She knew the meaning of that sound.

"It's the truth. I will show you the way. I will take you to Phyrexia—though, it's only fair to tell you that avengers stand guard around the Fourth Sphere ambulator fields and we'll be destroyed on the spot."

"It's gone. It's gotten away," her rescuer said, still laughing.

"The ambulator's nether end should be there—unless you let the searcher get away. The diggers, they don't know how to roll an ambulator, and the bearers can't."

Xantcha tried to rise and felt light-headed, felt light all over. It was not an unprecedented feeling. Every time she stepped into a new world there were changes: a different texture to the air, a different color to the light, a different sense between her feet and the ground. She took a deep breath to confirm her suspicions.

"The hill and shelter are where I remember them, but I am not any place that I remember?"

"Yes, my clever child, I brought you here, and I will take you back. The hill is there, but the shelter and this ambulator of which you speak, alas, is not."

Xantcha thought she understood. "You drew the prime end

through itself to bring me to this place?" She hesitated, but this man who had rescued her deserved the truth. "If you unanchored the ambulator, I don't know if I can take you to Phyrexia. I've seen the searcher-priests set the stones for Phyrexia, but I've never set them myself. I don't know what our fate will be if I set them wrong, but I'll go first."

"No, child, you will not go first," he said, grim and serious. "Though you have every reason to condemn Phyrexia, you have become a traitor to them, and traitors can never be trusted, must never be trusted."

Traitor. The word roused a hundred others from Xantcha's dreams. She supposed it was a truthful word, though not as truthful as it would have been if she weren't a newt who'd never been compleated. Insofar as kin pricked her conscience, it was safe to say that she had none.

"I was Orman'huzra when you found me, second of the dodgers. What is my position now? What is yours? What do I do, if I cannot be trusted and I cannot go first?"

The man paced the small, stark chamber in which she'd awakened. His eyes burned as he walked, reminding Xantcha of Gix. She lowered her head when he stopped in front of her. He put his hand beneath her chin to raise it. Her instinct was to resist, to avoid those eyes as she had avoided the eyes of Gix, but he overcame her resistance. Her rescuer had a demon's strength.

"Orman'huzra. That is not a name. What is your name?"

"In my dreams, I am Xantcha."

The answer failed to please him. Fingers tightened on either side of her jaw. She closed her eyes, but that made no difference. The many-colored light from his eyes burnt like fire in her thoughts.

"Your mind is empty, Xantcha," he said after an agonizing moment. "The Phyrexians took it all away from you."

He was wrong. Were it not for what the Phyrexians—Gix in particular—had done to her, Xantcha was sure she would have died right then. She didn't correct her new companion, no more than she'd corrected Gix, and took no small satisfaction in the knowledge that the sanctuary she'd created, when Gix had confronted her, remained intact.

"What is my place? What is yours?" she asked for the second time. "What do you do?"

"My place was Lord Protector of the Realm, and I failed to do what I should have done. You may call me Urza."

There were images for the word *Urza*, hideous images. Xantcha heard the voice of a teacher-priest: *If you meet Urza, destroy him.* The man in front of her didn't resemble the image. Even if he had, Xantcha would have denied the imperative. She wasn't about to destroy an enemy of Phyrexia.

"Urza," she repeated. "Urza, I will show you what I know of the ambulators."

Xantcha tried to rise from her pallet. The ambulator had to be beyond the chamber's closed door. It was too large for the chamber itself. She got as far as her knees. In addition to feeling light, she was weak. But there were no marks on her body. Her wounds had healed. Xantcha didn't understand; she'd been weak before, but never without wounds.

"Rest," Urza told her, offering her the corner of the blanket. "You have been very sick. Many days—at least a month—have passed since I brought you here . . . but not through any ambulator. I did, as you suggest, let the searcher get away. My error, Xantcha. I did not suspect your ambulators and seeing your kind on that other plane, I thought you had 'walked there. My grievous error: the emptiness between the planes is no place for a child without the necessary spark. You were less than a breath, less than a heartbeat, from death before I got you here—which is not where I'd intended to bring you."

"Do not touch that door!" he warned, then had an inspiration and pointed his forefinger at it.

The wood glowed and became dull, gray stone, like the rest of the chamber.

"The Phyrexians changed you Xantcha, and I could not undo their changes, but without what they did, you would not have lived long enough for me to do anything at all. This place is safe for you. It has air and a balance of heat and cold. Outside, there is nothing. Your skin will freeze and your blood will boil. Without the spark, you will not survive. Do you hear me, Xantcha? Can your empty mind understand?"

* * * * *

Xantcha had had no sense of modesty, not so soon after leaving Phyrexia, and the air in the chamber was comfortably warm, yet she'd clutched the blanket tight around her naked flesh—the same as she clutched it millennia later in a cold, dark cottage room while sleet pelted the roof overhead. Her empty mind never had a problem understanding Urza's words. It was the implications that often left her reeling.

* * * * *

"I understand," she assured Urza. "This is my place and I will remain here. But I do not know about *months*. I know days and seasons and years. What is a month?"

Urza closed his eyes and, after a dramatic sigh, told her about the many ways in which born-folk measured time. Xantcha told him that Phyrexia was a place where time went unmeasured. There was no sun by day nor stars by night. The First Sphere sky was an unchanging featureless gray. All the other spheres were nested within the First Sphere. Gix had been dropped into a fumarole that descended to the Seventh Sphere. The Ineffable dwelt in the ninth, at Phyrexia's core.

"Interesting," Urza said. "If you're telling the truth. I have heard the name Gix before, on my own plane, where it was the name of a mountain god before the Phyrexians stole it. In fifty years of searching, I have heard the name Gix many times. I've heard the name Urza, too, and several that sound like *Sancha*. There are only so many sounds that our mouths can make, so many words, so many names. At best, language is confusion. If you are to be useful to me, you must never lie. Are you telling me the truth, child?"

She nodded and added, truthfully, "I am not a child." The image was quite clear in her mind; the world for which she had

Xantcha continued walking, one step, another . . . misery stopped her before she took a third. Looking back over her shoulder, she caught the eyes of a slave who stared at her as if his condition were indeed her responsibility. Though they were at least a hundred paces apart, Xantcha saw that the slave was a dark-haired young man.

I asked my husband's brother how he'd come to lead the Fallaji horde, Kayla had written in *The Antiquity Wars*. *Mishra replied that he was their slave, not their leader. He laughed and added that I, too, was a slave to my people, but his eyes were haunted as he laughed, and there were scars around his wrists.*

In all the times Xantcha had read that passage, she'd followed Urza's lead and blamed Phyrexia for Mishra's scars and bitterness. But the Fallaji had been a slave-keeping folk, and looking across the Medran plaza, Xantcha suddenly believed that Mishra had told Kayla a simple, unvarnished truth.

Xantcha believed as well that she'd found her Mishra. With Urza's armor still around her, she strode over to the tavern.

"Are they spoken for?" she asked the only unchained man she saw, a balding man with a eunuch's unfinished face.

He wasn't in charge, but after a bow he scurried into the tavern to fetch his master, who proved to be a giant of a woman, garbed, like Xantcha, in men's clothing, though in the slave master's case, the effect was intimidation rather than disguise.

"They're bound for Almaaz," the slave master said. Her breath was thick with beer, but she wasn't nearly drunk. "You know it's against the law to sell flesh here."

By her posture, the slaver was right about the law and ripe for negotiation.

"I have Morvern gold," Xantcha said, which was true enough; money was never a problem for a planeswalker or his companion.

The slave master hawked and spat. "Mug's getting warm."

Xantcha thought fast. "For ransom, then. I recognize a distant cousin in your coffle. You've kept him safe, no doubt. I'll pay you for your trouble and take him off your hands."

"Him!" The slaver laughed until she belched.

There were women in the slave string, and Xantcha was

been destined—the world to which she had not gone—had children. "Children are born. Children grow. Phyrexians are decanted by vat-priests and compleated by the tender-priests. When I was decanted, I was exactly as I am now. I was not compleated, but I was never a child. Gix said he made me."

Urza shook his head sadly. "It is tempting, very tempting to believe that there is only one Gix, but I have made that mistake before. It is just a sound, a similar sound, filled with lies. You do not remember what you were before the Phyrexians claimed you, Xantcha, and that is just as well. To remember what you had lost . . ." He closed his eyes a moment. "You would not be strong enough. By your face, I'd say you were twelve, perhaps thirteen— " He shook a thought out of his mind and began to pace. "You were born, Xantcha. Life is born or it is not life. Not even the Phyrexians can change that. They steal, they corrupt, and they abominate, but they cannot create.

"You remember the decanting, and I am grateful that you remember nothing before that because I am certain that you were most horribly transformed. In my wanderings I have seen men and women in many variations, but I have never seen one such as you, who is neither."

Urza continued pacing the small chamber. He wouldn't look at her, which was just as well. Xantcha knew many words for madness and delusion, and they all described Urza. He had rescued her—saved her life—and he had strange powers, not merely in his glowing eyes, but an odd sort of passion that left her believing for a few distracted heartbeats that she had been born on the world at the bottom of her memories.

Xantcha ached in the missing places when Urza described her as neither man nor woman. After Gix's excoriation, while she'd hidden among the gremlins, she'd had opportunity to observe the differences between the two types of born-folk: men and women. If Urza was right, she had even more reason to wage war against Phyrexia.

But Urza had to be wrong. He didn't know Phyrexia. He'd never peeked into a vat to see the writhing shape of a half-grown newt. He'd never seen tender-priests throwing buckets of rendered flesh into those vats. Meat-sludge was the source of Xantcha's memories, meat-sludge and Gix's ambition. Nothing had been taken from her. She was empty, as Urza had told her, filled with memories that weren't her own.

Urza confirmed Xantcha's self-judgment as he paced. "Yes, it is better that you don't remember, better that your mind is empty and you have no imagination left that would fill it. Mishra knew what he had become, and it drove him mad. I will keep you, Xantcha, and avenge your loss as I avenge my brother. You will stay here."

Xantcha didn't argue. She was in a chamber that had neither windows nor doors. Her companion was a man-demon with glowing eyes. There was nothing at all to be gained by argument. Still, there was at least one question that had to be asked:

"May I eat?"

Urza stopped pacing. His eyes darkened to a mortal brown. "You eat? But, you're Phyrexian."

She shrugged and chose her words carefully. "They didn't take that. I ate from a cauldron when I was in Phyrexia, but I scrounged when I was excavating. I can scrounge here, if you'll show me where the living things are."

"Nothing lives here, Xantcha."

Urza muttered under his breath. His hands began to glow as his eyes had. He strode to the nearest wall and thrust his fingers into what had appeared to be solid stone. The glow transferred to the stone. The chamber filled with the hot, acrid smells Xantcha remembered from the furnaces. She eased backward, blindly clutching the blanket, as if it could protect her. There was a hollow in the wall now, and a radiant mass seething in Urza's hands.

"Bread," Urza said when the seething mass had cooled.

Xantcha had scrounged bread on a few of the worlds the searcher-priests had sent her to. The steaming loaf Urza handed her looked like bread and smelled a bit like bread, a bit more like overheated dust. Its taste was dusty, too, but she'd eaten worse, much worse, and gorged without complaint.

"Do you want more?"

She didn't answer. Want was an empty notion. Newts didn't want. Newts took what they could, what was available, and waited for another opportunity—which might come soon, or might not. Urza faded until he was a pale, translucent shadow; then he was gone. A heartbeat later, the chamber's light was gone, too.

Every world Xantcha had seen had spun to its own rhythms, and though she hadn't acquired an instinctive sense of day becoming night, she'd learned enough about time to be desperately afraid of the dark. She was ravenous when Urza finally returned, exhausted because she'd feared to close her eyes lest she sleep through his reappearance, and bleeding where she'd pinched herself to keep awake. Taking all her risk at once, Xantcha sprang across the chamber. She clung ferociously to Urza's sleeve.

"I won't remain here! Bring back the door. Let me out or destroy me!"

Urza stared at her hands. "I brought you something. Swallow it, and I can, as you say, bring back the door."

He held out his free arm and opened his hand which held a nearly transparent lump about half the size of her fist. Xantcha had eaten worse meals in the Fane of Flesh, but she didn't think Urza was offering her supper.

"What is it?" she asked, not letting go with either hand.

"Consider it a gift. I went back to the plane where I found you. The Phyrexians were careful to clean up after themselves, but I was more careful looking for them this time. I found a place where the soil had been transformed with black mana, much as you have been. So, I believe you, Xantcha. You are almost what you say you are, almost a Phyrexian. You believe the lies they told because when they transformed you they took your memory and your potential. You are a danger to others and to yourself but not to me. I will unlock your secrets and find answers I need for my vengeance."

"I'll help," Xantcha agreed. She'd agree to anything to get out of the chamber. After that . . .

After that would take care of itself.

Letting go of his sleeve with one hand but not the other, she reached for the lump. Urza swung it beyond her reach.

"You must understand, Xantcha, as much as you can understand anything. This is not bread to be wolfed down like a starving animal. This is an artifact. When you swallow it, it will settle in your stomach and harden into a cyst, a sort of stone that will remain there for as long as you live. Then, whenever we travel between planes or dwell on a plane where you could not otherwise survive, you will say a little rhyme that I shall teach you and yawn mightily at its end. The cyst will release an armor that will cover you completely to keep you alive."

"You will compleat me?"

Urza glowered. Xantcha felt him pursuing her thoughts, her suspicions about the cyst. He rummaged through her memories, yanking on them as if they were the loose ends of a stubborn knot. Did he believe Orman'huzra knew nothing about artifacts? She retreated into her private self.

He sensed her escape. She saw the questions and displeasure on his face. Urza wasn't flesh, no more than Gix, but he had the habits of flesh and all the subtlety of a freshly decanted newt.

"Like a rabbit flees into the brush," he said, and looked beyond the chamber. Tears leaked from Urza's eyes, especially his left eye. Then he shuddered, and the tear tracks vanished. "No, I don't compleat. That is abomination. My artifact will be inside you, because that is the best place for it, but is a tool, nothing more and never a part of you. Never! I cannot erase the memories of Phyrexia from your mind—and would not, because they will prove useful to my vengeance—but you are no longer Phyrexian, and you must not think of Phyrexian abominations."

"Artifacts are tools," she recited as she would have once recited to the teacher-priests. A tool that she would swallow, but that would remain in her belly forever but without becoming a part of her. It wasn't reasonable, but reason wasn't important to a Phyrexian, and she would be Phyrexian forever.

Urza let the lump flow into her hand. It was cold and clinging. Xantcha's stomach churned in protest. Gagging, she lost her grip on Urza's sleeve and nearly dropped the artifact as well.

"Swallow it whole. Don't chew on it!"

"Waste not, want not," Xantcha muttered. "Waste not, want not."

She raised her hand to her mouth and nearly fainted. She tried again, breathing out as she raised her hand. The artifact quivered and darkened. Then she closed her eyes and slurped it down without inhaling. It stuck in her throat. She slapped her hands over her lips, fighting the instinct to spit the lump across the chamber.

For something that was only a tool, Urza's artifact felt alive as it oozed down Xantcha's throat, got comfortable in her gut, and hardened into a stone. She was on her knees, banging her forehead on the floor when the horrifying process finally stopped.

"See? All over. Nothing to it."

She rested her head on the floor another moment before pushing herself upright.

"I'm ready."

Her voice felt different. The artifact had deposited a trail as it had moved down her throat. It still clung to her teeth and tongue. She coughed into her hand and studied drops of spittle that glistened briefly then turned to white powder. Urza taught her the rhyme that would release the cyst's power. Pressure built in her gut as she repeated it. The yawn that followed was involuntary, and the sensation of an oily liquid surging from within, covering her completely within two heartbeats, would have driven her to hysteria if it had lasted for a third.

Urza clutched her wrists. The cyst's liquid—her armor—tingled. He began to fade and, looking down, Xantcha saw herself fading as well.

She'd barely begun to scream when her substance was restored, covered by clothing less fine than Urza's, but finer than the rags she'd known all her life. Tempted to fondle the dark blue sleeve, she discovered it was illusion, visible but intangible.

"Later," Urza assured her. "Not long. I won't have a naked companion. Look upon this . . . Tell me: Have you ever seen its like before?"

Xantcha gathered her wits. They stood on a bare-rock plain. The sky was a cloudless pale blue; light came from an intensely white sun-star so high overhead that she thought she should have been hot and sweating. Yet the plain was cold, the wind colder. She could hear the wind and see the dust it raised. When she thought about it, Xantcha wasn't at all sure how she knew it was cold. With Urza's armor surrounding her, she felt nothing against her skin. The sensation, or lack of sensation, so intrigued her that Urza had to clear his throat twice before she saw the dragon.

"With that," he said, pride evident in his voice, "I shall destroy Phyrexia."

The dragon was dead black in the sunlight. Xantcha walked closer until she was certain that it was, indeed, made from a metal, though even when she touched a pillar-like hind leg, she couldn't say which metal. It was bipedal in structure, and her head came barely to its bent knees. Its torso, as yet unfinished, was a maze of tanks and tubes.

"Naphtha," Urza explained before she asked her question. "Phyrexians, the Phyrexians I mean to destroy, are sleeked with oil. They burn."

Xantcha nodded, recalling the Fourth Sphere lakes of slag and naphtha and the screams that sometimes arose from them. Scaffolding struts extruded from the dragon's counterbalancing tail. She seized one. Urza warned her to be careful; she had no intention of being anything else, but he'd asked a question and she meant to give him an honest answer.

The cyst-made armor moved with her however Xantcha contorted herself, even hanging by one knee to get a better look at the claws on the dragon's somewhat short arms. If its arms were short, its teeth were long and varied: sharp spikes, razor-edge wedges, rasps, and crushing anvils, all cunningly geared so that whoever sat in the Urza-sized gap between the dragon's shoulders could bring his best metal weapons to bear on a particular enemy—if a gout of flaming naphtha proved insufficient to destroy them.

More unfinished scaffolding rose above and behind the dragon's shoulders: protection, she guessed, for Urza, but possibly he intended to finish his engine with wings. She judged it little more than half finished and already heavier than anything she'd seen on the First Sphere. Perhaps he'd concocted a more potent fuel than glistening oil. Xantcha finished her exploration without finding the source of the engine's power.

After dangling from the dragon's forearm, Xantcha dropped three or four times her height. She was out of practice, hitting her chin on her knee as she absorbed the impact. Her lip should have been a bloody mess. She was pleasantly impressed with Urza's gift, but as for his dragon . . .

"If you had a hundred of them—" Her voice was definitely thicker, deeper, and distant-sounding to her armor-plugged ears. "You could take one of the Fanes and hold it against the demons, but not against the Ineffable."

"You don't appreciate what this is, Xantcha. I have built a dragon ten times stronger than anything Mishra or I had during our misbegotten war. When it is finished, not even the Thran could stand against it."

Xantcha shrugged. She didn't know the Thran. "It will have to be very powerful, then, when it is finished."

"You have been blinded, Xantcha, by what they did to you, by what you can't remember, but they are not as powerful as they've made you believe. When my dragon is finished—when I've found the rest of what I need—"

"Found?" Her scavenging curiosity had been aroused. "You found this? You did not make it, as you made the bread and tool?"

"I found the materials, Xantcha, and I shaped them to my needs. To make a dragon like this, to make it as I made your bread . . . even for me it would be exhausting, and in the end—" Urza lowered his voice—"not quite real."

Xantcha cocked her head.

"That bread filled your stomach and was nutritious. It would keep you alive, but you wouldn't thrive on it—at least, I don't think you would. When I was a man, I could not have thrived on it. Things that are made, whether they are made from nothing or something else, no matter how well made they are, aren't quite real. It's easier—better—to start with something similar to what you want to have at the end and change it, little by little."

"Compleat it?"

"Yes—" Urza began, then stopped suddenly and stared harshly at her, eyes a-shimmer. "No. Compleation is a Phyrexian taint. Do not use that word. Only artifacts can be made. Everything else must be born, must live and grow."

Xantcha studied her companion with equal intensity, though her eyes, of course, could not sparkle. "We were taught that the Ineffable made Phyrexia."

"Lies, Xantcha. They told you lies."

"I was told many lies," she agreed.

Urza took her wrists again.

"Until now," he said, "I have dwelt here beside my greatest artifact, but now that I have taken charge of you, I will have to have a dwelling in a more hospitable place. It is no great inconvenience. For every hospitable plane there are several out-of-the-way planes such as this. While these plains have supplied me with the ores I needed for my dragon's bones, they aren't where powerstones are to be found."

Xantcha had started to ask what a powerstone was when her armor began to tingle and Urza began to grow transparent in the stark sunlight. They were underway before Xantcha could ask where they were going, and though she'd already guessed that her image for a world was the same as Urza's image for a plane, getting dragged from one world to the next with his hands clamped around her wrists was worse than sinking through the ambulators.

Whether her eyes were open or closed, Xantcha saw the same many-colored streaks whirling around her. Every sense, every perception was stretched to its opposite extreme and held there for what might have been a single moment or might have been eternity. The silence was deafening, the cold so intense she feared she'd melt, the viselike pressure so great she feared she'd explode. And, to complete the experience, when Urza finally released Xantcha, her clinging armor transformed abruptly into a layer of white paste.

Pushed past her limit, Xantcha gave into the panic and terror, clawing the residue as she ran blindly away from Urza. She tripped, as was inevitable, and fell hard enough to knock the wind from her. Urza knelt and touched her. The armor residue was gone in an instant.

"I tested it on myself," he explained. He helped her to her feet and laid his hands on her scrapes and bruises, healing them with gentle heat.

Xantcha had endured much in her unmeasured life, none of it gentle. She pulled away when she could and realized he'd brought her back to the place where she'd been beaten. Parting her lips, she tasted the air; the tang of glistening oil was faint, stale.

"They're gone," she said.

"And not long after I rescued you. The locals would not know the Phyrexians had ever been here. I would not have known, if I had not found them first. This is the place, the very place, where they brought you and where the last of them stood before leaving."

Urza scuffed the ground with his boot. There was nothing visibly different, but movement released the scent of glistening oil to the air.

"It is a familiar place for you, isn't it? You lived here, found food here. Conquer your nightmares, Xantcha. The Phyrexians will not return. They are cowards, Xantcha; they only prey upon the weak. They grasped my brother, but they never came to me. They know me, Xantcha, and they will not return. This will be the place where you can dwell while I complete my dragon, the place where you can lay out your wretched memories for my understanding."

Xantcha tried to understand her new companion and failed. He was wrong, simply wrong, about so many things, yet he had the power to walk between worlds. No Phyrexian, not even a demon like Gix, could do that. Urza did not give orders, not in a Phyrexian sense. Still, Xantcha had no alternative but to obey him as she'd obeyed Gix, silently and without grace. She started up the path to the caves.

"Where are you going?"

Let him haul her back; he had that power. Or let him follow, which he did.

The cave was sealed, of course, and carefully, with stones, dirt, and plant life. The locals, as Urza had called them, wouldn't know the treasures of their ancestors had been plundered, but Xantcha knew. She began pulling weeds and hurling dirt with her bare hands.

Urza intervened. "Child, what are you doing?"

"I'm not a child," she reminded him. "They brought me here to extract an army. If it's gone, then you may be right that no Phyrexian will return. If it's not . . ." Xantcha went back to work.

"You'll be digging forever," Urza pulled her aside. "There are better ways."

For a moment, Urza stood stock-still with his eyes closed. When he opened them, they blazed with crimson light. A swirling cloud, about twice his height, bloomed in the air before the cave's sealed mouth. He spoke a single word whose meaning, if it had any, Xantcha didn't know, and the cloud rooted itself where she had been digging.

Fascinated, Xantcha attempted to put her hand in the small, bright windstorm. Urza touched her arm, and she could not move.

"We will come back tomorrow and see what is to be seen. Meanwhile, we will find food—it has been too long since I have enjoyed a meal—and you will begin telling me everything you remember."

Urza took Xantcha's wrists and pulled her into the between—worlds before she could recite her armor-releasing rhyme. The journey lasted less than a heartbeat, less than an airless breath. They emerged in what Urza called a *town*, where Xantcha found herself surrounded by born-folk: all flesh, like her, all different, too, and chattering a language she couldn't understand. He took her to an *inn*, gave orders in the born-folk language, told her to sit in a *chair* as he did, to drink from a *cup* and to use a *knife* and *fork* rather than her fingers when she ate.

It was difficult, but Urza was adamant. Xantcha ate until the knife, at least, was comfortable in her hands.

Later, there was music, exactly as Xantcha had dreamed it would be, and dancing which she would have joined if Urza had not said:

"Too soon, child. Your eyes are open, but you do not truly see."

When the music and dancing had ended, Urza led her from the inn to the night and through the between-worlds to the forest. He was gone when Xantcha awoke, long after sunrise. The scent of glistening oil was stronger, wafting down from the cave. She remembered the knife and wished she still had it in her hand, even though it would have been useless against a Phyrexian . . . or Urza.

Urza was inside the cave, and so were most of the artifacts. Tiptoeing to the brink of an excavation trench, Xantcha watched Urza dismantle one of the insect warriors. He was faster and more powerful. When its mandible claws closed over his ankle, they shattered. Antennae whips burned and melted when they touched his face.

Perhaps one dragon would be enough, if it was Urza's dragon, with Urza sitting between its shoulders.

Xantcha cleared her throat. "They're coming back. They wouldn't have left all this behind. Waste not, want not, that's our way."

Urza leapt into the air and hovered in front of her. "The Phyrexian way is not your way, Xantcha, not anymore, but otherwise, yes, I believe you're right. I'm ready for them tomorrow, though let us hope it isn't so soon. With time to study these automata, I'll be more than ready for them, Xantcha. These could almost be Thran design. They're pure artifice, no sentience at all, but perfectly adaptive. Look!" He held up a pearlescent ring. "A powerstone that isn't a powerstone. There is water in here, light, and simple mana, the essence of all things. I shall call it *phloton*, because it burns without consuming itself. It will give me power for my dragon! More power than I ever dreamed! I shall redesign it!

"Vengeance, Xantcha. I shall take vengeance for both of us. When the Phyrexians return, I will destroy them and pursue them all the way back to Phyrexia itself."

Chapter  10

Urza got his wish. The Phyrexians didn't return to the cave the next day, or the next after that. Seasons passed, and years. He dismantled the insect warriors, incorporating their parts into his redesigned dragon, linking their ring-shaped hearts into a single great power source.

Ten years passed, ten *Dominarian* years, according to Urza who claimed his attachment to his birth-world remained so strong that at any time he knew the sun's angle and the moon's phase above the cave he called Koilos, the Secret Heart.

"Come," Urza said one winter morning when Xantcha would have preferred to remain in her nest of pillows and blankets. "It is finished."

He held out his hand and, with a rhyme and a yawn, Xantcha clasped it. No more screaming through the between-worlds. She'd mastered her fears and the cyst in her stomach. Although she dwelt mostly in the forest where the Phyrexian portal had been laid out and where a cottage with a chicken coop and garden now stood Urza had insisted that she accompany him to every new world he discovered. Her nose for Phyrexians was indisputably better than his.

131

There were no Phyrexians on the world where Urza had built and rebuilt his dragon. There was no life at all and never had been. Urza's new dragon wasn't much taller than the old one, but he'd borrowed from the insect-warriors. The new dragon had a spider's eight-legged body. Any two of the eight legs could be the "front" legs, and any three could be destroyed without unbalancing it.

The many-toothed head remained from the dragon's previous incarnation, but the short arms had been lengthened, and the torso rotated freely behind whichever pair of legs led the rest. In addition to gouts of blazing naphtha, the new dragon spat lightning bolts and spheres of exploding fire.

"Phloton," Urza said, rubbing his hands together. "Unlimited power!"

Urza demonstrated each weapon, and though Xantcha still thought a hundred lesser war machines would be more effective, she was awed by the destruction Urza's new dragon brought to the barren, defenseless world. The sky was streaked with soot and dust. Slag lakes of amber and crimson pocked the plains. Everything that wasn't molten had been charred. It reminded her of nothing more or less than Phyrexia's Fourth Sphere, and she didn't think even a demon could stand against it. There was only one not-so-small problem.

"It's too big. It won't fit through an ambulator."

"It won't need an ambulator. It can walk the planes directly. Even you could guide it safely."

"I wouldn't know where to go."

Xantcha had conquered her fears, but no matter how hard she tried, she couldn't orient herself in the between-worlds emptiness. Worlds—planes—didn't call out to her the way they called out to Urza. If she lost her grip on Urza's hand, she fell like a stone to whatever world would have her. Urza's armor kept her alive through one failure after another, until Urza conceded that she'd never 'walk the planes.

"You won't have to do anything at all," Urza assured her. "After I've used the ambulator once, I'll know where Phyrexia is, and I'll 'walk the dragon there. You'll wait, safe and snug, until I return. Now, watch!"

Between blinks, Urza shifted from beside Xantcha to the dragon's saddle-seat. It came to life. No, not life, Xantcha reminded herself, never life! The dragon was an artifact, the tool of Urza's vengeance against the abominations of Phyrexia. Never mind that its eyes went from dark to blazing or that a ground-shaking roar accompanied each lightning bolt. The dragon was merely a tool that took aim at an already blackened hill and reduced it to slag in less time than it would have taken Xantcha to eat her breakfast.

"Do you still have doubts?" Urza asked when he'd returned to her side.

"Mountains don't defend themselves."

Urza took her words for a jest. His laughter rang between-worlds as he whisked her back to the forest cottage.

With the dragon finished, there was little to do but wait for the Phyrexians to return, and for Urza, waiting was difficult. Though he'd long since pried every story she was willing to tell from her memory, he continued to quiz her. How high were the First Sphere mountains? Where were the Fanes, the arenas? Which priests were the most dangerous and where did they dwell? Were the iron wyverns solitary creatures or pack hunters? In the Fourth Sphere, were the furnaces clumped together or did each stand alone? And were the fumaroles wide enough to allow his dragon to descend directly to the interior, or would he have to dismantle Phyrexia like a puzzle box?

Worse than the questions were the nights, about one in four or five, when Urza closed his eyes. Urza's terrible dreams were too large for his mind. His ghosts walked the forest when he slept, recreating a silent drama of anger and betrayal. Xantcha had built the cottage to protect herself from his dreams, but no wall was thick enough to insulate her from his anguish.

Urza's call for vengeance was something a Phyrexian could understand. From the beginning Xantcha's life had been full of threats and reprisals, broken promises and humiliation, but Urza needed more than vengeance. When his nightmares reached their inevitable climax, he'd cry out for mercy and beg someone he called *Mishra* to forgive him.

Urza wouldn't talk about his nightmares, which got worse once the dragon was complete. He wouldn't answer Xantcha's questions about the ghosts or their world or, especially, about *Mishra*, except to say the Phyrexians would pay for what they'd done to Mishra, or through Mishra—Xantcha couldn't be sure which. Whenever she dared mention the nightmare name, Urza would fly into a bleak rage. Ten or twelve days might pass without a word, without even a gesture. Then, without warning, he'd rouse from his stupor, and the questions would begin again.

Xantcha began to look forward to the times when restlessness got the better of Urza and he'd head off between-worlds, still hoping to stumble across Phyrexia, or an excavation team with its precious ambulators. He'd be gone for a month, even a season, and her life would be her own.

Long before the dragon was finished, Xantcha had learned how to control the substance that emerged from her cyst and expand it into a buoyant sphere instead of the clinging armor Urza had intended. Seated in the sphere, she'd traveled an irregular circuit of the hamlets and farms surrounding the forest, learning the local dialects and trading with women who accepted her claim that she lived with "an old man of the forest."

She still visited the local women, albeit carefully, lest they notice that she wasn't growing older the way they were, but with Urza gone for longer periods of time Xantcha gradually expanded her horizons. She was, after all, following Urza's orders. He didn't want her to remain near the cave while he was gone. Urza reasoned that Phyrexians might take her by surprise, extract his secrets from her empty mind, then ambush him when he returned. He designed an artifact that was attuned to his eyes. Though small enough to be worn as a sparkling pendant, the artifact could send a signal between-worlds.

"Come back frequently," he'd told Xantcha when he hung the jewel around her neck. "If they've returned, hide yourself far, far away from here, then break the crystal and I will return for my— for our—vengeance. Above all, once you've seen a Phyrexian, stay away from the forest until I come for you. Don't let your curiosity lead you into foolishness. If they find you, they will reclaim you, and you will betray me. You wouldn't want that to happen."

Twelve winters, twelve summers, and Urza still spoke to her as if she couldn't think for herself or hear through his lies. She swore she'd do as he asked. Whatever his reasons were, Xantcha didn't want to come face-to-face with anything Phyrexian, even though she suspected Urza wouldn't come back for her after he dealt with Phyrexia.

Urza's demands weren't a burden. The chaos and subtleties of born-folk societies fascinated her. Giving herself to the world's wind, Xantcha explored whatever struck her curiosity, so long as it didn't reek of Phyrexia's glistening oil. She learned to speak the born-folk languages, to read their writing, when it existed. The warrior-cave had a hundred different names, all of them archaic, all of them curses. In the world's larger towns, where more folk knew their history, she discovered it was better to invent a completely false history for herself than to admit she had roots near the warrior-cave.

After a few narrow escapes and near disasters, Xantcha decided that it was better to disguise herself as well. Born-folk had definite notion about the proper places of young men and women in their societies, and no place at all for a newt who was neither. An incorrigible lad, a rogue in the making, was an easier disguise than a young woman. At best when she wore a young woman's clothes, good-intentioned folk wanted to swallow her into their families. At worst . . . at worst, she'd been lucky to escape with her life. But Xantcha did escape and, hardened by Phyrexia, there was nothing in a born-folks' world that daunted her for long.

The forest world had one moon, which went from full to new to full again in thirty-six days. The born-folk marked time by their moon's phases, and Xantcha did, too, returning to the cave twice each month. Sometimes there was a message from Urza in the ruins of the neglected cottage. Sometimes he was there himself, waiting for her, eager to whisk her between-worlds to witness his latest accomplishment or discovery.

Urza had no one else. Although he said there were others who could walk between planes, he avoided them and born-folk alike.

Without Xantcha, there were only ghosts to break his silence. If anything would lure Urza back to her after Phyrexia, Xantcha expected it would be loneliness.

She pitied Urza; it seemed he'd lost more to his nightmares than he believed she'd lost to the Phyrexians. His artifact pendant was her most precious possession, a constant reminder that never left her neck. Yet, she was always a little relieved when she found the forest deserted, and except for one nagging worry, she would not have mourned the loss if Urza never reappeared in her life.

The worry was her heart, the lump Xantcha had held in her hand when the vat-priests decanted her, the lump they'd taken from her moments later, as they took it from every other newt. It had slipped through her memory sometime after she'd become a dodger, but it resurfaced when she encountered the Trien.

The Trien believed that their hearts could hold only so many misdeeds before they burst and consigned them to hell. To defend against eternal torment, the Trien purged their hearts of error through bloodletting and guilt dances. Urza had no more blood within him than a compleated Phyrexian, but she'd thought the guilt dance might defeat his nightmares, so she danced with the Trien—to test her theory—and in the midst of hysteria and ecstasy she'd remembered her own heart.

Xantcha tried to convince herself that the tale the vat-priests had told her was merely another of their countless lies. Her heart hadn't been very big, and no matter who might have done the counting, her or the Ineffable, she'd made a lot of mistakes that hadn't killed her. But Xantcha had never been particularly persuasive, not with Urza nor with herself. For the first time Xantcha's dreams were filled with her own ghosts: newts and priests, a plundered wind-crystal of music and beauty, insect warriors with baleful eyes, and even Gix as the other demons shoved him through the Fourth Sphere fumarole.

Worse than dreams, Xantcha began to worry what would happen if Urza succeeded, and all Phyrexia, including the heart vault beneath the Fane of Flesh, were destroyed.

She conquered her nightmares and worries; obsession wasn't part of her nature. Still, when the time came, after nearly two hundred summers of waiting, that Xantcha found diggers, bearers, and a handful of gremlin dodgers in the forest cave, she didn't retreat before breaking Urza's crystal artifact.

* * * * *

Urza arrived with his dragon less than a day later and caught the Phyrexians by surprise. From her bolt-hole in the hill above the warriors' cave, Xantcha heard the gremlins screaming and counted the flashes as the diggers and bearers exploded.

A handful of diggers made a stand in front of the cave. Urza toyed with them, tossing each again and again before crushing it. It was a display worthy of Phyrexia in its cruelty and single-minded arrogance. Xantcha couldn't watch. She looked away and saw, to her horror, a searcher-priest not ten paces away. She thought it was hiding, though it was difficult to imagine any compleat Phyrexian seeking shelter among living trees and animals.

Then insight struck. The searcher was fulfilling its destiny, watching an artifact Phyrexia would surely covet. Xantcha couldn't guess whether the priest had seen her before she saw it, but a moment later it began to run toward the ambulator, which it could—if it had the time and thought quickly enough—unanchor and suck to Phyrexia behind it.

Xantcha had no means to tell Urza that he was in danger of losing his way to Phyrexia and no reason to think she could stop the searcher-priest or even that she could catch it before it reached the ambulator, but if it paused to unanchor the nether end, she hoped she could delay it until Urza arrived. After a mnemonic yawn, she abandoned her bolt-hole.

The searcher-priest had no intention of unanchoring the ambulator's nether end or even slowing down. It had a score of strides on Xantcha when its brass foot touched the black circle. With its second step, it crossed the midpoint and sank between-worlds. *Too fast. Too fast*, memory warned from the back of Xantcha's mind; the priests had told them to enter the ambulators slowly, lest they get caught between two worlds.

Expecting an explosion, Xantcha skidded off the trail and hid behind the largest tree she saw. There was no explosion, but when she poked her head around the tree trunk fire rippled across the ambulator disk's surface. She had no idea if the priest had survived. For that matter, Xantcha didn't know if the ambulator had survived.

Urza wouldn't welcome the sight of her, not when he'd told her to stay far away, but Xantcha thought it best to warn him. She stepped in front of the dragon when it burnt a path through the trees. Urza shot flame to the left of her and flame to the right. Xantcha ran until she was breathless, then circled back. The dragon sat beside the ambulator; the saddle-seat between its shoulders was empty.

Urza had gone to Phyrexia alone.

Xantcha settled down to wait. Morning became afternoon. The sky darkened, and the dragon's eyes shone red.

Urza returned, not through the ambulator but in a blaze of lightning, and Xantcha did nothing to attract his attention as he remounted the dragon. Moments later they were gone.

The storm ended quickly. The ambulator beckoned. It wasn't broken. For the last time, Xantcha asked herself:

Was her heart important enough to risk everything to rescue it?

The priests lied about so many things; only a fool could believe they hadn't lied about newt hearts. Try as she might, Xantcha couldn't remember exactly what hers had looked like; mottled amber, perhaps, with bright rainbow inclusions. She'd only seen it that once and never seen another.

Only a fool . . .

And she was a fool.

On hands and knees, Xantcha crept up to the ambulator and was surprised to discover that the searchers had left the prime end in the forest. She began unanchoring it, careful not to disturb the hard panel where seven jet-black jewels were set in a silver matrix. When the ambulator was loose and rippling, Xantcha yawned. There was a single sharp pain in her gut as the cyst contracted— drawing the armor out twice in a single day wasn't what Urza had in mind when he made the cyst, but she could do it five times, at least, before the process failed. The not-quite-liquid flowed beneath her clothes.

She stepped into the unanchored ambulator. It swirled around her, not unlike the armor itself. By the time she'd reached the middle, the black disk had shrunk to half its size and risen to her waist. Xantcha had repressed how much she disliked the ambulators. The sinking and suffocating was worse than following Urza between-worlds, and the cyst made the passage worse. It swelled in her gut; she thought she might explode before her head emerged in Phyrexia.

Because she'd unanchored the prime end in the forest, the nether end in Phyrexia was also loose and shrank as Xantcha emerged. Any Phyrexian would have been suspicious of a newt who rolled up a ambulator behind it. The avengers that normally guarded the Fourth Sphere field, where scores of ambulators were anchored, would have annihilated her on sight, if there had been any left standing. Xantcha assumed that Urza had annihilated them as he emerged; at least, something had.

Waste not, want not, the Fourth Sphere was even uglier than she remembered with acrid air and oily ash drizzling from the soot clouds overhead. The roar of a thousand furnaces was less a sound than a presence, a vise tightened over her ribs. The hollow where the ambulator had been anchored was bright with bilious yellows, noxious greens, and an iridescent purple that was the very color of disease. Nothing was alive, of course; it was just filthy oil, slicked over an eon of detritus not fit for even the furnaces.

There wasn't a living Phyrexian, newt or otherwise, in sight.

Grateful, but suspicious of her good fortune, Xantcha retrieved the glossy disk from beneath her feet: the rolled-up ambulator. Holding it by its flexible rim, she twisted her wrists in opposite directions. The disk rippled and shrank until it was scarcely larger than her palm, with the jewels protruding on both sides.

After tucking the ambulator between her belt and her armor, Xantcha took her bearings. There was no sun-star for Phyrexia, especially not here, in the Fourth Sphere. Away from the furnaces, light came harsh, constant and without shadows. But the place was home, or it had been, and it came back to her.

A few strides up the greasy slope, the horizon expanded and Xantcha saw why her return to Phyrexia had been so easy: straight ahead, in the direction of the Fane of Flesh, the soot clouds had turned red and fire fell from the sky.

Urza? Xantcha asked herself and decided it was possible that Urza was burning his way through Phyrexia. The ambulators could be anchored anywhere. Once unrolled, they were tunnels, direct passages from one specific place to another, no detours allowed, but a 'walker made his own path here, there and everywhere. Urza could change his mind between-worlds, but whenever, wherever, he ended his 'walk, he stood on a world's surface. In Phyrexia, the surface was the First Sphere.

When she'd dwelt in Phyrexia, before she'd known the meaning of *silence*, Xantcha had been able to ignore the furnace roar. She reached within herself to remember the trick and realized she'd been gone from Phyrexia several times longer than she'd been a part of it. But the memory was there. Xantcha numbed herself to the ambient rumbling and heard the clanging alarms.

She smiled. Those alarms were struck when a furnace was about to blow. Every Phyrexian had an emergency place, and for newts that place was the Fane of Flesh, precisely where she wanted to go. Of course, the emergency wasn't a furnace, and the closer she got to the sprawled hulks of furnaces, fanes, and gremlin shanties, the clearer it was that in the absence of the expected disaster, panic had replaced plan.

Priests and other compleated types that Xantcha didn't remember, and possibly, had never seen, raced through gremlin town. Their voices were shrill enough to hurt. The challenge was staying out of their way; the shambles were already littered with gremlins who'd failed.

Urza's armor protected Xantcha from the sky; her sense of purpose did the rest. The Fane of Flesh wasn't the most impressive structure in the Fourth Sphere, but it stood near the glistening oil fountain, which had become a spire of blue-white flame.

A phalanx of demons made their appearance while Xantcha threaded her way through the maze of furnaces. Narrow beams of amber and orange shot upward from their torsos, into the reddest clouds. Urza answered with lightning. In the Fourth Sphere's filthy skies, the air itself ignited and a web of fire shot to every part of the horizon. Xantcha felt the heat through her armor. Her instinct was to run, but ash quickly followed the fire, and the Fourth Sphere went dark.

For a moment, flesh had the advantage over metal, at least flesh protected by Urza's armor. Neither ash nor smoke irritated Xantcha's eyes, and with a bit of effort she could see a body's length in front of her. As in the gremlin town alleys, the danger came from the panicked and the fallen: no one paid any attention to a stray newt, assuming they could see her.

Then the demons regrouped. A low humming sound began in the distance, followed by a cold wind that scoured the air. As it passed overhead, Xantcha looked up and saw the bottom of the Third Sphere, a sight she'd never seen before. She saw the flames, too, where Urza had burnt through the outer spheres. Another few moments and Xantcha might have seen Urza's dragon, if she hadn't started to run for the Fane.

The rusty doors on the far side of the Glistening Fountain were wide open as Xantcha entered the plaza where newts were compleated. She was in the final sprint for the Fane, when a vast shadow moved overhead. The last time Xantcha had seen Urza's new dragon, she hadn't noticed any wing struts and had assumed the artifact had grown too heavy for flight. She'd assumed incorrectly. Six of the dragon's eight legs supported wings that dwarfed the rest of its body and yet were highly flexible and maneuverable. The dragon swooped sideways to avoid a demon-flung bolt while belching a tongue of flame.

A furnace exploded. Metal shards and slag traced brilliant arcs beneath the Third Sphere ceiling. Impressed by beauty that was also terrifying and deadly, Xantcha considered the possibility that Urza would win. Then a tree-sized clot of slag crashed into the plaza. The flames of the Glistening Fountain sputtered and died while yellow fumes rose from the new crater beside it. Unless Xantcha wanted to die with Phyrexia, she had to find her heart and unroll the ambulator while there was still a solid place left to support the prime end.

Xantcha finished her run with no further distractions.

"Down! Go down!" a jittery vat-priest insisted as soon as she cleared the open doors. "Newts go down!" Its hooks and paddles clattered against each other as it indicated a deserted corridor.

The priests weren't flesh, but they weren't mindless artifacts, either. They might lack sufficient imagination to disobey a fatal command, but they had enough to be afraid.

"I go," Xantcha replied, the first time she'd spoken Phyrexian in centuries. She bungled the pronunciation; the priest didn't seem to notice.

She'd forgotten how big the Fane was. Maybe she'd never noticed; she'd never gone anywhere within it without a cadre of other newts and priests surrounding her. One corridor was as good as another when she had no idea where her heart might be, and the one the vat-priest had pointed toward was the broadest and best lit. She read the glyph inscriptions on the walls, hoping they would provide a clue, but they were only exhortations, lies, and empty promises, like everything else in Phyrexia.

The Fane of Flesh was quieter, cleaner than anything beyond its precincts. Its walls had, so far, resisted the outside flames. But it had taken damage. Turning a corner, Xantcha came upon a pile of rubble from a collapsed ceiling and a defunct vat-priest crushed beneath it. She wrenched one of the priest's long hooks from its shoulder socket and kept going.

A teacher-priest waited at another corner. Its eyes were flesh within a flat, bronze mask. They darted between the hook, Xantcha's face, her boots and her belt. "Newt?" it asked.

Xantcha had taken the hook as a weapon, but the priest assumed it was part of her, that it and her leather garments, were evidence that she'd begun her compleation.

"The hearts. Where are the hearts? I am sent to guard the hearts."

Flesh eyes blinked stupidly. "Hearts? What matter the hearts?"

"We are attacked; they are the future. I am sent to guard them."

"Who sent you?" it asked after another moment's hesitation.

"A demon," Xantcha replied. Small lies weren't worth the effort of defending them. "Where are the hearts?"

The teacher-priest continued to blink. Xantcha feared it didn't know where the hearts were stored, not a confession one priest would want to make to another, especially another under a demon's command. It asked, "Which demon?" as thunder waves pummeled the Fane and rust rained from the ceiling.

Xantcha had no time to wonder whether the strike was for Urza or against him. Gix was dead, thrust through a fumarole centuries ago. Still, any answer was better than none.

"The Great Gix sent me."

Her bluff worked. The teacher-priest just needed a name. It quaked as it gave her detailed directions to a vault so far beneath the Fourth Sphere floor it might actually have been on the Fifth. More blasts shook the Fane. A stairway she was supposed to use was clogged with debris and the scent of fire.

"I'll have to tell Urza that he's wrong," Xantcha complained as she put her hand on the portal artifact tucked beneath her belt. "I wouldn't be standing here, waiting to die, if I didn't have some damn fool useless imagination."

She could have gotten out. The corridor was wide enough to unroll the portal. She'd be back in the forest. Safe. Or not safe. Ambulators could only be rolled up from their prime end. If she left the ambulator's prime end here in the corridor and the Fane collapsed, the rubble might follow her to the forest . . . all of Phyrexia might follow her.

Waste not, want not! I never thought of that.

When she used the ambulator to escape, it would be a three-step process: first to the forest to anchor the nether end, back to Phyrexia to loosen the prime, and then another passage back to the forest. Timing had become even more critical.

Xantcha looked around for an intact stairway. She found one and found the vault, too. Measured by the world she'd left, Xantcha guessed she'd spent a morning in Phyrexia. Looking down at the mass of softly glowing hearts, she guessed it might take a lifetime to find her own.

The Ineffable's plan for Phyrexia was precise, even rigid, but the plan didn't cover every contingency. Vat-priests dutifully brought newt hearts to the vault, then simply heaved the little stones into a pit, one for every newt ever decanted. At the surface the pit was about twice the size of an unrolled ambulator. When she thrust the vat-priest's hook into the chaos, it went in all the way to the shoulder gears without striking anything solid.

The pit seethed. Countless glowing amber fists and a smaller number of dark ones were vibrating constantly against one another. On her knees, Xantcha could hear a steady chorus of sighs and gasps. She wondered about the dark ones and got lucky. She heard a pop! right in front of her, then watched as a glowing heart brightened, then went dark.

Death?

Phyrexians were dying in Urza's assault. Were their hearts, long detached from their compleated bodies, going dark as they did? Xantcha retrieved the newly darkened stone with the vat-priest's hook. Tiny scratches marred its surface: marks left as the heart stone clattered against its companions or a record of errors made by the Ineffable? She read the glyphs on the walls. They repeated the familiar teacher-priest lies.

Xantcha picked up a glowing stone. Its warmth and subtlety was tangible even through Urza's armor. She picked up a second glowing heart and found it just as warm, just as subtle, yet also different. But every dark stone felt as inert as the first she had touched.

The teacher-priests might not have told the whole truth, but they'd told enough. There was a vital bond between Phyrexians and their detached hearts. She hadn't been a total fool. There was good reason to rescue the stone she'd carried out of the vats.

And precious little hope of finding it among all the others.

Tears of frustration rolled down Xantcha's armored cheeks. They fumed when they landed on the glowing stones cradled in her lap. Another shudder rocked the Fane. When it ended, a score of hearts had popped and dimmed. More Phyrexian deaths to Urza's credit, but imagine what his dragon engine could do if Urza brought its weapons to bear where Xantcha sat. Imagine what she could do. The hearts weren't so hard that she couldn't break them, and if her tears could make the stones fume, what might her blood do if she chose to sacrifice herself for vengeance?

She'd been willing to die for much less before Urza rescued her, but she'd come to the Fane of Flesh because she wanted to live.

Choices and questions, all of them morbid, paralyzed Xantcha at the edge of the pit, and then she heard laughter. She scrambled to her feet, scattering hearts, crushing them in her frantic clumsiness. There was no one behind her. The laughter hadn't come from the corridor, it came from within . . . within her mind and within her heart.

Throwing the hook aside, Xantcha waded in the pit, sweeping her open hands in front of her, moving toward the laughter. She found what she was looking for not far below the surface, neither in the middle nor at the pit's edge. There was nothing to distinguish it from any other heart stone—a few scratches, but no more than any other stone she'd touched, glowing or dark. Yet it was hers; it had to be hers: Urza's armor absorbed it as it lay in her hand.

Another burst of popping hearts interrupted Xantcha's reverie. A hundred, perhaps several hundred, Phyrexians had died since she entered the vault, and the chamber was as bright as it had been when she entered. Xantcha tried to calculate how many glowing hearts lay on the surface, how many more might lay beneath. She gave up after a few attempts, but not before she'd decided that unless she told Urza about the heart vault, it would be a very long battle before he achieved vengeance.

Her heart was too big to swallow, too risky to carry in her hand. Xantcha tucked it carefully inside her boot before she headed off.

* * * * *

Finding her way out of the Fane was harder than finding Urza. Flames, smoke and sorcery ratcheted through one-quarter of what passed for the Fourth Sphere sky. While she'd been looking for her heart, the demons had mounted a counterattack.

Urza's hulking dragon was surrounded by Phyrexia's smaller defenders: dragons, wyverns and whatever else had been summoned from the First Sphere through the very hole Urza had burnt for himself. As she'd warned him, individually Phyrexia had nothing that could equal his devastating tool, but in Phyrexia, individuals weren't important. For every compleated priest, even for every scrap-made digger or bearer, there were twenty warriors: fleshless, obedient, and relentless. The demons aimed the warriors at Urza's dragon where they died by the score and occasionally did damage.

The dragon's wings were shredded and useless. Two of its legs had been disabled; a third burst into melting flames while Xantcha looked for a path through the Phyrexian lines. Urza could still defend himself in all quarters but if—when—he lost a fourth leg, there'd be gaps, and it wouldn't take imagination to exploit them.

You're lost! Xantcha shouted silently, adding an image of the vault of hearts, *There's a better way! 'Walk away now!* But though Urza could easily extract thoughts from her mind, she'd never been able to insert her thoughts into his.

There were hundreds of Phyrexians on the battlefield and even a few gremlins. All of them were in greater danger of being trampled by the relentless warriors than they were from anything in the dragon's arsenal, but their presence, a thin layer of chaos across the field, was Xantcha's best hope of getting to Urza.

Relying on Urza's armor to protect her from everything except her own stupidity, Xantcha dodged fire, lightning and the distortions of sorcery as she threaded her way through the Phyrexian circle. Once she came face to back with a demon. It was dark and asymmetric, with pincers on one arm and a six-fingered hand on the other, and it had eyes in several places, including the back of its head. Nothing like Gix, except for the malice and intelligence in its shiny red eyes. It studied her from boots to hair and vat-priest hook. Xantcha was sure it knew she wasn't what she was pretending to be, and equally sure Urza's armor wouldn't protect her from its wrath.

Just then a wyvern screamed, and the demon turned away.

A wall of sharp, noxious yellow crystals exploded from the ground between Xantcha and the demon. She staggered back and watched the demon uncoil like an angry serpent, writhing toward the dragon. Urza's armor protected Xantcha from flames and emptiness and corrosive vapors, too. She followed the wall of crystals as it extended across Phyrexia's Fourth Sphere toward Urza and his dragon. If Urza struck down the wall, Xantcha was meat. If he didn't, it would claim the fourth leg from his dragon.

But not before she swung up into the leg's scaffolding, climbing for her life and his.

Xantcha made an easy target, running across the dragon's back, but nothing attacked. The Phyrexians overhead didn't recognize her as an enemy, and Urza's attention was centered on the noxious wall. Xantcha fell hard when the leg collapsed. Worse, there was blood on her hands when she hauled herself back up. Either her armor was weakening, or Urza was.

She swung down between the dragon's shoulders expecting the worst.

Urza reclined in a wire shrouded couch. Smoke rose from his charred trousers. The dragon's wounds were reflected on his body. Bruises, contusions—bleeding contusions—covered Urza's hands and face.

Xantcha had never seen Urza hurt. She'd assumed he could be destroyed. She hadn't imagined that he could be wounded. She stood, confused and useless, for several moments before she found the courage to touch his shoulder.

"Urza? Urza, it's time to 'walk away from here, if you can."

No response.

"Urza? Urza, can you hear me? It's me, Xantcha." She put some strength into her hand. The whole couch rocked a bit, but there was no response from Urza. He was still in control of the dragon, still fighting. As mindless as any of the wyverns, Urza had abandoned sentience and become the tool. "Listen to me, Urza! Vengeance is slipping away. You've got to leave now!"

Urza's eyes opened. They were horrible to behold. He started to say the one word that would have been more horrible to hear than his eyes were to see, but he didn't finish: "Yawg— "

The Ineffable. The name that must not be spoken. Xantcha knew it; they all knew it. It was with them in the vats. But Urza should not have known it. He'd never gotten anything out of Xantcha's mind that she had not been willing to give him, and she'd never have given him that.

Every instinct said *run, now, alone*. Xantcha resisted. Urza had rescued her when she'd had no hope. She wouldn't leave him behind.

Xantcha reached across the couch and took Urza's wrists as he so often took hers. She steeled her nerves and stared into his seething eyes. "Now, Urza. We've got to leave now. 'Walk us somewhere safe—to the cave where you took me. And leave . . . leave that name behind."

"Yawg—"

"Xantcha!" she screamed her own name at his face.

His hands grasped hers and her vision went black.

Chater 11

The supplies were stowed, safe against mist, mice, and anything else the changeable climate of Ohran Ridge might drop on the cottage. Xantcha had checked them twice during the interminable night. She'd made herself a pot of tea and drunk it all. The herbs should have helped her relax, but they hadn't. Dawn's golden light fell sideways on the bed where she hadn't slept.

Her door was wide open, inviting shadows. Urza's wasn't. It wasn't warded with layers of "leave me alone" sorcery, but it wasn't leaking sound. The sounds had stopped coming through the wall in the unmeasured hours after midnight. Ratepe, Xantcha had told herself, had probably fallen asleep, and Urza rarely made noise when he was alone. Nothing unusual. Nothing to worry about. So why had she opened her door? Why had she spent the last of the night damp and shivering? Hadn't Ratepe demonstrated, if not an ability to take care of himself, then an inclination to ignore her advice?

And hadn't Urza welcomed Ratepe more enthusiastically than she'd dare hope? Whatever had brought silence to the far side of the wall, it wouldn't have been murder. No matter how annoying Ratepe got, he'd survive.

Xantcha unwound her blankets. Her joints creaked. Phyrexia was easier on flesh and bone than the Ohran Ridge. She broke the ice in her washstand, cleared her head with a few breath-taking splashes, then went outside and listened at the door. She'd give them until midday. If Ratepe hadn't reappeared by then, Xantcha planned to take a chisel to the cottage's common wall. Before that, she had one more gambit to try and put her chisel to work on the hardened ashes underneath her outdoor hearth.

When the fire was just right Xantcha covered it with an iron grate and covered the grate with a rasher of bacon. A friendly breeze carried the aromas into the cottage. She never knew when or if Urza would be in a mood to eat, but if Ratepe was alive, he'd be out the door before the bacon burnt.

Right on schedule Ratepe appeared in the doorway. "By the book! That smells good." He didn't have the cross-grained look of a man who'd just awakened, and he said something—Xantcha couldn't hear what—over his shoulder before closing the door behind him. "I'm starving."

"I see you survived." Xantcha hadn't realized how angry she was until she heard her own voice. "Here, eat. Starting tomorrow, you can cook your own." On his own hearth, too. Xantcha wasn't sharing, at least not until she'd calmed down.

Ratepe had the sense to approach her cautiously. "You're angry about last night?"

Xantcha slammed hot, crisp bacon on a wooden platter and thrust it at him. She didn't know why she was so upset and didn't want to discuss the matter.

"I guess it got out of hand. When I saw him—Urza. He is Urza, the Urza, Urza the Artificer. You were right, you know. Back in Efuan Pincar, I didn't believe you. I thought maybe you thought he was Urza, but I didn't think he could be the Urza, the by-the-holy-book Artificer!" Ratepe paused long enough to inhale a piece of bacon. "I thought I'd been as scared as I could get before I met you, but that was before he touched me. Avohir! I swear I'll never be afraid again."

"Don't make promises you can't keep."

"There can't be anything scarier." Ratepe shook his head and shoved another piece into his mouth.

This time he chewed before he swallowed. She was about to criticize his manners, but he was too fast for her.

"He's Urza. Urza is Urza, the real Urza. And I'm Mishra. I'm talking to a legend, watching things, hearing things I can't imagine, because Urza—Urza the Artificer, straight out of *The Antiquity Wars*, thinks I'm his brother, Mishra the Mighty, Mishra the Destroyer, and we're going to put what's wrong back to rights again."

Another pause. More bacon, more bad manners, but then he hadn't had manners before. His face was flushed and his eyes never stopped moving.

"I'm Mishra. Avohir! I'm Mishra. . . . He tries to trick me sometimes, says things he doesn't believe, things I shouldn't believe. I have to watch him close . . . watch him close. Did you see his eyes, Xantcha? Avohir! I think he's a little touched? But I stay ahead of him, nearly. I have to. I'm almighty Mishra—"

Xantcha had had enough of Ratepe's babbling. She wasn't as fast as Urza, but she was fast enough to seize a would-be Mishra by the neck of his tunic and whirl him against the nearest post. Damp debris from the thatching rained down on them both.

"You are not Mishra, you merely pretend to be Mishra. You are Ratepe, son of Mideah, and the day you forget that will be the day you die, because he is Urza and you cannot hope to 'stay ahead of him.' Do you understand?"

When a wide-eyed Ratepe didn't immediately say yes, Xantcha rattled his spine against the post. His chin bobbed vigorously. She released his tunic and stepped back. The greater part of her anger was gone.

"I know who I am, Xantcha," Ratepe insisted, sounding more like himself, more like the youth Xantcha thought she knew. "I'm Rat, just Rat. But if I don't forget, just a little—when he looks at me, Xantcha—when Urza the Artificer looks at me, if I don't let myself believe I am who he thinks I am—who you told me to be— then . . ." He stared at the closed door. "When I saw his eyes. I never believed that part, Xantcha. It's not in *The Antiquity Wars*.

Kayla wrote about Tawnos coming to tell her about how he'd seen Urza with the Weakstone and Mightstone embedded in his skull. She thought it was all lies, nice lies because Tawnos didn't want her to know the truth. The idea that the Weakstone or the Mightstone kept Urza alive, that's not even in Jarsyl. There's only one source for the stuff about Urza's eyes glowing with all the power of the sylex: four scraps of parchment bound by mistake at the back of the T'mill codex. They're supposed to be Tawnos's deathbed confession. My father said it was pure apocrypha. But it wasn't! Urza's eyes, they are the Weakstone and the Mightstone, aren't they? They're what've kept him alive, if Urza really is alive, if he's not just something the stones have created."

Waste not, want not, Xantcha hadn't found Mishra the Destroyer, she'd found Mishra the skeptic and Mishra the babbling pedant! She shot him a disbelieving look. "Don't ask me. Last night, you were the one who said that the Weakstone was singing to you."

Ratepe winced and walked past the bacon without taking any.

"Two eyes, two stones," Xantcha continued. "I thought you'd gotten lucky."

"I heard something, not with my ears, but inside my head." He stopped and faced her, confusion painfully evident on his face. "I called it singing, 'cause that's the best word I had. And it came from his left eye." He sat down on the ash bucket, staring at his feet. "Do you want to know how I knew which eye was which?"

Measured by his expression, she wouldn't like the answer but, "Go ahead, enlighten me."

"It told me. It told me what it was and that it had been waiting for someone who could hear it. When Urza said Harbin wasn't his son, it was, it was . . ." Ratepe made a helpless gesture that ended with his fingertips pressed against his temples. "Not pain, but like the feeling that comes after pain." He stopped again and closed his eyes before continuing. "Xantcha, I heard Mishra. Well, not quite heard him. It was just there, in my mind, from the stone. I knew what Mishra thought, what he would have said. Not his words, exactly. My words." His eyes opened. He stared at Xantcha with only a shadow of his usual cockiness. "I know who I am, Xantcha.

I'm Ratepe, son of Mideah, or, just Rat now, 'cause I lost everything when I became a slave. I was born almost eighteen years ago in the city of Pincar, on the sixth day after the Festival of Fruits in the sixth year of Tabarna's reign. I'm me. But, Xantcha, pretending to be Mishra, the way you asked me to—" He broke the stare. "It's not pretend. I could get lost. I could wind up thinking I am Mishra before this is over."

Xantcha bit her lip and sighed. Ratepe wasn't looking, didn't seem to have heard. "Right now, while you're sitting there, can you hear the Weakstone singing Mishra's thoughts in your mind?"

He shook his head. "Only when I'm looking at Urza's eyes, or when he's looking at me."

She began another sigh, of relief this time, but she began too soon.

"I'm worried, Xantcha. It's so real, so easy to imagine him, and that's after just one night. By next year when I'm supposed to go back to Efuan Pincar . . . ? You should've warned me."

Trust Rat—or Ratepe—or Mishra—or whatever he wanted to call himself to go for the guilt. "I didn't know about the singing. I knew about Urza's eyes, where they came from anyway, and I did warn you about that. But singing and Mishra? Beyond *The Antiquity Wars*, I don't know anything but what Urza's told me, and I guess there's a lot he didn't."

The rest of Xantcha's anger went with that admission. She leaned against a porch post, grateful that no one was looking at her. All those times Urza had glowered at her, eyes ablaze—had the voice of Mishra's Weakstone tried to make itself heard in her mind? Why, really, had she gone in search of a false Mishra? What had drawn her to Ratepe? She'd known he was the one to fulfill her plans before she'd gotten a good look at him.

"Can I trust myself?"

Xantcha had no assurances, not for herself or for him. "I don't know."

Ratepe folded his arms tightly across his ribs and shrank within himself. Xantcha had spent all her life with Phyrexians or Urza. She wasn't accustomed to expressive faces and wasn't prepared for the gust of empathy that blew from Ratepe to her. She tried to shake it off with a change of subject and a touch of humor.

"What were the three of you talking about all night?"

Ratepe wasn't interested. "A year from now, will there be anything left of me? Will I be myself?"

"I'm still me," Xantcha answered.

"Right. We talked, some, about you."

She should have expected that, but hadn't. "I haven't lied to you, Ratepe, not about the important things. The Phyrexians are real, and Urza's the only one with the power to defeat them."

"But Urza's wits are addled, aren't they? And you thought you'd cure him if you scrounged up someone who'd remind him of his brother. You thought you could make him stop living in the past."

"I told you that before we left Medran."

"Are you as old as he is?"

Xantcha found the question surprisingly difficult to answer. "Younger, a bit . . . I think. You're not the only one who doesn't know who or what to trust inside. He told you I was Phyrexian?"

"Repeatedly. But, since he thinks I'm Mishra, he's not infallible."

The bacon was burning. Xantcha scraped the charred rashers onto the platter and made of show of eating one, swallowing time while she decided how to answer.

"You can believe him." She took a deep breath and recited—in Phyrexian squeals, squeaks, and chattering, as best she could remember them—the first lesson she'd learned from the vat-priests. "Newts you are, and newts you shall remain. Obey and learn. Pay attention. Make no mistakes."

Ratepe gaped. "That day, in the sphere, when you cut yourself—If I'd taken the knife from you—"

"I'd bleed no matter where you cut me. It would have hurt. You could have killed me, you were inside the sphere. I'm not Urza. I don't think Urza can be killed. I don't think he's alive, not the way you and I are."

"You and I, Xantcha? No one I know lives for three thousand years."

"Closer to thirty-four hundred, I think. Urza believes I was born on another plane and that the Phyrexians stole me while I was still a child then compleated me the way they compleated Mishra.

But that can't be true. I don't know what happened to Mishra, but with newts, we've got to be compleated while we're still new. Urza's never accepted that I was dragged out of a vat in the Fane of Flesh."

"So, in addition to everything else, Phyrexians are immortal?"

"To survive the compleation, newts have to be very resilient, immortally resilient. But Phyrexians can die, especially newts, just not of age or anything else that born-folk might call natural."

"And after thirty-four hundred years, Urza still doesn't believe you?"

"Urza's mad, Ratepe. What he knows and what he believes aren't always the same. Most of the time it doesn't make any difference, as long as he acts to defeat Phyrexia and stops trying to recreate the past on a tabletop."

Ratepe nodded. "He showed me what he was working on."

"Again?" Xantcha couldn't muster surprise or indignation, only weariness.

"I guess, if you say so. Funny thing, with the Weakstone, I get a sense of everything that happened to Mishra." He fell silent until Xantcha looked at him. "You're half-right about what happened. Urza's half-right, too. Phyrexians wanted the Weakstone. When Mishra wouldn't surrender it, one of them tried to kill him. The Weakstone kept him alive then and even when they took him apart later, but it couldn't keep him sane." Ratepe strangled a laugh. "Maybe burning his own mind was the last sane thing Mishra did. After that, there're only images, like paintings on a wall, and waiting, endless waiting, for Urza to listen."

"And now Mishra, or the Weakstone, or both of them together have you to speak for them."

"So far, I listen, but I speak for myself."

"What does that mean?"

Ratepe began to pace. He made a fist with his right hand and pounded it against his left palm. "It means I'd do anything to have my life back. I wish I'd never seen you. I wish I was still a slave in Medran. Tucktah and Garve only had my body. My thoughts were safe. I didn't know the meaning of powerless until I looked into Urza's eyes. I'm as dead as he is, as Mishra, as you."

The self-proclaimed dead man stopped beside the bacon platter and ate a rasher.

"I'm not dead."

"No, you're Phyrexian," Ratepe retorted between swallows. "You weren't born, you were immortal when you were decanted. How could you ever be dead?"

Xantcha ignored the question. "A year, Ratepe, or less. As soon as Urza turns away from the past, I'll take you back to Efuan Pincar. You have my word for that."

Silence, then: "Urza doesn't trust you."

That stung, even if Ratepe was only repeating something that Xantcha had heard countless times before. "I would never betray him . . . or you."

"But you're Phyrexian. If I believe you, you've never been anything but Phyrexian. They're your kin. My father once told me not to trust a man who led a fight against his kin. Betrayal is a nasty habit that once acquired is never cast aside."

"Your father is dead." When it came to cruelty, Xantcha had been taught by masters.

Ratepe stiffened. Leaving the last rashers of bacon on the platter, he walked a straight path away from the cottage. Xantcha let him go. She banked the fire, ate the last of the soggy bacon, and retreated to her room. Her treasured copies of *The Antiquity Wars* offered no solace, not against the turmoil she'd invited into her life when she'd bought herself a slave. And though there was no chance that she'd fall asleep, Xantcha threw herself down on her mattress and pillows.

She was still there, weary, lost in time, and wallowing in an endless array of painful memories, when she sensed a darkening and heard a gentle tapping on her open door.

"Are you awake?"

If Xantcha hadn't been awake, she wouldn't have heard Ratepe's question. If she'd had her wits, she could have answered him with unmoving silence and he might have gone away. But Xantcha couldn't remember the last time anyone had knocked on her door. Sheer surprise lifted her onto her elbows, revealing her secret before she had a chance to keep it.

Ratepe crossed her threshold and settled himself at her table, on her stool. There was only one in the room. Xantcha sat up on the mattress, not entirely pleased with the situation. Ratepe stiffened. He seemed to reconsider his visit, but spoke softly instead.

"I'm sorry. I'm angry and I'm scared and just plain stupid. You're the closest I've got to a friend right now. I shouldn't've said what I said. I'm sorry." He held out his hand.

Xantcha knew the signal. It was oddly consistent across the planes where men and women abounded. Smile if you're happy, frown when you're not. Make a fist when you're angry, but offer your open hand for trust. It was as if men and women were born knowing the same gestures.

She kept her hands wrapped around her pillow. "Betrayed by the truth?"

He winced and lowered his hand. "Not the truth. Just words I knew would hurt. You did it, too. Call it square?"

"Why not?"

Xantcha offered her hand which Ratepe seized and shook vigorously, then released as if he was glad to have the ritual behind him. A suspicion he confirmed with his next remark.

"Urza's gone. I knocked on his door. I thought I'd talk to him and ask his advice. I know, that was stupid, too. But, the door opened . . . and he's not in there."

Xantcha spun herself off the bed and toward the door. "He's gone 'walking."

"I didn't see him leave, Xantcha, and I would've. I didn't go far, not out of sight. He's vanished."

"Planeswalking," she explained, leading the way to the porch and the door to Urza's larger quarters. "Dominaria's a plane, Moag, Vatraquaz, Equilor, Serra's realm, even Phyrexia, they're all planes, all worlds, and Urza can 'walk among them. Don't ask how. I don't know. I just close my eyes and die a little every time. The sphere that I brought you here in started off as armor, so I could survive when he pulled me after him."

"But? You're Phyrexian. The Phyrexians . . . how do they get here?"

"Ambulators . . . artifacts."

Xantcha put her weight against the door and shoved it open. Not a moment's doubt that Urza was gone, but one of surprise when she saw that the table was clear.

"You said you saw him working at the table?"

Ratepe barreled into her, keeping his balance only by grabbing her shoulders. He let go quickly, as he had when their hands had touched. "It was a battlefield, "The Dawn of Fire." Can you tell where he's gone?"

Xantcha shrugged and hurried to the table. No dust, no silver droplets, no gnats stuck in the wood grain or stranded on the floor. She tried to remember another time when Urza had cleaned up after himself so thoroughly. She couldn't.

"Phyrexia?" Ratepe asked, at her side again.

"He wasn't ready for a battle, and there'll be a battle, if he ever goes back to Phyrexia. No, I think he's still here, somewhere on Dominaria."

"But you said 'among worlds.' "

"The fastest way from here and there on Dominaria is to go between-worlds. Did he mention Baszerat or Morvern?"

Ratepe made a sour face. "No. Why would anyone mention Baszerat and Morvern?"

"Because the Phyrexians are there, on both sides of a war. I told him to go and see for himself. With all the excitement last night, I forgot to ask him what he learned."

"That the Baszerati are swine and the Morvernish are sheep?"

After so many worlds and so many years of wandering, Xantcha tended to see similarities. Ratepe had a one-worlder's perspective,which she tried to change. "They are equally besieged, equally vulnerable. The Phyrexians are the enemy; nothing else matters. It was smelling them in Baszerat and Morvern that convinced me the time was right to go looking for you. Urza's got to hold the line in Baszerat and Morvern or it will be too late."

Ratepe sulked. "Why not hold the line in Efuan Pincar? The Phyrexians are there, too, aren't they?"

"I haven't talked to him about Efuan Pincar."

"I did." He saw her gasp and added, "You didn't say I shouldn't."

When Xantcha had hatched her scheme to end Urza's madness by bringing him face-to-face with his brother, she'd imagined that she'd be setting the pace, planning the strategies until Urza's wits were sharp again. Her plans had been going awry almost from the beginning, certainly since the burning village. While she came to terms with her error, Ratepe attacked the silence.

"He didn't seem to know our history, so I tried to tell him everything from the Landings on. He seemed interested. He asked questions and I answered them. He seemed surprised that I could, because he said my mind was empty. But he paid the closest attention toward the end when I told him about the Shratta and the Red-Stripes. Especially the Shratta and Avohir and our holy book. I told him our family wasn't religious, that if he really wanted to know, he should visit the temples of Pincar and listen to the priests. There are still wise priests in Pincar, I think. The Shratta can't have gotten them all."

"Enough, Ratepe," Xantcha said with a sigh and a finger laid on Ratepe's upper lip. He flinched again. They both took a step back. The increased distance made conversation a little easier; eye contact, too, if he'd been willing to look at her. "It's not your fault."

"I shouldn't have told him about the temples?"

Xantcha raised her eyebrows.

Ratepe corrected himself. "I shouldn't have told him about the Phyrexians. I should have asked you first?"

"And I would have told you to wait, even though there's nothing I want more than to get Urza moving. You did what you thought was right, and it was right. It's not what I would have done. I've got to get used to that. I warn you, it won't be easy."

"He'll come back, won't he? Urza won't just roar through Efuan Pincar, killing every Red-Stripe Phyrexian he can find."

With a last look at the table, Xantcha headed out. "There's no second guessing Urza the Artificer, Ratepe—but if he did, it wouldn't be a bad thing, would it?"

"Killing all the Red-Stripes would leave the Shratta without any enemies."

Xantcha paused beside the door. "You're assuming that there aren't any Phyrexians among the Shratta. Remember what I told you about the Baszerati and the Morvernish—the sheep and the swine? I wouldn't count on it."

She left Ratepe standing in the empty room and had gotten as far as the wellhead, beyond the hearth, before he came chasing after her.

"What do we do now?" Ratepe's cheeks were red above the dark stubble of a two-day beard. "Follow him?"

"We wait." Xantcha unknotted the winch and let the bucket drop.

"Something could go wrong."

"All the more reason to wait." She began cranking. "We'd only make it worse."

"Urza hadn't ever heard of Efuan Pincar. He didn't know where it was. He doesn't know our language."

Xantcha let go of the winch. "What language do you think you two have been speaking since you got here?" Ratepe's mouth fell open, but no sound came out, so she went on. "I don't know why he says our minds are empty. He's willing to plunder them when it suits him. Urza doesn't know everything you know. You can keep a secret by just not thinking about it, or by imagining a wall around it, but in the beginning—and maybe all the time—best think that Urza knows what you know."

Ratepe stood motionless except for his breathing, which was shallow with shock. His flush had faded to waxy pale. Xantcha cranked the bucket up and offered him sweet water from the ladle. Most of it went down his chin, but he found his voice.

"He knows what I was thinking? The Weakstone and Mishra? How I thought I was outwitting Urza the Artificer? Avohir's mercy . . ."

Xantcha refilled the ladle and drank. "Maybe. Urza's mad, Ratepe. He hears what he wants to hear, whether it's your voice or your thoughts, and he might not hear you at all—but he could. That's what you've got to remember. I should've told you sooner."

"Do you know what I'm thinking?"

"Only when your mouth is open."

He closed it immediately, and Xantcha walked away, chuckling. She'd gone about ten steps when Ratepe raced past and stopped, facing her.

"All right. I've had enough . . . You're Phyrexian. You weren't born, you crawled out of a pit. You're more than three thousand years old, even though you look about twelve. You dress like a man—a boy. You talk like a man, but Efuand's a tricky language. We talk about things as if they were men or women—a dog is a man, but a cat is a lady. Among ourselves, though, when you say 'I did this,' or 'I did that,' the form's the same, whether I'm a man or woman. Usually, the difference is obvious." He swallowed hard, and Xantcha knew what he was thinking before he opened his mouth again. "Last night, Urza, when he'd talk about you, he'd say *she* and *her*. What are you, Xantcha, a man or a woman?"

"Is it important?"

"Yes, it's important."

"Neither."

She walked past him and didn't break his arm when he spun her back to face him.

"That's not an answer!"

"It's not the answer you want." She wrenched free.

"But, Urza . . . ? Why?"

"Phyrexian's not a tricky language. There are no families, no need for men or women, no words for them, either—except in dreams. I had no need for those words until I met a demon. He invaded my mind. After that and because of it, I've thought of myself as *she*."

"Urza?" Ratepe's voice had harshened. He was indignant, angry.

Xantcha laughed. "No, not Urza. Long before Urza."

"So, you and Urza . . . ?"

"Urza? You did read *The Antiquity Wars*, didn't you? Urza didn't even notice Kayla Bin-Kroog!"

She left Ratepe gaping and closed the door behind her.

Chapter 12

Urza was an honorable man, and an honest one. Even when he'd been an ordinary man, if the word ordinary had ever applied to Urza the Artificer, Urza had had no great use for romance or affection, but he'd tolerated friendship, one friend at a time.

After Xantcha had pushed him out of Phyrexia, he'd accepted her as a friend.

In the three thousand years since, Xantcha had never asked for more nor settled for less.

* * * * *

They'd stumbled through three worlds before the day during which Urza had ridden his dragon into Phyrexia, ended. Xantcha was seedier than Urza by then, which meant they were leaning against each other when Xantcha released her armor to the cool, night mist. There were unfamiliar stars peeking through the mist and a trio of blue-white moons.

"Far enough," she whispered. Her voice had been wrecked by the bad air of four different worlds. "I've got to rest."

"It's not safe! I hear him, Yawg—"

Xantcha cringed whenever Urza started to say that word. She seized the crumbling substance of his ornately armored tunic. "You're calling the Ineffable! Never say that, never do that. Every time you say that name, the Ineffable can hear you. Of all the things I was taught in the Fane of Flesh, that one I believe with all my strength. We'll never be safe until you burn that name from your memory."

Sparks danced across Urza's eyes, which had been a featureless black since he'd dragged them away from Phyrexia. Xantcha didn't know what he saw, except it had him spooked, and anything that unnerved Urza was more than enough for her.

Urza took her suggestion to heart. Heat radiated from his face. Waste not, want not, if he could literally burn something from his memory, he could probably survive it, too. Still, she put more distance between them, leading him by the wrist to a rock where he could sit.

"Water, Xantcha. Could you bring me water?"

He was blind, at least to real things. His vision, he'd said, was all spots and bubbles, as if he'd stared too long at the sun. There'd been no sun above the Fourth Sphere, but the dragon had been the target of all the weapons, sorcerous and elemental, that the demons could aim.

"You'll stay right here?" she asked.

"I'll try."

Xantcha didn't ask what he meant. She'd set her feet on enough worlds to have a sharp sense of where she could survive and where she couldn't. Phyrexia and the three worlds after Phyrexia were inhospitable, but this three-moon world was viable. She had her cyst, her heart, and, tucked inside her tunic, an ambulator. If Urza vanished before she returned, it wouldn't be the end of her.

Heavy rains had fallen recently. Xantcha saw water at the base of the hill where they emerged from between-worlds. Carrying it was another matter. She quenched her thirst from her own cupped hands, but for Urza she stripped off her tunic, sopped it in the water, and carried it, dripping, up the hill.

Urza's attempt to remain seated atop the rock had been successful. Silhouetted against the softly lit night sky, his shoulders were slumped forward, and his chin had disappeared in the shadows of his armored tunic. His hands lay inert in his lap.

"Urza?"

His chin rose.

"I've brought you water, without grace or dignity."

"As long as it is wet."

She guided his hand to the sopping cloth. "Quite wet."

Urza sucked moisture from the cloth, then wiped his face. When he'd finished, he let her tunic fall. Xantcha sat at his feet.

"Is there anything more I can do for you? Will you eat? Food might help. I smell berries. It's summer here."

He shook his head. "Just sit beside me. Sleep, if you can, child. Morning will come, a summer morning."

Xantcha fought into her tunic. The night was cool, not cold. The garment was uncomfortable, nothing worse. Discomfort was nothing unfamiliar. She got comfortable against the rock. Urza shifted his hand to the top of her head.

"I told you to stay behind."

"I did, for a little while."

"You could have been hurt. I might have left you in Phyrexia forever."

Urza was Urza, at the very center of his world and every other. On a night like this, after the day they'd survived, his vainglory was reassuring. Xantcha relaxed.

"It went otherwise, Urza. I was neither hurt nor left behind."

"I'd still be there but for you."

"You'd be dead, Urza, if you can die, or in the Seventh Sphere, if you can't, wishing that you could."

"The Seventh Sphere is the place where—" He hesitated. "Where the Ineffable punishes demons?"

"Yes."

"Then I should thank you."

"Yes," Xantcha repeated. "And you should have listened to me when I told you what waited in Phyrexia."

"I will build another dragon, bigger and stronger. I know where

Phyrexia is now, tucked across a fathomless chasm. I would never have seen it 'walking. I wouldn't see it now, but I know and I can go back. They will die, Xantcha. I will reap them like a field of overripe grain. The day of Mishra's vengeance is closer today than yesterday."

Xantcha swallowed an ordinary yawn. "You were surrounded, Urza. The fourth leg went right after I climbed it. You'd destroyed hundreds of Phyrexians, and yet there were as many around you at the end as there had been at the beginning."

"I will change my design."

"A thousand legs wouldn't be enough. You can't destroy every Phyrexian by fighting. You'll need allies and an army three times the size of Phyrexia. Tactics. Strategy." Xantcha thought of the heart vault. "Or, the perfect target for a stealthy attack."

"And since when did you become my war consul, child?"

Urza could be disdainful. Strategy and tactics indeed. She'd need be careful when she mentioned the heart vault. Tonight, while Urza was blind and she was exhausted, wasn't the right time to reveal her discoveries. Another yawn escaped, entirely normal. Without the mnemonic, the cyst was just a lump in her stomach.

"Sleep, child. I am grateful. I underestimated my enemy. I'll never do that again."

Xantcha was too tired to celebrate what little victory she'd achieved. She fell asleep thinking she'd be alone when she awoke.

She was, but Urza hadn't gone far. With nothing more than grass, twigs and small stones, Xantcha's companion had recreated the Fourth Sphere battleground in an area no more than two-paces square. His dragon, made from twigs and woven grass, towered over the other replicas in precisely the proportions she remembered. She expected it to move.

"I'm awed," she admitted before her shadow fell across Urza's small wonders. "You must be feeling better?"

"As good as a fool can feel."

It was a comment that begged questions, but Xantcha had learned to tread softly through confusion. "You can see again?"

"Yes, yes." He looked up: black pupils, hazel irises, white sclera. "You had the right of it, Xantcha. Burn that name out of my mind.

As soon as I did, I began to feel like myself again, ignorant and foolish. No one was hurt. No planes were damaged."

"A few spheres. The priests will be a long time repairing the damage. And you destroyed a score of their dragons and wyverns. Better than I expected, honestly."

"But not good enough. If I'd come down here—" Urza touched the ground behind the stone-shaped furnaces then quickly rearranged the delicate figures—"I'd have had a wall of fire at my back, and they couldn't have encircled me."

Xantcha studied the new array. "How would that be better? With the furnaces behind you, you'd have been held in one place almost from the start." Urza gave her a look that sparkled. She changed the subject. "Are we staying here while you build another dragon?"

"No. The multiverse is real, Xantcha. At least every plane I'd ever found before was real, until yesterday when I found Phyrexia. Going there and leaving, those were 'walking strides like I've never taken before. It was as if I'd leapt a vast chasm in a single bound. The chasm, I realize now, is everywhere, and Phyrexia is its far side. No matter where we are, we're only one leap away from our enemy and it from us. Even so, I'll feel better when I've put a few knots in my trail."

She had no argument with that plan. "Then what? Another dragon? An army? Allies? I found something yesterday, Urza, something I thought was probably lies. I found my heart."

Xantcha slid her hand into her boot. The amber continued to glow. She offered it to Urza.

"That is—well, it's not your heart, Xantcha." He didn't take it. "Your heart beats behind your ribs, child. The Phyrexians lied to you. They took your past and your future, but they didn't take your heart." Urza guided her empty hand to her breastbone. "There, can you feel it?"

She nodded. All flesh had a blood-heart in its breast. Newts in the Fane of Flesh had hearts until they were compleated. "This is different," she insisted and described the vault where countless hearts shimmered. "We are connected to our hearts. We are taught that the Ineffable keeps watch over our hearts and records our errors on their surface. Too many errors and—" She drew a line across her throat.

Urza took the amber and held it to the sun. Xantcha couldn't see his face or his eyes but a strangeness not unlike the between-worlds tightened around her. She couldn't breathe, couldn't even muster the strength or will to gasp until Urza lowered his hand. His face, when he turned toward her again, was not pleased.

"Of all abominations, this is the greatest." Urza held the amber above her still-outstretched hand but did not release it. "I would not call it a heart, yet it falls short of a powerstone. I can imagine no purpose for it, except the one you describe. And you knew where the vault was?"

Xantcha sensed Urza had asked a critical question and that her life might depend on her answer. She would have lied, if she'd been certain a lie would satisfy him. "I knew it was somewhere in the Fane of Flesh."

"You didn't tell me?"

"I didn't want to die with all the rest of Phyrexia. I wasn't certain. I thought you'd laugh and call me a child again, and I would have been too ashamed to follow you."

Not quite an answer, but the truth and, apparently, satisfactory. Urza dropped the amber into her hand. Without conscious thought, Xantcha clutched it against her blood-heart.

"I wouldn't have—" Urza began, then stopped abruptly and looked down at his grass-and-twig dragon. "No, very possibly your concerns were justified. I do not imagine abominations and have discouraged you, thinking you imagined them. I allowed myself to forget that your mind is empty. Phyrexians have no imagination." He crushed the dragon beneath his boot. "Another mistake. Another error. Forgive me, Mishra, I cannot see when I need most to see and opportunity slips away forever. If only I could relive yesterday instead of tomorrow."

"You can go back as soon as you've restored your strength. If I could find the vault . . ."

Urza shuddered. "They know me now. Your Ineffable knows me, I cannot return to Phyrexia, not without absolute certainty of success and overwhelming strength. For the sake of vengeance, I must be cautious. I cannot make any more mistakes. I would be found out before I set foot on your First Sphere."

Xantcha kept her mouth shut. It wasn't *her* First Sphere. Urza had powers that Phyrexia coveted, but he was oddly reluctant to use them. He had to overwhelm whatever lay before him, and when he made one of his mistakes, that mistake became a fortress.

"I could go. I have an ambulator." She lifted the hem of her tunic, revealing the small black disk tucked beneath her belt. "If you made a smaller dragon, I could turn it loose in the vault."

Urza smiled. "Your courage is laudable, child, but you couldn't hope to succeed. We will talk no more about it." He reached for the portal. Xantcha retreated, folding her arms defensively over her belly. "Come child, you have no need for such an artifact. It is beyond your understanding. Let me have it."

"I'm not a child," she warned, the least incendiary comment seething on the back of her tongue.

"You see, simply having a Phyrexian artifact so close to you taints you, as that name, yesterday, threatened to taint me. You haven't the strength to resist its corruption. You've become willful. Between that and your heart . . . You're overwhelmed, Xantcha. I should take them both from you, for your own safety, but I will leave you your heart, if you give me the ambulator."

"It's mine!" Xantcha protested. "I rolled it up."

She'd seen born-children in her travels and recognized her behavior. Urza didn't have to say another word. Xantcha handed the ambulator over.

"Thank you, Xantcha. I will study it closely."

Urza held the ambulator between his fingertips where it vanished. Perhaps he would study it. Perhaps he would find a way to add its properties to her cyst. Whichever or whatever, Xantcha didn't think she'd see it again, but she kept her heart. Urza could have everything else, not that.

He 'walked through two more worlds that day and two more the next and the next after that, making knots in their trail. After two score worlds in half as many days, Xantcha swore the next would be her last, that she'd let go of his hands and remain behind. Any world would be better than another between-worlds passage. But the next world was yellow gas, wind, and lightning that seemed particularly attracted to her armor, and the world after that had no air. Urza made an underground chamber where Xantcha could breathe without her armor and catch up on her sleep.

They came to a swamp with cone-shaped insects as long as her forearm and an abundance of frogs, not Xantcha's favorite sort of place. It reminded her of Phyrexia's First Sphere, but she could breathe and eat and the water, though brackish, didn't make her sick.

"This is far enough for me," she announced when Urza held out his hand. "I don't need to visit every world."

"Only a few more," Urza protested.

He'd begun to pace. Since Phyrexia, his restlessness had steadily worsened until he could scarcely stand still. He didn't even try to sleep.

"I'm tired," she told him.

"You slept last night."

"Last night! When was last night? Where was last night? The world with the yellow trees or the one with two suns? I want to stay put long enough see the seasons change."

"Farmer," Urza chided her, a distinct improvement over 'child' and the truth as well. She'd spent too much time scratching in Phyrexia's sterile soil not to appreciate worlds where plants grew naturally.

"I want a home."

"So do I." An admission she hadn't expected. "It's here, Xantcha. Dominaria . . . home. I can feel it each time we 'walk, but at every step, a darkness blocks me. The darkness was here the last time, before I found you. It was like nothing I'd encountered before. I was sure it would pass, but it hasn't. It's still here, and stronger than before."

"Like a knife?" she asked, remembering the rumors of newts trapped on the nether side of broken portals.

"A knife? No, it is as if multiverse itself had shattered, as if Dominaria and all the planes that are bound to it have been broken apart. I have 'walked all around, approaching it from every vantage, yet each time it is the same. There is a darkness that is also cold and repels me. I've been making a map in my mind, a shape beyond words. When it's done, I will know that Dominaria is completely sealed from me and Phyrexia.

"It is my fault, you know. It's not merely vengeance that I require from Phyrexia. I require atonement The Phyrexians corrupted and destroyed my brother; that's vengeance. But we, my brother and I, let them back into Dominaria when we destroyed the Thran safeguards. The land itself has not forgiven me, won't forgive me until I have atoned for our error by destroying Phyrexia. Dominaria locks me out, as it locks out the Phyrexians. I cannot go home until I have done what not even the Thran could do: destroy Phyrexia!

"I want to go home, Xantcha. You, who cannot remember where you were born, cannot know true homesickness as I know it. I had not thought it would be so difficult. The land does not forgive. It has sealed itself against me. But it has sealed itself against Phyrexia, too, and though my heart aches, I am content with my exile, knowing that my home is safe."

Xantcha rubbed her temples. There was truth, usually, tangled through Urza's self-centered delusions. "Searcher-priests don't 'walk between-worlds," she said cautiously, when she thought she had the wheat separated from the chaff. When conversation touched Mishra, Dominaria or the mysterious Thran, Urza's moods became less predictable than they usually were. "They use ambulators, but I don't know how they set the stones to find new worlds. Maybe you can't be quite certain that Dominaria is safe?"

"I'm certain," he insisted.

Her thoughts raced along a bright tangent. "You figured out how to set the stones on my ambulator?"

"Yes. I set it for Dominaria, and it was destroyed."

Xantcha's mind went dark. There was much she could have said and no reason to say any of it. She turned away with a sigh.

"When I know, beyond doubt, that Dominaria is inaccessible, then I will look for a hospitable plane. I mean to take your advice, Xantcha. I will build an army three times the size of Phyrexia, and ambulators large enough to transport them by the thousand! I examined your ambulator quite thoroughly before it was destroyed. I can make you another once I find the right materials, and can make it better."

Urza expected her to rejoice, so she tried. She took his arm and followed to a "few" more worlds, thirty-three, before he was satisfied that Dominaria was inaccessible behind what he called a shard of the multiverse. Urza insisted that, compared to the multiverse, a thousand worlds could be properly termed a "few" worlds. The multiverse meant little to her. Urza's efforts to explain the planes and nexi that comprised it meant less. But the fact that Urza did try to explain it meant a lot.

"I need a friend," he explained one lonely night on a world where the air was old and nothing remained alive. "I need to talk with someone who has seen what I have seen, some of it, enough to listen without going numb from despair. And, after I have talked, I need to hear a voice that is not my own."

"But you never listen to me!"

"I always listen, Xantcha. You are rarely correct. I cannot replace what the Phyrexians took away from you. Your mind is mostly empty, and what isn't empty is filled with Phyrexian rubbish. You recite their lies because you cannot know better. Your advice, child, is untrustworthy, but you, yourself, are my friend."

Urza hadn't called her child since they 'walked away from Dominaria, and Xantcha didn't like to think that after so much time together, he continued to distrust her, but an offer of friendship, true friendship, was a gift not to be overlooked.

"I will never betray you," Xantcha said softly, taking his hand between hers.

It was like stone at first, flexible stone. Then it softened, warmed, and became flesh.

"I want nothing more than to be your friend, Urza."

He smiled, a rare and mortal gesture. "I will take you wherever you want, but I would rather you wanted to remain with me until we find a plane that satisfies both of us."

Late that night, when the fire was cold and Urza had gone wandering, as he usually did while she slept, Xantcha sharpened her knife and made an incision in her left flank, the side opposite the cyst. She tucked her amber heart into the gap, sealed it with a paste of ashes, then bound it tightly with cloth torn from her spare clothes.

Urza knew immediately. She'd been a fool to think he wouldn't.

"I swallowed it my own way," she told him, in no mood for a lengthy argument. "It's part of me now, where it belongs. I'll never lose it, no matter where you take me."

* * * * *

Xantcha wanted a world where she could pretend she'd been born. Never mind that by their best guess, she was living near the end of her sixth century and no more than seven decades younger than Urza himself. Urza wanted a plane where he could recruit an army. Their wants, she thought, should not have been incompatible, and perhaps they wouldn't have been, if Urza had been able to sleep. To give him his due, Xantcha granted that Urza tried to sleep. He knew he needed to dream, but whenever he attempted that treacherous descent from wakefulness, he found nightmares instead, screaming nightmares that spread like the stench of rotting fish on a summer's day. Until anyone within a half-day's journey could see the flames of Phyrexia and the metal and flesh apparition that Urza called *Mishra*.

Strangers did not welcome them for long. Recruiting an army was impossible. When she was lucky, Xantcha nursed a single harvest from the ground before they went 'walking again. When they found a truly hospitable world with abundant, rich soil, a broad swath of temperate climates and a wealth of vigorous cultures, Xantcha suggested that Urza build himself a tower on the loneliest island in the largest sea. He could 'walk to such a tower without difficulty and sleep, she'd hoped, without disturbing anyone.

Urza called the world Moag, and it became the home Xantcha had dreamed about. He built a sheer-walled tower with neither windows nor doors and filled it with artifacts. Within a decade, its rocky shores had become a place of prophecy and learning where

Urza warned pilgrims of Phyrexian evil and laid the foundations for the army he hoped eventually to raise.

Xantcha built a cottage with a garden, and in the seasons when it didn't need tending, she yawned and went exploring. Urza had made her another summoning crystal, which she wore in friendship but never expected to use. They met at his island whenever the moon was full, nowhere else, no other time. They'd become friends who could talk about anything because they knew which questions to avoid.

For thirty years, life—Xantcha's apparently immortal life— could not have been better. Until the bright autumn day on Moag's most intriguing southern continent when Xantcha caught the unexpected, unforgettable scent of glistening oil. She followed it to the source: the newly refurbished temple of a fire god with a taste for gold and blood sacrifice.

A born-flesh novice sat beside a burning alms box. For the hearths of the poor, he said, and though it looked like extortion, Xantcha threw copper into the flames. She yawned out her armor before entering the sanctuary. Trouble found her, one Phyrexian to another, before she reached the fire-bound altar.

Wrapped in concealing robes, it showed only its face which had the jowls and grizzled beard of a mature man and the reek of the compleated. In its gloved hand it carried a gnarled wooden staff that immediately roused Xantcha's suspicion. She had a small sword on her hip. A mace would have been more useful, but out of keeping with the rest of her dandy's disguise.

"Where have you been?" it asked in a Phyrexian whisper that could have been mistaken for insects buzzing.

"Waiting," Xantcha replied with a newt's soft inflection. Waiting to see what would happen next.

It came faster than she'd expected. There was a priest of some new type inside those robes, and its staff was as false as its face. A web of golden power struck her armor. The priest wasn't expecting surprises, not from a newt. Xantcha kicked it once in the midsection and again on the chin as it fell. Its head separated from its neck, leaving its flesh-face behind. Xantcha understood instantly why Urza could not purge his brother's last memory from his mind. She reached for the not-wooden staff and realized, belatedly, that there'd been witnesses.

Phyrexian witnesses. Four of them were surging out of the recesses to block her path. They all had staves, and she'd lost the advantage of surprise. The sanctuary roof had a smoke vent above the altar. Xantcha grabbed the priest's head instead of its staff as she braced herself for the agony of wringing a sphere from the cyst while the armor was still in place around her. There was blood in the sphere, but it resisted the efforts of the Phyrexians and their staves to bring it down as it expanded and lifted her out of immediate danger.

Willpower got Xantcha drifting silently just above the rooftops south of the temple. But willpower couldn't lift her high enough to catch the winds that would carry her to true safety beyond the walls. The cyst couldn't maintain both the sphere and the armor for long. Already, knife pains ripped through her stomach, and her mouth had filled with blood.

Woozy and desperate, Xantcha went to ground in the foulest midden she could find: a gaping pit behind a boneyard. She thought she'd die when the sphere dissolved on contact with the midden scum, and she found herself shoulder-deep in fermenting filth. With a death grip on the metal-mesh head—if she dropped it, she'd never have the courage to fish it out—Xantcha released her armor as well and hoped that uncontrolled nausea wouldn't prevent the cyst from recharging itself.

By sunset, when swarms of insects mistook her for their evening meal, Xantcha was ready to surrender to any Phyrexian brave enough to haul her out of her hiding place. She thought about gods and the inconvenience of not believing in any of them, then filled her lungs for a yawn. With a single, sharp pain that threatened, for one horrible moment, to fold her in half, the cyst discharged. Xantcha gasped her way through the mnemonic that would create the sphere, and just when she thought she had no endurance left, it began to swell.

She was seen—certainly she was scented—rising above the shambles' roofs, slowly at first, then faster as fresh air lifted her up. There were screams, clanging alarms and, from the open roof of the fire god's temple, a diaphanous gout of black sorcery that fell short of its moving target. The winds blew westward, into the sunset. Xantcha let them carry her, until the moon was high, before she began the long tacks that would take her to Urza's tower.

The moon was a waxing crescent when Xantcha set down on the tower roof five nights later. Urza wasn't expecting her and wasn't pleased to have her within his tower walls. Xantcha had abandoned her clothes and scrubbed herself raw with sand and water without quite ridding herself of the midden's aroma. But Urza reserved his greatest displeasure for the metal-mesh head she stood on his work table.

"Where did you find that?" he demanded and stood like stone while Xantcha raced through an account of her misadventure in the southern city.

"You struck it down, before witnesses? And you brought it here, as a trophy? What were you thinking?"

Urza's enraged eyes lit up the chamber. The air around him shimmered with between-worlds light. Xantcha thought it wise to armor herself, but when she opened her mouth Urza enveloped her in stifling paralysis. Naked and defenseless, she endured a scathing lecture about the stupidity of newts who exposed themselves to their enemies and jeopardized the delicate plans of their friends.

"I smelled glistening oil," Xantcha countered when, toward dawn, Urza released her from his spell. She was angry by then and incautious. "I was curious. I didn't know it came from Phyrexian priests. Maybe it was just a coincidental cooking sauce! I didn't plan to destroy a Phyrexian, but it seemed better than letting it kill me, and as for witnesses, well, I am sorry about that. I didn't notice them standing there until it was too late. And I brought the head because I thought I'd better have proof, because I wasn't sure you'd believe me without it. Should I have let myself be killed? Or captured? Maybe they could have dropped my head on the roof before they attacked! Would that have been better? Wiser, on my part?"

A silver globe appeared in Urza's hand. He cocked his arm.

"Go ahead, throw it. Then what? Make me into another mistake you can mourn? You can't change the past, Urza. The Phyrexians were here before I found them. Empty-headed fool that I am, I thought you'd want to know whatever I could learn, however I learned it. Waste not, want not, I thought you'd be glad I survived!"

The globe vanished in a shower of bright red sparks. "I am. Truly. But they will have found me."

"Phyrexians are here, Urza. It's not necessarily the same thing. How do you suppose they found Dominaria in the first place? Searcher-priests look for more than artifacts. That thing—" Xantcha gestured at the metal-mesh head—"had a face no one would look twice at. The searchers have found a nice, little world, ripe for the plucking. They've set themselves up in the fire god's cult because what Phyrexia needs more than artifacts is ore for its furnaces, and Moag's a metal-rich world."

"They'll destroy Moag, Xantcha. It will all happen again."

"Well, isn't that what you've been waiting for, a chance to right old wrongs?"

"No. No, the price is too high."

"Urza!" Xantcha lost patience with him. "Forget about listening to me, do you ever listen to yourself?"

He stared at her, mortal-eyed, but as if she were a stranger rather than his companion of the centuries. "Go, Xantcha. I need to think. I will come for you at the full moon."

"Maybe I don't want to 'walk away from this. Maybe I want my vengeance!"

"Go, child! You're disturbing me. I must think. I will tell you my decision when I've made it, not before."

They were back to child again, and he *had* made his decision. Xantcha had been with Urza too long not to know when he was lying to her. He'd made a hole in the roof, and she took advantage of it. She gathered the weapons she hadn't discarded and the sack that held her traveling stash of gold and gems, these things the midden hadn't damaged at all. Only the sack desperately needed replacing, so she took one of Urza's and swapped the contents before yawning out the sphere. The hole closed as soon as she'd passed through it.

Morning had come, a beautiful morning with mackerel clouds streaking north by northeast, the direction Xantcha needed, if she were going back to her cottage, which she decided after a heart-beat's thought that she wasn't. Xantcha set her mind south, to the fire god's city. Urza was going to leave Moag, and despite her threats, Xantcha knew she'd go with him, but if he'd intended simply to leave, they could have 'walked already. They'd left other worlds with less warning. No, Urza had something planned, and Xantcha wanted to witness it.

As soon as Xantcha reached the coast, she found a prosperous villa and sneaked into it by moonlight. She left two silver coins and another world's garnet brooch on a night stand, in exchange for her pick of the young heir's wardrobe. His britches were tight and his boots too big, but overall she considered it a fair swap. She didn't linger until sunrise to learn the household's opinion.

Xantcha scuffed up her fine clothes when she reached the southern city and wove a tale of tragedy and coincidence for the apothecary whose shop window had the best view of the fire god's temple. The owl-eyed merchant didn't believe a word Xantcha said, but she could read, count, and compound a script better than either of his journeymen. He took her in with the promise of two meals a day, one hot, one cold, and a night-pallet across the threshold, which was what she'd wanted from the start.

She settled in to wait: one day, two days, three, four. Urza came on the fifth. Or rather, a ball of fire descended from the stars during the fifth night. It struck the temple with hideous force. Masonry, stone and burning timbers flew across the plaza, smashing through shutters and walls. Xantcha got her sword from its hiding place, bid an unobserved farewell to the apothecary, then went hunting for Phyrexians through the smoke.

Xantcha found a few, as terrified as any born-folk, or more so since glistening oil burnt with a hot blue flame. She put an end to their misery and with her armor to protect her from both flames and smoke made her way into the sanctuary. The journeymen had succumbed to her questions, and told her where the fire god's priests had their private quarters. Which was where Xantcha expected to find—and steal—another ambulator.

She found a passage back to Phyrexia, but it was unlike any ambulator she'd seen before. Instead of a bottomless black pool, the flesh-faced priests had a solid-seeming disk that rose edgewise from the stone floor. Face on, it was as black as the ambulators Xantcha was familiar with. From behind, it simply wasn't there. One thing hadn't changed; it still had a palm-sized panel with seven black jewels where the disk emerged from the floor. Since she couldn't roll the standing-portal up and take it with her, Xantcha smashed the panel with her sword.

Smoke and screams belched out of the black disk before it collapsed. Xantcha guessed she'd closed it just in time. A pair of lines gouged into the stone was all that remained when the smoke cleared. She was rummaging through shelves and cabinets, hoping to find a familiar ambulator, when the air grew heavy. The other kind of between-worlds passage, Urza's kind of 'walking passage, was opening.

"It's me!" she shouted as he came into view.

"Xantcha! What are you doing here? I could have killed you."

They never had established whether Urza's armor would protect her from Urza's wrath or Urza's mistakes.

"I came for the ambulator. I knew they'd have one, and I wasn't sure you'd think to roll it." He hadn't when he rode the dragon into Phyrexia. "It was a new kind," she admitted. "I couldn't roll it up."

Urza stared at the lines in the floor. "No, it was a very old kind. Did you destroy it?"

He was so calm and reasonable, it worried her. "Yes. I broke the gems. There were screams, then nothing."

"Well, perhaps it is enough. If not, I have left my mark above, and I will leave a trail. Are you ready to 'walk, or are you staying here?"

"You want the Phyrexians to follow us?"

Urza nodded, smiling, and held out his hand. "I want them to pursue us with all their strength and leave Moag in peace."

Xantcha took his hand and said, "I don't think it works that way," but they were between-worlds and her words were lost.

* * * * *

Xantcha never knew if the second part of Urza's plan bore fruit, but the first was successful beyond his wildest dreams. He stopped laying a deliberate trail after the fourth world beyond Moag, but that didn't stop the searcher-priests and the avenger teams they led.

Sometimes she and Urza got a year's respite between attacks, never more. Urza reached into his past for sentries he called Yotians, never-fail guardians shaped from whatever materials a new world offered: clay, stone, wood, or ice.

He'd 'walked her to ice worlds before. They were dark, airless places where the sun was lost among the stars and the ice as hard as steel. Save for the gas worlds, where there was no solid ground at all, ice worlds were the least hospitable worlds in the multiverse. They never stayed long on ice, no matter how close the pursuit.

Then, years after Moag by Urza's reckoning, he found a world where the ice was melting, and the air was cold but breathable. Once it had been a world like Moag. Whole forests and cities could be glimpsed through the ice when the light was right. Now it was a brutal place, with men who'd forgotten what cities were.

Xantcha thought it was as inhospitable as any airless world, but Urza disagreed and she was disinclined to argue. He hadn't slept soundly since they left Moag. The simple act of closing his eyes was enough to trigger the nightmares—hallucinations of the past, of the Ineffable. To Xantcha's abiding horror, the forbidden name had returned to Urza's memory and came easily to him when he battled through his nightmares.

Years without proper sleep had taken their toll. Urza's restlessness had grown into a sort of frenzy. He was never still, always pacing or wringing his hands. He babbled constantly. Xantcha fashioned wax earplugs so she could sleep. With Phyrexians on their trail, they never strayed far apart.

And Urza needed her. Without her, Urza often didn't know what was real from what was not. Without her gentle nagging, he would have forgotten to carve the Yotians or given them the appropriate orders. Without her willingness to brave his hallucinations he would have gouged the gemstone eyes from his skull and put an end to his misery.

Sitting on the opposite side of a fire, with a score of icy Yotians clanking patrol through the frigid night, Xantcha wondered if she should let him die. They were each over eight hundred years old and though she could still pass for an unbearded youth, Urza looked his age, or worse. The arcane power that enabled him to change his appearance at will had become erratic. On nights like tonight, even though he wasn't hallucinating, Urza seemed to be surrounded by a between-worlds miasma. Viewed from some angles, he had no substance at all, just seething light that hurt her eyes.

"Will you eat? Can you eat?" Xantcha asked gently, trying to ignore the way the hearth flames were visible through his robes.

Food was no substitute for sleep and dreams, but it helped keep Urza looking mortal. She'd seasoned the stew pot with the aromatic herbs that had tempted him before. But it didn't work this time.

"I'm hollow," he said, a disturbingly accurate assessment. "Food won't fill me, Xantcha. Eat all you can. Pack the rest. I feel the eyes of the multiverse upon us."

Xantcha lost her appetite. When Urza thought the multiverse was watching him, Phyrexians weren't usually far behind. She forced down a small portion—the between-worlds was easier on a near-empty stomach—and filled a waterskin with the rest. The ice-shaped Yotians were almost as restless as Urza. Xantcha slung the waterskin and other essentials from a shoulder harness and checked her weapons. The second-best way to deal with Phyrexians was to batter them apart. She'd long since abandoned her Moag sword in favor of a short club with a jagged chunk of pure iron for its head.

The best way to deal with Phyrexian avengers, however, was to hide, and let Urza demolish them with sorcery and artifice, then wait until he shaped himself into a man again. Waiting was the difficult part. As the years and worlds and ambushes accumulated, Urza had never had a problem vanquishing the avengers, but increasingly he lost himself in the aftermath. Two ambushes ago, he'd devolved into a pillar of rainbow light that shimmered for three days before condensing into a solid, familiar form. Considering the brutal, backwater worlds they frequented, Xantcha desperately wanted an ambulator and the wherewithal to set its black stones for a hospitable world.

She'd raised the subject as often as she'd dared, which didn't include this night with the ice Yotians clattering like crystals through the shadows.

The ambush came at dawn, in gusts of hot, sour Phyrexian wind. There were a score of them, not counting the two searcher-priests who squatted beside the flat-black ambulator. This time the avengers resembled huge turtles with bowl-shaped carapaces and four broad, shovel-like feet, ideal for churning through snow and ice. Instead of claws or teeth, their weapons were beams of dark radiance that shot through an opening where a turtle's head would emerge from its shell.

Xantcha left the turtles for Urza and the Yotians. Safe in her armor and screaming loudly, she charged the searcher-priests instead, hoping to steal their ambulator. They took one look at her and retreated into the ambulator, rolling it up behind them, abandoning the avengers. She cursed them for their cowardice, but searchers were hard to replace. They were subtle for Phyrexians, far more subtle than avengers who, because they were so powerful, were also stupid.

She supposed the searchers could bring reinforcements, though, so far, once they left, they'd stayed gone. But the other skirmishes had been over sooner. Ice was not the ideal defense when the avengers' weapon was heat. The Yotians had been utterly destroyed without bringing down a single Phyrexian, which meant that Urza had to face them all. He had the skill and power, though the turtles were a bit tougher, a bit nastier they'd been in the last ambush, as if Phyrexia were learning from its failures—a frightening notion in and of itself.

There were only eight of the avengers left. Urza had destroyed two of those with dazzling streaks of raw power from his jeweled eyes. No one learned faster than Urza. He never tired nor depleted his resources. So long as there was substance beneath his feet or stars in the sky overhead, Urza the Artificer could work his uniquely potent magic.

Then, suddenly, his strikes became indecisive.

A turtle scuttled forward unchallenged and knocked Urza backward; the first time Xantcha had ever seen him touched in battle. He destroyed it with a glut of flame, but not before the other turtles pelted him with bursts of darkness.

After that Xantcha expected Urza to make short work of the enemy. Instead he became vaporous, a man of light and shadow. A turtle paw passed directly through him. Xantcha thought it was another of Urza's tactical surprises, until she watched his counterstrike pass through the turtle.

Xantcha had imagined the end many times, but she never thought the end would come from turtles on an ice-bound world.

Her armor would protect her . . . probably. Her club would almost certainly have no effect on avengers meant to destroy Urza the Artificer, but Xantcha would sooner face her personal end right here, right now, than risk capture and return to Phyrexia, or—even worse—eternity on this ice-bound world. She leapt onto the back of the nearest turtle and took aim at the forward gap in its carapace.

The turtle proved quite agile, bucking like an unbroken horse in its efforts to throw Xantcha off. She held on until two of the other avengers began targeting her instead of Urza. The armor held, barely. Xantcha felt the heat of dark magic, front and back, and the crack of her ribs as they began to break, one by one, under the hammer-and-anvil pressure.

The last thing Xantcha saw was Urza, brighter than the sun. . . .

Not a bad sight to carry into the darkness.

Chapter 13

Summer had come to the Ohran ridge some two months after Ratepe arrived. Grass in every shade of green rippled in the wind beneath a blue crystal sky. Xantcha's sphere rose easily, caught a westward breeze, and began the journey to Efuan Pincar.

"Do you think this is going to work?" Ratepe asked when the cottage had disappeared into the folded foothills.

She didn't answer. Ratepe gave her a sulky look, which she also ignored. Still sulking, he began rearranging their traveling gear. Xantcha's head brushed the inner curve. Ratepe, who was a head-plus taller, was at a much greater disadvantage. With a dramatic show of determination, he shoved the largest, heaviest box behind them and upholstered it with food sacks. Although his efforts made the sphere easier to maneuver, if he didn't settle down Xantcha thought she might finish the journey alone.

"I don't think I've ever had cushions up here before," she said, trying to be pleasant, hoping pleasantry would be enough to calm her companion.

"I do what I can," he replied, still sulking.

Ratepe had a flair for solving problems, which didn't seem to depend on the images he gleaned from Urza's Weakstone eye.

Even Urza had noticed it and made a point of discussing things with him that he'd never have mentioned to her. Xantcha told herself this was exactly what she'd wanted—an Urza who paid attention to the world around him. Of course, Urza thought he was talking to his long-dead brother, and Ratepe, though he played his part well, wanted more than conversation.

These days, Ratepe's mind swam in the memories of a man who'd been Urza's peer in artifice. He'd absorbed all the theories of artifact creation, but as clever as he was with sacks and boxes, he was awkward at the worktable. Perhaps if he'd been willing to start with simple things . . . but if Ratepe had had the temperament for easy beginnings, the Weakstone probably would have ignored him, as it had always ignored Xantcha.

He'd tried pure magic where Xantcha had been certain he would succeed. Urza always said that magic was rooted in the land. Ratepe's devotion to Efuan Pincar was the touchstone of his life, and magic often came both late and sudden into a mortal's life, but it wouldn't enter Ratepe's, no matter how earnestly he invited it. The lowest blow, however, had come after he'd badgered Urza into concocting another cyst.

Ratepe had gulped the lump without a heartbeat's hesitation and writhed in agony for two days before he let Urza dissolve it. One artifact poisoning wasn't enough. He'd tried twice more, until Urza—who knew somewhere in the fathomless depths of his being that Ratepe was an ordinary young man and not his brother—refused to brew up another one.

"I don't mind doing the heavy work," Xantcha said. The sphere was moving nicely on its own. She laid her hand on his arm. "I like the company . . . the friendship."

Ratepe was more than a friend, though both of them were careful not to put the difference into words. The cottage had only two rooms. Her room had only one bed. The difference had come suddenly. One moment they were each alone, ignoring another rainy night. The next, they were on the bed, sitting near each other, then touching. For warmth, he'd said, and Xantcha had agreed, as if curiosity had never gotten her into trouble before. As if she hadn't known the difference between curiosity and need and been coldly willing to take advantage of it.

It had been awkward at first. Xantcha was, as she'd warned, a Phyrexian newt, a vat-grown creature whose purpose had never been to love another or beget children. But Ratepe was nothing if not persistent in the face of challenge, and the problems, though inconvenient, had been surmounted without artifice or magic. He was satisfied. Xantcha was surprised—astonished beyond all the words in all the languages she knew—to discover that being in love had nothing to do with being born.

Ratepe laced his fingers through hers. "I could do more. You never made good on your threat to make me cook my own food."

"There's only one hearth. I haven't had time to make another."

"That's what I mean." Ratepe tightened his hand. "You do everything. Urza doesn't notice, but I do. You're the one who makes the decisions."

Xantcha laughed. "You don't know Urza very well."

"I wouldn't know him at all if you hadn't decided to bring me here. I wake up in the morning, and for a few moments I think I'm back in Efuan Pincar with my family and that it's all been a dream. I think about telling my little brother, then I look over at you—"

She made an unnecessary adjustment to the sphere's drift, an excuse to reclaim her hand. "Urza's coming back to life, letting go of his obsessions. That's your doing."

Ratepe sighed. "I hadn't noticed."

Ratepe, like Mishra, had a tendency to sulk. Xantcha had re-read *The Antiquity Wars* looking for ways to buoy his spirits. She'd even asked Urza what could put an end to Ratepe—or Mishra's—black, self-defeating moods. Silence, Urza had replied, had always been the best tactic when his brother sulked. Mishra couldn't bear to be ignored. Be patient, out wait him and his quicksilver temper would find another target.

Xantcha had learned endurance without mastering patience. "For the first time in two and a half centuries, Urza's worktable isn't covered with mountains. He's making artifacts again." Xantcha thumped the box behind her. "New artifacts, not the same gnats. He pays attention when *you* talk to him. Why do you think we're going up to Efuan Pincar?"

"To appease me? To keep me in my place?"

Xantcha's temper rose. "Don't be ridiculous."

"No? I've done what you wanted. He calls me Mishra and I answer. I listen to the Weakstone and remember things I never lived, that no one should have lived. When you or he says that I'm so much like Mishra . . . by Avohir's book, I want to go outside and smash my skull with a rock. It's no compliment to be compared with a cold-blooded murderer, and that's what they both are, Xantcha. That's what they always were. They care more about things than people. But I don't do it, because all I've got to replace everything I've lost is you. You asked me to be Mishra, so I am. All I've asked of Urza is that he care enough to send a few of his precious artifacts for Efuan Pincar."

"He does. He has. We're taking these to Pincar City, aren't we?"

"Admit it, you'd both rather be rooting around in Baszerat or Morvern. You've been down there, what, seven, eight times?"

"Six, and you could have come. The lines are clearer there. Urza recognizes the strategies. It's your war all over again, just smaller."

"Not my war, damn it! If I were going to fight a war it wouldn't be in Baszerat or Morvern!"

Xantcha made the sphere tumble and swerve, but those tricks no longer worked. Ratepe had overcome his fear of the open sky. He kept his balance as easily as she did and knew perfectly well that she wasn't going to let them drop to the ground.

"You're wasting your time. Get rid of the Phyrexians in Baszerat or Morvern, and they'll keep on fighting each other. That's what they do."

"And Efuands are so much better than Baszerati swine and Morvernish sheep, or have I got that backward? Are the Baszerati the swine or the sheep?"

"They're all pig-keepers."

Belatedly, Xantcha clamped her teeth together and said nothing. She should have taken Urza's advice, hard as ignoring Rat was when they couldn't get more than a handspan apart. The sphere came around on two long tacks before he saw fit to speak again.

"Do you think it will work?"

The same question he'd asked as they'd risen up from the cottage, but the whiny edge was gone from his voice. Xantcha risked an honest answer.

"Maybe. The artifacts will work. They'll be our eyes and ears and noses in the walls. We'll find out where the Phyrexians are, and if we know that, maybe we'll be able to figure out what they're up to, what can be done to thwart them."

"We know they're in the Red-Stripes and we know the Red-Stripes are doing the Shratta's dirty work. If there are any Shratta left. I want to get to Pincar City and get you into Avohir's temple. I want to know what kinds of oils you smell there. I want you in the palace, so I'll know what's happened to Tabarna. Has he become another Mishra, a man on the outside, a Phyrexian on the inside? Avohir's mercy—I was so certain Urza would listen when I said, 'Brother, don't let the Phyrexians do to another man what they did to me!' And what was his response? Pebbles! We're going to scatter *pebbles* then come back, who knows when, and see if any of the pebbles have changed color!" Ratepe took a breath and began speaking in a dead-on imitation of Urza, "That way I will know for certain if my enemy has come to Efuan Pincar. . . .

"Sometimes I'm not so sure he is Urza. Maybe he was once someone like me, then the Mightstone took over his life. Avohir! If a man's a murderer, what's the use of a conscience? During the war, the real Urza and the real Mishra both made hunter-killers, none of this pebbles-on-the-path, wait-and-see nonsense. They went right after each other."

"Urza doesn't want to repeat his old mistakes." Waste not, want not—she was defending Urza with the very arguments that had infuriated her for millennia. "The situation in Efuan Pincar is different. He's not sure what's going on, so he's being careful."

"And putting all his real efforts into Baszerat and Morvern! Avohir! How many Efuand villages have to burn before they're important?"

"I wouldn't know," Xantcha snarled. "Dominaria's the only world he's ever come back to. Everyplace else, he's just 'walked off and left to its fate. Urza may not be doing what you'd like him to do, but he is doing something. He listens to you, Ratepe. He's never really *listened* to anyone before. You should be pleased with yourself."

"Not while my people are dying. Urza's got the power, Xantcha, and the obligation to use it."

Xantcha was going to mutter something about men who put ideas first, but resisted the impulse. Prickly silence persisted throughout the afternoon. She brought the sphere down with the sun. Ratepe made an abortive attempt to help set up their camp, but they weren't ready to talk civilly to each other. Xantcha banished him to nearby trees until she got the fire lit.

The sky was radiant lavender before she went looking for her troublesome companion. Ratepe had seated himself on the west-facing bole of a fallen tree. Xantcha got no reaction as she approached and was rekindling her irritation when she realized his cheeks were wet. Compleat Phyrexians didn't cry, but newts sometimes did, until they learned it didn't help.

"Supper's on the fire."

Ratepe started, realized he'd been weeping, and wiped his face roughly on his sleeve before meeting her eyes. "I'm not hungry."

"Still angry with me?"

He turned west again. "The Sea-star's above the sun. The Festival of Fruits is over."

A single yellow star shone in the lavender.

"Berulu," she said, giving it the old Argivian name that Urza used. It would be another week before it rose high enough to be seen from the cottage.

"I'm eighteen."

Born-folk, being mortal and having parents and usually living their whole lives on a single world, kept close track of their ages. "Is that a significant age?" she asked politely. Some years were more important than others.

Ratepe swallowed and spoke in a husky voice. "You and Urza don't live by any calendar. One day's the same as the next. There isn't any reason . . . I—I forgot my birthday. It must have been three, maybe four days ago. Last year—last year we were together. My mother roasted a duck, and my little brother gave me a honey-cake that was full of sand. My father gave me a book, Suppulan's *Philosophy*. The Shratta burnt it. For them, there is only one book. Or it wasn't the Shratta but the Red-Stripes doing Shratta work who burnt it. It got burnt, that's enough. Burnt and gone." Ratepe hid his face in his hands as memory got the better of him. "Go away."

"You think about them?"

"Go away," he repeated, then added, "Please."

Urza's grief had hardened into obsession. Xantcha understood obsession. Ratepe's flowed freely from his heart and mystified her. "I could roast a duck for you, if I can find one. Will that help?"

"Not now, Xantcha. I know you care, but not now. Whatever you say, it only reminds me of what's gone."

She retreated. "I'll be by the fire until it is good and truly dark. Then I will come back here, if you will not come down. This is wild country, Ratepe, and you're not . . ." The right word, the word that wouldn't offend him, failed to spring into her mind.

"I'm not what? Not clever enough to take care of myself? Not strong enough? Not immortal or Phyrexian? You call me Ratepe now, and you say that you love me, but I'm still a slave, still Rat."

Agreeing with him would start a war. "Come down to the fire. I promise I will not say anything."

Xantcha kept her promise. It wasn't difficult. Ratepe wrapped himself in a blanket and curled up with his back to her. She couldn't easily count the nights she'd spent in silence and alone. None of them had seemed as long. When he stretched himself awake after dawn, Xantcha waited for him to speak first.

"I'm going into the palace when we get to Pincar."

She'd hoped for a less inflammatory start to the day. "No. Impossible. You agreed to stay at an inn with our supplies while I scattered Urza's pebbles in the places where we don't want to find Phyrexians. Your task is to help me find the Shratta strongholds in the countryside once I'm done in the city. We need to know if there are any real Shratta left."

"I know, but I'm going to the palace. Straight to Tabarna, if he's there, whether he's a man or something else. Every Efuand has the right to petition our king. If he's a man, I'll tell him the truth."

Xantcha planned her reply as she set aside a mug of cold tea. "And if he isn't?" She'd learned from Urza, truth and logic were worthless with madmen. It was always better to let them rant until they ran themselves down.

"Then they'll kill me, and you'll have to tell Urza what happenen, and maybe then he'll do something."

She grimaced into her tea. "That's a burden I don't want to carry. So, let's assume you survive. Let's assume you're face-to-face with Tabarna. What truth will you tell your king?"

"I will tell him that Efuands must stop killing Efuands. I'll tell Tabarna what the Red-Stripes have done."

"Very bold, but with or without Phyrexians, your king already knows what the Red-Stripes are doing in the Shratta's name."

"He can't . . ." Ratepe's voice trailed off. He'd seen too much in his short life to dismiss her out of hand.

"He must."

"Not Tabarna. He wouldn't. If he's still in Pincar City, if he's still a man, then he thinks what I thought, that it's all the Shratta. He doesn't know the truth. He can't."

Xantcha sipped her tea. "All right, Rat, assume you're right. The king of Efuan Pincar, a man like yourself, still sits on his throne. He doesn't know that there are Phyrexians among his Red-Stripe guards. He doesn't know what those red-striped thugs have done. He doesn't know that, in all likelihood, the Shratta were the first to be exterminated. If Tabarna doesn't know any of this exists, then who else in Efuan Pincar does? And how has this nameless, faceless person kept your king in ignorance all these years?"

Ratepe's whole face tightened in uncomfortable silence. "No." not a denial, but a prayer, "Not Tabarna."

"Best hope that Tabarna is skin stretched over metal. You'll hurt less, when the time comes, if you're not fighting a man who sold his soul to Phyrexia. In the meantime, until I know where the Phyrexians are and who they are, we will rely on Urza's pebbles and you will stay out of trouble and danger."

Ratepe wasn't happy. He wasn't stupid, either. After a slight nod, he busied himself folding his blanket.

That day's journey was easier and much quieter. Ratepe spent most of their time aloft staring at the horizon, but there were no tears and Xantcha let him be. Most of her journeys had been taken in silence, and though she'd quickly grown accustomed to Ratepe's company and conversation, old habits returned quickly.

She brought them over the Pincar City walls in the darkness between moon set and sunrise six days later. The sky was clear, the streets were deserted, and the guards they could see were more interested in staying awake until the end of their watch than in a dark speck moving across a dark sky. Xantcha decided to risk a pass above the palace. Few things were as useful as a bird's eye view of unfamiliar territory.

A few slow-moving servants were at work in the courtyards, getting a jump on their chores before the sun rose. Sea breezes and frequent showers kept the coastal city livable in the summer, but the air was always moist and if a person had the choice, work was easier done before dawn than in mid-afternoon.

Xantcha was building a mind-map of the royal apartments, servant quarters, and bureaucratic halls when Ratepe tugged on her sleeve and drew her attention to the stables. His lips touched her hair as he whispered.

"Trouble."

Six men, cloaked head to toe but otherwise unmarked, led their horses toward the postern gate—the palace's private gate. Probably it wasn't anything significant. Palaces throughout the multiverse had similarly placed gates because royal affairs sometimes required the sort of discretion that others might call deceit. But while it was still dark they were in no danger of being seen. Xantcha wove her fingers, and the sphere floated behind the men.

The tide was out, exposing a narrow rocky spit between the ocean and the harbor. The not-unpleasant tang of seaweed and salt-water mud permeated the sphere. Xantcha took a deep breath. No glistening oil. Whoever the six cloaked men were, they weren't Phyrexian.

"Messengers," she decided softly and the sphere began to drift backward with the sea breeze.

"Follow them."

"They're nothing, Rat."

"They're trouble. I smell it."

He knew she detected Phyrexians by scent. She knew his nose wasn't sensitive. "You can't smell trouble, and you can't see it, either. We've got to find an alley where we can set ourselves down without drawing a crowd."

"Xantcha, please? I've just got a feeling about them. I want to know where they're going. I'll stay at the inn. I won't give you any hassle, just—follow them?"

"No complaints when we're stuck hiding in a gully somewhere until after sundown?"

"Not a word."

"Not a sound or a gesture, either," she grumbled, but she shifted her hand and they scooted over the palace wall.

Their quarry stayed along the shoreline, out of side of the guards on the Pincar walls. Ratepe was likely right. They weren't up to any good, but that could mean almost anything, maybe even a meeting with the Shratta. That would be worth knowing about, but she wasn't prepared for confrontation.

"We're not getting involved," Xantcha warned.

They'd fallen far enough behind the six men that Xantcha wasn't worried about being overheard. She did worry about sun. Dominaria wasn't a world where large man-made objects routinely whizzed through the sky. Urza's ornithopters, like Urza himself, were remembered mostly for their wrongheadedness. She'd followed men for days and never been noticed, but men who were, as Ratepe proclaimed, trouble, tended to looked over their shoulder frequently and might notice a shadow where one shouldn't be.

"Not unless we have to."

"No unlesses, Rat. We're not getting involved."

"We've got more than we had when you sent me into a burning village."

True enough. Since she knew there were Phyrexians loose in Efuan Pincar, Xantcha had fattened their arsenal with a variety of exploding artifacts and a pair of firepots. Having protection wasn't the same as using it. She hadn't survived all these centuries by blundering into someone else's trouble.

"We're following them, that's all. In the very unlikely event that they're going to meet with a Phyrexian demon, I'll think about it." She thought about it as long as it took her to spin the sphere around and push it, with all of her might, toward the opposite horizon.

Although Xantcha and Ratepe could still see the city walls, the riders had reached a point where they were beyond the Pincar guards' sight. Accordingly, they mounted and galloped their horses south.

"They're in a hurry," Ratepe said as Xantcha pushed the loaded sphere to its limit. "I wonder where they're going."

"Not far. Not at that speed."

The laden sphere couldn't keep pace. They lost sight of the riders, but not the dust cloud their horses raised. Xantcha took the opportunity to tack behind them and be in the east with the sun when they caught up again.

"You said you'd follow them!" Ratepe said, as the sphere veered sunward.

"You said no complaints."

"If we were on their tails."

"We're on their sun-side flank, it's safer. Trust me."

As expected, the horses slowed, the dust ebbed, and the sphere carried Xantcha and Ratepe close enough to see that the men had reined in at the grassy edge of an abandoned orchard and dismounted.

"That's odd," Xantcha muttered. A warrior's sunrise ceremony? She'd seen far stranger traditions.

Ratepe had no ideas or comments. Perhaps he was feeling foolish or thinking about the long day ahead of him, hunkered down in a gully, forbidden by his honor to complain. Xantcha tapped him on the shoulder.

"See that spot down there on the grass?"

She pointed at a dark splotch in the west. Ratepe nodded.

"That's our shadow. I want you to keep a watch on it, and if I get careless and it gets close to those men or, especially, their horses, I want you to tell me. We're going in for a closer look."

"I concede that you were right, and I'm a fool. Let's find some shade. The sun's just come up, and I'm sweating already."

"Keep an eye on our shadow."

Xantcha kept the sun squarely on their backs as they floated closer. There was no real danger. She'd been seen elsewhere, even shot at with arrows and spears, none of which could pierce the sphere. Sorcerers were more of a problem. But sorcerers—sorcerers with the power to damage with one of Urza's artifacts—were almost as easy to detect as Phyrexians and rarer than Phyrexians in Efuan Pincar.

As they approached hearing distance, Xantcha reminded Ratepe to be quiet and brought the sphere into the orchard nearest the men who were trampling the grass in a rough circle about ten paces across. She didn't like what she saw.

"If you sincerely believe in your god," she said softly, "start praying that I'm wrong."

"What?"

She held a finger to her lips.

Ratepe wasn't successful with his prayers, or Avohir, the all-powerful Efuand god, was listening elsewhere that morning. They hadn't hovered among the trees for very long when one of the men pulled something black, shiny, and disk-shaped from his saddlebags.

Xantcha made a fist with her non-navigational hand and swore in the lilting language of a pink-sky world where curses were considered art.

"Trouble?" Ratepe asked.

The six men had each grabbed onto the disk and were beginning to stretch it across the trampled grass, not the way she'd learned to open an ambulator, but it had been nearly two thousand years since she'd last seen one. Undoubtedly there'd been changes.

"Big trouble. We're going to get involved. That's a passageway to Phyrexia that they're rolling out. Maybe they're going to visit the Ineffable, but more likely, there're *sleepers* coming in, and we're going to stop them, or die trying. You understand me?"

Xantcha seized Ratepe's shoulder and forced him to look at her. "We either stop those men, or you make damn sure you don't survive, 'cause *sleepers* won't come through alone, and anything else that comes through that ambulator you don't ever want to meet."

He went bloodless pale beneath his sweat and neither nodded nor spoke.

"Understand?"

"W-what can I do?"

"They're not watching their backs. If we're lucky, we can set up the firepots, then you keep dropping Urza's toys into them, one after another."

Ratepe nodded, and Xantcha curled her fingers, raising the sphere slightly, then backing off to the far edge of the orchard, out of sight of the six men, but well within the firepots' range. She brought it down carefully. The thump of their supplies hitting the ground as the sphere collapsed wasn't loud enough to disturb the birds in the nearest trees.

Xantcha kissed Ratepe once before she yawned out a layer of armor that would make affection pointless. The firepots were tubes shaped roughly like men's boots, with the important difference that when Xantcha unlaced them, their phloton linings glowed. She aimed them from memory. Close would be good enough with the canisters they'd be using. After she'd piled the fist-sized canisters at Ratepe's feet and dumped a pair—one filled with compressed naphtha, the other with glass shards—into the rapidly heating firepots, she handed Ratepe her smaller coin pouch.

"Anyone gets too close, don't bother with your sword, just throw one of these at him and duck."

Then the firepots let loose, and it was time to draw her sword and run.

The Efuands were sword-armed but not armored. Xantcha planned to take one, maybe two, of them by surprise, and hoped that the firepots would do the same, but mostly she hoped that the Efuands would abandon the ambulator before it spat out reinforcements. The first part of her plan went well. She met a man charging through the trees, struggling to draw his sword. Xantcha slew him with a side cut across the gut. It was loud and messy but successful.

One down, five to go.

The firepots, whose trajectory was more height than distance, delivered both of Urza's exploding artifacts within twenty paces of the ambulator. They'd spooked the horses; all six had torn free and bolted, but the naphtha had fallen beyond the black pool, and the glass hadn't disabled any of the four men—two still at work anchoring the ambulator, two with their swords drawn and coming after her—that Xantcha could see.

Two more canisters came hissing out of the morning sunlight. One fell on the rippling pool and vanished before it exploded. No time to imagine where it might have gone or what it might accomplish when it arrived. The second spread more glass shards near the two men working on the portal's rim. If she survived, Xantcha planned to tell Urza that glass shards weren't effective against Efuands. Though bloodied and clearly in pain, the pair stayed put.

Four plus one was only five. Xantcha hoped Ratepe remembered the coins. Then she put him out of her mind. The swordsmen positioned themselves between her and the other pair of Efuands. She knew what they saw: an undersized youth with an undersized sword and no apparent armor. She knew how to take advantage of misperception. Her arm trembled, the tip of her sword pointed at the ground, and then she ran at the nearer of the pair.

He thought he could beat her attack aside with a simple parry. That was his last mistake. The other thought he had an easy stroke across the back of her neck. He struck hard enough to drop Xantcha to one knee, but he'd been expecting more and failed to press what little advantage he had. Xantcha pivoted on her knee, got her weight behind the hilt, and thrust the blade up through his stomach to his heart.

She left her sword in the corpse and took up his instead.

Of the two remaining Efuands, one was on his knees fussing with the ambulator while the other stood guard over him. Black on black patterns flowed across the portal's surface. Xantcha didn't dare run across it.

She could smell Phyrexia as the Efuand beat aside her first attack. He was the best of the men she'd faced so far and respectful. He stayed calm and balanced behind his sword, not in any hurry. Xantcha was in a hurry, and led with her empty, off-weapon hand, seizing his sword midway down the blade. It was a risky move. Urza's armor couldn't make her bigger or heavier than she naturally was. She couldn't always maintain her grip, and more than once she'd wound up with a dislocated shoulder.

This time, surprise and luck were with her, at least long enough to plunge her sword in the swordsman's gut before she shoved him backward, off the blade and into the black pool. She kicked the kneeling Efuand in the chin, not a crippling, much less a killing blow, except that he, too, fell backward, into the now seething ambulator.

Two more exploding artifacts arrived. One was simply loud and hurled her backward, away from the ambulator, but still the last direction she wanted to move. The other was fire that spread evenly across the black surface.

Xantcha staggered back to the place where the last Efuand had been kneeling, the place where she expected to find a palm-sized panel with seven black jewels. The priests had changed the design. There was neither panel nor jewels. In their place Xantcha saw a smooth black stone, like Urza's magnifying lens, or like the ambulator itself. The fire still burnt. Nothing had emerged. She brought her sword down on the stone.

The sword shattered.

The fire vanished as if someone had inhaled it.

And the black on black patterns had turned silver.

"Run, Ratepe!" she shouted as loud as the armor permitted, and ignored her own advice.

A Phyrexian emerged from the black pool moments later. It was a priest of some sort. There was too much metal, all of it articulated, for it to be anything less than a searcher, definitely not the scrap-made tender or teacher Xantcha had expected with a band of *sleepers*. It had a triangular head with faceted eyes, a bit like Urza's gemstone eyes, though large enough that she couldn't have covered one with splayed fingers. The design needed improvement. The priest raised a nozzle-tipped arm and exterminated a flying bird an instant after it was fully erupted, but ignored Xantcha who crouched unmoving some three paces from the ambulator's edge.

The nozzle arm was also new to Xantcha. She thought she'd seen a thin black thread reach out to the bird, but the attack had been so quick that she couldn't be sure of anything except the bird had disappeared in a burst of red light. Nothing, not even a feather, had fallen from the sky.

No doubt Xantcha would find out exactly what it could do, and since the priest's arms were mismatched, what surprises lurked on its right side. Urza's armor had never failed.

"Over here, meatling!" Few epithets would get a priest's attention quicker than calling it a newt. Xantcha stood up, brandishing her broken sword.

The nozzle weapon sent something very sharp, very hot at the hollow of Xantcha's neck, and she felt as though it had come out through her spine. Urza's armor flashed a radiant cobalt blue, astonishing both her and the priest.

"What is your place?" the priest demanded through mouth-parts hidden within its triangle head. It was not an avenger, modeled after fleshly predators, it was, despite its weapons, a thinker, a planner.

"Xantcha."

The right arm came up and shot forth a segmented cable, the tip of which was a fast-spinning flower with razored petals. It struck Xantcha's face. She felt bones give, but the flower took greater damage. Steel petals clattered to the ground, and pulses of glistening oil spurted from the still-spinning hub. Xantcha struck quickly with the broken sword, enveloping the cable and yanked hard. It had two metal legs and a top-heavy torso. In the Phyrexia she remembered, such bipedal priests had a tendency to topple.

And it nearly did, though nearly was worse than not at all. Xantcha had simply pulled it closer, and it lashed the severed cable of its right arm around her waist. It began using its metal arms as clubs. Xantcha could neither retreat nor make good use of her sword. Her right elbow got clobbered and broken within the armor. She managed to get the sword free of the cable and transferred to her left hand before her right went numb within the armor. Xantcha took the only stroke she had, a sideswipe at the priest's right eye.

Two more of Urza's canisters rained down. One was concussive; the other screamed so loud Xantcha's ears hurt through the armor. Together, the canisters jarred something loose inside the priest. Glistening oil poured from the downward point of its triangle head. It struck one final time, another blow to her already mangled elbow—they truly had no imagination—before it expired.

He'd saved her life.

Ratepe, son of Mideah, had saved her life.

The damn fool either hadn't heard her shout or, most likely, had ignored it.

Xantcha writhed free of the cable. Numbness had spread up her right arm to her shoulder. She'd survive. Urza himself had said that a Phyrexian newt's ability to heal itself was nothing less than miraculous, but she wasn't looking forward to releasing the armor and wouldn't consider doing it until she'd dealt with the ambulator.

She got down on her knees and cursed. New designs or no, the black pool in front of her was definitely the nether end of an ambulator, and unless she wanted to poke her head into Phyrexia to loosen the prime end, there was no way Xantcha could destroy it completely. But she could make it very dangerous to use, if she could get it rolled and find some way to break or reset the black lens. She had half the rim unanchored when yet another pair of canisters showered her with glass and fire.

"Enough, already!"

She moved on to the next anchor.

Ratepe arrived moments later. "Xantcha!"

"Stay away!" she warned harshly. The pain was bearable but numbness was making her groggy. She could have used help, but not from someone who was pure, mortal flesh. "It's not done. Not yet. I *told* you to run!"

"Xan—"

Xantcha realized she must look bad, broken bones bruising her face, her right arm, mangled and useless. "Don't worry about me.

I'll be fine in a couple of days. Just . . . get away from here. More can come through, even now. Make yourself unnoticeable. I've to create an inconvenience."

"I'll help—"

"You'll hide."

She popped another anchor. The pool rippled, black on black. Ratepe retreated, but not far. She didn't have the strength to argue with him.

"There, by the priest, you'll see a little black glass-circle thing. Don't touch it! Don't touch anything. But think about breaking that glass." Xantcha crawled to the next anchor.

"Priest? Shratta?"

"No." She pointed at the heap of metal that had been the Phyrexian and went back to work on the anchor. Another eight or ten, and she'd have it loose.

"Merciful Avohir! Xantcha, what is it?"

"Phyrexian. A priest. I don't know what kind, something new since I left. That's what we're fighting. Except, that's a priest and not a Phyrexian meant for fighting."

"Not like you, then—"

Xantcha looked up. He was bent over, reaching out. "I said, don't touch it!" He straightened. "And I'm not a fighter. I'm not anything, a newt, nothing started, nothing compleated. Just a newt."

"The six—I killed the last one, myself, with those coins you left me." She hadn't heard the explosions. Well, there'd been other things on her mind. "They called this . . . a priest? They invited it here, to Efuan Pincar?"

"Big trouble, just like you said. And don't kid yourself. Assume they've got more ambulators." She remembered the upright disk in the Moag temple. "Assume they've got worse. Assume that some of the sleepers are awake, that there are priests inside the palace, and that some of your own have been corrupted, starting with your king." Xantcha released another anchor. "Look at the glass, will you? My sword broke when I hit it."

A moment or two of silence. She was down to her last three anchors when Ratepe said, "I've got an idea," and ran into the trees.

He came back with the firepots and the rest of Urza's canisters. "We can put it in one of the pots with the bangers, put one pot on top of the other and let it rip."

All the anchors were up and Xantcha had no better idea, except to send Ratepe to the far end of the orchard before she followed his suggestions.

Afterward, she remembered flying through the air and landing in a tree.

Chapter 14

It had happened before in the between-worlds: a sensation of falling that lasted until Xantcha opened her eyes and found herself looking at nothing familiar.

"Ah, awake at last."

The voice was not quite a man's voice, yet deeper than most female voices and quite melodious, though Xantcha suspected that an acid personality powered it. She could almost picture a Phyrexian with that voice, though this place wasn't Phyrexia. Not a whiff of glistening oil accompanied the voice, and the air was quiet. There was music, in the distance, music such as might be made by glass chimes or bells.

Xantcha remembered the wind-crystal on another world.

She realized she was not in a bedroom, not in a building of any sort. The wall to her left and the ceiling above were a shallow, wind-eroded cave. Elsewhere, the world was grass. Grass with a woman's voice?

"Where am I? How did I get here? Urza? Where's Urza? We were together on the ice, fighting Phyrexians." She propped herself up on one elbow. "I have to find him." She was dizzy. Xantcha was rarely dizzy.

"As you were!"

By its tone, the voice was accustomed to obedience.

Xantcha lay flat and returned to her first question. "Where am I?"

"You are here. You are being cared for. There is nothing more you need to know."

She'd been so many places, picked up so many languages. Xantcha had to lie very still, listening to her thoughts and memories, before she could be sure she did not know the language she was speaking. It was simply there in her mind, implanted rather than acquired by listening. Another reason to think of Phyrexia.

Xantcha considered it unlucky to think of Phyrexia once before breakfast and here she'd thought of it three times. She realized she was very hungry.

"If I'm being cared for, I'd like something to eat, if you please."

Urza said manners were important among strangers, especially when one was at a stranger's mercy. Of course, he rarely bothered with such niceties. With his power, Urza was never at a stranger's mercy.

Xantcha remembered the turtles, the Phyrexians they'd been fighting before—before what? She couldn't remember how the skirmish had ended, only a bright light and a sense that she'd been falling for a long time before she woke up here, wherever here was.

"The air will sustain you," the voice said. "You do not need to fill yourself with death."

Another thought of Phyrexia, where compleat Phyrexians neither ate nor breathed but were sustained by glistening oil.

"I need food. I'll hunt it myself."

"You'll do no such thing!"

Xantcha pushed herself into a sitting position and got her first look at the voice: a tall woman, thin through the body, even thinner through the face. Her eyes were gray, her hair was pale gold, and her lips were a tight, disapproving line beneath a large, but narrow nose. She seemed young, at least to Xantcha. It seemed, as well, that she had never smiled or laughed.

"Who are you?" Xantcha asked. Though, *what are you?* was the question foremost in her mind.

The multiverse might well contain an infinite number of worlds, but it had no more than two-score of sentient types, if Xantcha followed Urza's example and disregarded those types that, though clearly sentient, were also completely feral and without the hope of civilization. Or nearly four-score, if she followed her own inclination to regard men and women of every type as distinct species.

Urza's type was the most common and with the arrogance of the clear majority. He called himself simply a man where others were elf-men, or dwarf-men, or gremlin-men. His wife, Kayla Bin-Kroog had been a woman, a very beautiful woman. When Xantcha had asked Urza for a single word that united men and women, as elves united elf-man and elf-woman, he'd answered mankind, which seemed to her a better way of uniting all the men, common and rare rather than common men with their wives and daughters.

When she'd demanded a better word, Urza had snarled and 'walked away. Xantcha wondered what he'd make of the woman standing in front of her. Wonder sparked a hope he was still alive, and that she'd find him here, but another thought crowded Urza from Xantcha's mind. She and the stranger were both dressed in long white gowns.

Where had her clothes gone? Her sword and knives? The shoulder sack filled with stew and treasure? Except for the gown, Xantcha was naked. She wondered if the stern-faced woman was naked, if she was really a woman after all. Her voice was quite deep, and her breasts were a far cry from generous.

That was very nearly a fifth Phyrexian thought before breakfast, and since the stranger had given no indication that she was going to answer any of her questions, Xantcha got her feet under her and pushed herself upright. Another bout of dizziness left her grateful for the nearby rock.

She rested with her back against the stone and took a measure of the world where she'd awakened. It was a golden place of rolling hills and ripened grasses, all caught in the afterglow of a brilliant sunset, with clear air and layers upon layers of clouds overhead. It was difficult, though, to discern where west lay. Urza had explained it to her in the earliest days. Wherever men dwelt, the sun set in the west and rose in the east. In all quarters the horizon was marked with dazzling amber peaks that might have been mountains or might have been clouds. It was achingly beautiful and almost as strange.

On impulse, Xantcha looked for her shadow and found it huddled close by her feet, where she'd expect to find it at high noon. Curiosity became suspicion that got the better of her manners, "Does this world mark time by the sun?" she asked with a scowl, a sixth Phyrexian thought. "Or do you live in immortal sunset?"

The stranger drew back and seemed, somehow, taller. "We think of it as sunrise."

"Does the sun ever get risen?"

"Our Lady has created all that you can see, each cloud, each breeze, each stone, each tree and blade of grass. She has created them all at their moment of greatest beauty. There is peace here and no need for change."

Xantcha let out a long, disbelieving breath. "Waste not, want not."

"Exactly," the stranger replied, though Xantcha had not intended the Phyrexian maxim as a compliment.

"Are we alone?"

"No."

"Where are the others?"

"Not here."

Xantcha's dizziness had passed. If there were others elsewhere, she was ready to look for them. She took a deep breath, opened her mouth, and yawned.

"Not here!" the woman repeated, an emphatic command this time.

Listen and obey the vat-priests had told Xantcha in the beginning, and despite the passage of time, she still found it difficult to disobey, especially when the cyst felt heavy in her gut, heavy and oddly unreliable. She swallowed the lump that was part unemerged sphere and part rising panic.

"How did I get here?"

"I don't know."

"How long have I been here."

"Since you arrived."

"Where am I?"

"Where you are."

Panic surged again, and this time Xantcha couldn't fight it down. "What manner of world is this?" she shouted. "The sun doesn't rise or set. You give me answers that aren't answers. Is this Phyrexia? Is that it? Have I been brought back to Phyrexia?"

The stranger blinked but said nothing.

"Can I leave? Is Urza here? Can I find Urza?"

More silence. Xantcha wanted to run. She was lucky she could walk. Her legs had become the legs of a lethargic stranger. Every step required concentration, calculation, and blind faith as she transferred weight from one foot to the other. After ten strides, Xantcha was panting and needed to rest. She didn't dare sit down for fear she wouldn't have the strength to stand again, so she bent from the hips and kept her balance by bracing clammy, shaking hands on her gown-covered knees.

The stranger wasn't following her. Xantcha pulled herself erect and started walking again. She took nearly twenty cautious steps before her strength gave out. The stranger hadn't moved at all.

Urza! Xantcha thought his name with the same precision she used with her mnemonics when she yawned. Urza had never admitted that he was open to her thoughts, but he'd never denied it, either. *Urza, I'm in a strange place. Nothing is all wrong, but it's not right, either and I'm not myself. If you're nearby—?*

She stopped short of begging or pleading. If he had survived their last battle . . . and Xantcha was unwilling to believe that she had outlived Urza the Artificer, and she certainly couldn't have gotten here on her own. If Urza weren't busy with problems of his own, then he would come. Until then, she would walk.

The heaviness and lethargy didn't go away as the dizziness had, but Xantcha became accustomed to them, as she would have accustomed herself to the rise and fall of a boat's deck. Xantcha might not know where she was or where she was going, but when she looked over her shoulder, she'd left a clean line through the ripe grass.

The stranger had told at least one truth. The air was enough. Xantcha forgot her hunger and never became thirsty, even though, she worked up a considerable sweat forcing herself across the hills. Up and down and up again. Eventually Xantcha lost sight of the stranger and the rock where she'd awakened. There were other rocks along her chosen path, all dun-colored and eroded into curves that were the same, yet also unique.

Once, and once only, Xantcha saw a bush and veered off her straight path to examine it. The bush was shoulder-high and sprawling. Its leaves were tiny but intensely green—the first green she'd found on this sunset-colored world. Pale berries clustered on inner branches. Xantcha considered picking a handful, then noticed the thorns, too, a lot of them and each as long as her thumb.

The stranger had been appalled when she'd mentioned hunting for her food, as if nothing here needed anything more than air to survive. But if that were true, then why the thorns, and why were there berries only on the inner branches? The stranger had spoken of a Lady and of creation and perfection. Someone somewhere was telling lies.

Xantcha left the berries alone. She rejoined her trail through the grass. If there were predators, they'd have no trouble finding her. The golden grass was ripe and brittle. She'd left a wake of broken stalks and wished she still had her sword or at least a knife. Aside from the stranger, Xantcha had seen nothing living that wasn't also rooted in the ground, no birds or animals, not even insects. A place that had berries should have insects.

Even Phyrexia had insects.

Xantcha walked until her body told her it was time to sleep. How long she'd walked or how far were unanswerable questions. She made herself a grass mattress beside another rock, because habit said a rock provided more shelter than open grass. If the stranger could be believed, night never fell, the air wouldn't turn cold, and there was no reason not to sleep soundly, but Xantcha didn't trust the stranger. She couldn't keep her eyes closed long enough for the grass beneath her to make impressions in her skin and after a handful of failed naps, she started walking again.

If walking and fitful napping were a day, then Xantcha walked for three days before she came upon a familiar stranger waiting beside a weathered rock. Even remembering that she, herself, had been one of several thousand identical newts, Xantcha was sure it was the same stranger. The rock was the same, and a wake of broken grass began nearby.

The stranger had moved. She was sitting rather than standing, and she was aware that Xantcha had returned, following her closely with her gray eyes, but she didn't speak. Silence reigned until Xantcha couldn't bear it.

"You said there were others. Where? How can I find them?"

"You can't."

"Why not? How big is this world? What happened to me? Did I trick myself into walking in a circle? Answer me! Answer my questions! Is this some sort of punishment?" Manners be damned, Xantcha threatened the seated woman with her fists. "Is this Phyrexia? Are you some new kind of priest?"

The woman's expression froze between shock and disdain. She blinked, but her gray eyes didn't become flashing jewels as Urza's would have done. Nor did she raise any other defense, yet Xantcha backed away, lowered her arms, and unclenched her hands.

"So, you can control yourself. Can you learn? Can you sit and wait?"

Xantcha had learned harder lessons than sitting opposite an enigmatic stranger, though few that seemed more useless. Other than the slowly shifting cloud layers, the occasionally rippling grass and the gray-eyed woman, there was nothing to look at, nothing to occupy Xantcha's thoughts. And if the goal were self-reflection . . .

"Urza says that I have no imagination," Xantcha explained when her legs had begun to twitch so badly she'd had to get up and walk around the rock a few times. "My mind is empty. I can't see myself without a mirror. It's because I'm Phyrexian."

"Lies," the stranger said without looking up.

"Lies!" Xantcha retorted, ready for an argument, ready for anything that would cut the boredom. "You're a fine one to complain about lies!"

But the stranger didn't take Xantcha's bait, and Xantcha returned to her chosen place. Days were longer beside the rock. Sitting was less strenuous than walking and despite her suspicions, Xantcha slept soundly with the stranger nearby. They had a conversational breakthrough on the fourth day of unrelenting boredom when a line of black dots appeared beneath the lowest cloud layer.

"The others?" Xantcha asked. She would have soared off in the sphere days earlier and over her companion's objections, if the cyst weren't still churning and awkward in her gut.

The stranger stood up, a first since Xantcha had returned from her walk. Gray eyes rapt on the moving specks, she walked into the unbroken grass. She reached out toward them with both arms stretched to the fingertips. But the specks moved on, her arms fell, and she returned to Xantcha, all sagging shoulders and weariness.

In this world without night, it finally dawned on Xantcha that she might have leapt to the wrong conclusions. "How long have you been here?" A friend's concern rather than a prisoner's accusation.

"I came with you."

Still a circular answer, but the tone had been less aloof. Xantcha persisted. "How long ago was that? How much time has passed since we've both been here?"

"Time is. Time cannot be cut and measured."

"As long as we've been sitting here, was I lying under the rock longer than that, or not as long?"

The stranger's brow furrowed. She looked at her hands. "Longer. Yes, much longer."

"Longer than you expected?"

"Very much longer."

"The air sustains us, but otherwise we've been forgotten?"

More furrowed brows, more silence, but the language implanted in her mind had words for time and forgetting. Meaning came before words. The stranger had to understand the question.

"Why are we both here, beside this rock and forgotten? What happened?"

"The angels found you and another—"

"Urza? I was with Urza?"

"With another not like you. His eyes see everything."

Xantcha slouched back against the rock. Raw fear drained down her spine. "Urza." She'd been found with Urza. Everything would be resolved; it was only a matter of time. "What happened to Urza?"

"The angels brought you both to the Lady's palace. The Lady held onto *Urza*. But you, you are not like Urza. She said she could do nothing with you, and you would die. The Lady does not look upon death."

"I was stuck out here to die, and you were put here to watch me until I did. But I didn't, and so we're both stuck here. Is that it?"

"We will wait."

"For what?"

"The palace."

Xantcha pressed her hands over her mouth, lest her temper escape. A newt, she told herself. The gray-eyed stranger was a newt. She listened, she obeyed, she had no imagination and didn't know how to leap from one thought to another. Xantcha herself had been like that until Gix had come to the First Sphere, probing her mind, making her defend herself, changing her forever. Xantcha had no intention of invading the stranger's privacy. She didn't have the ability, even if she'd had the intention. All she wanted was the answers that would reunite her with Urza.

And if her questions changed the stranger, did that make Xantcha herself another Gix? No, she decided and lowered her hands. She would not have poured acid down the fumarole to Gix's grave if he'd done nothing more than awaken her self-awareness.

"What if we didn't wait," Xantcha asked with all the enthusiasm of a conspirator in pursuit of a partner. "What if we went to the palace ourselves."

"We can't."

"Why not? Urza gave me a gift once. If you could tell me where the palace is, it could take us both there."

"No. Impossible. We shouldn't be speaking of this. I shouldn't be speaking with you at all. The Lady herself could do nothing with you. Enough. We will wait . . . in perfect silence."

The stranger bowed her head and folded her hands in her lap. Her lips moved rapidly as she recited something—Xantcha guessed a prayer—to herself. No matter. The wall had been breached. Xantcha *was* a conspirator in search of a partner, and she had nothing else to do but plan her next attack.

Within two days she had the stranger's name, Sosinna, and the certainty that Sosinna considered herself a woman. Two days more and she had the name of the Lady, Serra. After that, it was quite easy to keep Sosinna talking, although the sad truth was that Sosinna knew no more about Serra's world than Xantcha had known about Phyrexia when Urza first rescued her.

Sosinna was a Sister of Serra, one of many woman who served that lady in her palace. If Xantcha had not walked for three days straight and found herself back where she'd started, she would have laughed aloud when Sosinna described Serra's palace as a wondrous island floating forever among the golden clouds. But it did seem true that Serra's world had no land, not as other worlds where men and women dwelt had great masses of rocks rising from their oceans. Xantcha had already learned that she could-n't walk to the edge of the floating island where she and Sosinna sat in exile, but once she had the thought of a floating island in her mind, Xantcha could see that many of the darker clouds around them weren't clouds at all but miniature worlds of grass and stone.

The others Sosinna had mentioned were angels, winged folk who did Serra's bidding away from the palace. Angels had found Urza and Xantcha, though Sosinna didn't know where, and angels had brought Xantcha and Sosinna to their exile island because the Sisters of Serra were unable to leave the floating palace on their own. The angels' wings weren't like Urza's cyst—the idea of having an artifact reside permanently in her stomach appalled Sosinna so much that she stopped talking for three full days. Nor

were the wings added in some floating-island equivalent of the
Fane of Flesh. That notion roused Sosinna's anger.

"Angels," she informed Xantcha emphatically, "are born. Here
we are all born. The Lady reveres life. She would not ever coun-
tenance that—that—Fane. Filth. Waste. Death! No wonder—no
wonder that the Lady said you could not be helped! I will have
nothing more to do with you. Nothing at all!"

Sosinna couldn't keep her vow. The woman who'd sat silently
for days on end, could not resist telling Xantcha in great detail
about the perfect way in which the Lady raised her realm's children.

Births, it seemed, were rare. Incipient parents dwelt in the
palace under the Lady's immediate care, and their precious children, once they were born and weaned, went to the nursery where
the Lady personally undertook their education. Sosinna's voice
thickened with nostalgia as she described the tranquil cloister
where she'd learned the arts of meditation and service. Privately,
Xantcha thought Lady Serra's nursery sounded as grim as the Fane
of Flesh, but she kept those thoughts to herself, smiling politely,
even wistfully, at each new revelation.

On the twentieth day of forced smiles, Xantcha's conspirator-
ial campaign achieved its greatest victory when Sosinna confessed
that she was in love, perfectly and eternally, with one of her nursery peers: an angel.

"Is that permitted?" Xantcha interrupted before she had the wit
to censor herself. The notion of love fascinated her, and spending
most of her life in Urza's shadow or hiding her unformed flesh
beneath a young man's clothes, she'd had very little opportunity
to learn love's secrets. "You don't have wings."

Xantcha's curiosity was ill-timed and rude. It jeopardized everything she'd gained through long days of patient questions, but it
was sincere. On worlds where mankind lived side by side with
elves or dwarves or any other sentients, love, with all its compli-
cations was rarely encouraged, more frequently forbidden. She
hardly expected love between the Sisters of Serra and winged
angels to flourish in a place where the mere appearance of the sun
would have spoilt the perfection of the sunrise.

But Sosinna surprised Xantcha with a furious blush that stretched from the collar of her white gown into her pale gold hair.

"Wings," Sosinna exclaimed, "have nothing to do with it!" A lie, if ever Xantcha had heard one. "We are all born the same, raised the same. Our parentage is not important to Lady Serra. We are all equal in her service. She encourages us to cherish each other openly and to follow our hearts, not our eyes, when we declare our one true love."

More lies, though Sosinna's passion was real. "Kenidiern is a paragon," she confided in a whisper. "No one serves the Lady with more bravery and vigor. He has examined every aspect of his being and cast out all trace of imperfection. There is not one mote of him that isn't pure and devoted to duty. He stands above all the other angels, and no one would fault him if he were proud, but he isn't. Kenidiern has embraced humility. There isn't a woman alive who wouldn't exchange tokens with him, but he has given his to me."

Sosinna removed her veil and, sweeping her hair aside, revealed a tiny golden earring in the lobe of her left ear.

"Beautiful. An honor above all others," Xantcha agreed, trying to imitate Sosinna's lofty tone while she wracked her mind for a way to turn this latest revelation toward a reunion with Urza and escape from Serra's too-perfect realm. "It must be difficult for you to be apart from him. You can't know what he's doing, or where. If something had happened to him, you wouldn't know and, well, if he's given you his token, it's not likely that he'd have forgotten you, so you have to think that he's looking for you, if he can." Xantcha smiled a very Phyrexian smile. Urza would disapprove, although there was no reason for him to ever know. "Of course, sometimes, even paragons get distracted."

Several long moments of nervous fiddling passed before Sosinna said, "We have our duties. We both serve the Lady. Everyone serves the Lady first and foremost." She sat up straight and looked very uncomfortable. "I have strayed from the path. We will speak of these things no more."

But the damage had been done. Sosinna had lost the ability to stare endlessly at nothing. She watched the clouds. Xantcha supposed Sosinna was looking for angels and hoped, for her own selfish reasons, that they appeared. In the end, though, it wasn't angels that got them moving.

Once she'd learned that Serra's realm was composed of islands drifting in a cloudy sea, Xantcha had quickly realized that each island had its own rhythm and path. With a persistent ache in her stomach, Xantcha wasn't tempted to yawn out the sphere and become her own island, but she thought she could hop from one island to another if a more interesting one drifted near. She dismissed the possibility of a collision between two of the Lady's islands as an unimaginable imperfection, until the ground bucked beneath them.

One moment Xantcha and Sosinna were laying flat, clinging to the rooted grass. The next, they were both thrown into the air while the land beneath shattered. For an instant they floated weightless; then the falling began. Without thinking or hesitating, Xantcha yawned and grabbed Sosinna's ankle. The cyst was slow to release its power, and the sphere, when it finally emerged, was midnight black.

Chapter 15

Xantcha and Sosinna both screamed as the darkness sealed around them. Navigation was impossible, and they became one more tumbling object in the chaos raining down from the colliding islands. Sosinna called her lady's name, begging for deliverance. Xantcha hoped Serra could hear. The sphere wasn't like Urza's armor. The armor lasted until Xantcha willed it away, but once the sphere had risen, it collapsed as soon as it touched the ground. At least that was what had always happened. It might do something different this time when it had come out black.

The jostling, which seemed to last forever, ended when they struck a decisive bottom. The sphere collapsed, as it always had, coating Xantcha in soot and leaving them in a shower of rocks. Xantcha was stunned when a stone struck her head. But mind-stars were all she saw through the sticky soot. Sosinna's hand closed over hers. Xantcha let herself be guided to a place where the air was quiet.

"So, what next?" Xantcha asked when she'd wiped away enough soot to open her eyes.

There wasn't much to see. The air was dusty, and the overhead island—the island from which they'd fallen and that continued to

215

rain chunks of itself onto the island where they were standing—remained close enough to keep them in twilight darkness. She feared another collision.

"We can't stay here," she added, in case Sosinna had missed the obvious.

They were both nursing bruises. Xantcha's hand came away bloody when she touched the throbbing spot where the rock had hit her skull. The left sleeve of Sosinna's gown was torn to rags, and she was dripping soot-streaked blood from a gash on her forearm. Xantcha never worried her own cuts. She healed quick, and the infections or illnesses that plagued born-folk weren't interested in newt-flesh. She worried about Sosinna, instead.

Although Sosinna had gotten them to safety beyond the rock fall, she was dazed and unresponsive. She held her bleeding arm in front of her and stared at it with glassy eyes. The folk of Serra's realm were born, or so Sosinna had claimed. Despite the strangeness of the floating-island realm and the way Serra's air sustained them, Sosinna might be as fragile as the born-folk usually were. The soot alone might kill her. Blood poisoning wasn't an easy death or a quick one. But unless she had hidden injuries, Sosinna's problem had to be shock and fear.

"Waste not, want not, you're not near dead yet. Pull yourself—"

"It was black," Sosinna interrupted.

"I noticed," Xantcha said with a shrug. "It's always been clear before. But it kept us alive, and we'll use it again."

Sosinna wrenched free. "No! You don't understand. It was black! Nothing here is black. The Lady doesn't permit it." She began to weep. "I told you, you couldn't call on black mana here."

"Black mana? I'm no sorcerer, Sosinna. I've never called to the land in my life." But the cyst had felt wrong since she'd awakened, worse since she'd used it, and the sphere had been black.

"You shattered the land. Shattered it!"

Xantcha didn't demand gratitude, but she wouldn't stand for abuse. "I didn't shatter anything. Two islands collided, and I kept us alive the only way I knew how. Would you rather I'd left you to be crushed by the rocks?"

"Yes! Yes, they'll come for you because of what you've done, and they'll come for me because what you've done is all over me."

"If I'd known that, I'd've done it sooner," Xantcha lied.

Xantcha wasn't in pain. If anything, she was numb. For the first time in centuries, she wasn't aware of Urza's cyst. Her hand felt cloth when she rubbed below her waist, but the rest of her couldn't feel her hand. The numbness wasn't spreading. The part of her mind that knew when she was healthy said that she was numb because she was empty. She didn't know what would happen if she called on the cyst while her gut was numb and didn't want to find out unless she had to.

"How long before your Lady gets here?"

"The Lady won't come. She takes no part in death, even when she knows it must be done. The archangels will come." Sosinna looked up at the still-crumbling underside of their original floating island. "Soon."

Sosinna dried her tears, leaving fresh streaks of blood and soot on her face. Then she did what Serra's folk seemed to do best: she sat down, folded her hands in her lap, and settled in to wait. The gash on her arm continued to bleed. Maybe Sosinna didn't feel pain, or maybe she hoped she'd bleed to death before the dreaded archangels arrived.

If her own life hadn't hung in the balance, Xantcha would have laughed at the absurdity. She grabbed Sosinna below the shoulders and hauled the taller woman to her feet.

"You want to live, Sosinna. You got us both away from the falling rocks and dirt—" She shook the other woman, hoping for reaction. "You want to live. You want to see Kenidiern again."

A blink. A frown. Nothing.

"This is not perfection!" Xantcha shouted and then let Sosinna go.

The taller woman balanced on her own feet a moment, then calmly sat down again. Xantcha walked away in disgust. She'd gone about ten paces before the light of understanding brightened in her mind.

"You knew!" Xantcha shouted as she ran back. "You've known from the beginning! You've been expecting these arch-whatever-angels since I woke up . . . since before I woke up. Your precious, perfect

Lady sent me here to be killed and sent you as what? A witness? 'Come back to the floating palace when everything's taken care of.'? All this time, waiting for the archangels—"

"I never wanted them to come!" Sosinna shouted back.

It was the first time Xantcha had heard the other woman raise her voice—perhaps the first time Sosinna had raised it. She seemed aghast by her outburst.

"Why not? Didn't you want to get back to the palace and Kenidiern?"

Sosinna gasped and fumbled for words. "Don't you understand? I can't go back."

"Because I saved your life with my black mana." Xantcha thought she understood, perfectly. "If only the archangels had been a little quicker. Is that what you've been doing while you sat all the time. Praying to the archangels: get here soon?"

"I didn't want you to wake up because while you were asleep there was no chance you'd use your black powers, and nothing would draw the archangels to us. Once you were awake . . . You are . . . You are so difficult. I was afraid to tell you anything."

"I'd be much less difficult," Xantcha said with exaggerated politeness, "if I knew the truth." She sat down opposite Sosinna. "The perfect truth."

"Kenidiern—"

Xantcha rolled her eyes. "Why am I not surprised that he is at the heart of the truth?"

"You are very difficult. It is the black mana in you. It rules you. The Lady said so."

Xantcha wondered what the Lady had said about Urza, but that would have been a truly difficult question. "I know nothing about black mana, but I won't argue with your Lady's judgment. Go on . . . please . . . before we run out of time."

"How can you run out of time?"

Xantcha shrugged. "Just talk."

"The Lady smiled on Kenidiern and I. She has never encouraged the divisions between the sisterhood and the angels. We had her blessing to come to the palace, but before we could be together he was sent away, and I was chosen to accompany you. I would not have objected," Sosinna continued quickly and emphatically. "I serve Lady Serra proudly, willingly. We all know how she sacrifices herself to maintain the realm. It would be the worst sort of pride and arrogance to question her decisions. . . . But I could not, cannot believe this was her decision."

"To send me away to die or to send you away to die with me?"

Sosinna had the decency to look uncomfortable. "You are difficult, and you are devious. You imagine dark corners and then you make them real."

That was a criticism Xantcha had never heard from Urza's lips.

"You would never do among the sisters or the angels, but if I were to speak to the Lady, I would tell her that except for your black mana you would make a most excellent archangel, and I think she would agree. I was—am—young among the sisters, but I have—had—the Lady's confidence. I know she would not have sent me away without seeing me or telling me why."

"Then why hasn't she come looking for you? Wouldn't she notice you were missing, you and Kenidiern, both?"

Sosinna shivered. "You ask such questions, Xantcha! I would never think to ask such questions myself." She paused and Xantcha raised her eyebrows expectantly. "Until I met you. Now, I ask myself such questions, and I do not like my own answers! I ask myself if the Lady has been deceived by those who were displeased that Kenidiern had given me his token, and no matter how hard I try to purge my thoughts, I cannot convince myself that she hasn't."

"Or maybe your Lady's not perfect?"

Sosinna's thin-lipped mouth opened, closed, and opened again. "I don't know if she never looked for me or if she could not find me but in either case, yes, there would be imperfection. So you see I cannot go back to the palace, not with these thoughts in my heart. Kenidiern is lost. You mock me, Xantcha, do not bother to lie about it, but Kenidiern is a paragon. He would have looked for me and since he hasn't—"

"Hasn't found you, but maybe he is looking. How many of these floating islands are there? A thousand? Ten thousand? You shouldn't give up. He might be just one rock away. Think of the look on his face when he finds you here dead because you stopped trying to stay alive."

"Difficult."

"But right."

"Half right." A faint smile cracked the dirt on Sosinna's face, then vanished. "We couldn't go back to the palace."

"Seems to me that's exactly the place we should be going."

"We wouldn't be welcomed."

"Waste not, want not, Sosinna, your precious Lady is being lied to, and you'd roll over and die without your lover because your enemies won't welcome you."

"Not enemies."

"Enemies. Anyone who wants you dead, Sosinna, is an enemy, yours and your Lady's. If you're determined to die, let's at least try to find this floating palace where your Lady is surrounded by silent enemies. Urza will support you."

That was a promise Xantcha didn't know if she'd be able to keep, but it had to be made. Anything that would get Sosinna thinking had to be done, because even if the archangels didn't show up, the islands were likely to collide again. The upper island had taken the worst damage in the first collision and might again in the second, but anything on the surface of the lower island was going to get squashed like a bug.

"Difficult," Sosinna repeated.

Xantcha stood up and offered her hand. "But right."

"I don't know where the palace is. Only the angels know."

"Didn't Kenidiern ever tell you how he flew in and out?"

"We never talked about such things."

Xantcha almost asked what did they talk about, but Sosinna might have answered, and she didn't truly want to know. "Come on, let's at least start walking. We've got to walk ourselves clear of what's overhead. Maybe when we get to an edge we'll get lucky and see this wondrous palace."

"We can't."

"Can't what?"

"We can't walk to the edge of an island. I don't think we can walk out from under the one overhead. I tried, Xantcha, before you woke up. I tried to abandon you. I knew when you walked away that you'd have to come back."

"No apologies. I'd've done the same," Xantcha said and offered her hand again. "Come on. I've lived with worlds over my head, but not this close. Makes me nervous."

Sosinna reached, and winced as the gash on her arm began bleeding again. It was ugly now and would only get worse if they didn't find water soon. Xantcha hadn't seen free-running water since she'd first opened her eyes in Serra's realm, but now that Sosinna was moving again, she didn't seem worried about her wounds, so Xantcha said nothing either.

Xantcha kept an eye on the island overhead to measure their progress. The lethargy that had slowed her on her previous walk was worse. They weren't covering ground the way she would have liked. Even so, they were getting nowhere relative to the convoluted underside above them. Sosinna looked at her every time she looked up, a look that expected concessions and defeat, but Xantcha kept walking.

Sosinna's remarks about black mana had confirmed Xantcha's suspicion that Serra's floating-island realm was a magical place, as unnatural in its way as Phyrexia. The forces that made Phyrexia a world of concentric spheres were as inexplicable as the ones that shaped Serra's realm into thousands of floating islands . . . and, perhaps, not all that different from each other. She'd have questions for Urza when they met again. If they met again. If she and Sosinna could walk to a place where the opening between the collided islands was large enough that she'd risk casting them adrift in the sphere.

The thought of waking up the cyst brought an end to gut numbness. Xantcha dropped to one knee.

"The archangels will find us," Sosinna said, not the words Xantcha wanted to hear at that moment. "Every time you call on black mana, it brings them closer."

"I didn't call on black mana," Xantcha insisted.

Xantcha used a mnemonic to awaken Urza's artifact. She didn't know how the cyst made the sphere or armor. Urza knew mana-based sorcery; the necessary insights had come with his eyes. He said the Thran hadn't used mana so he wouldn't either, but the Thran had made Urza's eyes. Sosinna thought Xantcha imagined dark corners. Xantcha didn't need imagination so long as she had Urza.

The pain had faded, and numbness returned. Xantcha's legs were leaden when she stood. She could barely lift her feet when she tried to walk. "There's got to be another way."

"We wait until the archangels find us. There is no other way."

"Is your lady sensitive to black mana, or just the archangels?"

"Black mana has no place here. It hurts. We can all feel it, the Lady most of all. She is aware of the whole realm as you are aware of your body. The archangels patrol the islands looking for black mana and other evil miasmas. They eliminate evil before it can affect the Lady, but when they found you and the other—Urza—together, they called Lady Serra for a judgment. You've already been judged. When the archangels find us, they won't call Lady Serra again. They won't risk her health. None of us would risk it. If the Lady sickened, we would all die."

Another unfortunate choice of words, given the state of Xantcha's gut, but she had an idea. "I'm going to get everyone's attention, the archangels and, with any luck, your Lady herself."

Xantcha yawned and thought the mnemonic for her armor. At first there was nothing, and she thought she'd lost the cyst altogether. Then the pain began and she felt something acid rising through her throat. Sosinna screamed, but by then Xantcha couldn't have stopped the process if she'd wanted to. The armor burned as it flowed over her skin. It spared her eyes. When Xantcha looked down what she saw was blacker than the darkest night, as black and featureless as the walls of an unlit cave. She brought her hands together, saw them touch, and felt absolutely nothing.

"You got the archangels, that's all." Sosinna pointed through the narrow opening between the islands. "We're doomed."

Sosinna stood no more than two arm's lengths away, but with the black armor covering Xantcha's ears, she sounded distant and under water. Xantcha looked in the indicated direction. A dazzling white diamond had appeared in the ribbon of golden light between the two islands. A moment's observation revealed that it was growing, moving toward them at considerable speed. From the air, then, the floating islands had edges. It was only from the ground that the horizon never became an edge.

As the diamond grew larger, it became apparent that it had five parts: four smaller lights, one each in the narrow and oblique points, and a much larger light in the center.

"The Aegis," Sosinna said.

The Aegis was also diamond shaped and too bright to look at directly. Xantcha held her black-armored hand in front of her eyes and squinted through the pinhole gaps between her fingers. She saw writhing plumes of yellow fire emerging from a hole that reminded her of a portal, a portal to the sun. Moving her hand slightly she observed the smaller lights, the archangels themselves: radiant, elongated creatures with dazzling wings that didn't move and smooth, featureless faces. They resembled Sosinna the same way many compleat Phyrexians resembled newts. Not an encouraging thought.

Xantcha didn't think Urza's armor, in its present condition, would be proof against the Aegis. She tried to say good-bye to Sosinna and discovered the armor had taken away her voice.

Wind preceded the archangels. It shook boulders loose from the overhead island and lifted the island itself out of the way. One loosened boulder struck the ground so near to Xantcha's feet that she felt the ground shudder. The wind died when the archangels brought the Aegis to a hovering halt. As good warriors anywhere, the archangels tested their weapon before they put it to use. A beam of light as hot as a Phyrexian furnace and many times as bright seared the land directly below the Aegis. Then the beam began to move toward Xantcha and Sosinna.

It made no difference whether Xantcha's eyes were open or shut. She was blind, and it felt as if the back of her skull were on fire. Xantcha had never believed in gods or souls, but facing the end of her life, Xantcha found she believed in curses. She'd roundly cursed Lady Serra's notion of perfection when she was struck down by a sideways wind.

The wind was a word and the word was:

Halt!

A woman's voice. This time there could be no mistaking it, even through Xantcha's blackened armor. The great Lady of the realm reined in her archangels. The heat ebbed at once, but Xantcha remained blind. A more ordinary voice, a man's voice, shouted, "Sosinna!" Xantcha guessed that Kenidiern had found his beloved. She hoped Sosinna was still alive. She'd hoped, too, that Urza might be part of the rescue party, but no one called her name. Someone did lift her to her feet and into the air—at least Xantcha thought that she'd been lifted—she presumed she was being carried by an angel or archangel. Blind and numb as she was, it was impossible to be certain, and she was in no way tempted to release Urza's armor, assuming she could release it.

The journey lasted long enough for Xantcha's vision to recover from its Aegis searing. She was moving through the air of Serra's realm, tucked under the arm of the right side archangel. Craning her neck as much as she dared, Xantcha caught a glimpse of a silver face with angles for nose, chin, and not so much as a slit for vision.

A mask she thought, because the hand she could see at her waist was flesh with stretched sinew and pulsing arteries apparent beneath normal-hued skin. Xantcha could understand why the archangels might choose to cover their eyes. Even when it was shut down, the Aegis—one golden tether to which her archangel held in his, hers? its? other hand—was nothing Xantcha wanted to look at. Easily four times as high as her archangel, it reminded Xantcha of nothing so much as a piece of the sun, that Serra's realm did not otherwise possess.

They left the Aegis behind, shining among the floating islands, once the great island that could only be Lady Serra's palace came into view.

The palace was many times the size of any other island Xantcha had seen, and if she'd had to make a guess, she'd have said that it was the very center of the lady's creation.

As all Phyrexia had formed in spheres around the Ineffable?

But Xantcha had seen nothing like the palace in Phyrexia.

Lady Serra's home leaped and soared in fantastic curves. Xantcha could think of no stone or brick that would glisten as the palace walls and ribs glistened in the Aegis's light. The underlying color was white, or possibly a golden gray. It was difficult to be certain. A myriad of rainbows moved constantly along every arch and into every corner. There was sound in all timbres to accompany the kaleidoscopic light, and not an echo of discord.

The total experience, which could have been as overwhelming as the Aegis, was instead subtle and unspeakably beautiful. It was also pushing Xantcha and her archangel away. They were falling behind the others, including the fifth, unmasked angel carrying Sosinna. Xantcha would have preferred to keep her armor, black as it was, around her but she didn't want to be left alone either. Perhaps releasing the armor would be the most foolish thing she'd ever done, and the last, but she recited the mnemonic that made it melt away.

Black dust streamed away from her. It dirtied the archangel's pure white robes, but he regained his right side place in the formation moments before they began a dizzying ascent to the rainbow lace ornament atop the palace's highest, most improbable arch.

With nothing else to guide her eye, Xantcha had misjudged the scale of Serra's palace. She'd seen snow-capped mountains that weren't as high as that single, soaring arch, and mighty temples that were smaller than the deceptively delicate edifice on whose jeweled porch the archangel landed.

Her knees buckled when her feet touched the ground. She was numb the same way the palace was many-colored: awash in shifting waves of sensation. She kept her balance by keeping a close watch on her feet and the floor.

"Follow me."

Xantcha looked up quickly, a mistake under the circumstances. The archangels had already vanished, and Kenidiern, assuming the unmasked angel was Kenidiern, had no hands to spare. Xantcha broke her fall with her arms and stayed where she was, crouched on the glass-smooth floor.

"I can send someone out for you," Kenidiern said in a tone that clearly conveyed the notion that he wouldn't recommend accepting the offer.

He had a friendly, honest voice. Xantcha had never paid much attention to the handsomeness of men, but even she could see that Kenidiern was, as Sosinna had claimed, a very attractive paragon. She guessed he knew how to laugh, although his face was anxious at that moment. If Sosinna wasn't dead, she was clinging to life by a very delicate thread. The Aegis had burned the tall woman badly. Her flesh was seared and weeping beneath its crust of dirt.

"Go," Xantcha told him. "I'll follow." She started to stand and abandoned the attempt. "I'll find a way."

Chapter 16

Xantcha watched Kenidiern carry Sosinna through one of the many open doorways, and made sure she'd remembered which one before rising to her feet. Speed, she decided, mattered. The palace didn't like her and especially didn't like her when she moved quickly. Slow, gliding movements, as if she were crossing a frozen pond, offended it least. She made steady progress from the porch through the door and down a majestic corridor. There was no one to stop or question her, at least no one that Xantcha could see, which was not to say that she didn't believe her every step was scrutinized.

The corridor ended in a chamber of breathtaking beauty. Unlike the rest of the palace, which seemed to be made from crystal and stone, this inner chamber was a place of life and growth. A maze of columns that might be trees, all graceful, but asymmetric and entrancing, hid the walls. Each tree or column was taller than her eye could measure.

Xantcha lost her thoughts in the overhead tangle of green-gold branches, and the music, which was no longer the austere interplay of wind and light, but the more playful sounds of water and the bright-feathered birds she glimpsed among the high branches. She was startled witless when someone grabbed her from behind.

"Xantcha! I did not know you still lived!"

"Urza!"

They'd never been much for backslapping embraces or other shows of affection, but any tradition needed its exception. And Urza was more animated, more alive, than Xantcha could remember him. His hands were warm and supple on her shoulders. They banished the lethargy that had plagued her since she'd first awakened and ended the numbness in her gut around the cyst.

"Let me look at you!" he said, straightening his arms. His eyes glittered but only with reflections from Serra's palace. "A bit worn and dirty at the edges—" Urza winked as he tightened his fingers—"but still the same Xantcha."

There was the faintest hint of a question in his statement. The sense that they were being watched hadn't faded with the numbness and lethargy. If anything, Xantcha was more aware than ever that she was in strange, perhaps hostile, surroundings.

"As stubborn and suspicious as ever," Xantcha replied with a wink of her own.

"We will talk, child. There is much to talk about. But, first you must meet our host." His arm urged her to walk beside him.

"I did once, already." Xantcha slipped free and into one of the many, many other languages they both knew. If they were back to child, then she was going to be very stubborn and twice as suspicious. Lowering her voice, she added, "Serra sent me away to die, Urza, and sent one of her own to die with me. That's why you didn't know I was alive."

"We will talk, child," Urza repeated in Serra's language. "This is not a good time to have a tantrum."

She switched to another language. "I'm not a child, I'm not having a tantrum, and you know it!"

Urza could put thoughts into Xantcha's head with only a little more discomfort than when he removed them. *Yes, I know, and I will ask Serra why she misled me. I'm sure the answer will amuse us both. But for now you are safe with me, and it will be better all around if you behave graciously.*

Xantcha replied with a thought of her own. *Graciously be damned! Serra didn't mislead you . . . she lied!*

But Xantcha couldn't put a thought in Urza's mind, and her indignation went unshared. Urza walked away, and faced with a choice between keeping up with him or staying by herself, she caught up, as he'd almost certainly known she would.

He said the chamber was known as Serra's Aviary and that she had seldom left it since creating her floating island realm.

"Then you know this isn't a natural world?" Xantcha asked, still refusing to speak Serra's language.

"Yes," Urza replied, ignoring her choice of language.

"Does it remind you of my home as much as it reminds me?" She was careful not to speak the word Phyrexia.

"There are no abominations here. The angels' wings are no more a part of them than your cyst is part of you. Serra's realm is slow and not without its flaws, but it is a living, natural place."

"For you. I haven't eaten since I got here. That's not natural for me."

"She has paid a price for her creation. Now, be gracious."

Urza took Xantcha's hand as they wound around another organic column. A narrow spiral stairway opened in front of them. Xantcha looked up and up and up.

"There's another way—?"

"We are guests."

Urza began climbing. Xantcha fell in behind him and into a kind of trance. The spiral was a tight one and each step a bit different in height and width than its neighbors. An odd sort of perfection that made each one unique, Xantcha thought, when she dared to think. Each step required concentration lest she lose her balance and tumble to the floor, which through the tangle of branches around them had come to look like twinkling stars on a warm, humid night. Urza surged ahead of her, but a hand awaited at the top of the stairway.

Not Urza. Kenidiern. She recognized him by his stained robe.

"She asked me to wait until you were here."

Xantcha was breathing hard, but Urza's embrace had revitalized her. She didn't need anyone's help to follow the angel along a suspended walkway to a somewhat more intimate chamber than any she'd yet seen in the palace. It was only ten or twenty times the size that a room needed to be. Urza was there already, talking with a woman who could only be the lady, Serra, herself.

Having seen angels, archangels and Sosinna, Xantcha had expected a tall, slender and remote woman, but Serra could have walked through any man-made village without attracting a second glance. Her face, though pleasant, was plain, and she had the sturdy silhouette of a woman who'd borne children and done many a hard day's work. She was also one of two light sources in the chamber, surrounded by a gently flickering white nimbus. If she'd created this realm, as Urza said, then, like him, she could change her appearance to suit her whims.

The chamber's other light source was incomprehensible at first glance: a jumble of golden light and angular crystals bound together into two overlapping spheres. An artifact, certainly— Xantcha's dodger instincts had never deserted her—and beautiful, but its purpose, except as a source of light, eluded her.

"Please." Kenidiern offered his hand again. "She is very weak, and she must be alive when the cocoon is closed or there is no reason to close it."

Be gracious, Urza had said, so Xantcha let the angel have her hand, and before she could object he'd swept her up in both arms and carried her into the crystal lights. The wingless sisters of Serra were, perhaps, accustomed to being swooped about the palace, but Xantcha had rarely felt as helpless or as grateful to have her own feet under her once they'd reached a tiny enclosure where the spheres met.

Cocoon, Kenidiern called it, and that was as good a word as any for the vaguely egg-shaped compartment in which Sosinna lay. Her stained gown was gone, replaced by a shining quilt, but the Aegis had seared her face and hair. Her eyes were terrible, frightened and frightening. Sosinna was blind. At least, Xantcha hoped Sosinna was blind.

"Xantcha?" Sosinna's voice was a pain-wracked whisper. Her breathing was shallow and liquid.

Xantcha had seen worse, done worse, though few things in her life had been more difficult than reaching out to touch the quilt-bandaged lump that was, or had been, Sosinna's hand.

"I'm here."

"We made it. You were right."

"Difficult, but right."

Sosinna tried to smile, pain defeated her. "We will name our child for you."

Be gracious, that was easy. "I'm honored." Optimism came harder. "I'll show her, or him, how to be difficult."

Another failed smile on Sosinna's swollen lips and an agonizing attempt to shake her head. "You will go outside where you belong. Kenidiern and I will remember you."

With the sound of his name, Kenidiern came closer. His wings were soft, plumes rather than feathers. He rested his hand on Xantcha's shoulders. A shiver ran down Xantcha's spine, reminding her that, unlike Serra, the Ineffable had decreed that Phyrexians would not be born, and she was neither a man nor woman. Xantcha couldn't know if Kenidiern were a true paragon of anything useful, but she believed he had been looking for his beloved, and she envied Sosinna as she had never envied anyone before.

"We must close the cocoon," Kenidiern whispered, urging her to retreat.

Better call it a coffin. Some hurts were beyond even Urza's healing talents, and Sosinna's would be among them. It wasn't just her skin that had been charred and blistered. Sosinna had breathed fire and her insides were burnt as well. Xantcha took a backward step.

"Good-bye . . . friend." Sosinna whispered.

"Good-bye, friend."

The upper sphere had begun to descend. Sosinna might be blind, but the cocoon wasn't silent. Surely she knew it was closing around her. She met her end without a whimper.

"Until you rise again," Kenidiern added, a euphemism, if ever Xantcha had heard one, though Sosinna managed a trembling smile just before the spheres blocked Xantcha's view.

There was a click, the golden light intensified, and, through her feet, Xantcha felt the whir of a distant engine. She thought of the Fane of Flesh, of the vats where discarded flesh was rendered and newts were decanted.

"You didn't say good-bye," she said to Kenidiern.

"Sosinna will rise again. The Lady does not offer her cocoon to everyone, but when she does, it never fails."

He swept Xantcha up again before she could protest and brought her down to Urza and Serra, whose conversation died as they approached.

"Sosinna is a special child to me," Serra said before Xantcha's feet were on the floor. "I didn't know what had become of her. I'm grateful that you showed us where she was, even though I'm not grateful for your methods!"

The lady had Urza's voice, the voice of someone who treated everyone as children, someone whom mortals might mistake for a god. Xantcha had never been mortal, never believed in gods, and she'd used up all her graciousness.

"Sosinna didn't believe in mistakes, she never lost faith in you. All the time we were together on that forsaken, floating island, she was hoping you or Kenidiern would rescue her before the archangels came to kill her. If that was you who called the Aegis off, then when it comes to rescuing your special children, you cut very close to the edge." Urza was appalled. His eyes glowed dark. Kenidiern stared at his sandaled feet. "Things here aren't as perfect as she believed they were."

"You are Phyrexian, are you not?" Serra asked, a tone short of accusation.

Urza's displeasure rumbled through the empty part of Xantcha's mind. The important part, the part she'd kept for herself since Gix had taught her how to build mental walls, remained unbowed. "You know I am."

"Your leave, my lady," Kenidiern interrupted. "My love is in your hands now. There is no need for me to stay."

Serra dipped her chin. Kenidiern was in the air before she raised it again. There were only three of them left in the branch-framed chamber: a man and a woman with the powers of gods, and a Phyrexian newt. Well, Xantcha was used to being overmatched.

"There is no need for this, Xantcha." Urza attempted to impose peace. "I think Lady Serra will concede there have been certain imperfections in our condition here." He turned toward Serra.

"Your arrival was so unexpected—" Serra began.

Xantcha cut her off. "That reminds me. How did we get here? The last thing I remember was beating on the shell of a Phyrexian turtle."

"I destroyed that abomination and all the others," Urza answered quickly. "But my enemies were lurking, watching from nether places, and before I could escape, they sent through reinforcements. It threatened to become the Fourth Sphere battle all over again, so I decided to retreat. I 'walked away, grabbing you as I left. But you were badly injured, and my grasp was not firm. I sensed the chasm to Phyrexia, of course—it is always there—but I sensed another, too, and threw myself across it. It was a terrible passage, Xantcha. I lost you. I would not have survived myself if Lady Serra had not found me and put me inside that cocoon you just saw.

"Such a marvelous artifact! If there is life, any life at all, the cocoon will sustain it and nurture it until the whole is healed. I am well again, Xantcha, well and whole as I have not been since I left Phyrexia, since before Phyrexia . . . since I met you. The principle is ingenious. To make her plane, Serra has treated time itself as a liquid, as a stream where water flows at different speed. . . ."

Xantcha swallowed hard. It didn't help. She stopped listening to Urza ramble about the wonders of Serra's cocoon. His recounting of events was laced through with simplifications that were no better than lies: *so I decided to retreat* and *I 'walked away* didn't accurately describe what she remembered of Urza's Phyrexian invasion and was probably no better at describing how the skirmish with the turtle-avengers ended or how they'd come to Serra's realm, but Urza remembered what he wanted to remember and forgot the rest.

He had rescued her from the turtles. Never mind asking if he'd cared about anything beyond keeping her away from Phyrexian scrutiny. His grasp might not have been firm. He might have lost her by accident. And he had been ill . . . since Phyrexia, but not before.

Xantcha was relieved to see Urza looking vigorous again, pleased to see him talking and moving in a mortal way, but she could not escape the implications of those few words: *since I met you*. They echoed ominously in her own thoughts. Had Urza decided something, perhaps everything, was her fault?

That warm greeting in the lower hall had been less relief or enthusiasm, than guilt.

Xantcha glanced at Serra, wondering what role she had played. Romance? That seemed unlikely with Urza . . . unnecessary, too, when she could distract him with the cocoon. After she'd gotten rid of Urza's annoying, Phyrexian companion?

"You want to know what I did when you were found?" Serra asked, an indication that she was sensitive to thought and, perhaps, did not find Xantcha's mind as empty as Urza did.

"I know what you did, why did you do it? What had I done to you or your perfect realm?"

"All things, natural or artifact, are created around a single essence. Your essence is black mana. When I created my plane, I created it around white mana, because the underlying essence plays a pivotal role in determining the character of a thing. White mana is serene, harmonic. It has the constancy that allows my plane to be the safe haven I desired. Black mana is discord, suspicion, and darkness. There is black mana here—it was not possible to eliminate it entirely—but it is only the small remainder that balances the rest—"

"I told you it is not so simple," Urza interrupted their host. "Lady Serra turned away from all that was real to make this place. She created it out of sheer will. But it seems there is a flaw, a fallacy, in willful creation. Outside, in the multiverse which is unbounded, balance simply is and all planes are balanced among all the essences. Inside, when a plane is created by an act of single will, balance is impossible. One essence must dominate and another become the odd fellow."

"I knew this place reminded me of Phyrexia!" Momentarily forgetting everything else, Xantcha savored the satisfaction of solving a thorny puzzle. "The teacher-priests said the Ineffable made Phyrexia. I thought they meant that we all answered to him, that we were all part of his plan, but it was more than that. The Ineffable created Phyrexia. It was nothing, nothing at all, before he made it."

"Precisely," Urza agreed. "I had reached the same conclusion. A created plane, cut off from the rest of the multiverse by an unfathomable chasm, no wonder it was so hard to find! But, inherently unbalanced! Think of it, Xantcha. Lady Serra retreats to her cocoon where she adds her will to her plane's flux, constantly keeping it almost in balance, but never quite and never for long. It always slips away. She prunes it to keep it small—"

"Small's never been a part of the Ineffable's plan—"

"Excuse me!" Serra said firmly and in her own language, which neither Xantcha nor Urza had been using.

The air in Xantcha's lungs became so heavy she couldn't speak and even Urza seemed to be at a loss for words.

"As I was saying." The lady's tone implied she'd tolerate no more interruptions. "The only black mana here is here because it cannot be eliminated. Nothing here has black mana as its underlying essence. Such a thing, natural or artifact, would disrupt everything around it. When the archangels found you and Urza, both near death and unable to speak for yourselves, they—I— determined that you had swallowed a piece of him. You were clinging to him. And your essence was black—is black.

"They have standing orders. Safe haven cannot be extended to anything with an underlying black mana essence. Because you had a piece of him, and we did not know then if it was a vital piece, I sent you away—put you in quarantine—while my cocoon restored Urza. His underlying essence is white mana, the same as ours. There was no risk. The cocoon purged him of a black mana curse."

The Ineffable, Xantcha thought. The Ineffable had place a spark in Urza's skull as surely as Gix had placed one in hers all those centuries ago. She said nothing, though, because Serra would object, and because she wanted to hear Urza's version of events before proposing her own.

If black mana was suspicion, then Xantcha had become black mana incarnate.

"It was not a vital piece, of course," Serra continued. "Urza explained how he'd enabled you to survive the journeys between planes when he emerged from the cocoon, but by then . . ."

By then, *what?* Xantcha asked silently, eager to hear how Serra would wriggle free of the truth.

The lady hesitated and Urza plunged into the silence. "By then, her plane needed tending. She needed tending! Your presence alone had been enough to disrupt the balance more than it had ever been disrupted. You were well and truly lost by then, and I had no idea that you'd survived at all. My grasp had been weak to begin with. I asked the elders here, and they said I'd been alone when archangels brought me to the palace."

"They lied," Xantcha snapped, unable to stifle her indignation. She wished Kenidiern had not taken his leave. She'd liked to have seen his face when he'd heard that remark.

"Misinformed," Urza prevaricated. "I was alone. The archangels separated us, took us in different directions. The sisterhood had no idea what I was talking about."

"They knew, Urza. They sent Sosinna to die with me—" At least that was what Sosinna had assumed. But there were other possibilities. Serra said she had decided what would be done with her and Urza both. Xantcha looked straight at Serra. "Someone sent Sosinna to die with me."

"I cannot keep up with you!" the lady complained. "Either of you. You should hear yourselves, switching languages every other phrase, every other word. You have been together too long. No one else could possibly understand you." She took Urza's hand. "My friend, my offer stands, I will take her wherever you think best, but this is something for you to work out between yourselves. That piece of you she holds within her, surely it is a vital part of your memory, Urza. You should consider carefully before abandoning it."

Serra faded, 'walking somewhere else within her realm, leaving Urza and Xantcha alone in the golden light from the cocoon.

"What offer, Urza? Abandon it? Abandon me?"

But Urza was staring at the place where Serra had stood. "She was angry. I had no notion, no notion at all. You should not have done that, Xantcha. It was very ungracious to speak your mind in a way that Lady Serra couldn't understand. She doesn't understand that the Phyrexians emptied your mind. I must find her and apologize."

He started to fade as well.

"Urza!" Xantcha called him back. "Waste not, want not—you don't hear the words or their meanings! She said both of us. We were both speaking whatever words fit best. We do that, we've done it from the beginning. We've been too many places and seen too many things that no one else has seen. We have our own way of talking. We might just as well be one mind with two bodies."

"No! That can't be," he insisted. "Lady Serra is a Planeswalker. You aren't. She saw great tragedy, as I did on Dominaria, and she made this place, this plane, as a memorial to what she'd lost. She understands me, Xantcha. No one else has understood me. I've been happy here with her."

"Who wouldn't be happy in a world of their own making? The Ineffable is happy. The Ineffable understood you."

Urza whirled around. "Don't try to tempt me. That trap is sprung, Xantcha."

"What trap?" she retorted, but beneath the surface her fears and suspicions had intensified. "What offer, Urza? What's happened to you while I was floating on that island? What changed your mind about me?"

"Lady Serra healed me. Her cocoon healed me of all the taint and curse that Phyrexia has laid on me since Mishra and I let them back into Dominaria."

He reached for her. Xantcha eluded him.

"It's not your fault, Xantcha. No one is blaming you, least of all me. The one you call the Ineffable used you. He could not tempt me directly, so he made you to tempt me, to lead me to him. Oh, I knew you were dangerous, I've known that since I rescued you. I knew you could never be completely trusted, but I thought I was strong enough, clever enough to use you myself.

"Your Ineffable has lost his power over me, Xantcha. You were merely his tool, his arrow aimed at my heart. All these centuries that you've been beside me, I have been obsessed with simple vengeance. I didn't see the larger patterns until you were gone. It is all Lady Serra can to do keep her plane balanced. She knows that some day she will grow tired and it will fail. She does not let it expand. Created planes fail. They cannot evolve. They dare not grow. They are doomed from the moment of their creation. I understand that now, only natural planes endure. Yawg—"

"Don't—"

"Your Ineffable was exiled from some other plane before Dominaria. He thinks of Phyrexia not as a safe haven, as Serra thinks of her realm, but as a place to build a conquering army. Twice he has tried to conquer Dominaria, and he will try again. I know it. And I have wasted all my time looking for Phyrexia, trying to conquer Phyrexia—"

"I told you it couldn't be done."

"Yes. Yes, you did. Your creator knew I would not believe you. He is mad, but he is also cunning and clever. That is why he emptied your mind. That is how he tempted me off the path."

And if the Ineffable was mad, but cunning, what did that leave Urza? There was truth and logic wound through Urza's argument. Phyrexia was the Ineffable's creation as this world of floating islands was Serra's creation, and Phyrexia was the rallying point for a conquering army. If all had gone according to plan, Xantcha would have been part of that army, at least as the demon Gix had conceived the army while the Ineffable slept. . . .

Serra slept in the cocoon to keep her world alive. Had the Ineffable slept for the same reason? Was that why the priests warned the newts, *Never speak the Ineffable's name lest he be awakened?*

"You awoke him," Xantcha said incredulously, interrupting Urza's diatribe which had gone on while she asked herself questions. "When you rode your dragon into Phyrexia you must have awakened the Ineffable."

"No, Xantcha, you will not lead me astray again. I know what must be done. Yawgmoth is a Planeswalker, like Serra and me. Only Planeswalkers can create planes, and Planeswalkers are born in natural worlds. No one born here can 'walk, no Phyrexian can 'walk. So Yawgmoth was born on a natural plane and driven out. I will find that plane where Yawgmoth was born, and when I do, I will know his secrets and his weaknesses. I will find the records of those who cast him out, and I will learn how they won their victory. I will find the tools that I need to build the artifacts that will keep Yawgmoth away from Dominaria and away from any other natural plane he might covet."

"That's reasonable," Xantcha conceded. "If we knew when the Ineffable created Phyrexia—"

"No! I have said too much already! You have no thoughts of your own, Xantcha. Whatever you think, whatever you say, comes from Yawgmoth. It is not your fault, but I dare not listen to you. We must go our separate ways, you and I. Lady Serra discussed this before you arrived. She is willing to take you to a natural plane she knows. That's the offer she mentioned. I have not seen it, but she says it is a green plane, with much water and many different races. I think it must be like the Dominaria of my youth. You will do well there, Xantcha."

Xantcha was a breath short of speechless. "You can't mean that. You can't. Look at me, Urza. I am what I am, what I've always been. What would a newt like me do forever on a single world?" Never mind that it had been her destiny to *sleep* on such a world. . . .

Urza reached for her and this time caught her. "You've always done very well for yourself. You trade, you travel, you learn all their languages, you scratch a little garden in the dirt. When I rescued you, I never imagined we'd be together as long as we have been."

"I've never imagined anything else."

"Xantcha, you don't imagine anything that Yawgmoth didn't put inside your skull. I will win your vengeance, trust me. You cannot climb into the Lady's cocoon. Black mana is your underlying essence. The cocoon would destroy you, or you would destroy it. I'm sorry, but it has to be this way."

"You can't just abandon me . . . not to Serra! Who will you talk to? Who else understands, truly understands."

"I will miss you, Xantcha, more than you can imagine. You have been my ward against loneliness and, yes, even madness. You have a good heart, Xantcha. Even Lady Serra admits that. She finds no fault with your heart."

Heart.

Xantcha wriggled out of his embrace. "Give me your knife." She had nothing but her ragged, dirty robe and a pair of sandals.

Urza had a leather sheath slung from his belt. If it wasn't real, he could make it real with a thought. "Please, Urza let me have your knife, any knife."

"Xantcha, don't be foolish. You were always happiest when we settled in one place."

"I'm not going to be foolish. I just want to borrow your knife! I'll find something else that's sharp—"

She eyed the cocoon's golden crystals, and Urza relented. The knife he handed her had a blade no longer than her longest finger—which would have been plenty long enough to slash her throat, if she'd been determined to bleed to death. But Xantcha had never in her life wanted to die. She wasn't fond of pain, either, when there were other alternatives, which, at that moment there weren't.

Xantcha put a few paces between them. Then, with a steady hand, she plunged the short knife into her flank where she'd tucked her heart away. Her hand was shaking as she lengthened the incision. Urza tried to stop her. Panic gave her the strength to reach inside.

"My heart," she said, offering him the bloodstained amber. "If you think I'm untrustworthy, if you think I belong to the Ineffable, crush it and I'll die. I swore I'd never betray you. I'd rather die than live knowing that you've abandoned me."

"Xantcha!" Urza reached for the wound, which he could heal with a touch.

She staggered backward. "Take it! If I am what you say I am, I don't want to live. But if you won't kill me, then take me with you."

Chapter 17

Xantcha awoke with her butt on the ground and her back against an apple tree's broken trunk. Torn branches with upside-down leaves blocked her view of the world. There were green apples piled in her lap and the crook of her throbbing arm. The portal explosion had thrown her so hard she'd shattered a tree when she fell, but Urza's armor had kept her whole.

Ratepe stood among the branches, looking anxious, but not at her.

"How long was I out?" she asked, reaching for the waterskin he dangled with her good arm.

"A bit . . ."

He dropped the waterskin in her lap. Whatever had his attention wasn't letting it go. She pulled the cork with her teeth and took a swallow before asking:

"What's out there?"

"He came out of nowhere, as soon as you'd fallen. His eyes blazed lightning and fire."

Xantcha imagined the worst. "Another Phyrexian?"

She tried to stand but armor or no armor, Phyrexian or no Phyrexian, she'd taken a beating, and her body wasn't ready for anything. Latching onto the hem of Ratepe's tunic, Xantcha dragged herself upright.

The awe-inspiring invader had been Urza, not another Phyrexian. Garbed in stiff armor and looking like a painted statue, he contemplated the metal-and-oil wreckage. He carried an ornate staff, the source of the lightning web that ebbed and flowed around him. Xantcha thought Urza had lost that staff ages ago when they were dodging Phyrexian ambushes. She wasn't entirely pleased to see it again.

Her battered arm wanted out of the armor. Xantcha would have preferred to wait until she had a better sense of Urza's mood, but there wasn't time for that. She silently recited the mnemonic that dissolved the armor. Her arm swelled immediately.

"Has he said anything?" she asked.

"Not a word. The way he looked, I got out of his way. Might've been better if there had been another Phyrexian for him to fry?"

"Might've," Xantcha agreed.

If there'd been an upright Phyrexian in the vicinity, Urza would have had another target besides her. She couldn't remember the last time he'd come charging to her rescue. In point of fact, she didn't think he had come to her rescue. Since they'd gotten to Dominaria, Xantcha's heart had sat gathering dust on a shelf in Urza's alcove. She didn't think Urza had given it a second thought in over a century, but she wasn't surprised that he'd been watching it closely while she and Ratepe were away. She imagined it had flashed when she hit the tree.

Best get it over with, she decided and said to Ratepe, "You wait here," though there was no chance that he'd pay attention, and she was grateful for the help clambering through the tangled branches.

"Been a long time since I've seen a compleat one," she said casually, starting the conversation in the middle, which was sometimes the best way when Urza was rigid and wrapped in power.

"You should have known better than to engage a Phyrexian with my brother beside you!"

Urza was angry. His eyes were fire, his breath sulfur smoke and sparks. Xantcha winced when they landed on her face. He either hadn't noticed—or didn't care—that she wasn't encased in his armor. She was groping for the words that would calm him when Ratepe spoke up.

"This was my idea. We wouldn't have gotten into trouble if I hadn't badgered her into tracking the riders away from Tabarna's palace."

Urza turned without moving. "Palace?" He'd followed her heart between-worlds and didn't know where, precisely, they were.

"Pincar City's a short, hard ride for six men on good horses," Xantcha said and pointed northwest. "We spotted the riders going out a sea gate at sunrise. It was my decision to get involved when I saw them laying down an ambulator's nether end."

"An ambulator, here?"

Urza turned his head, looking for one. He was in the here and now again. Xantcha relaxed.

"We blew it up in the firepots. They had the nether end here. I sure didn't want to go through to get the prime, and I didn't want to risk carrying a loose nether around with me, especially not after what came out. I swear I was expecting *sleepers* and, at the outside, a tender-priest. Nothing like this."

Urza rolled the wreckage with his staff. Bright, compound eyes looked up at the sun, metal parts clattered, and Ratepe leapt a foot in the air, thinking it was still alive.

"They've sent a demon," Urza mused, slipping out of Efuand, into his oldest language, pure ancient Argivian.

"Not a demon," Xantcha corrected, sticking with Efuand. "Some new kind of priest. Not as bad as a demon, but pretty bad when you were expecting a cadre of *sleepers*."

"How do you know what it was if you've never seen it before?" Ratepe asked. A reasonable question, though Xantcha wished he hadn't been staring at Urza's eyes as he asked it.

"Yes," Urza added, back to Efuand. "How can you be sure?" He tipped his staff toward one of the two Efuand corpses lying near the Phyrexian. "Are they sleepers? They have the smell of Phyrexia around them."

Xantcha swallowed her shock. Urza had long admitted that she was better at scenting out Phyrexians, but he'd never hinted how much better, and she'd never tried to put the distinctions into words, any words from any language, including Phyrexian. "This is a priest—" she nudged the wreckage with her foot—"because it looks like a priest."

"That's not an answer," Ratepe chided.

"I'm not finished!"

Xantcha got on her knees and with her good hand attempted to loosen the Phyrexian's triangular face-plate. It was a struggle. The tenders had compleated it carefully, and it had recently received a generous allocation of glistening oil to bind what remained of its flesh to its metal carapace. Once she'd got her fingertips under one sharp corner, Ratepe helped her pry it off.

Shredded leather clung to the interior of the plate, matching the shreds of a skinless but still recognizably childish face that it had covered.

"It had compleated eyes," Xantcha explained, indicating the coiled wires emerging from the empty sockets. "Only the higher priests and warriors have compleat eyes. And it had an articulated mouth; that's definitely priest-compleat. Diggers and such, they just have boxes in their chests. And all the metal's the same, not scraps. That's priest-compleat, too. It's got no guts, just an oil bladder. A priest's got muscles and nerves, compleated, of course, joined with gears and wire, but it's got the brain it was decanted with. The brain makes it go. That's why most Phyrexians have two arms, two legs, its brain knows two arms, two legs—"

"You said they weren't flesh," Ratepe interrupted, a bit breathless and green-cheeked. He'd told her once that he hadn't been able to help with the butchering on his family's farm. Probably he wished he hadn't helped her now.

"This isn't flesh." She tore off a shredded bit. Not surprisingly, he wouldn't take it from her hand, but Urza did. "This is what flesh becomes when it is compleated."

"They start with a living man and transform him into this," Urza's voice was flat and cold as he ground the shred between his fingers.

"They start with a newt," Xantcha said flatly.

"So, this is what would have happened to . . ." Ratepe couldn't finish his thought aloud.

"If I'd been destined to become a priest."

She could remember the Xantcha who'd waited, hope against hope, for the tender-priests to come for her. Would she have been happier if they had? There was no Phyrexian word for happiness.

"And my brother?" Urza flicked the shred into the weeds. "Did he become a priest? Is that what I fought in Argoth? His skin had been stretched over metal plates, over coiled wire. What was he?"

"A victim," Ratepe answered before Xantcha had a chance. "What about the demons and the *sleepers?*"

She chose to answer the easy part first. "*Sleepers* are newts, uncompleated, the way we came out of the vats. But there's oil in the vats, and the smell never goes away. That's how I spot them."

"This one recognized you?" Ratepe always had another question.

Xantcha shrugged. "Maybe, if I hadn't gotten its attention first." She rubbed the hollow of her neck. "That left arm, Urza. It shot something new at me. Your armor barely stopped it, and for a moment I was glowing blue. And those canisters you made for the firepots? The glass shards are worthless, but the shrieking ones, they brought this priest to its knees."

Urza snapped the wreck's left arm at the shoulder with no more apparent effort than she'd need to break a twig. He angled it this way and that in the sun as glistening oil poured over his hand.

"Do *sleepers* know what they are?" Yet another question from Ratepe.

"I was destined to sleep and I knew, so I assume they know, but I think, lately, that I'm wrong. The *sleepers* I've seen don't seem to recognize one another, don't seem to know they weren't born. And if you were going to ask—" she pointed to the Efuand corpses—"they're not *sleepers.*"

"How do you know?" Urza demanded. "How can you be certain? They're man-shaped, not like you. And they smell."

Xantcha rolled her eyes. "Gix corrected the man-woman mistake before they excoriated him. *Sleepers* were men and women before I left the First Sphere. Phyrexians know about gender,

Urza, they've just decided it's the way of flesh and not the way they're going to follow. These Efuands, they've got oil on the outside from handling the ambulator. Right now, you smell of glistening oil. *Sleepers* have oil on the inside, in their breath."

"So you cover your mouth?" Ratepe asked.

She nodded. He'd watched her do that more than once. "If they're not breathing, you might have to cut them open to be sure."

"Have you cut them open, to be sure?" Urza asked.

Xantcha answered. "I've always been sure."

She met Urza's eyes, they were mortal-brown just then. How many times in the past two hundred years had she sent him out to confirm her sightings? He always said she'd been correct, always told her never to risk encountering them again, but had he ever scented a Dominarian sleeper?

"I have cut them open," Urza confessed. "I've killed and eviscerated men and women because they smelled, faintly, of Phyrexia. But when I examined them outside, I saw only men and women, not what you have become, what my brother became. Even on the inside, there was nothing unusual about them. They had a black mana essence, but essence isn't everything. It doesn't make a man or woman a Phyrexian."

Xantcha didn't know what to say and was grateful when Ratepe asked:

"What about demons?"

"The demons are what they are—and that is an answer. They're as old as Phyrexia, as old as the Ineffable. They're powerful, they're evil. They smell of oil, of course, but, in Phyrexia, I knew a demon when I saw one because I felt fear inside me."

"Mishra met a demon." Ratepe's eyes were glazed. His attention was focused between his ears where he heard the Weakstone sing. "Gix."

The bees in the orchard were louder than Ratepe's whispered declaration, but he got Xantcha's attention and Urza's too.

"Names are just sounds," Urza said, the same as he'd said when Xantcha told him—long before she read *The Antiquity Wars*—the only demon's name she knew. "The Brotherhood of Gix was ancient before I was born. They venerated mountains, gears, and clockwork. They were susceptible to Phyrexian corruption after my brother and I inadvertently broke the Thran lock against Phyrexia, but neither they nor their god could have been Phyrexian."

"Gix promised everything. He knew how to bring metal to life and life to metal." Ratepe's voice remained soft. It was hard to tell if he was frightened by what he heard in his mind or dangerously tempted by it.

"Ratepe?" Xantcha reached across the wrecked priest to take Ratepe's hand. It was limp and cold. "Those things didn't happen to you. Don't let Gix into your memory. Gix was excoriated more than three thousand years ago, immersed in steaming acid and thrown into the pit. He can't touch you."

"You cannot seriously think that there is a connection between the memories placed in your mind and those in Mishra's," Urza argued. "At best there is a coincidence of sound, at worst . . . remember, Xantcha, your thoughts are not your own! Haven't you learned?"

Still clinging to Ratepe's hand, Xantcha faced Urza. "Why is it that everything you believe is the absolute truth and anything I believe is foolishness? I was meant to sleep here—right here in Dominaria. I dreamed of this place. I was decanted knowing the language that you and Mishra spoke as children. There is something about this world, above all the others, that draws Phyrexia back. They tried to conquer the Thran. That didn't work so they tried to get you and Mishra to conquer each other. Now they're trying a third time. Big wars didn't work, so they're trying lots of little wars. If you would listen to someone else for a change instead of always having to be the only one with the right answers—"

Ratepe squeezed Xantcha's hand and helped her to her feet. "Xantcha's got a point, Urza. Why here? Why do the Phyrexians come back to this world?"

Urza 'walked away rather than answer, and this time he didn't come back.

"I shouldn't have challenged him." Xantcha leaned against Ratepe, grateful to have someone to share her misery with, and aware, too, that she would have spoken much differently if there hadn't been three of them gathered around the Phyrexia wreckage. "I always lose my temper at the wrong time. He was so close to seeing the truth, but I had to have it all."

"You're more like Mishra than I am." Ratepe wrapped his arms around her. "Must've been something Gix poured in your vat."

He was jesting, but the joke made Xantcha's heart skip a beat. What had Gix said on the First Sphere plain? She remembered the spark and walling herself within herself, but the words hung outside of memory's reach. What had happened to Mishra's flesh? Flesh was rendered, never wasted. Had she been growing in the vats while Urza and Mishra fought? She'd thought she had.

Xantcha leaned back against Ratepe's arms and saw the thoughtful look on his face.

"Don't," she said, a plea more than a command. "Don't say anything more. Don't think anything more."

Arms tightened around her, one at her waist, the other cradling her head. She couldn't see his face, but she knew he hadn't stopped thinking.

Xantcha hadn't either, though there was neither joy nor satisfaction in any of her conclusions.

"We've got to leave," she said many silent moments later. "Someone's going to wonder what happened to the riders."

"If we're lucky, someone. Something, if we're not."

Xantcha grimaced. Ratepe's humor was missing its mark, and her arm, compressed between them, kept her edgy with its throbbing. "Whichever, we're going to have to leave this for someone else to sort out. I should've shoved the priest through before we destroyed the ambulator."

"Then there wouldn't have been anything for Urza to look at."

"Not sure whether that was good or bad."

Ratepe let her go and did most of the work assembling their supplies in a pile for the sphere to flow around. One look at his face and Xantcha knew he was disappointed that they weren't returning to Pincar City, but he never raised the subject. Her elbow had swollen to the size of a winter melon and her arm, from the shoulder down, looked as if it had been pumped full of water.

Her fingers resembled five purple sausages. Her arm was rigid, too. It had been centuries since she'd had an injury Urza hadn't healed, She'd almost forgotten how newts stiffened when they broke their bones.

If Xantcha had the nerves Ratepe had been born with, she would have been curled up, whimpering, on the ground. As it was, she was grateful for Ratepe's company, sought the calmest windstreams through the air, and brought them down frequently.

Twice over the following several days they spotted gangs of bearded men riding good horses through the summer heat. She grit her teeth and followed them, still hoping to find a Shratta stronghold, but both times the men ended their treks peaceably in palisaded villages. Either the religious fanatics had gone to ground or they'd gone from dreaded to welcome in little more than a season. She thought of going up to the gates and inviting herself into their councils, as she had scarcely a season earlier. Her arm kept her from acting on those thoughts.

"It was your idea to disperse those villagers, let them spread the word that it was Red-Stripes who were killing and burning in the Shratta's name," Xantcha reminded Ratepe as she guided the sphere to its prior course. "You're the one who told me that I was a friend because I was the enemy of your enemy. What did you expect?"

"Not this," Ratepe replied with a scowl. "Maybe I'm wiser now. The enemy of my enemy still has his own plans for me."

Xantcha let the provocative comment slide.

High summer was a season of clear, dry weather on Gulmany's north coast. They rounded the western prong of the Ohran Ridge without excitement and hit the first of the big southern coast storms at sunrise the next day. For three days they camped in a bear's hillside den waiting for the rain to stop. Xantcha's arm turned yellow. Her fingers came back to life, knuckle by spasmed knuckle.

Xantcha was in no hurry to get back to the cottage. Once her elbow recovered from its battering, she could enjoy Ratepe's company, and his attentions. There was always a bit of frustration. She simply didn't have the instincts for romance, or even pleasure, that Ratepe expected her to have. They loved and laughed and argued, walked as much as they soared the windstreams. They didn't see the cottage roof until the moon had swung twice through its phases, and there was a hint of frosts to come in the mountains' morning air.

"He's there," Ratepe said, pointing at the lone figure.

Xantcha blinked to assure herself that her eyes weren't lying, but it was Urza, tall, pale-haired and stripped to the waist beside the hearth, vigorously stirring something that bubbled and glowed in her best stew pot.

She'd always thought of Urza as a scholar, a man whose strength came from his mind, not his body, though Kayla had written that her husband built his own artifacts and had the stamina of an ox. Over the centuries, Urza had become dependent on abstract power, using sorcery or artifice rather than his hands whenever possible. The sight of a tanned, muscular, and sweating Urza left Xantcha speechless.

She would have preferred to approach this unfamiliar Urza cautiously from the side, but he spotted the sphere and waved.

"He seems glad to see us." Ratepe's voice was guarded.

Maybe it wasn't that Phyrexians had no imagination, but that their imaginations never prepared them for the truth. Xantcha reminded herself that Urza had her heart on a shelf. He'd followed it to Efuan Pincar. He could have found her again or crushed the amber stone in his fist.

She brought the sphere down beside the well. Urza ran toward them—ran, as a born-man might run to greet his family. He embraced Ratepe first, slapping him heartily on the back and calling him "brother." Xantcha turned away, telling herself she'd learned her lesson in the apple orchard. Urza didn't have to be sane, he didn't have to see anything except as he wished to see it, as long as he fought the Phyrexians. She hadn't quite finished the self-lecture when Urza put his hands on her shoulders.

"I've been busy," he said. "I went back to all those places I'd been before. I trusted my instincts. If I thought it was Phyrexian, I believed it was Phyrexian. I didn't need outside proof.

They have a new strategy, Xantcha. Instead of fighting their own war, or pulling the strings on one big war, they've stirred a hornet's nest of little wars just in Old Terisiare alone. I have no notion what they might be doing elsewhere.

"But I'll find out, Xantcha. I know Dominaria less well than I know a score of other planes, but that's going to change, too. Come, let me show you—"

He pulled Xantcha toward the cottage. She dug in her heels, a futile, but necessary protest.

"No, Xantcha, this time—this time I swear to the Thran, it is not like before." He gestured to Ratepe. "Brother! You come too. I have a plan!"

Urza did have a plan, and it truly was like nothing he'd done before. He'd drawn maps on his walls, maps on the floor, a map on the worktable, and maps on every other reasonably smooth surface in the workroom. No wonder he was working outside. The many-colored maps were annotated with numerals she could read and a script she couldn't. None of them made particular sense until she recognized the crescent-shaped capital of Baszerat on their common wall. After that she recognized several towns and cities, drawn upside down by her instincts, but accurate, so far as she could remember. She guessed the annotations included the number of *sleepers* he'd found in each city and asked:

"Are you going to drive the *sleepers* back to Phyrexia?"

"Yes, in proper time. The first time no one was left and the message was lost. The last time, no one knew what we faced until the very end and as you pointed out—" Urza included Ratepe in the discussion—"nobody believed the message. This time I will take no chances. The Phyrexians have chosen to fight a myriad of wars. I will fight them the same way, with a myriad of weapons. I will expose them! Watch!"

Urza left her and Ratepe standing in the middle of the room while he fussed with a tattered basket. His eagerness and delight would have been contagious, if Xantcha hadn't watched too many times before. She'd exchanged a worried-hopeful glance with Ratepe when the world erupted into chaos.

The chaos was a sound like Xantcha had never experienced, sound more piercing than the howling winds between-worlds. She tried to draw breath to yawn out her armor, but the sound had taken possession of her body. It shook her as a dog shook its fur after the rain and threw her to the floor. Her bones had turned to jelly before it reached into her skull and shook her mind out of her brain.

Control and reason returned as suddenly as they had departed. Except for a few bruises and a badly bitten tongue, Xantcha was no worse than dazed. She knew her name and where she was, but the rest was muddled. Ratepe stood a little distance away. Xantcha realized he hadn't been affected by the attack, but before she could consider the implications, Urza was beside her, cupping her chin in his hands, taking the pain away.

"It worked!" he exalted before she could stand. "I'm sorry, but there was no other way, and I had to be sure."

"You? You did that to me?" She propped herself up on one elbow.

"Wind, words, they're both the same. Sound is merely air in motion, like the sea. You said the priest collapsed because of the whistling shot. I have made a new artifact, Xantcha, a potent new weapon. It has no edge, no weight, no fire. It is sound."

Urza opened his hand, revealing a lump roughly the size and shape of a ceiling spider. Xantcha couldn't accept that something so simple had laid her low.

"It's too small," she complained. "Nothing so small could hurt so much."

"You gave me the idea when you said the oil was inside the *sleepers*. Sound, if it is the right sound, can move things, break things. The sound this artifact makes is one that shakes glistening oil until it breaks apart."

Xantcha would have said oil could not be broken if she had not just endured a sound that had proven otherwise.

"Do we throw them at the *sleepers*?"

"We plant them in all the places where Xantcha's scented *sleepers*," Ratepe said from the wall where he had studied several of the maps.

"Yes! Yes, exactly right, Brother!" Urza left Xantcha on the floor. "We will scatter them like raindrops!"

"What will set them off? They're too small for a wick or fuse."

"Ah, the Glimmer Moon, brother. A strange thing, the Glimmer Moon. It has virtually no effect on tides, but on sorcery— white-mana sorcery—it is like a magnet, pulling the mana toward itself, sometimes strong, sometimes not so strong, but strongest when the Glimmer Moon reaches its zenith. So, very simple, I make a spindly crystal and charge one end with white mana. I put the crystal inside the spider, in a drop of water where it floats on its side. When the Glimmer Moon goes high, it tugs the charged end of the crystal, which stands up in the drop of water, and my little spider makes the noise that affected Xantcha, but not you or I. It is as good as an arrow!"

"But just a bit more complicated," Ratepe warned.

"Geometry, brother," Urza laughed. "Astronomy. Mathematics. You never liked mathematics! Never learned to think in numbers. I have done all the calculations." He gestured at the writing-covered walls.

Xantcha had pulled herself to her feet. Her anger at being tricked had vanished. This was the Urza she'd been waiting for, the artifacts she'd been waiting for. "How powerful are they? I was what, maybe four paces away? How many will we need to flush out all the *sleepers* in a city? Hundreds, thousands?"

"Hundreds, maybe, in a town. Thousands, yes, in a city. The more you have, the greater the effect, though you must be very precise when you attach them to the walls. Too far is bad, too close is worse. They'll cancel each other out, and nothing at all will happen. I will show you in each town we pass through. And I will continue to refine them."

Ratepe's face had turned pensive. Xantcha thought it was because he'd play no part in Urza's grand plan, but he proved her wrong, as usual.

"We could just make things worse. I know Xantcha's Phyrexian, but when she fell just now I didn't guess she fell because she was Phyrexian. You're going to have something make a noise born-folks can hardly hear, but a few are going to collapse on the ground. People won't know why. They don't cut up corpses, they've never seen a Phyrexian priest. They'll think it's a god's doings and there's no guessing what they'll think after that."

"The *sleepers* will be gone, Brother. Dead. Lying on the ground. Let men and women think a god has spoken, if that's their desire. Phyrexia will know that Dominaria has struck back; and that's what matters: the message we send to Phyrexia. It is as good as saying that the Thran have returned."

"I'm only saying that if no one knows why, no one will understand, and ignorance is dangerous."

"Then, Brother, what would you have me do?" Urza demanded. "Handwriting in the sky? A whisper in every Dominarian ear? Would you have another war? Is that what you want, Mishra— another war across Terisiare? This way there is no war. The land is not raped. No one dies."

"The *sleepers* will die," Xantcha said.

In her mind's eye she saw the First Sphere and the other newts, the other Xantcha with its orange hair. She'd slain newts herself—she'd slain that other Xantcha when it got between her and food—but when she thought about vengeance against Phyrexia, she thought about priests and demons, not newts or *sleepers*. Her head said they had to be eliminated—killed. The artifact-spider's sound had gripped her. She believed it could kill, but not quickly or painlessly, and if her hunch was correct, that many of the *sleepers* didn't know they were Phyrexian, they wouldn't know why they suffered.

Ratepe and Urza were watching her.

"They have to die," she said quickly, defensively. "There's no place for them. . . ." A shiver ran down her back. Place, one of the oldest words in her memory. Her cadre never had a place. They were oxen, deprived of everything except their strength, used ruthlessly, discarded as meat when there was nothing left. "I'll do it," she snarled. "Don't worry. Waste not, want not. I'll do whatever has to be done until Phyrexia is rolled up like an ambulator and disappears." Her voice had thickened as it did when she yawned, but her throat was tight with tears, not armor. "But it's not true that no one will die."

Urza strode toward her. "Xantcha," he said softly, insincerely.

The open door beckoned. She ran through it. Urza tried to call her back:

"Xantcha, no one's talking about you . . . !"

She ran too far to hear the rest.

Chapter 18

There were other discussions, some less volatile, a few that had the three of them storming off in different directions, but in the end Ratepe and Xantcha fell in with Urza's plan to broadcast the screaming spiders—Ratepe named them—throughout Old Terisiare and anywhere else that Urza or Xantcha might sniff a Phyrexian in the air.

They had about three seasons to get the spiders arrayed on dusty walls and ceilings. By Urza's calculations the Glimmer Moon would strike its zenith above Old Terisiare a few days short of next year's midsummer's eve. Xantcha had little time for visiting unfamiliar places or searching out new Phyrexian infestations. The windstreams weren't fast enough. Urza 'walked her to realms where glistening oil tainted the air. Then he left her with a cache of spiders while he 'walked on with several thousand more. Nine days later, he'd examine her glowing amber heart, find her, and take her back to the cottage where Ratepe waited for them.

In a compromise between delusion and practicality, Urza had decided his brother's talents were uniquely suited to constructing spiders. Ratepe had tried to argue his way out of the responsibility, but Urza's instructions were clear and, aside from charging the white mana crystals, making the small artifacts was more tedious than difficult. Every nine days, when they were together at the cottage, Urza banished Ratepe and Xantcha from his workroom while he grew and charged the crystals.

Summer ended, autumn vanished, winter came, all without disrupting their cycles.

"Not that you couldn't do it," Urza would say, the same words every time he and Xantcha returned, as if they were written on the instructions he'd given Ratepe. "But you've been alone all this time, and Xantcha likes to talk to you. And I've got another idea or two I'd like to tinker with. I can make them better, make them louder, wider, more powerful. So, you two go on. Let me work. Go next door. Talk, eat, do as you like. I'll be busy here until tomorrow night."

"He's as mad as he ever was," Xantcha said as Ratepe put his weight against the workroom door, cracking the late-winter ice that had sealed it since Urza and Xantcha had left nine days earlier.

"He was mad long before the real Mishra died," Ratepe said lightly and regretted his nonchalance as he lost his footing on the slick wood. "You didn't really think anything was going to change that, did you?"

Like Urza, the two of them had fallen into habits and scripts, at least until they'd lit the oil lamp and the brazier and warmed the blankets of Xantcha's old bed. They seldom talked much or ate after that until the lamp needed replenishing.

"I want a favor from you," Ratepe said while Xantcha re-lit the lamp with a coal from the brazier.

Xantcha looked up silently.

"It's getting on toward a year."

She'd been expecting that. Winter lingered on the Ridge. It was spring in the lowlands, a bit more than two months shy of the year she'd asked of Ratepe in Medran. She and Urza were three-quarters through the workroom maps, but their chances of finishing the job before midsummer were nil, and none if Ratepe demanded the freedom she'd sworn to give him.

"You want to go back to Efuan Pincar." A statement, not a question. She made tea from the steaming water atop the brazier.

"No, I can count as well as you—better, usually. Urza needs me here until midsummer, at least. I have my doubts, so do you, but nobody knows what happens next. We agreed to take the risks."

"So, what's the favor?"

"I want you to go back to Efuan Pincar."

"Me?"

"Everywhere else the Phyrexians are all *sleepers*—everywhere, except Baszerat and Morvern, and they'll keep fighting each other with or without Phyrexian meddling. But I'm still worried about Efuan Pincar and the Shratta. We never went back—"

She interrupted. "I did. I plastered the walls of Medran and seven other towns while Urza did Pincar City. You said midsummer's the biggest holy day of Avohir's year and everybody goes to the temples, so I put a few spiders in the sanctuaries, just in case, but I didn't smell anything suspicious. My guess is that the Red-Stripes wiped out the Shratta years ago. Maybe they had Phyrexian help, maybe not. It's history now."

"I figured that, and that's why I want a favor. I've tinkered with the spiders—studied the changes that Urza's made since last summer, even made a few of my own and tested them, too."

Xantcha raised her eyebrows as she strained the tea.

"It's not like you didn't experiment with the cyst after Urza gave it to you," Ratepe retorted.

Xantcha decided not to pursue the argument.

"Urza doesn't count the crystals. I think he expects me to damage a few—and, anyway, we know the crystals work. It's the other part that I modified."

"You're not trying them out on me." She slammed the straining bowl on the table for emphasis.

"No, they're not like that, but I did change the sound they make. The way Urza had them set, the sound makes things boil. What I did makes solid things like rocks and especially mortar break down into sand and dust. And I want you to plant my spiders in the foundation of the Red-Stripe barracks and under the high altar of Avohir's temple in Pincar City. When the Glimmer

Moon passes overhead, the sound will rattle the stones until they come apart."

It would work, but, "Waste not, want not—why? Even if I could do it, why? Not that I care, personally, but Avohir is your god. Why would you want to turn Avohir's altar into rubble?"

"And the Red-Stripe barracks. Both. I want to make a sign for every Efuand to see that whatever strikes down the *sleepers* strikes down the Shratta, too. If there's any left anywhere, I don't want some bearded fanatic to take advantage of what we've done. All right, the Shratta didn't kill my family, but they drove us out of the city. They burnt the schools and the libraries. If the Phyrexians got rid of them, well, that's a mark in their favor, but I don't want to take the chance. Will you do it, Xantcha? For me?"

She followed the steam rising from her mug. "I'll talk to Urza."

"Urza can't know."

"Ratepe! I'm not just wandering out there. I 'walk out of here with Urza and nine days later I 'walk back with him. What am I supposed to do, yawn and hightail it up to Efuan Pincar the moment he sets me down and then hightail it back again?"

"That's what I thought you'd do."

"And when he asks about the spiders I was supposed to be planting?"

"I thought of that. You'll tell him they didn't feel right so you didn't spread 'em around. I've learned how to make duds, too. If he gets angry, he'll be angry at me for being careless."

"Wonderful."

"You'll do it?"

"Let me think about it. Lying to Urza. I can get angry with him, I can yell at him and keep secrets, but I don't know if I can outright lie to him."

Ratepe didn't push, not that night, but he asked again the next time they were together and alone. If he'd gotten her angry, just once, she'd have put the whole cockeyed notion behind her, but Ratepe was too canny for that. Passionate, yet totally in control. Xantcha wondered what Kayla Bin-Kroog would have thought. She wondered whether Kayla would have stood under the stars as she herself did a few visits later and said:

"We're getting to the end. He's taking me to Russiore tomorrow. It's not infested with *sleepers*. More important, it's not far from Efuan Pincar. I can get down the coast to Pincar City, plant your spiders and cover Russiore, too."

Ratepe lifted Xantcha off the ground and, before she had a chance to protest, spun on his heels, whirling her around three times while he laughed out loud. She was gasping and giddy when her feet touched down.

"I knew you would!"

He kissed her, a kiss that began in joy and ended in passion as he lifted her up again.

* * * * *

The next evening, when Urza took her wrist for 'walking, Xantcha was sure that he knew she had extra spiders in her sack and deceit in her heart. She couldn't meet his eyes at their most ordinary.

"There is no shame to it, Xantcha," Urza said moments later when they stood on a hillside above the seacoast principality of Russiore. "He is a young man and you prefer yourself as a woman. I heard you laughing with him last night. I racked my memory but I don't think I've ever heard you or him so happy. It does my old bones good. After Russiore, I shall go off and leave you two alone together."

Urza vanished then, which was just as well, Xantcha needed to breathe and couldn't until he was gone.

Urza's bones, she thought with a shudder. Urza doesn't have any bones, she chided herself and yawned out the sphere.

The sphere rose swiftly through the ground breezes until the ocean windstreams caught it and threw it south, an abrupt reminder—as if Xantcha needed one—that she made mistakes when she was distracted. She wove her hand through the wind, pushing the sphere to its limit. Dawn's light revealed Efuand villages. Morning found her walking the market road into Pincar City.

Xantcha had scattered spiders all winter without once breaking a sweat, but she was damp and pasty-mouthed when a Red-Stripe guard asked her particulars at the city gate. He had a mortally unpleasant face, a mortally unpleasant smell.

"Ratepe," she told him, "son of Mideah of Medran." Despite anxiety, Xantcha's accent was flawless, and the coins of Russiore were common enough along Gulmany's northern coast that she could offer a few as a bribe, if needs be.

"Here for?"

"I've come to pray before Avohir's holy book on the fifth anniversary of my father's death."

Ratepe had said there was no more solemn obligation in a Efuand son's life. No born Red-Stripe would question it, and no Phyrexian would last long if it did.

"Peace go with you," the Red-Stripe said and touched Xantcha on both cheeks, a gesture which Ratepe had warned het to expect. "May your burdens be lifted."

Xantcha went through the gate in peace, her burdens hung from her shoulder, exactly as she'd packed them. She knew where the garrison barracks were and that they'd be swarming with Red-Stripes most of the day. That left the temple, which might be just as busy but was open to anyone who needed Avohir's grace. Ratepe had taught her the necessary prayers, when and where to wash her hands, and not to jump if anyone sprinkled seawater on her head while she was on her knees.

Three thousand years, more worlds than she could count, and always—always—an outsider.

The square altar was as tall as a man and stood on a stairway dais that was almost as high. Xantcha could barely see the holy book laid open atop it, although it was the largest book she'd ever seen—bigger than her bed. A huge cloth of red velvet covered the altar from the book to the dais. As Xantcha watched from the back of the sanctuary, an old man climbed the dais steps on his knees. At the top he lifted the velvet over his head and shoulders. He was letting Avohir dry his tears; she would be affixing Ratepe's spiders.

Xantcha claimed a space at the end of the line of mourners, petitioners, and cripples shuffling along a marked path to the dais where a red-robed priest guarded the steps. She was under the great dome, halfway to the altar, when a second priest came to take the place of the first. The second priest also wore a red robe with its cowl drawn up. His beard, as black as Ratepe's hair, spilled onto his chest.

Shratta, Xantcha thought, remembering what Ratepe had told her in the burning village.

He'd been at his post a few moments before the air brought her the scent of glistening oil.

Xantcha tried to get a look within the priest's cowl as her turn on the dais stairway neared. The oil scent was strong, but no stronger than with other *sleepers*. She didn't expect to see glowing or lidless eyes and his—its—hands, which she tried unsuccessfully to avoid, had a fleshy feel around hers.

"Peace be with you," he said, more sincere than the guard. Xantcha held her breath when he touched her cheeks. "May your burdens be lifted."

The path was clear, as simple as that, as simple as Ratepe had promised it would be. She hobbled on her knees, like everyone else, raised the velvet drape and flattened an artifact against the dark stone. A second spider on the opposite side would be a good idea, four would be better. Xantcha gazed up into the dome as she left, looking for a sphere-sized escape hole.

There were no holes in the roof, but there was one in the wall—an archway into a cloister where a few laymen in plain clothes appeared to be continuing their prayers. Xantcha took the chance and joined them. No one challenged her, and after she bruised her knees a while longer, she yawned out Urza's armor and left the cloister through a different door.

The smell of oil was stronger in the corridor beyond the cloister. Not a great surprise. She was in the priests' private quarters now. The corridors were poorly ventilated, and under such circumstances she'd expected the taint to thicken, but there was something more. Xantcha palmed a handful of screaming spiders from her sack, affixed them to the wall, and pressed deeper into the tangled chambers behind the sanctuary. The scent grew stronger and more complex. She suspected there was an ambulator nearby, or perhaps one of the vertical disks she'd seen so long ago in Moag.

We call them priests, she reminded herself, although there were no gods in Phyrexia, only the Ineffable, and blind obedience wasn't religion.

Midway down a spiral stairway, Xantcha encountered a priest rushing for the surface. Without a gesture or apology, he shoved her against the spiral's spine. She slipped down two, treacherously narrow, steps before catching her balance. The scent of glistening oil was heavy in his wake, but except in rudeness, he hadn't noticed her.

In her mind, Xantcha heard Ratepe muttering, *Phyrexians: no imagination!* Ratepe was young. He hid his fears in sarcasm. She put one of his stone-shattering spiders on the spiral's spine.

The stairway ended in a vaulted crypt. Light came from a pair of filthy lanterns and Phyrexian glows attached haphazardly to the stone ribs overhead. The sight of Phyrexian artifacts answered a wealth of questions and left her feeling anxious within Urza's armor. Xantcha thought again of Moag and wondered if she shouldn't scurry back to Russiore, confess her deceit when Urza came for her, and let him explore the crypt instead of her. But the truth was that Xantcha feared Urza's anger more than she feared Phyrexia.

Tiptoeing forward, Xantcha silently apologized to Ratepe. The crypt's air was pure Phyrexia. Not only was there some sort of passageway in Avohir's temple, it was wide open. She might have to tell Urza what she'd found, after she knew what it was, after she'd shared her discoveries with Ratepe, with Mishra.

Xantcha came to another door, the source of a fetid Phyrexian breeze. She hesitated. She had her armor, a boot knife and a handful of fuming coins, a passive defense and no offense worth mentioning. Wisdom said, this is foolish, then she heard a sound behind her, on the spiral stairs, and wisdom said, *hide!*

Three steps beyond the door the corridor jogged sharply to the right and into utter darkness. Xantcha put one hand behind her back and finger-walked into the unknown. The loudest sound was the pulsing in her ears. She had a sense that she'd entered a larger chamber when the breeze died.

She had a sense, too, that she wasn't alone; she was right.

"Meatling."

Thirty-four hundred years, give or take a few decades, and Xantcha knew that voice instantly.

"Gix."

Light bloomed around him, gray, heavy light such as shone on the First Sphere, light that wasn't truly light, but visible darkness. Xantcha thought the demon was the light's source and needed a moment to discern the upright disk gleaming behind him.

Gix had changed since the last time she'd seen him, corroded, crumbling, and thrust into a fumarole. He'd changed since the first time, too—taller. She looked at his waist when she looked straight ahead; symmetric, altogether more man-shaped, though his metal "skin" didn't completely hide the glistening sinews and tubes—like a born-man's veins only filled with glistening oil— that wound over his green-gold skin. Gix's forehead was monumental and framed a rubine gem that was almost certainly a weapon. His skull seemed to have been pivoted open along his brow ridge. A black-metal serrated spike ran from the base of his neck to the now-raised base of his skull. From the side, it looked like the spike was rooted in his spine and attached to a red, blue, and yellow fish.

In another circumstance, the demon would have been ludicrous or absurd. Far beneath Avohir's altar, he was the image of malignity and horror. Xantcha stood transfixed as a narrow beam of blood-red light shone between her and Gix's bulging forehead. She felt surprise, then a command:

Obey. Listen and obey.

"Never." Urza's armor wasn't perfect protection against the demon's invasion of her mind, but added to her own stubbornness and to the walls she'd made ages ago, Xantcha defied the demon. "I'll die first."

Gix grinned, all glistening teeth and malice. "Your wish—"

He probed her mind again, brutally. Xantcha fed him images of his excoriation. The demon withdrew suddenly, his metallic chin tucked in a parody of mortal surprise.

"So old?"

Light sprang up in the portal chamber, a catacomb, with desiccated bodies heaped here and there, all male, all bearded. The Shratta, if not all of them, then at least a hundred of them, and probably their leaders. Replaced with Phyrexians or simply exterminated? Like as not, she'd never know. Whatever their crimes, Xantcha knew the Shratta would have suffered horribly before they died; that would have to suffice for Rat's vengeance.

"Yes, I remember you," Gix whispered. "One of the first, and still here?" His metal-sheathed shoulders jerked. "No. Not sent. I saved you back . . . Waiting. Waiting . . ." The demon's voice faded. The light in its forehead flickered. "Xantcha." He made her name long and sibilant, like a snake sliding over dried leaves. "My special one. Here . . . in Dominaria?"

Before Gix had needed cables and talons to caress Xantcha chin. Now he used light and encountered Urza's armor.

"What is this?"

The light bored into her right eye, seeking Xantcha's past, her history. Defiantly, she threw out images of Urza's dragon burning through the Fourth Sphere ceiling.

"Yes. Yes, of course. Locked out of Dominaria, where else would you go? I gave you purpose and you pursued it. You pursue it still."

The light became softer. It caressed Xantcha's mind. She shivered within Urza's armor.

"I'll tell Urza that the demon who destroyed his brother has returned."

It was a guess on Xantcha's part, Ratepe had seen Gix in Mishra's Weakstone recordings, but he'd never said anything about the Phyrexians who'd undertaken Mishra's compleation. But it was a good guess.

"Yes," Gix sighed. "Tell Urza that Gix has returned. Tell him the Thran are waiting for him."

Xantcha didn't understand. The Phyrexians had fought the Thran. Her mind swirled with echoes of Urza's lectures about Koilos and a noble race that sacrificed itself for Dominaria's future.

Gix laughed. All the raucous birds and chittering insects of summer couldn't have equaled the sound. "Did he tell you that? He knows better. He was there."

The statement made no sense. Urza had found his eyes at Koilos and through them, remembered the final battle between the Thran and the Phyrexians, but he hadn't been there. Gix was toying with her, feeding on her confusion and terror, waiting for her to make the mistake that would let him into her secret places.

"You have no secrets, Xantcha." More laughter. "I made the stone the brothers broke, and I made the brothers, too, and then I made you."

"Lies," Xantcha shot back and remembered standing beside a vat. A body floated below the surface: dark haired, angular, sexless . . . her. "There were a thousand of us," she shot back.

"Seven thousand, and only one like you. I looked for you . . . after."

After he escaped the Seventh Sphere? "I have my own heart."

"Yes. You have done well, Xantcha. Better than I hoped. I had plans for you. I still have them. Come back. Listen and obey!"

Gix pulled a string in Xantcha's mind. She felt herself begin to unravel. Newts had no importance. Newts did what they were told. Newts listened and obeyed. She belonged with Gix, to Gix, in Phyrexia, her home. Gix would take care of her. The demon was the center. She would do as he wished.

Urza's armor was in the way. . . .

Xantcha was about to release the armor when she thought of Ratepe. Suddenly there was nothing else except his face, laughing, scowling, watching her as she walked across the Medran plaza with a purse of gold on her belt. The sensations lasted less than a heartbeat, then Gix was back, but Xantcha hadn't needed a whole heartbeat to retreat from the destructive folly she'd been about to commit.

"So, you found him," Gix said after he'd retreated from her mind. "Does he please you?"

The red light continued to shine in her eye. Gix would pull another string, and this time there'd be no Ratepe, son of Mideah, to surprise the demon. Ratepe had given Xantcha a second chance, but she had to seize it. And Xantcha did, diving to her left, toward the corridor. Something hard and heavy struck her back. It threw her forward. She skidded face-first along the floor-stones, surrounded by red light, but the armor held. Xantcha scrambled to her feet and ran for her life. Demons weren't accustomed to defiance. They had no reflex response to stop a newt's desperate escape. Gix chased her, but he didn't catch her before she reached the spiral stairway.

He howled and clawed the stones, but the passage was too tight, too narrow. A fireball engulfed Xantcha in an acid wind. She clung to the spine until it passed, then ran again, through the corridor, the cloister and into Avohir's sanctuary.

Night had fallen on the plaza. Xantcha wasted no time asking herself where the day had gone. She released the armor, yawned out the sphere as soon as she dared, and headed up the coast to Russiore.

Chapter 19

Urza and Xantcha 'walked away from Serra's realm not long after Xantcha gave him her heart. Xantcha was scarcely wiser about the imperfections of Serra's creation than she'd been when she'd walked into the palace, though it was clear that her presence, so close to the Cocoon, affected not only the realm as a whole but Sosinna's recovery from the Aegis burns. For Sosinna and Kenidiern, Xantcha would have accepted Serra's offer of transit to another, natural and inherently balanced world, but the offer was not made a second time. Urza accepted Serra's judgment. Even though he distrusted Xantcha as a Phyrexian, he'd been through too much with her to go on alone.

He held Xantcha in his arms for that first terrible step across the chasm that separated a willfully created plane from the natural multiverse. She held a sealed chest nearly filled with gifts from Lady Serra. The gifts included a miniature cocoon that was the perfect size for Xantcha's amber heart.

Their first natural world was a tiny, airless moon circling another world that appeared to be one vast blue-green ocean, though Urza said otherwise. He made a chamber beneath the moon's surface and filled it with breathable air, his usual course in a place where he could survive indefinitely but Xantcha could not.

"A terrible thing, this," he said, removing Xantcha's heart from the chest and placing it in a niche he had just finished. "I believe it contains everything they took away from you, even your soul."

Despite his incursion into Phyrexia, and Lady Serra's assertion that Xantcha wholly and entirely differed from any born man or woman, Urza wouldn't surrender his belief that she'd been stolen from her parents and abominably transformed by her Phyrexian captors. She no longer bothered arguing the point with him. It was reassuring to be treated as he had always treated her.

"I would destroy it, if I could find a way to return what it has taken. But that mystery does not solve itself easily, and I cannot devote my energies to it until I have determined the first plane of the Phyrexians and my vengeance has feasted on their entrails. You will understand that vengeance must come first."

Xantcha nodded unnecessarily. Urza had not asked her a question. His concentration did not extend beyond his own thoughts, and he didn't notice her head moving.

"Serra and I determined that the true number of natural planes in the multiverse cannot be counted, even by an immortal. If one started at the beginning, new planes would have emerged, and old planes would have disappeared before the count was concluded. This is not, however, an insurmountable problem, as we can be certain that the Phyrexians were not driven away from a freshly engendered plane, and while it would be a tragedy if their keystone plane had succumbed to entropy and reorganization, we need not blame ourselves for the loss. Thus, it is only necessary that I start somewhere and proceed with great precision until I reach the end, which, with the multiverse, is also the beginning. Do you understand what this means?"

Xantcha nodded again, confident that Urza would continue explaining himself until her answer was truthful.

"Good. I will, of necessity, 'walk lightly. I had thought of creating my own plane, since such planes are always accessible across the chasm, but I would have to create a plane in which both you and I could thrive, and Serra told me that such a creation would be quite difficult to manage. Black essence, which is to say your essence, and white, which is mine, are deeply opposed to each other and virtually impossible to balance in the microcosm of a created plane. Now, I do not shirk challenges, but I must avenge my brother before I allow myself the pleasures of pure research, thus I have put creation out of my mind. I will make do with bolt-holes such as this, which I will forge and relocate as I have need of them. There is an element of proximity in the multiverse, and eventually one is within an easy 'walk of a particular plane.

"This should be an especial relief to you, Xantcha, since I will keep your heart in such a place where it cannot be lost or disturbed. It is also useful for me, since when I know where you are, I also know where your heart is, and contrariwise as well. And Serra has returned that crystal pendant I gave you while I was fleeing Phyrexia." He fished it out of one of the many boxes and draped it around Xantcha's neck. "You, I, and your heart and my pendant together make a single unit, a triangle, the strongest of angled structures. None of us can get lost."

Triangles . . . triangles with four points? It had to be mathematics. . . . Of all the lessons Xantcha had been taught in the Fane of Flesh, mathematics had come hardest. She'd long since learned that she didn't need to understand the why of mathematics if she simply followed all the rules. If the rules turned her heart into one of a triangle's four parts, she'd keep quiet about it. And she'd survive with her heart in a niche on an airless moon the same way she'd survived the centuries when it had lain in the Phyrexian vault.

"What do you need of me?" she asked, hoping to forestall any further discussion of unimaginable triangles.

"You are good at sniffing out Phyrexians. When we reach a plane, I want you to explore it, as you would anyway, looking for infestations."

"I'll need to use the sphere, is that all right?" The modifications remained a sore point between them. "You'll fix it so it isn't black anymore?"

Urza ignored her questions. "For me, being somewhere quickly is easier than getting there slowly. I will search for the victors, the folk who drove the Phyrexians out and forced them to create Phyrexia."

You will do what you want, Xantcha thought in the most private corner of her mind. Of course, so would she. Life was never better than when she was soaring the windstreams, chasing her curiosity, trading trinkets with strangers, and collecting the stories that born-folk told.

"What do I do if I find a Phyrexian infestation?" She liked the word, her mind filled with possible ways to drive out an infestation.

"You run away. The moment you are aware of Phyrexians, you hide yourself in the meeting place I'll point out to you, and you wait for me. I'll take no more chances with you and Phyrexians. You are vulnerable to them, Xantcha. It's no fault of yours—you're brave and good-spirited—but they tainted you. You are a bell goat and after you followed me to Phyrexia, my enemies were able to use you to find me—much as I will use your heart to find you."

I never told you the Ineffable's name. That's how they found you. Xantcha thought, but said nothing. She'd made her choice to stay with Urza, even knowing his obsessions and madness. If he reordered his memories of the past to absolve himself of blame or responsibility, well—he'd done it before and he'd do it again. Xantcha believed in vengeance against Phyrexia and believed that Urza, with all his flaws, stood a better chance of achieving it than she.

So they began their quest for the victors, the folk who'd driven the Phyrexians out of the natural multiverse. Urza set his mark on each world they visited, regardless of its hospitality. That way, he said, they would know when they'd come full circle. Xantcha wasn't certain about the full circle notion; it raised some of the same problems as a four-pointed triangle, but the marks kept them from accidentally exploring the same world twice.

It was no surprise to Xantcha that they found very few hospitable worlds where the Phyrexians had not made an appearance. She'd been a dodger. She knew about the relentless explorations carried out by the searcher-priests. The first few decades after leaving Serra's realm, she'd spent most of her time huddled up at whatever meeting place Urza designated, then gradually Urza had relaxed his rules. She could wander freely, provided she encountered no *active* Phyrexians.

Thus began a long, golden period of wandering the multiverse. Every handful of worlds held one that was hospitable enough for Xantcha to exchange Urza's armor for the sphere. Every ten or twelve handfuls of hospitable worlds revealed one that was interesting, at least to Xantcha. She became the tourist who delighted in minor variations, while Urza was on a single-minded quest.

"They were here," he said when they rejoined each other. They met in a white stone grotto of a world where elves were the dominant species and civilization was measured by forests, not cities.

"I know," Xantcha agreed, having found the spoor of two searcher expeditions and heard tales of demons with glistening, metallic skin in several languages. "Searchers came through a good long time ago. They're remembered as demons and the bringers of chaos. They came through again, maybe a thousand local years ago, but only in a few places. They collected beasts both times, I think. There's metal here, but no mines. The searchers will come back again. They're waiting for the elves to do the hard work of opening the ground."

Urza nodded though he wasn't happy. "How did you learn such things? There are no centers of learning here, few records in the ground or above it. I have found it most frustrating!"

"I talk to everyone, Urza. I trade with them," she explained, handing Urza a sack filled with trinkets and treasures, her profits from three seasons' wandering. He'd take them to the bolt-hole where he kept her heart. "Everyone has a story."

"A story, Xantcha—what I want is the truth! The hard-edged truth."

She squared her shoulders. "The truth is, this is not the victor's world. I could have told you that before the sun set twice."

"And how could you have done that?"

"No one here knows a word for war."

Urza stiffened. A planeswalker didn't have to listen with his ears. He could skim thought and meaning directly off the surface of another mind and drink down a new language like water. As a result, Urza seldom paid attention to the actual words he heard or spoke. He handled surprise poorly, embarrassment, worse. His breathing stopped, and his eyes shed their mortal illusion.

"I have encountered a new world," he snapped after a pensive moment. *Equilor.* His lips hadn't moved.

Xantcha didn't disbelieve him, although Equilor wasn't a word that she remembered hearing on this or any other world. "Is it a name?" she asked cautiously.

"An old name. The oldest name. The farthest plane. It belongs to a plane on the edge of time."

"Another created world, like Phyrexia or Serra's realm?"

"No, I think not. I hope not."

She'd wager, if she'd ever been the wagering sort, that Urza hadn't learned of Equilor from the elves of the forest world but had heard of it years ago and forgotten it until just now when she'd challenged him.

They set out at once, with no more preparation than Urza made for any between-worlds journey. He explained that preparation and, especially, directions weren't important. 'Walking the between-worlds wasn't like walking down a path. There was no north or south, left or right, only the background glow of all the planes that were and, rising out of the glow, a sense of those planes that a 'walker could reach in a single stride. By choosing the faintest of the rising planes at each step, Urza insisted they would in time arrive at Equilor, the plane on the edge of time.

Xantcha couldn't imagine a place where direction didn't matter, but then, for her the between-worlds remained as hostile as it had been the first time Urza dragged her through it. For her the between-worlds was a changeless place of paradox and sheer terror.

At first, the only evidence she had that Urza was doing anything different was indirect. Her armor crumbled, the instant Urza released her, in the air of the next, new world. There was breathable air in each new world they 'walked to, as if he'd at last given up the notion that the Phyrexians could have begun on a world without air. And Urza himself was exhausted when they arrived. He would go into the ground and sleep as much as a local year while she explored.

They were some thirty worlds beyond the elven forest world when Urza announced, as Xantcha shook herself free of flaking armor:

"Here you do not need to look for Phyrexians. Here we will find others of my kind."

Urza didn't mean that he'd brought her to Dominaria. Every so often, he journeyed alone to the brink of his birth-world to assure himself that it remained safe within the Shard they'd discovered long ago. Urza meant, instead, that he'd broken an age-old habit and set them down on a plane where other 'walkers congregated.

He'd never insinuated that he was unique, at least as far as 'walking between-worlds. Serra was a 'walker and so, Xantcha suspected, had been the Ineffable. But Urza had avoided other 'walkers until they came to the abandoned world he called Gastal.

"Be wary," he warned Xantcha. "I do not trust them. Without a plane to bind them, 'walkers forget what they were. They become predators, unless they go mad."

Knowing Urza fell in the latter category, Xantcha stayed carefully in his shadow as they approached a small, fanciful, and entirely illusory pavilion standing by itself on a barren, twilight plain, but the three men and two women they met there seemed unthreatening. They knew Urza—or knew of him—and welcomed him as a prodigal brother, though Xantcha couldn't actually follow their conversation: planeswalkers conversed directly in one another's minds.

But Urza was not the only 'walker who tempered his solitary life with a more ordinary companion. Outside the pavilion, Xantcha met two other women, one of them a blind dwarf, who braved the between-worlds on a 'walker's arm. Throughout the balmy night, the three of them sought a common language through which to share experience and advice. By dawn they'd made progress in a creole that was mixed mostly from elven dialects from a hundred or more worlds. Xantcha had just pieced together that Varrastu, a dwarf, had heard of Phyrexia when Urza emerged to say it was time to move on.

Xantcha rose reluctantly. "Varrastu said that she and Manatarqua have crossed swords with folk made from flesh and metal—"

Words failed as a second sun, yellowish-green in color, loomed suddenly high overhead. The air exploded as it hurtled toward them. Xantcha had the wit to be frightened but hadn't begun to guess why or to yawn Urza's armor from the cyst, when the pavilion burst into screaming flames, and Urza seized her against his chest. He pulled her between-worlds. Without the armor to protect her, she was bleeding and gasping when they re-emerged.

Urza laid her on the ground then cradled her face in his hands. "Don't go," he whispered.

It seemed an incongruous request. Xantcha wasn't about to go anywhere. The between-worlds had battered her to exhaustion. Her body seemed to have already fallen asleep. She wanted only to close her eyes and join it.

"No!" Urza pinched her cheeks. "Stay awake! Stay with me!"

Power like fire or countless sharp needles swirled around her. Xantcha fought feebly to escape the pain. She pleaded with him to release her.

"Live!" he shouted. "I won't let you die now."

Death would have been preferable to the torture flowing from Urza's fingers, but Xantcha hadn't the strength to resist his will. Mote by mote, he healed her and dragged her back from the brink.

"Sleep now, if you wish."

His hand passed over her eyes. For an instant, there was darkness and oblivion, then there was light, and Xantcha was herself again. She exhaled a pent-up breath and sat up.

"I don't know what came over me."

"Death," Urza said calmly. "I nearly lost you."

She remembered the yellow-green sun. "We must go back, Varrastu—Manatarqua—"

"Crossed swords with the Phyrexians. Yes. Manatarqua was the pavilion. She died on Gastal."

A shudder raced down Xantcha's spine. There was more that Urza wasn't saying. "How long ago?"

"In the time of this plane, nearly two years."

Xantcha noticed her surroundings: a bare-walled chamber with a window but not a door. She noticed herself. Her skin was white. It cracked and flaked when she moved, as if her armor clung in dead layers around her. Her hair, which she always hacked short around her face, hung below her shoulders. "Two years," she repeated, needing to say the words herself to make them true in her mind. "Long years?"

"Very long," Urza assured her. "You've recovered. I never doubted that you would, if I stayed beside you. You'll be hungry soon. I'll get food now. Tomorrow or the next day we'll move on toward Equilor."

Already Xantcha felt her stomach churning to life—after two empty years. Food would be nice, but there was another question: "At Gastal, Manatarqua—you said she 'was the pavilion.' Do you mean that she was Phyrexian and that you slew her?"

"No, Manatarqua was a 'walker like myself, but much younger. I have no idea why she presented herself as an object. I didn't ask, it was her choice. Perhaps she hoped to hide from her enemies."

"Phyrexians?"

"Other planeswalkers. I told you, they—we—can become predatory, especially toward the newly sparked. I was nearly taken myself in the beginning—Meshuvel was her name. She was no threat to me. My eyes reveal sights no other 'walker can see. Until Serra, I avoided my own kind. They had no part to play in my quest for vengeance. I'd been thinking about 'walkers since leaving Serra's realm. I thought I might need someone more like myself."

"But they died."

"Manatarqua died. I suspect the others escaped unharmed, as I did. They prey on the young and the mortal because a mature 'walker is no easy target. But I had made up my mind almost from the start. I don't need another 'walker. I need you. To finally realize that and then feel you die so soon afterward—it was almost enough to make me worship the fickle gods."

Xantcha imagined Urza on his knees or in a temple. She closed her eyes and laughed. He was gone when she reopened them, and she was too stiff yet to climb through the window. Her saner self insisted that Urza wouldn't abandon her, not after sitting beside her for two years, not after what he'd just said about needing her. Then this world's sun passed beyond the window. Sanity's voice grew weaker as shadows lengthened. Of all the ways Xantcha knew to die, starvation was among the worst. She had dragged herself to the window and was hauling herself over the sill when she felt a breeze at her back. The breeze was thick with fresh bread, roasted meat, and fruit. Urza had returned.

He called the meal a celebration and ate with her, at least until a more ordinary sort of tiredness drove Xantcha back to the bed where she'd lain for so long. She awoke with the sun. There was a door beside the window, more food and, somewhere beyond the sun, near the edge of time, a world called Equilor.

* * * * *

Later, after they'd gotten to Dominaria, when Xantcha sorted through her memories, the largest pile belonged to the years they had searched for Equilor. Every season, for much more than a thousand Dominarian years, she and Urza wandered the multiverse, taking other worlds' measure. There were surprises and excitement, mostly of the minor variety. After Serra's realm, Phyrexia seemed to lose interest in them—or, at least, had lost their trail. Though they sometimes found evidence of searcher-priests and excavations. Eventually, everything they found was long abandoned.

"I'm headed in the right direction," Urza would say whenever they came upon eroded ruins no one else would have noticed. "I'm headed toward the world that cast them out."

Xantcha was never so confident, but she never understood how Urza found anything in the between-worlds, much less how he distinguished hospitable worlds from inhospitable ones, near from far. She was content to follow a path that led endlessly away from the Phyrexia she knew and toward the vengeance that seemed equally distant. Until the day when they came to a quiet, twilight world.

"The edge of time itself," Urza said as he released Xantcha's wrists.

She shed her armor and filled her lungs with air that was unlike any other. "Old," she said after a few moments. "It's as if everything's finished—not dead, just done growing and changing. Even the mountains are smoothed down, like they've been standing too long, but nothing's come to replace them." She gestured toward the great, dark lump that dominated the landscape like a risen loaf of bread. "Somehow, I expected an edge to have sharp angles."

Urza nodded. "I expected a plane where everything had been put to use, not like this, neglected and left fallow."

Yet not completely fallow. As twilight deepened, lights winked open near the solitary mountain. There was a road, too: a ribbon of worn gray stone, cut in chevrons and fitted so precisely that not a blade of grass grew between them. Urza insisted he had no advance idea of what a new plane was like, no way at all of selecting the exact place where his feet would touch the ground, yet, more often than not, he 'walked out of the between-worlds in sight of a road and a town.

They began to travel down the road.

A carpet of bats took flight from the mountain, passing directly over their heads. When their shrill chirping had subsided, other noises punctuated the night: howls, growls and a bird with a sweet, yet mournful song. Stars appeared, unfamiliar, of course, and scattered sparsely across the clear, black sky. No moon outshone them, but it was the nature of moons to produce moonless nights now and again. What surprised Xantcha was the scarcity of stars, as if time were stars and the black sky were itself the edge of time.

"A strange place," Xantcha decided as they strode down the road. "Not ominous or inhospitable, but filled with secrets."

"So long as one of them is Phyrexia, I won't care about the rest."

The light came from cobweb globes hovering above the road and the three-score graceful houses of an unfortified town. Urza lifted himself into the air to examine them and reported solemnly that he had not a clue to their construction or operation.

"They simply are," he said, "and my instinct is to leave them alone."

Xantcha smiled to herself. If that was Urza's instinct then whatever the globes were, they weren't simple.

A man came out to meet them. He appeared ordinary enough,

though Xantcha understood how deceptive an ordinary appearance could be, and it bothered her that she hadn't noticed him leave any one of the nearby houses, hadn't noticed him at all until he was some fifty paces ahead and walking toward them. He wore a knee-length robe over loose trousers, both woven from a pale, lightweight fiber that rippled as he moved and sparkled as if it were shot with silver. His hair and beard were dark auburn in the globe light and neatly trimmed. A few wrinkles creased the outer corners of his eyes. Xantcha placed him in the prime of mortal life, but she'd place Urza there, too.

"Welcome, Urza," the stranger said. "Welcome to Equilor. We've been waiting for you."

Chapter 20

Xantcha had understood every word the auburn-haired man had said, an unprecedented happening on a new world. She dug deep into her memory trying to recognize the language and missed the obvious: the stranger spoke Argivian, the sounds of Urza's long-lost boyhood and of her newt-ish dreams, the foundation of the argot she and Urza spoke to each other. But if this were Dominaria, then Urza would have recognized the stars, and if the stranger were another 'walker with the power to absorb languages without time or effort, then why had he said, We've been waiting?

The stranger touched his forehead, lips, and heart before embracing Urza, cheek against cheek. Urza bent into the gesture, as he would not have done if he were suspicious.

"And you're . . . Xantcha."

The stranger turned his attention to her. He'd hesitated before stating her name. Taking it from her mind? Not unless he were much better at such things than Urza was; she'd felt no violation. Once again the stranger touched himself three times before embracing her exactly as he'd embraced Urza. His hands were warm, with the texture of flesh and bone. His breath was warm, too, and faintly redolent of onions.

"Waiting for us?" Urza demanded before asking the stranger's name or any other pleasantry. "Before sunset I was elsewhere, very much elsewhere. And until now, I did not know for certain that I had found the place I have been seeking for so long."

"Yes, waiting," the stranger insisted, keeping one hand beneath Xantcha's elbow and guiding Urza toward one of the houses with the other. "You 'walk the planes. We have been aware of your approach for quite some time now. It is good to have you here at last."

Xantcha glanced behind the stranger's shoulders. Urza had devised a code, simple hand and facial movements for moments when they were among mind-skimmers. She made the sign for danger and received the sign for negation in response. Urza wasn't worried as the stranger led them through a simple stone-built gate and into a tall, open-roofed atrium.

There were others in the atrium, a woman at an open hearth, stirring a pot of stew that was the source of the onions Xantcha had smelled earlier, two other women and a man, all adults, all individuals, yet bound by a familial resemblance. An ancient sat in a wicker chair—wrinkled, toothless, and nearly bald. Xantcha couldn't guess if she beheld a man or a woman. Beyond the ancient, in another atrium, two half-grown children dangled strings for a litter of kittens, while a round-faced toddling child watched her from behind the banister at the top of a stairway.

Of them all, only the toddler betrayed even a faint distrust of uninvited guests. Where moments earlier Xantcha had warned Urza of danger, she now began to wonder why the household seemed so unconcerned. Didn't they see her knives and sword? Had they no idea what a 'walker could do—especially a 'walker named Urza?

"There is a portion for you," the hearth-side woman said specifically to Xantcha, as she ladled out a solitary bowl and set it on the table that ran the length of the atrium. Like the man who'd met them on the road, she spoke Argivian, but with a faint accent. "You must be hungry after your journey here."

Xantcha was hungry. She caught Urza's eyes again and passed the general sign that asked, What should I do?

"Eat," he said. "The food smells delicious."

But a second bowl wasn't offered—as if they knew a 'walker never needed to eat.

Xantcha sat in a white chair at a white table, eating stew from a white bowl. Everything that could have had a chosen color, including the floors and the walls, was white and sparkling clean. Except for the spoon in the bowl. It was plain wood, rubbed until it was satin smooth. She used it self-consciously, afraid she'd dribble and embarrass herself—both distinct possibilities, distracted as she was by conversations between Urza and the others that she couldn't quite overhear.

The stew was plain but tasty. If there was time, she'd like to see the garden where they grew their vegetables and the fields where they harvested their grain. It was a meatless stew—somehow that didn't surprise her—with egg drizzled in the broth, and pale chunks, like cubes of soft cheese, a bit smaller than her thumb, taking the place of meat. The chunks had the texture of soft cheese, but not the taste; indeed, they had no taste that Xantcha could discern, and she was tempted to leave them in the bowl until the woman asked her if the meal was pleasing to a wanderer's palate.

The auburn-haired man's name was Romom, the cook was Tessu, the other names left no impression in Xantcha's mind, save for Brya, the toddler at the top of the stairs. When Xantcha had finished her second bowl of stew and a mug of excellent cider, Tessu suggested a hot bath in an open, steaming pool. Xantcha had no wish to display her newt's undifferentiated flesh before strangers and declined the offer. Tessu suggested sleep in a room of her own—

"Facing the mountain."

It was a privilege of some sort, but Xantcha declined a second time. She pushed away from the spotless white table and took a cautious stride toward the pillow-sitting knot of folk gathered around Urza. Opposition never materialized. The family made room for her between the two women whose names Xantcha couldn't remember. Urza gave her the finger sign for silence. The family discussed stars and myths. They used unfamiliar names, but all the other words were accented Argivian with only a few lapses of syntax or vocabulary. It wasn't their native language, yet they'd all learned it well-enough for an esoteric conversation that couldn't, in any meaningful sense, include her or Urza.

Xantcha twisted her fingers into an open question, and Urza replied with the sign for silence. Silence wasn't difficult for Xantcha, unless it was imposed. She fidgeted and considered joining the youngsters still playing with the kittens until Tessu shuttled them upstairs. The conversation began to flag and for the first time since they'd entered the austerely decorated atrium, the air charged with anticipation. Even at the edge of time there were, apparently, conversations that could be held only after the children had gone to bed.

Tessu and Romom together brought the ancient to what had been Romom's place on Urza's right. Then everyone shuffled about to make room for the pair—who Xantcha had decided were husband and wife, if not lord and lady—on the opposite side of the circle.

"You have questions," the ancient said. The voice gave no clues to the grizzled figure's sex, but the accent was thick. Xantcha had to listen closely to distinguish the words. "No one comes to Equilor without questions."

Urza made two signs, one with each hand, silence and observe, before he said, "I have come to learn my enemies' weakness."

The two men exchanged glances, one triumphant, an ongoing dispute settled at last. Against all reason, these folk had been expecting them, exactly them: Urza from Argive and a companion who'd been glad of a hot meal at the end of a long day. But they hadn't known for certain why, and that made less sense. If you knew Urza well enough to know his name and where he was headed, then surely you knew what had driven him through the multiverse to Equilor.

The men, however, said nothing. Like Xantcha, they seemed relegated to silence, waiting for the ancient to speak again.

"Equilor is not your enemy. Equilor has no enemies. If you were an enemy of Equilor, you would not have found us."

Another created plane like Phyrexia and Serra's realm, accessible only across a fathomless chasm—which Urza hadn't mentioned?

"I am a seeker, nothing more," Urza countered, as formal and constrained as Xantcha had ever heard him. "I sensed no defenses as I 'walked."

"We would not intimidate our enemies, Urza. We would not encourage them to test their courage. We knew you were a seeker. We permitted you to find what you sought. The elders will see you."

By which the ancient implied that he, or she, was not one of the elders. Perhaps the term was an honorific, not dependent on age. Xantcha would have liked to ask an impertinent question or two, but Urza's fingers remained loosely in their silence and observe positions.

"And I will ask them about Phyrexia. Have you heard of it?"

There was considerable movement in the circle. Xantcha couldn't observe it all, but Phyrexia was not unknown to the household.

The ancient said one word, "Misguided," which seemed sufficient to everyone but Urza and Xantcha.

"More than misguided," Urza sputtered. "They are a force of abomination, of destruction. They have set themselves against my plane, and I have sworn vengeance against them in the name of my brother, my people, and the Thran."

That word, "Thran," also brought an exchange of glances, less profound than what had followed Phyrexia.

"Misguided," the ancient repeated. "Foolish and doomed. The elders will tell you more."

"So, you know of them! I'm convinced that they were banished from their natal plane before they created Phyrexia. I am looking for that plane. If it is not Equilor, I hope that you can tell me where it is. I have heard that whatever is known in the multiverse is known to Equilor."

The ancient nodded. "The ones you seek have never come to Equilor. They are young, as you are young. Youth does not often come to Equilor."

"They fought the Thran over six thousand of my years ago, and I myself have walked the planes for over two millennia."

The ancient fired a question to Romom in a language Xantcha couldn't understand.

Romom replied, in Argivian, "Shorter, Pakuya, by at least a third."

"You are old, Urza, for a young man, but compared to Equilor, you are scarcely weaned from your mother's breast. In Equilor, we began our search for enlightenment a hundred millennia ago. Do not wonder, then, that you could not see our defenses as you passed through them."

"You will think differently when the Phyrexians arrive!"

"They are a small folk with small ambitions, smaller dreams. We have nothing to offer them. Perhaps we were wrong about you."

The ancient added something short and decisive in the other language. Watching Urza as closely as she watched the household, Xantcha realized that Urza couldn't skim the thoughts of these deceptively simple folk.

"It is late," Tessu said, putting a polite, yet unmistakable end to the discussion. She rose to her feet. Romom rose beside her. "Time to rest and sleep. The sun will rise."

The rest of the household stood and bowed their heads as Romom and Tessu helped the ancient from the atrium. Moments later, Urza and Xantcha were alone.

"This is the place!" Urza said directly in her mind.

"The old one said not."

"She is testing us. Tomorrow, when I meet with these elders, I will have what I have long wished to learn."

In her private thoughts, Xantcha wondered how Urza knew the ancient was a woman, then chided herself for thinking he could be right about such a small thing when he seemed so wrong about the rest. The ancient had talked to Urza as Urza often talked to her, but he hadn't noticed the slights.

"They have secrets," Xantcha warned but no reply formed in her mind, and she couldn't know if Urza had retrieved her thought.

Tessu and Romom returned. Romom said there was a special chamber where those who would speak to the elders waited for the sun to rise. For Xantcha, who was just as glad not be included, there was a narrow bedchamber at the end of a cloistered corridor, a change of clothes, and a worried question:

"You will bathe before sunrise?"

She answered in the same tone, "If I may bathe unobserved?"

"The mountain will see you."

There were no roofs over any of the chambers. Xantcha wondered what they did when it rained, but, "The mountain is not a problem."

"You have customs that inhibit you?"

Xantcha nodded. If that explanation would satisfy Tessu, she'd provide no other.

"I will not interfere, but I cannot sleep until you have bathed."

"Your customs?"

Tessu nodded, and with her clean clothes under her arm Xantcha followed her host to the dark and quiet atrium. If Tessu failed to contain her curiosity, Xantcha was none the wiser. As smooth and hairless as the day she crawled out of her vat, Xantcha eased herself into the starlit, steaming pool. A natural hot spring kept the water pleasantly warm. A gutter—white, of course, and elegantly simple—carried the overflow away. She'd scrubbed herself clean in a matter of moments and, knowing that Tessu waited in the atrium, should have toweled herself off immediately, but the mountain was watching her and she watched back.

It had many eyes—Xantcha lost count at thirty-three—and, remembering the bats, the eyes were probably nothing more than caves, still, the sense of observation was inescapable. After staring so intently at shades of black and darkness, Xantcha thought she saw flickering lights in some of the cave eyes, thought the lights formed a rippling web across the mountain. Xantcha thought a number of things until she realized she was standing naked beside the pool, at which point all her thoughts shattered and vanished. She grabbed her clothes, both clean and filthy, and retreated into the atrium.

"You are unwell?" Tessu asked discreetly from the shadows as Xantcha wrestled with unfamiliar clasps and plackets.

"It did see me."

Tessu failed to repress a chuckle. "They will not harm you, Xantcha."

Urza was right. They were being tested. Xantcha hoped she had passed.

Xantcha slept well and awoke to the unmistakable sounds of children being quiet outside her door. They were not so fluent in Argivian as the household's adult members, but the tallest of the three boys—who understandably took himself to be older than Xantcha and therefore entitled to give her orders—made it clear that sunrise was coming and it was time for guests to come outside and join the family in its morning rituals.

The eastern horizon had barely begun to brighten when Xantcha settled into what was evidently a place of honor between Tessu and the ancient. They faced west toward the mountain, which was as monolithic black in the pre-dawn light as it was during Xantcha's bath. There were no prayers, a relief, and no Urza or Romom or Brya, either. Brya's absence could be explained by the motionless serenity with which the household awaited the coming of daylight. No toddler could sit so still for so long.

Xantcha herself was challenged by the discipline. Her mind ached with unasked questions, her nose itched, then her toes, and the nearly unreachable spot between her shoulder blades. She was ready to explode when light struck the mountain's rounded crest. As sunrises went, it was not spectacular. The air was clear. There were no clouds anywhere to add contrast or movement to the surprisingly slow progression of color and light on the mountainside.

But that, Xantcha realized, was Equilor's mystery and revelation. Those who dwelt at the edge of time had gone past a need for the spectacular; they'd learned to appreciate the subtlest differences. They'd conquered boredom even more effectively than the perfect folk of Serra's realm. They could wait forever and a day, which Xantcha supposed was a considerable accomplishment, though nothing she wished to emulate.

Find what you're looking for! she urged the absent Urza, moments before the dawn revealed two white-clad figures moving among the mountain's many caves.

The ancient rapped Xantcha sharply on the back. "Pay attention! Watch close!"

Guessing that some rite of choosing or choice was about to take place, Xantcha did her best to follow the ancient's advice, but it proved impossible. Brilliant lights suddenly began to flash from the cave mouths, as if each contained a mirror. She blinked rapidly and to no useful effect. Each cave mouth had its own rhythm, no matter how Xantcha tried, her eyes were quickly, painfully blinded by reflected sunlight.

"You'll learn," the ancient chortled, while tears ran down Xantcha's cheeks.

The dazzle ended.

Tessu embraced Xantcha with a hearty "Good morning" and pulled her to her feet before releasing her. Xantcha had scarcely dried her face on her sleeve before the rest of the household followed Tessu's example and greeted her with the same embrace they used with one another. She had never been so carefully included in a family gathering, and seldom felt so out of place. Her vision was still awash in purple and green blobs when she and Tessu were alone in the atrium.

"You aren't used to it yet," Tessu said gently. "You'll learn."

"That's what the ancient said."

"Ancient? Oh, Pakuya. She'll go up the mountain herself, I think, after you and Urza leave. We've been waiting quite a long time, even for us, for you to arrive."

The certainty in Tessu's voice was an unexpected relief. "Urza's in one of the caves, right?"

"Keodoz, I think. Romom will say for certain when he returns this afternoon."

Keodoz, the name of the cave or the elder who occupied it? Xantcha stifled idle curiosity in favor of a more important question: "Do you know when Urza will return?"

"Tomorrow or the next day. Whenever he and Keodoz have finished."

It was nearly twenty days before neighbors spotted a white-robed man coming down the mountain. By then Xantcha knew that there was no difference between the cave and the elder—or more accurately, elders—who dwelt within it. Romom, Tessu, and the rest of the Equilor community—and there was only the one community at the edge of time—lived their mortal lives in expectation of the day when they'd climb the mountain one last time to merge with their ancestors.

Despite their focus on their cave-dwelling ancestors, the folk of Equilor weren't a morbid people. They laughed with one another, loved their children, and took genuine delight in the small events of daily life. They argued, held grudges, and gossiped among themselves and about the elders, who, despite their collective spirits, were not without individual foibles. Keodoz, Xantcha learned, was known to be long-winded and supremely self-confident. As Urza's time in the caves had lengthened, the household began to joke that Keodoz had found a soulmate—a notion that distressed Xantcha. Idyllic ways notwithstanding, Equilor was not a place where she wanted to spend eternity.

When she heard that Urza had been spotted, she left the house at once and jogged along the stone road until she met up with him.

"Did you get your answers?" she asked, adding, "I can be ready to leave before sundown."

"I have only scratched the surface, Xantcha. We are young compared to them. We know so little, and they have been collecting knowledge for so long. A thousand years wouldn't be enough time. Ten thousand, even a hundred thousand wouldn't be too much. You cannot imagine what the elders know."

Of course she couldn't imagine. She was Phyrexian. "Remember why we came here. What about vengeance? Your brother? Dominaria? Phyrexia!"

He grabbed her and lifted her into the air. "Keodoz knows so much, Xantcha! Do you remember, after we left Phyrexia, how I was unable to return to Dominaria? I said it was as if the portion of the multiverse that held Dominaria had been squeezed and sealed away from the rest. I was right, Xantcha. Not only was I right, but I was the one who had squeezed and twisted it when I emptied the sylex bowl! It wasn't evident at first—well, it was. Dominaria was cooler when I left, but I didn't understand how the two were related. But it was in my mind, when I used the sylex, to protect my home for all time, and the bowl's power was so great that my wish was granted. No artifact device, nor planeswalker's will, can breach the Shard that the sylex created. The elders here at Equilor could not breach it."

"You turned your home into Phy– " Xantcha caught herself before she finished the fatal word and substituted, "Serra's realm?" instead.

"Better, Xantcha. Much better! The Shard is more than a chasm, and Dominaria is an entire nexus of planes, all natural and balanced. Dominaria is safe, and I saved it with the sylex."

"But the Phyrexians? Phyrexia? The Ineffable?"

"They are doomed, Xantcha. Accidents and anomalies, not worth the effort of destroying them, now that I am sure Dominaria is safe. There are more important questions, Xantcha. I see that now. I've found my place. Equilor is where I belong. Keodoz and the others have so much knowledge, but they've done nothing with it. Look around us, Xantcha. These folk need leadership— vision!—and I will give it to them. When I am finished, Equilor will be the jewel of the multiverse."

Xantcha thought of Tessu and Romom waiting to merge with all their ancestors. She wriggled free and said, cautiously, "I don't think that's what anyone here wants."

"They have not dreamed with me, Xantcha. Keodoz has only begun to dream with me. It will take time, but we have time. Equilor has time. They are not immortal, but they might as well be. Did you know that if Brya, Romom's youngest, had been born where I was born, she would be an old woman in her eighties?"

Xantcha hadn't known and wasn't comfortable with the knowledge. Urza, however, was radiant, as intoxicated by his ambitions as she would have been by a jug of wine. "Urza, You haven't found your place," she said, retreating into the grass. "You've lost it. We came here to find the first home for the

Phyrexians. They've never been here, and if the elders don't know where they're from, then we should leave . . . soon."

"Nonsense!" Urza retorted and started walking toward the white houses.

Nonsense was also the first word out of Pakuya's toothless mouth when Urza regaled the household with his notions over supper. Tessu, Romom, and the others were too polite—or perhaps too astonished—to say anything until Urza had 'walked back to Keodoz's cave, and then they spoke in their own language. Xantcha had learned only a few words of Equiloran—she suspected they spoke her Argivian dialect precisely to keep their own language a mystery—but she didn't need a translator to catch that they were unhappy with Urza's plans or to decide that their politeness masked a strong, even rigid, culture.

Tessu confirmed Xantcha's suspicions. "It might be best," she said in a supremely mild tone, "if you spoke with Urza."

"I've already told him but Urza doesn't listen to me unless I'm telling him what he wants to hear. If I were you, I'd send someone up the mountain to talk with Keodoz."

"Keodoz is not much for listening."

"Then we've got a problem."

"No, Xantcha, Urza's got a problem, because the other elders will get Keodoz's attention, sooner or later."

"Is Urza in danger? I mean . . . would you . . . would they?" Tessu was such a calm, rational woman that Xantcha had difficulty getting her question out, though she knew from other worlds that the most ruthless folk she'd ever met were invariably calm and rational.

"Those who go up the mountain, do not always come down," Tessu said simply.

"Urza's a 'walker, I've seen him melt mountains with his eyes."

"Not here."

Xantcha absorbed that in silence. "I'll talk to Urza, the next time he comes down . . . assuming he comes back down."

"Assuming," Tessu agreed.

Urza did return to the white houses after forty days in Keodoz's cave. He summoned the entire community and made the air shimmer with visions of artifacts and cities. Xantcha had learned a bit more Equiloran by then. When she spoke to Urza afterward, her concerns were real.

"They're not interested. They say they've put greatness behind them and they're angry with Romom and Tessu for letting you stay with them so long. They say something's got to be done."

"Of course something's got to be done! And I'll get Keodoz to do it. He's on the brink. He's been on the brink for days now. I left him alone to get his thoughts in order. They're a collective mind, you know, each elder separately and all the elders together. They've become stagnant, but I'm getting them moving again. Once I get Keodoz persuaded, he'll give the sign to the others, and the dam will burst. You'll see."

"Tessu said, those who go up the mountain don't always return. Be careful, Urza. These people have power."

"Tessu and Romom! Forget Tessu and Romom, they might as well be blind. Yes, they've got power. All Equilor had undreamed power, but they turned their back on power and they've forgotten how to use it. Even Keodoz. I'm going to show them what greatness truly is!"

Xantcha walked away wondering if Tessu had enough power to take her between-worlds once Urza stayed in the mountains with Keodoz. The adults were missing, though, and the children wouldn't meet Xantcha's eyes when she asked where they'd gone, not even eighty-year-old Brya. Xantcha went outside, to the place where they gathered to watch sunrise light the mountain each morning. The skies were clear. It had rained just four times since she'd arrived—torrential downpours that soaked everything and recharged the cisterns. During the storms they'd taken shelter in the underground larders. She'd thought the adult community might be meeting there, or outside one of the other houses. Xantcha listened closely for conversation but heard nothing, and though she'd never heard or seen anything to suggest that the gardens and fields beyond the white houses were dangerous at night, she decided she was safest near the children.

Tessu's children took harmless advantage of her absence. They raided the larder, lured the kittens onto the forbidden cushions and, one by one, fell asleep away from their beds. Xantcha guessed they'd slipped into the long hours between midnight and dawn. She decided to try another conversation with Urza, but he was gone, 'walked back to Keodoz, most likely. She sensed that the Equilorans didn't approve of skipping between-worlds to get from the house to the cave. They didn't say anything, though; they weren't inclined toward warnings or ultimatums. Not that either would have mattered with Urza.

Xantcha went outside again. She paced and stared at the mountain, then paced some more, stared some more. The sky brightened: dawn, at last. The adults would come back for the sunrise. She'd talk to Tessu. They'd work something out.

But the brightening wasn't dawn. The new light came from a single point overhead, a star, Xantcha thought—there weren't so many of them in the Equilor sky that she hadn't already memorized the brightest patterns. She'd never seen a star grow brighter before, except on Gastal when the star had been a predatory planeswalker.

Xantcha ran inside, awakened the children, and was herding them to the larders when Tessu raced through the always-open door.

"I was sending them to shelter, before that thing—" Xantcha pointed at the brightness overhead—"crashes on top of us."

The children had rushed to their mother, babbling in their own language—offering apologies and excuses for why they weren't in bed, Xantcha guessed, and maybe blaming her, though there were no pointed fingers or condemning glances. Tessu calmed them quickly. If the youngest was indeed eighty, Tessu had had several lifetimes in which to learn the tricks of motherhood. She didn't urge them into the larder, however, but outside to the sunrise gathering place.

"Thank you for thinking first of the children," Tessu said. It wasn't what she'd come running home to say, but the words seemed sincere. "Nothing will crash down on Equilor. A star is dying."

Xantcha shook her head, unable to comprehend the notion.

"It happens frequently, or so the elders say, but only twice when

293

we on the ground could see it, and never as bright as this." Tessu took Xantcha's hands gently between hers. "It is an omen."

"Urza? Is Urza—?"

"There will be a change. I can't say more than that. Change doesn't come easily to Equilor. We will go outside and see what the sunrise brings."

Xantcha freed herself. "You know more. Tell me . . . please?"

"I know no more, Xantcha. I suspect—yes, I suspect the elders have gotten Keodoz's attention. The problem with Urza will be resolved, quickly."

Xantcha stared at her hands. She didn't grieve or wail. Urza had brought this on himself, but when she tried to imagine her life without him she began to shiver.

"Don't borrow trouble," Tessu advised, draping a length of cloth over Xantcha's shoulders. "The sun hasn't risen yet. Come outside and wait with us."

No night had ever been longer. The dying star continued to brighten until it cast shadows all around. It remained visible after the other stars had dimmed and when the dawn began. Xantcha worried the hem loose from her borrowed shawl and began to mindlessly unravel it.

There was change, more noticeable than anyone had imagined. As dawn's perimeter moved down the mountain, the caves flashed in unison and in complex rhythm that could only be a code. Xantcha tugged on Tessu's sleeve.

"What does it mean?" she whispered.

"It means they've come to their senses," Pakuya snapped. "If that fool wants to change a world, let him change his own!"

To which Tessu added, "You'll be leaving soon."

"Urza's alive?"

"No more than he was yesterday, and I'd be surprised if he's learned anything. Keodoz certainly hasn't. But that's for the best, isn't it, if they both think they've made the changes for themselves?"

Xantcha thought a moment, then nodded. Urza 'walked up a few moments later.

"The future's ended before it began," he began, talking to her, talking to the household and talking to himself equally. "I cannot stay to lead you, and Keodoz has already begun to waver in the face of stagnant opposition. But they have lifted me into the night and shown me a frightening sight. The fortress I made around the planes where I was born has been brought down by a misguided fool! As my brother and I undid the Thran, so I have been undone by ignorance. But I can go back, and I will go back.

"Equilor, however, is on its own. You will have to complete my visions without my guidance."

The household made a fair show of grief. From Pakuya to Brya, they said how sorry they were that they wouldn't get to live the future Urza and Keodoz had promised them. The entire community flattered Urza's righteousness and strength of character. They wished him well and offered to make him a feast in honor of his departure for Dominaria. Xantcha was relieved when Urza declined. She didn't think she'd have the stomach for an extended display of insincerity.

Tessu had been right. It was for the best that Urza left Equilor thinking the decision had been his own.

It took them a hundred Dominarian years to 'walk the between-worlds from Equilor to Dominaria, but in the spring of the 3,210th year after Urza's birth, Xantcha finally stood on the world where she'd been destined to sleep.

Chapter 21

"If Gix could find me, he would find me. He would have found me before I left Pincar City. He would have come for me while I slept. If he didn't want to be seen, he would have sent *sleepers* after me."

Eight days after her narrow escape, Xantcha sat in the branches of a oak tree. The sun would set sometime during the thunderstorm that was bearing in from the ocean. She'd been watching the clouds pile up all afternoon, watching the lightning since she left Russiore with the day-traders. Her armor tended to attract lightning even as it protected her from the bolts, and a big, old tree, standing by itself on a hillside, wouldn't be a good hiding place much longer.

Once the storm struck, Xantcha figured she'd find a saner place to wait for Urza. With all that metal and exposed sinew, Gix wasn't apt to come looking for her in the rain.

"He didn't know we were here. He didn't recognize me until he found the spark in my mind."

The spark. She'd had a headache the first day away from Pincar City, but her back had ached, too, along with her neck and jaw and every other part of her body: the aftermath of total terror.

There were uglier beasts in the multiverse, meaner ones, and possibly more dangerous ones. None of them had a demon's malignant aura. Born-folk had a word, rape. It occurred on every world, in every language. In Phyrexian, as Xantcha understood it, the word for rape was Gix.

Xantcha had scrubbed her skin raw even though Gix hadn't touched her because she couldn't scour her mind. She'd rehearsed a score of confessions, too, and her greatest fear as the wind whipped the branches around her wasn't that Gix would find her but that he'd already found Urza . . . or Ratepe.

Urza could take care of himself. Xantcha had to believe that; she couldn't let herself believe, even for a heartbeat, that Gix had told the truth when he'd said "I made the brothers, too, and then I made you." And if she believed that Urza's mind was his own, then she could be confident it would take the Ineffable to challenge him in single combat. But whatever she managed to believe about herself and Urza, it didn't help when she thought of Ratepe, alone and unsuspecting on the Ohran ridge. Rat wouldn't have a chance, whether Gix came to kill or corrupt.

And when all those memories of Ratepe's face had freed her from Gix's thrall, surely some of them had given away the cottage's location, if Gix were inclined to find the man who went with that face.

"Gix doesn't care," she told the oak tree. "Phyrexians have no imagination."

Rain pelted, driven by the wind, and Xantcha was drenched in an instant. Urza's armor was strange that way. It would protect her from fire or the complete absence of breathable air, but it was entirely vulnerable to plain water. Xantcha clambered down a branch or two, then dropped straight to the ground. She found an illusion of shelter among the briar bushes tangled at the bottom of the hill.

Urza would find her no matter where she hid. Her heart, he said, pulled him between-worlds. He'd grumble about the rain, if he arrived before the storm died out. Not that any weather affected him; Urza simply didn't like surprises. He wouldn't like her confession.

The storm moved south without clearing the air. A steady rain continued to fall, as a starless night closed in around the briars. Xantcha tried to stay awake, but it was a losing struggle. She hadn't slept much in Russiore. She'd been busy, for one thing, distributing nine days' worth of screaming spiders in less than eight and afraid to close her eyes for the other. The briars were secure and friendly by comparison and the rain's patter, a lullaby.

Xantcha had no idea how long she'd been asleep when Urza awoke her with her name.

"Over here!" she called back.

The rain had stopped, save for drips from the leaves around her. A few stars shone through the thinning clouds, silhouetting Urza as he strode down the hill.

"Ready to go home?" He sounded cheerful. Xantcha told herself that confession would be easier with Urza in a good mood. "No sacks?" He cocked his head at her empty hands and shoulders. "You couldn't get his food and such?" Urza generally avoided choosing a name for Ratepe.

"Urza, I have to talk to you—"

"Problems in Russiore? Are they in the midst of a famine?"

"Not exactly. I didn't have time to scrounge supplies. Something came up—"

"Not to worry. I have other plans, anyway. We'll talk at the cottage."

He seized Xantcha's wrist, and before she could protest they were between-worlds. The journey was swift, as always. Two strides through nothing, and they were on the Ohran ridge. It was also, as always, disorienting. Urza stepped out several hundred paces from the cottage to give Xantcha a chance to gather her wits before they greeted Ratepe.

Xantcha's nerves reassembled themselves slowly, in part because she had to assure herself that the cottage was unharmed. Urza had gotten ahead of her. She ran to catch up.

"Urza, I said we have to talk. There's a problem. You. Ratepe. Your brother. The spiders—" All her carefully rehearsed statements had vanished in the between-worlds.

"I've thought it through. I can do the work of all three of us for the next nine days. I'll distribute the artifacts that he's made for us, yours and mine together, and get the next batch assembled. It's another aspect of time: I'll live a little faster. It's good practice, crawling before walking. The spiders won't end this war, Xantcha. They'll only buy time until I solve the Phyrexian problem at its source."

Urza had gotten over his obsession with righting his brother's fate, but he still talked of traveling back in time, much further back in time. Urza wanted to meet the Thran and fight beside them in their final battle against the Phyrexians. He thought they might know enemy's true home and, although he didn't say it, Xantcha believed Urza hoped go behind the Thran, all the way to the Phyrexians' first world to annihilate rather than exile them.

Gix had said the Thran were waiting. The demon could have rummaged the name out of her memories or out of Mishra during the war. Almost certainly Gix wasn't telling the truth; at least not the important parts of it, but Urza needed to know what had happened in the catacomb beneath Avohir's temple in Pincar City.

"I met . . . I found . . ." She was still tongue-tied. Had the demon left something in her that left her able to think but not to speak? It wasn't impossible. Gix savored fear spiced with helplessness and frustration. She didn't know the measure of the red light's power, but she'd lost an entire afternoon in the catacomb, and when Ratepe burst out of memory to save her, she'd been doing the unthinkable: walking toward Phyrexia.

"Xantcha?" Urza stopped. He faced her and gave her his full attention.

"We have to go back to Pincar City."

"No, Efuan Pincar is out of the question. Anywhere we've found *sleepers* is out of the question. You and he have to go someplace, of course. I don't want anyone around while I'm working this time. I could wait. I should wait until after the Glimmer Moon rises. We can never know the future, Xantcha. I'm sure of that. Only the past is forever, and only now gives us choices. I choose to give the next nine days to you and him so you will always have them. Tell me where you want to be, and I'll 'walk you both there in the morning."

Nine days. Nine days in hiding while she sorted out her tangled thoughts? It was the coward's way, but Xantcha seized it. "I'll talk to him." A lie. Xantcha could feel that confessing to Ratepe would be no easier than confessing to Urza. "We'll decide where we want to go."

Ratepe welcomed them with the enthusiasm and relief of any talkative youth who'd kept company with himself for entirely too long. He cast several inquiring glances Xantcha's way. She pretended not to notice them while Urza announced his intention to reclaim his workroom for the next nine days.

"You told Urza," Ratepe snapped to Xantcha the moment they were alone together. "Now he's taking over everything! Just tell me, did you get my artifacts attached to Avohir's altar?"

"One," Xantcha answered truthfully. "There were *sleepers* in the temple, made up as Shratta. And Shratta dead in the catacombs. They were finished years ago, Ratepe. If there are Shratta left, they're like the Efuands in the Red-Stripes. They're in league, consciously or not, with Phyrexia." She thought of Gix; this wasn't the time to tell him, not when they were both angry. "I put your shatter-spiders, and screamers, too, in places where the glistening scent was strong. I didn't get to the barracks."

Ratepe threw his head back and swore at the ceiling. "What were you thinking! I don't want to bring Avohir's sanctuary down—not while the Red-Stripe barracks is still standing!" He shook his head and stood with his back to her. "When it wasn't what I expected, you should've waited. Sweet Avohir, what did you tell Urza?"

Xantcha's guilt and anxiety evaporated. "I didn't tell him anything!" she shouted.

"Then keep your voice down!"

"Stop telling me what to do!"

They were on opposite sides of the table, ready to lunge at each other, and not with the passion that normally accompanied their reunions. Ratepe seemed to have outrun himself. Jaw clenched, eyes pleading, he looked across the table, but Xantcha was similarly paralyzed. It was her nature, created in Phyrexia and shaped over time in Urza's company, to back down or explode when cornered. This was a moment when she couldn't see a clear path in either direction.

The door was at her back. Xantcha ducked and ran out, leaving it open behind her, listening for the sounds that never came. She settled in the darkness, wrestling with her conscience, until the lamps in her shared room had flickered and died. Approaching the door through starlight, she saw a dark silhouette at the table, where Ratepe had fallen asleep with his head on his arms. She crept past him, as silently as she'd crept toward the Pincar catacomb. Her bed was strung with a creaking rope mattress. Xantcha quietly tucked herself in a corner by her treasure chest.

Ratepe was sprawled on the bed when she awoke. Urza was in the doorway, the golden light of dawn behind him.

"Are you ready to 'walk?" he asked.

Urza never came into her side of the cottage. Perhaps he thought she'd been sleeping in the corner since Ratepe arrived. They weren't ready to 'walk anyway; Ratepe wasn't ready to wake up. He was cross-grained from the moment his eyes opened. Xantcha expected him to start something they'd all regret, but instead he just said, "You decide," as he slipped past Urza on his way to the well.

"We don't need you to 'walk us anywhere," Xantcha said to Urza as she stretched the kinks out of her legs. Her foot felt as if her boot was lined with hot, sharp needles.

"I don't want you near here while I work."

"We won't be."

"Don't dawdle, then. I want to get started!"

Ratepe stayed away while Xantcha rearranged her traveling gear. She packed a good deal of gold and silver, which could be traded wherever they went, but included copper, too, in case they got no farther than their closest neighbors along the frontier between the ridge and the coast. She threw in flour for journey bread, as well, and thought about the hunter's bow suspended from the rafters. Nine days could be an uncomfortably long time to live off journey bread, but a bow could be troublesome in a city. In the end Xantcha put a few more coins in her belt purse, left the bow on its hook, and met a sulking Ratepe beside the well.

Urza either didn't notice or didn't care that Xantcha and Ratepe were scarcely speaking to each other. He'd been away from his workroom for nearly a half-year and didn't wait to see the sphere rise before sealing himself in with his ideas.

The morning sun was framed with fair weather clouds against a rich blue sky. Prairie wildflowers blanketed the land above which the sphere soared. It was difficult, in the face of such natural beauty, to remain sullen and sour, but Xantcha and Ratepe both rose to the challenge. A northwest wind stream caught the sphere and carried it toward Kovria, southeast of the ridge. There was nothing in the Kovrian barrens to hold Xantcha's attention, no destinations worth mentioning, but changing their course meant choosing their course, so they drifted into Kovria.

By mid-afternoon, the tall-grass prairies of the ridge had given way to badlands.

"Where are we going?" Ratepe asked, virtually the first full sentence he'd uttered since the sphere rose.

"Where does it look like we're going?"

"Nowhere."

"Then nowhere, it is. Nowhere's good enough for me."

"Put us down. You're crazed, Xantcha. Something happened in Efuan Pincar, and it's left you crazed. I don't want to be up here with you."

Xantcha brought them down on a plain of baked dirt and weedy scrub. They were both silent while the sphere collapsed and powdered.

"What went wrong?" Ratepe asked as he brushed the last of the white stuff from his face. "It's not just *sleepers*. *Sleepers* wouldn't frighten you, and you're afraid. I didn't think there was anything that could do that."

"Lots of things frighten me. Urza frightens me, sometimes. You frighten me. The between-worlds frightens me. Demons frighten me." Xantcha tore a handful of leaves off the nearest bush and began shredding them. Let Ratepe guess; let him choose, if he could.

"There was a demon in Avohir's temple? In the catacombs with the dead Shratta? A Phyrexian demon?"

Ratepe was uncommonly good at guessing and choosing.

"I don't know any other kind."

"Avohir's mercy! You and Urza didn't find demons anywhere else, did you?"

"I didn't."

"Why Efuan Pincar? If a Phyrexian demon was going to come to Dominaria, why come to Efuan Pincar. We keep to ourselves. When our ancestors left Argive, they never looked back. They settled on the north shore of Gulmany because it's so far away from everywhere else. We're not rich. We don't bother our neighbors, and they've never bothered us. We don't even have an army—which is probably why we had trouble with the Shratta and the Red-Stripes, but why would that interest Phyrexia? I don't understand. Do you?"

"I told you, demons frighten me. I didn't ask questions, just . . . just got away." She stripped another handful of leaves. Xantcha wanted to tell Ratepe everything, but the words to get her started weren't in her mind.

"The day you bought me, I told you that you were a lousy liar. You may be three thousand years old, Xantcha, but my eight-year-old brother could fib better than you. When he got into trouble, though, I could guess what he was hiding, 'cause I'd hidden it myself. I can't guess about demons."

Xantcha scattered the leafy bits and faced Ratepe. "It was Gix. I smelled *sleepers* in the sanctuary, I followed the smell, planting spiders as I went, yours and Urza's both. I wound up way underground, in the dark. There was a passageway, one of the big, old, upright ones, and there was Gix."

"You said Gix had been killed in the Sixth Sphere."

"The Seventh. He was excoriated, consigned to endless torment. We were taught that nothing escapes the Seventh Sphere."

"Another Phyrexian lie? You're sure it was Gix, not some other demon?"

"Yes." One answer for both questions.

"Did he hurt you?"

Ratepe never failed to ask the question Xantcha wasn't expecting. "I'm here, aren't I?"

"Then, what's got you so riled? Why were we headed 'nowhere'? Unless . . . wait, I get it now. Urza's sent you off with the mere mortal. He's not that crazed. He knows what I am, who I'm not. He's going back after Gix, and you're here with me instead of—"

"I didn't tell Urza." The words belched out of her.

"You found a Phyrexian demon under Avohir's temple and you didn't tell Urza?"

She turned away in shame.

"Of course," Ratepe sighed. "He'd yell at you and blame you, just as I've yelled at you and blamed you. And you are a lot like my little brother when you get accused of something that's not your fault. And Gix. Gix was the one who got Mishra. Mishra didn't know—not until it was too late. Strange thing. They fought over those two stones that are Urza's eyes now, but I don't think either brother could hear the stones sing."

Xantcha took a deep breath. "Do you wonder why you can hear them."

"I can't hear them. I only hear Mishra's stone. I don't know for sure that the Mightstone sings, but—yes, I do wonder. I think about it a lot, more than I want to. Why? Did Gix say something about the stones?"

"Yes. He said he made them, and then he said something about you." And Urza, Xantcha's mind added, but not her tongue.

Ratepe was pale and speechless.

"He could have gotten your name out of my mind. I was careful what I gave him, enough to keep him from digging too deep. But I got in trouble. Serious trouble." Xantcha's hands were shaking. She clasped them together behind her back. "He had me, Rat. I was walking toward the passageway. I would've gone into Phyrexia, and that would've been the end of me, I'm sure. Then, suddenly, all I could think of was you."

"Me?"

"You're the first 'mere mortal' I've gotten to know. You've . . ." Blood rushed to Xantcha's face. She was hot, embarrassed, but she stumbled on. "Thinking about you pulled me back. But Gix was in my mind when I did, so he could have taken your name and made a lie around it. Everything he said could've been lies . probably was lies." And why share Gix's lies with anyone? "He didn't tell me anything I didn't know, except, maybe, about the Thran. And, well, Mishra knew some things about the Thran."

Though Xantcha could feel the blood draining from her own face, Ratepe's was still dangerously pale.

"Tell me what Gix said about me, then what he said about Mishra and the Thran. Maybe I can tell you if it's lies or not."

"Gix said he wondered if I'd found you, as if he'd planned that we were supposed to meet."

"And about the Thran?"

"When I said that Urza would finish what the Thran had started against the Phyrexians, he laughed and said the Thran were waiting for Urza and that they'd take back what was theirs. Gix was thinking about Urza's eyes—at least, I started thinking about Urza's eyes and how they were the last of the Thran powerstones. Gix laughed louder, and the next thing I knew, I was thinking about you and not walking toward the portal. What he said about you and what he said about me, they're lies. Even if Mishra was compleated in Phyrexia . . . even if his flesh and blood were rendered for the vats . . . I was one of thousands. We were exactly alike. We don't even scar, Ratepe. We couldn't tell ourselves apart!"

"Lies," Ratepe said so softly that Xantcha wasn't sure she'd heard him correctly and asked him to repeat himself. "Lies. The Weakstone's a sort of memory. Mostly it's Mishra's memory, but I've been hit with some Thran memories and some of Urza's, too, though not as strong. With Mishra, there's personality. I'm thankful I never met him while he was alive. He'd've killed me for sure. With the Thran and Urza, it's like faded paintings. But if you were Mishra—if any part of you was Mishra—the Weakstone would have recognized him in you, even though you're Phyrexian. And if I'd been touched by Gix, I'd be dead. The Weakstone doesn't like Phyrexians, Xantcha, and it especially doesn't like Gix."

"Urza's eye doesn't like me?"

Ratepe shook his head, "Sorry, no. It sees you, sometimes, but if Urza doesn't trust you, the Weakstone could be responsible because it doesn't trust you."

"The Weakstone has opinions?"

"Influence. It tries to influence."

Xantcha considered Urza's eyes watching her and Ratepe each time they retreated to her side of the wall. "It must be overjoyed when we're together."

Color returned to Ratepe's face in a single heartbeat. "I'm not Mishra. I make my own opinions."

"What do you know from Mishra and the Weakstone about the Thran and the Phyrexians?" Xantcha asked when Ratepe's blush had spread past his ears.

"They hate each other, with a deep, blinding hate that gives no quarter. But I'll tell you honestly, in the images I've gotten of their war, I can't tell one side from the other. The Thran weren't flesh and blood, no more than the Phyrexians. Even Mishra's just something the Weakstone uses. Urza's notion that the Thran sacrificed themselves to save Dominaria, maybe that's the Mightstone's influence, but it's not true. My world's better off without both of them, Thran and Phyrexians together."

They'd wandered away from their gear. Xantcha headed back. "Maybe Urza will succeed someday in 'walking between times as easily as he 'walks between worlds. I'd like to know what really happened back there at Koilos. I'd like to see it for myself. It's a shadow over everything I've ever known, all the way back to the vats."

Ratepe corrected her pronunciation of Koilos, reducing the three syllables to two and moving the accent to the first.

"I heard it from Urza and he's the one who named it," she retorted.

"I guess language drifts in three thousand years. It's still there, you know—well, it was three hundred years ago when the ancestors left Argive."

Xantcha stopped short. "I thought it wasn't recorded where the first Efuands came from. That's part of your myth."

"It is . . . part of the myth, that is. But Father said our language is mostly Argivian and the oldest books, before the Shratta burnt them, had been written in Argivian. And, if you look at a map, Efuan Pincar is about as far away from Argive as you can get without sailing right off the edge."

"And Koilos?" Xantcha stuck with Urza's pronunciation. "It's still there in Argive?"

"It's not in Argivia. It never was, but folk knew where it was three hundred years ago. It's like *The Antiquity Wars*, something that's not supposed to be forgotten. I guess it was inaccessible for most of the Ice Age, but when the world got warmer again, the kings of Argivia and their neighbors sent folk up on the Kher to make sure the ruins were still ruins."

"Urza's never mentioned them. I just assumed Koilos vanished with Argoth."

"You've seen a map of what's left of Terisiare?"

Xantcha shrugged. There were maps in her copies of *The Antiquity Wars*. She'd assumed they were wrong and paid no attention to them.

"We'd have to go over the Sea of Laments. We'd never make it there and back in nine days," Ratepe said with a smile that invited conspiracy. Waste not, want not. If Gix hadn't lied about the young Efuand, they were all doomed.

"We'd make landfall on Argivia in two very cold days and colder nights. Getting back would be more difficult, but it's that or go back to the cottage and tell Urza that I saw Gix in Pincar City."

"He wouldn't be pleased to see us."

* * * * *

The journey over the Sea of Laments was as uneventful as it was unpleasant. They'd traded for blankets and an oil-cloth sail in a village on Gulmany's south coast. The fisherman who took Xantcha's silver thought she was insane; a little while later, both Ratepe and Xantcha agreed with him, but by then it was too late. They were in the wash of a roaring wind river and remained there until they saw land again. For two days and nights there was nothing to do but huddle beneath blankets and the sail.

"Don't you have to keep one hand free?" Ratepe had shouted early on, as they struggled to wrap the blankets evenly around their feet.

"Tack across this?" she shouted back. "We're here for the ride."

"How many times have you crossed the sea?"

"Once, by mistake."

"Sorry I asked."

Misery ended after sunrise on the third day. There was land below, land as far as the eye could see. Xantcha thought down and thrust her hand through the sphere for good measure. Her hand turned white as they plummeted down to familiar altitudes.

As her hand began to thaw, Xantcha asked, "Now, which way to Koilos?"

"Where are we?"

"Don't you recognize anything from your maps?"

"Avohir's sweet mercy, Xantcha, maps don't look like the ground!"

They found an oasis and a goatherd who seemed unfazed by the sight of two strangers in a place where strangers couldn't be common. He spoke a language neither of them had heard before but recognized the word Koilos in its older, three-syllable form. He rattled off a long speech before pointing to the southeast. The only words they recognized, beside Koilos, were Urza and Mishra. Xantcha traded a silver-set agate for all the food the youth was carrying. He strode away, whistling and laughing.

"What do you think he said?" Xantcha asked when they'd returned to the gulch where their gear was hidden. "Other than that we're fools and idiots."

"The usual curses against Urza and Mishra."

The sphere flowed over them and they were rising before Ratepe continued.

"Haven't you ever noticed how empty everything is? Even in Efuan Pincar, which was as far from Argoth as it could be, it's nothing to ride through wilderness and find yourself in the middle of ruins from the time before the ice and the war. Here in Argivia, according to the books the Ancestors brought to Pincar, they were still living in the shadows of the past—literally. They didn't have the wherewithal to build the buildings like the old ruins. Not enough people, not enough stone, not enough metal, not enough knowledge of how it was done. Urza talks about the mysteries of the Thran. The books my father studied talked about the mysteries of Urza and Mishra. They all talk about Koilos. It's the place in Terisiare, new or old, where everything comes to an end. It's a name to conjure darkness."

Xantcha caught a tamer wind stream and adjusted their drift. "Does everyone in Efuan Pincar talk about such things? Are you a nation of storytellers?"

Ratepe laughed bitterly. "No, just my father, and he taught me. My father was a scholar, and both my grandfathers, too. The first things I remember are the three of them arguing about men and women who'd died a thousand years ago. I was ashamed of them. I hated lessons; I wanted to be anything but a scholar. Then the Shratta came. My grandfathers were dead by then, Avohir's mercy. My father did whatever he had to do to take care of us. When we got to the country, he learned farming as if it were a Sumifan chronicle, but he missed Pincar. He missed not having students to teach or someone to argue with. My mother told me to sit at his feet and learn or she'd take her belt to me. I never argued with my mother."

Xantcha stared at Ratepe who was staring at the horizon, eyes glazed and fists clenched, the way he looked whenever he remembered what he'd lost. Urza had buried Mishra beneath layers of obsession, and there was little enough in Xantcha's own life worth cherishing. Looking at Ratepe, trying to imagine his grief, all she felt was envy.

The winds were steady, the sky was clear, and the moon was bright. They soared until midnight and were in the air again after a sunrise breakfast. By midday they saw the reflection of a giant lake to their south, and by the end of a long afternoon they were over the foothills of the Kher Ridge. There were no villages, no roads, not even the bright green dot of an oasis.

Ratepe closed his eyes and folded his hands.

"Now what?" Xantcha asked.

"I'm praying for a sign."

"I thought you knew!"

"I do, somewhat. The landscape's changed a bit since Mishra was here last. But I think I'll recognize the mountains when I see them."

"We're fools, you know. At most we'll have a day at Koilos—if we find it."

"Look for a saddle-back mountain with three smaller peaks in front of it."

"A saddle-back," Xantcha muttered, and lowered her hand to get a better look.

The setting sun threw mountain-sized shadows that obscured as much as they revealed, but there was nothing that looked like a double-peaked mountain, and the wind streams were starting to get treacherous as the air cooled. Xantcha looked for a place to set up their night camp. A patch of flat ground, a bit lighter than its surroundings and shaped like an arrowhead, beckoned.

"I'm taking us down there for the night," she told Ratepe, dropping the sphere out of the wind stream.

He said something in reply. Xantcha didn't catch the words. They'd caught a crosswind that was determined to keep her off the arrowhead. She felt like she'd been the victor in a bare-knuckle brawl by the time the sphere collapsed.

Ratepe sprang immediately to his feet. "Avohir answers prayers!" he shouted, running toward a stone near the arrowhead's tip.

Time had taken a toll on the stone, which stood a bit taller than Ratepe himself. The spiraled carvings were weathered to illegibility, but to find such a stone in this place could only mean one thing.

Ratepe lifted Xantcha into the air. "We've found the path! Are you sure you don't want to keep going?"

She thought about it a moment. "I'm sure." Wriggling free, she explored the marks with her fingertips. Here and there, it was still possible to discern a curve or angle, places that might have been parallel grooves or raised dot patterns that struck deep in memory. "Koilos isn't a place I want to see first by moonlight."

"Good point. Too many ghosts," Ratepe agreed with a sigh. "But we will see it—Koilos, with my own eyes. Seven thousand years. My father . . ." He shook his head and walked away from the stone.

Xantcha didn't need to ask to know what he hadn't said.

The desert air didn't hold its heat. They were cold and hungry before the stars unveiled themselves. Xantcha doled out small portions of journey bread and green-glowing goat cheese, the last of the dubious edibles they'd traded from the goatherd. The cheese and its indescribable taste clung to the roof of Xantcha's mouth. Ratepe wisely stuck to the journey bread. He fell asleep while Xantcha sat listening to her stomach complain, as she watched the sky and the weathered stone and thought—a lot—of water.

The sphere reeked of cheese when she yawned it at dawn. Ratepe, displaying a healthy sense of self-preservation, said nothing about the smell.

It was all willpower that morning. The wind streams flowed out of the mountains, not into them. She'd been about to give up and let the sphere drift back to the desert when Ratepe spotted another stone, toppled by age. Xantcha banked the sphere into the valley it seemed to mark. They hadn't been in it long when it doglegged to the right and they saw, in the distance, a saddle-back mountain overshadowing three smaller peaks.

With Mishra's memories to guide them, they had no trouble weaving through the mountain spurs until they came to the cleft and hollowed plateau Urza had named Koilos, the Secret Heart. Xantcha could have sought the higher streams and brought them over the top. She chose to follow the cleft instead and couldn't have said why if Ratepe had asked. But he stayed silent.

Seven thousand years, and the battle scars remained: giant pockings in the cliffs on either side of them, cottage-sized chunks of rubble littering the valley floor. Here and there was a shadow left by fire, not sun. And finally there was the cavern fortress itself, built by the Thran, rediscovered by two brothers, then laid bare during the war: ruins within ruins.

"That's where they hid from the dragons," Ratepe said, pointing to a smaller cave nearly hidden behind a hill of rubble.

"I didn't expect it to be so big."

"Everything's smaller now. Smell anything?"

"Time," Xantcha replied, and not facetiously. The sense of age was everywhere, in the plateau, the cleft which had shattered it, the Thran, and the brothers. But nowhere did she sense Phyrexia.

"You're sure?"

"It will be enough if I know that Gix lied."

Xantcha started up the path to the cavern mouth. Ratepe fell behind as he paused to examine whatever caught his eye. He jogged up the path, catching her just before she entered the shadows. "There's nothing left. I thought for sure there'd be something."

"Urza and I, we're older than forever, Ratepe, and Koilos is older than us."

Her eyes needed a moment to adjust to the darkness. Ratepe found the past he was looking for strewn across the stone: hammers and chisels preserved by the cavern itself. He hefted a mallet, its wood dark with age but still sturdy.

"Mishra might have held this."

"In your dreams, Ratepe," Xantcha retorted, unable to conceal her disappointment.

Koilos was big and old but as dead as an airless world. It offered no insights to her about the Thran or the Phyrexians or even about the brothers, no matter how many discarded tools or pots Ratepe eagerly examined.

"We may as well leave," she said when the afternoon was still young and Ratepe had just found a scrap of cloth.

"Leave? We haven't seen everything yet."

"There's no water, and we don't have a lot of food with us, unless you want to try some of that cheese. What's here to see?"

"I don't know. That's why we have to stay. I'm only halfway around this room, and there's an open passage at the back! And I want to see Koilos by moonlight."

Urza's idea, in the beginning, had been to get her and Ratepe away from the cottage, to give them some time together. Koilos surely wasn't what Urza had in mind, but Ratepe was enjoying himself. Whether they left now or in the morning wasn't going to make much difference in the return trip to Gulmany, and considering what that journey home was going to take out of her, Xantcha decided she could use some rest.

"All right. Wake me at sunset, then."

Xantcha didn't think she'd fall asleep on the stone but she did until Ratepe shook her shoulder.

"Come see. It's really beautiful, in a stark way, like a giant's tomb."

Sunset light flooded through the cavern mouth. Ratepe had stirred enough dust to turn the air into ruddy curtains streaked with shadows. They walked hand in hand to the ledge where the path ended and the cavern began. The hollowed plateau appeared drenched in blood. Xantcha was transfixed by the sight, but Ratepe wanted her to turn around.

"There are carvings everywhere," he said. "They appeared like magic out of the shadows once the sunlight came in."

Xantcha turned and would have collapsed if Ratepe hadn't been holding her.

"What's wrong?"

"It's writing, Ratepe. It's writing, and I can read it, most of it. It's like the lessons carved into the walls of the Fane of Flesh."

"What does it say?"

"Names. Mostly names and numbers—places. Battles, who fought who. . . ." Her eyes followed the column carvings. She'd gone cold and scarcely had the strength to fill her lungs.

"What names? Any that I'd recognize?"

"Gix," she said, though there was another that she recognized: Yawgmoth, which she didn't—couldn't—say aloud. "And Xantcha, among the numbers."

"Phyrexian?"

"Thran."

"We know they fought." Ratepe freed his fingers from her death grip.

Xantcha grabbed them again. "No, they didn't fight. Not the Phyrexians against the Thran. The Thran fought themselves."

"You can't be reading it right."

"I'm reading it because it's the same writing that's carved in the walls of every Fane in Phyrexia! Some of the words are unfamiliar, but—Ratepe! My name is up there. My name is up there because Xantcha is a number carved in the floor of the Fane of Flesh to mark where I was supposed to stand!" She made the familiar marks in the dust then pointed to similar carvings on the cavern walls.

Ratepe resisted. "All right, maybe this was the Phyrexian stronghold and the Thran attacked it, instead of the other way around. I mean, nobody really knows."

"I know! It says Gix, the silver-something, strong-something of the Thran. Of the Thran, Ratepe. If Urza could go back in time, he'd find Gix here waiting for him. That's what Gix meant! Waste not, want not, Ratepe. Gix was here seven thousand years ago! He wasn't lying, not completely. Those are Thran powerstones that you and Urza call the Mightstone and the Weakstone. The stones made the brothers what they were, Ratepe, and Gix might well have made the stones!"

"The Phyrexians stole powerstones from the Thran?"

"You're not listening!" Xantcha waved her arms at a heavily carved wall. "It's all there. Two factions. Sheep and pigs, Red-Stripes and Shratta, Urza and Mishra, take your pick. 'The glory and destiny is compleation'—compleation, the word, Ratepe, the exact angle-for-angle word that's carved on the doors of the Fane of Flesh. And there." She pointed at another section. " 'Life served, never weakened' and the word Thran, Rat, is the first glyph of the word for life." She recited them in Phyrexian, so he could hear the similarities, as strong as the similarities between their pronunciation of Koilos. "If language drifts in three thousand years, imagine what it could do in seven, once everyone's compleat and only newts have flesh cords in their throats."

The sun had slipped below the mountain tops. The marks, the words, were fading. Xantcha turned in Ratepe's arms to face him.

"He's been wrong. All this time—almost all his life—Urza's been wrong. The Phyrexians never invaded Dominaria! There was no Phyrexia until Gix and the Ineffable left here. Winners, losers, I can't tell. We knew that. We spent over a thousand years looking for the world where the Phyrexians came from, so we could learn from those who defeated them . . . and all the time, it was Urza's own world."

Xantcha was shaking, sobbing. Ratepe tried to comfort her, but it was too soon.

"Urza would say to me, that's Phyrexian, that's abomination. Only the Thran way is the right way, the pure way. And I always thought to myself, the difference isn't that great. The Phyrexians aren't evil because they're compleat. They'd be evil no matter what they were, and those automata he was making, he was growing them in a jar. Is it right to grow gnats in a jar but not newts in a vat?"

Ratepe held her tight against his chest before she pulled away. "The Red-Stripes and the Shratta were both bad luck for everybody who crossed either one of them," he said gently. "And so were Urza and Mishra. Any time there's only one right way, ordinary people get crushed— maybe even the Morvernish and the Baszerati."

"But all our lives, Ratepe. All our lives, we've been chasing shadows! It's like someone reached inside and pulled everything out."

"You just said it: the Phyrexians are evil. Urza's crazed, but he's not evil, and he's the only one here who can beat the Phyrexians at their own game. We wanted to find the truth. Well, it wasn't what we expected, but we found a truth. And we've still got to go back to Urza. The truth here doesn't change that, does it?"

"We can't tell him. If he knew his Thran weren't the great and noble heroes of Dominaria . . . If he knew that the Thran destroyed Mishra . . ."

"You're right, but Mishra would laugh. I can hear him."

"I can't believe that."

"It's laugh or cry, Xantcha." Ratepe dried her tears. "If you've truly wasted three thousand years and you're stuck fighting a war that was stupid four thousand years before that, then either you laugh and keep going, or you cry and give it up."

Chapter 22

There was no laughter three days later over the Sea of Laments. The weather had been chancy since Xantcha had put the Argivian coast at her back. From the start, thick clouds had blocked her view of the sun and stars. She navigated against a wind she knew wasn't steady and with an innate sense of direction that grew less reliable as she tired. They hadn't seen land for two days, not even a boat.

Xantcha would have brought the sphere down on a raft just then and taken her chances with strangers. A black wall-cloud had formed, leaking lightning, to the northeast. The waves below were stiff with cross winds and froth. She knew better than to try to soar above the impending storm, didn't have the strength to outrun it, and didn't know what would happen to the sphere if—when—downdrafts slammed it into the ocean.

Ratepe had his arms around her, keeping Xantcha warm and upright, the most he could do. He'd spotted the storm but hadn't said anything, other than that he knew how to swim. Ratepe was one up on Xantcha there; the long-ago seamen who'd taught her how to sail had warned her never to get friendly with the sea. If—when—they went down, she'd yawn out Urza's armor. Maybe it would keep her afloat, though it never had kept her dry.

The storm was bigger than the wall-cloud, and fickle, too. In a matter of minutes it spawned smaller clouds, one to the north, the other directly overhead. The first wind was a downdraft that hit the sphere so hard Xantcha and Ratepe were weightless, floating and screaming within it. Then, as Xantcha fought to keep them above the waves, a vagrant wind struck from the south. The south wind pushed them into sheets of noisy, blinding rain.

The squall died as suddenly as it had been born. Xantcha could see again and wished she couldn't. The distance between them and the storm's heart had been halved and, worse, a waterspout had spun out. Rooted in both the ocean and the clouds, the sinuous column of seawater and wind bore down on them as if it had eyes and they were prey.

"What is that?" Ratepe whispered.

"Waterspout," she told him and felt his fingers lock into her arms like talons.

"Is it going to eat us?"

The waterspout wasn't alive and didn't really have an appetite for fools, but that scarcely mattered as they were caught and spun with such force that the sphere flattened against them. It flattened but held, even when they slammed into the raging waves. At one point Xantcha thought they were underwater, if only because everything had become dark and quiet. Then the ocean spat them out, and they hurtled through wind and rain.

Wind, rain, and, above all, lightning. Whatever the cyst produced, whether it was Urza's armor or the sphere, it attracted lightning. Bolts struck continuously. The air within the sphere turned acrid and odd. It pulled their hair and clothes away from their bodies and set everything aglow with blue-white light. Xantcha lost all sense of north or south and counted herself lucky that she still knew up from down.

Every few moments the storm paused, as if regrouping its strength for the next assault. In one such breather, Ratepe leaned close to her ear and said, "I love you,"

She shouted back, "We're not dead yet!" and surrendered the sphere to an updraft that carried them into the storm's heart.

They rose until the rain became ice and froze around the sphere, making it heavy and driving it down to the sea. Xantcha thought for sure they'd hit the waves, sink, and drown, but the storm wasn't done playing with them. As lightning boiled off the ice, the winds launched them upward again. Xantcha tried to break the cycle, but her efforts were useless. They rose and froze, plummeted, and rose again, not once or twice, but nine times before they fell one last time and found themselves floating on the ocean as the storm passed on to the south.

The pitch and roll among the choppy waves was the insult after injury. Ratepe's grip on Xantcha's arms weakened, and she suffered nausea.

"I can't lift us up," she said, having tried and failed. "I'm going to have to let go of the sphere."

"No!" Ratepe's plea should have been a shout; it was a barely coherent moan instead.

"I'll make another—"

"Too sick. Can't float."

She tried to ignite his spirit. "A little seasickness won't kill you."

"Can't."

"Waste not, want not. I'm the one who can't swim! I'm counting on you to keep me afloat until I can make another sphere."

Ratepe slumped beside her. His face was gray and sweaty. His eyes were closed. Whatever strength he had left was dedicated to fighting the spasms in his gut. A little bit of seasickness would kill them both if she released the sphere. And if she didn't release it?

Xantcha tried to make it rise, but lifting the sphere had always been something that simply happened as it formed and not anything she'd ever consciously controlled.

"Urza," Ratepe said through clenched teeth. "Urza'll come. Your heart."

Urza had come when she'd nearly blown herself up with the Phyrexian ambulator, but now she wasn't in any immediate danger. The sky overhead was a brilliant blue, and the sphere bobbed like a driftwood log.

"Sorry, Ratepe. If he didn't pull us out of that storm we were riding, then he's not going to pull us out of here. I'm not close enough to dying to get his attention."

"Gotta be a way."

Xantcha peeled Ratepe's sweat-soaked hair away from his eyes. He'd said he loved her, in a moment of sheer panic, of course, but there was a chance he'd been telling the truth. Sexless, parentless newt that she was, Xantcha didn't imagine she could love as born-folk did, but she felt something for the miserable young man beside her that she'd never felt before, something worth more than all her books and other treasures.

"Hold on," she urged, grasping his hand. "I'll think of something."

Xantcha couldn't think of anything she hadn't already tried, and the sphere remained mired in the water. The waves had lessened, and she enjoyed the gentle movement, but Ratepe was as miserable as when the storm had dropped them, and by the way he was sweating out his misery, he'd be parched before long, too.

"Come morning, we'll be late," she said as the sky darkened. "Maybe Urza will come looking for us, but maybe not right away."

"Can't you . . . do something . . . to make him look?" Ratepe asked.

A whole sentence exhausted him. He rested with his eyes closed. Xantcha tried to tell Ratepe that the motion would bother him less if he sat up and looked at the horizon, as he'd learned to do when they were soaring. Ratepe insisted the motions were totally dissimilar and refused to try.

"How does . . . Urza know when you . . . need him?"

"He doesn't," Xantcha answered. "When we were dodging Phyrexians we stayed close, but the rest of the time, I never gave much thought to needing Urza, and he certainly never needed me."

"Never? Three thousand years . . . and you never . . . needed each other?"

"Never."

Ratepe sighed and curled around his knees. He began to shiver, a bad sign considering how warm the Sea of Laments was in the summer. Xantcha tucked their blankets around him, then, because she'd worked up a sweat herself, and stripped off her outer tunic. It got tangled in her hair and in the thong of a pendant she'd worn so long she'd forgotten why she wore it.

"You can hit me now," she said, breaking the thong.

"What?"

"I said, you can hit me now . . . or you can wait until after we find out if this thing still works."

"What?"

"A long time ago—and I mean a long time ago—Urza did make me an artifact that would get his attention. I used something like it just once, before Urza invaded Phyrexia. I have to break it."

That time Xantcha had crushed the little crystal between two rocks. This time she tried biting it and broke a tooth before it cracked. Waste not, want not. At least she'd been farsighted enough to use her back teeth which grew back quicker than the front ones.

That time, between the rocks, there'd been a small flash of light as whatever power or sorcery Urza had sealed within the crystal was released. This time Xantcha neither saw nor felt anything, and when she examined the broken pieces, they were lined with a sooty residue that didn't look promising.

"How long?" Ratepe asked.

"A day before he got there with his dragon."

Ratepe groaned, "Too long."

Xantcha was inclined to agree. Urza must have come back to the forest before he went after the dragon. He wouldn't have taken the chance that the Phyrexians might get away, and after he'd finished with the diggers, he'd known where the ambulator was. If Urza was going to haul them out of the Sea of Laments, they'd be on dry land before moonrise. If the crystal hadn't lost its power. If Urza recognized its signal and remembered what it meant.

Those were worries Xantcha kept to herself. The stars came out. Xantcha began to fear the worst, at least about Urza, and for Ratepe. They had enough food and water for two more days. Taking advantage of her newt's resilience, Xantcha could get to land either way. She wasn't sure about Ratepe.

It would be a stupid way for anyone to die, but the same could be said about most deaths.

Ratepe fell asleep. His breathing steadied, his skin grew warmer and drier. He might be over his seasickness by morning; he had adapted to soaring, and there was nothing to be gained by premature despair. Xantcha settled in around him. It was remarkable that two bodies could be more comfortable curled around each other than either was alone. She closed her eyes.

Xantcha woke up with a stabbing pain in her gut, water sloshing against her armpits, and Urza shouting in her ear:

"What misbegotten scheme put you in the middle of an ocean!"

He had her by the nape of the neck, like a cat carrying a kitten, and held Ratepe the same way. The sphere was burst, obviously. Xantcha knew she should yawn out the armor, but Urza moved too fast. They were a split instant between-worlds, a heartbeat longer in the wintry winds of a nearby world, then back through the between-worlds to the cottage. Xantcha was gasping, mostly because Urza dropped her before turning his attention to Ratepe who'd turned blue during the three-stride 'walk. She knew his color because they'd traveled west and the sun wasn't close to setting behind the Ohran Ridge.

A bit of healing and a few sips from a green bottle off Urza's shelves brought Ratepe around.

"Change your clothes, Brother," Urza commanded in a tone that had surely started battles in their long-ago nursery. "Wash. Get something to eat. Xantcha and I need to talk."

Mishra, of course, stood his ground. "Don't blame Xantcha, and don't think you can ignore me . . . again. I'm the one who wanted to see Koilos."

Ratepe pronounced the word in the old-fashioned way. Xantcha dared a glance at Urza's eyes, thinking her lover was getting advice from the Weakstone. Both of Urza's eyes were glossy black from lid to lid. She hadn't seen them like that since they'd left Phyrexia, which made her think of Gix and the Thran and a score of other things she quickly stifled. Xantcha tried to catch Ratepe's eye and pass him a warning to tread cautiously, if he couldn't figure that for himself.

With his bold remark, Ratepe had effectively changed the landscape of recrimination. If Xantcha could have seized control of the argument at that moment, she could have guaranteed there'd be no revelations about the fate of the Thran. If she could have seized control. She didn't catch Ratepe's eye, and Urza had lost interest in her as well.

"Koilos is dead. There's nothing left. We took it all, Brother. Us and the Phyrexians," Urza said, leaving Xantcha to wonder if he'd visited the cave since his return to Dominaria.

"I needed to see it with my own eyes," Ratepe replied, a comment that, considering the circumstances, could have many layers of meaning. "You told me to go away for a while, so I did."

"I never meant you to go to Koilos. If it was Koilos you wanted, we could have gone together."

"That was never a good idea, Urza," Ratepe said with finality as he walked out the open door, following the near-orders Urza had already given.

"You should have stopped him," Urza hissed at Xantcha when they were alone. "My brother is . . . fragile. Koilos could have torn him apart."

"It's just another place, Urza," Xantcha countered, resisting the urge to add that Ratepe was just another man. Neither statement was true. After a year on the Ohran Ridge, Ratepe might not be Mishra, but he'd become more than a willful, onetime slave.

" 'Just another place,' " Urza mocked her. "For one like you, yes, I suppose it would be. What would you see? A cave, some ruins? What did my brother see? He isn't quite himself yet. The next one will be better, stronger. I expected it would be several Mishras before I'd take one back to Koilos."

"There won't be another Mishra, Urza."

Urza turned away. He puttered at his worktable, scraping up residues and dumping them in a bucket. He'd been working on something when the crystal struck his mind. Xantcha's anger, always quick to flare, was also quick to fade.

"Thank you for picking us out of the ocean."

"I didn't know at first. It took me a moment to remember what it was that I was hearing. I made that crystal for you so long ago, when I still thought I could invade and destroy Phyrexia. My ambitions have grown smaller. Since Equilor, it's all I can do to protect Dominaria from them. I'll make you another."

"Make it easier to break. I lost a tooth on this one. Make one for Ratepe, too."

"Ratepe?" Urza looked up, puzzled, then nodded. "When this is over, when I've exposed the *sleepers* and put Phyrexia on notice that Dominaria is prepared to fight them, it will be time to talk about the future. I've thought about it while you were gone. This cottage isn't big enough. I've begun to envision permanent defenses for all Dominaria, for Old Terisiare and all the other great islands. Artifacts on a scale to dwarf any that I've made before. I'll build them in place, and when I've finished one of my new sentries, I'll move on to the next. I'll need assistants, of course—"

"Other than me and . . . ?" Xantcha left her thought dangling.

"What I've planned will take a generation, maybe ten before it is complete. And the assistants I have in mind will become the guardians of my sentries. They'll become the patriarchs and matriarchs of permanent communities. You understand that can't include you. As for him, he is mortal, not like you or me. We are what the Phyrexians made us. I can't change that, or him. I wouldn't, even if I could. That would be adding abomination to abomination. But he—Ratepe, my brother—will age and die. I thought, I hoped you would choose, while you were together these last few days, to remain together, with him—"

"Somewhere else?"

"Yes. It would be best. For me. For what I have to do."

Urza wasn't mad, not the way he'd been mad and locked in the past for so long. Bringing him face-to-face with Mishra had set him free to be the man Kayla Bin-Kroog had known: self-centered, self-confident, and selfish, blithely convinced, until the world came to an end, that whatever he wanted was best for everyone else.

Xantcha was too weary for anger. "We'll talk," she agreed. Maybe she'd tell him what she'd learned at Koilos. More likely, she wouldn't bother. Urza was immune to truth. "Do you still need either of us, or should we make ourselves scarce again?" she asked.

"No, not at all! I have work for you, Xantcha." He gestured toward one wall where boxes were piled high. "They've all got to be put in place. I'll 'walk you there. You know, it's quite fortunate, in a way, that you broke that crystal. I'd forgotten them completely; I'll make up a score by dawn. Think of it, no more waiting, no more wasted time. As soon as you're finished, you can summon me, and I'll 'walk you to the next place!"

"Tomorrow," she said, heading for the door. Xantcha had gotten what she wanted; if she'd been born with true imagination, she would have known that getting what she wanted wouldn't be the same as what she had expected. "Tonight I've got to rest."

Ratepe was waiting for her in the other room. "Did you tell him?"

Xantcha shook her head. She sat down heavily on her stool. The chest with her copies of *The Antiquity Wars* caught her eye. What would Kayla have said? Urza never really changes. His friends never really learn.

"There wasn't any need to tell Urza anything. He's got his visions, his future. Nothing I'd tell him would make any difference, just like you said. We're going to be busy until the Glimmer Moon goes high. I am, at least. He's got a pile of spiders for me to plant and great plans for that crystal I broke. Watch and see, by tomorrow Urza will have decided that it was his idea for us to get stuck in the Sea of Laments."

Ratepe stood behind her, rubbing her neck and shoulders. It had taken only a year, after more than three thousand, to become dependent on the touch of living fingers. She'd miss him.

"I should've stayed?" he asked. "I hoped if I took the blame—if I made Mishra take it—he'd calm down quicker. Guess I was wrong."

"Not entirely. You had a good idea, and you handled it well." She shrugged off his hands and stood. "Has Urza ever told you that he thinks you're the first of many Mishras who're going to walk back into his life?"

"Never in those words, but, sometimes I know he's frustrated with me. Scares me sometimes, because if he decided he didn't want me around, there'd be nothing I could do about it. But I've gotten used to not having charge of my own life. I've forgotten Ratepe. I'm just Rat, trying to live another day and not always sure why . . . except for you."

Xantcha studied her hands, not Ratepe's face. "Maybe you should think about taking charge of your life again."

"He's decided it's time for a new Mishra? Do I get to help find my replacement?"

"No." That didn't sound right. "I mean, I'm not going to look for another Mishra." She took a deep breath. "And I won't be here if another Mishra comes walking over the Ridge."

Ratepe pushed air through his teeth. "He's sending us both away because we went to Koilos?"

She shook her head. "Because my plan worked. Urza's not thinking about the past anymore, and you and I, we're part of his past."

"I'll go back to Efuan Pincar, to Pincar City," Ratepe spoke aloud, but mostly to himself. "After we expose the *sleepers* and all, Tabarna's going to need good men. If Tabarna's not a sleeper himself. If he is, I don't know who'll become king, and we'll need good men even more. What about you? We could work together for Efuan Pincar. You're smarter than you think you are. You leap sometimes, when you should think, as if a part of you is as young as you look. But you know things that never got written down."

Xantcha walked to the window. "I am part of the past, Ratepe, and I'm tired. I never realized just how tired."

"It's been a too-long day and the worst always falls on you." He was behind her again, rubbing her shoulders and guiding her toward the bed.

Xantcha's weariness wasn't anything that sleep or Ratepe's passion could cure, but she wasn't about to discuss the point.

Urza 'walked her to Morvern shortly after dawn. He left her with two sacks of improved spiders, explicit instructions for where they should be placed, and a plain-looking crystal he promised wouldn't break her teeth. Four days later Xantcha took no chances and crushed the crystal between two stones. Urza 'walked her to Baszerat, then to other sleeper-ridden city-states on Gulmany's southern and eastern coasts. There wasn't time, he said, for side trips to the cottage. They had eighteen days until the Glimmer Moon struck its zenith.

"What about Efuan Pincar?" she asked before he left her and a sack of spiders in the hills beyond another southern town. "Will there be time to put the new ones there?"

"You and him!" Urza complained. "Yes, I've taken care of that myself. When the night comes, that's where you'll be, in the plaza outside the palace in Pincar City. I wouldn't dare suggest any place else! Now, you understand what has to be done here? The spiders in that sack, they're for open spaces, for plazas, markets, and temple precincts. You've got to put them where there are at least twenty paces all around. Less and the vibrations will start to cancel each other out. And make sure you put them where they won't attract attention or be trampled. You understand, that's important. They mustn't be trampled. They might break, or worse, they'll trigger prematurely."

They'd come a long way from screaming spiders. Xantcha supposed she'd find out exactly how far in Pincar City. Until then, "Twenty paces all around, no attention, no big feet. How long?"

"Two days, less, if you can. There are some places in the west that we've missed, and it wouldn't hurt to put a few across the sea in Argivia—"

"Urza, we've never even looked for Phyrexians there!"

"It couldn't hurt, if there's time."

With that, Urza 'walked away.

* * * * *

Seventeen days later, the eastern city of Narjabul in which Xantcha was planting spiders had begun to fill with revelers for the coming mid-summer festival. Finding the privacy she needed to plant them was becoming more difficult by the hour. At last a tall, blond-haired man stepped out of the crowd and said, "I think there's nothing more to be done. Let's 'walk home."

The man was Urza, looking like a man in his mid-twenties and dressed in a rich merchant's silks that felt as real as they looked.

Xantcha hadn't expected to see him for another day. She hadn't felt she could break the crystal before then. "I'm nowhere near finished," she confessed. "There aren't enough rooms. The crowds just stay on the streets. It's been difficult, and it's getting worse. They sleep in the plazas where I'm trying to plant the spiders."

"No matter," Urza assured her. "One spider more or less won't win the day, or the night. There's always next month, next year."

He was in one of his benign and generous moods. Xantcha found herself instantly suspicious.

"Has something gone wrong?" she asked. "With the spiders? At the cottage?" She hesitated to say Ratepe's name.

"No, no . . . I thought you and he might want to celebrate. I thought I'd 'walk you both to Pincar City and leave you there tonight."

Urza had his arm draped across Xantcha's shoulder and was steering her through the crowd when they were accosted by three rowdy youths, considerably worse for the wine and ale that flowed freely in the guild tents pitched across plaza. The soberest of the trio complimented Urza's wide-cuffed boots while one of his companions grabbed Xantcha from behind and the third tried to steal Urza's coin pouch. Xantcha stomped her boot heel on her attacker's instep and rammed her elbow against his ribs to free herself.

The youth, remarkably sobered by his pain, immediately shouted, "Help! Thief! He's taken my purse and my father's sack! Help! Stop him before he gets away!"

Xantcha had no intention of running or of surrendering the spider-filled sack. She had a fighting knife and could have put a swift end to her attacker, but they'd drawn attention, and the middle of a mob was a dangerous place to make a defensive stand, even with Urza's armor. If she'd been alone, Xantcha would have used her sphere and made a spectacular exit. She wasn't alone, though, Urza was a few steps away in the midst of his own fracas, so she yawned out her armor instead and hoped he'd get them free before too many revelers got hurt.

Justice was swift and presumptive. A bystander grabbed her from behind again and put a knife against her throat. He'd probably guessed that something wasn't quite right before she stomped and elbowed him as she'd done with her first attacker, but everyone knew she was more than she seemed when they saw that the knife hadn't drawn blood. Most folk retreated, making ward-signs as they went, but a few rose to the challenge. One of challengers, a thick-set man in long robes and pounding a silver-banded ebony staff against the cobblestones, was also a sorcerer.

"Urza!" Xantcha shouted, a name that was apt to get everyone's attention anywhere in Dominaria. It didn't matter what language she used after that to add, "Let's go!"

The sorcerer cast a spell, a serpentine rope of crimson fire that fizzled in a sigh of dark, foul-smelling smoke when it touched the armor. He'd readied another when Urza ended the confrontation.

Urza had abandoned his merchant's finery for imposing robes that made him seem taller and more massive. He didn't have his staff—it was absolutely real and couldn't be hidden—but Urza the Artificer didn't need a staff. Mana flowed to him easily. Even Xantcha could feel it moving beneath her armored feet, in such abundance that he could afford to target his spells precisely: small, but not fatal, lightning jolts for the three troublemakers and a mana-leaching miasma for the sorcerer who'd intervened on the wrong side of a brawl.

Then Urza clapped his hand around Xantcha's and 'walked with her into the between-worlds.

"Between us and the spiders, everyone in Narjabul's going to remember this year's mid-summer festival," Xantcha laughed when her feet were on solid ground outside the cottage.

Urza grimaced. "They'll remember my name. The *sleepers* and who knows what else might get suspicious before tomorrow night. I didn't want to be connected with this, not yet. I want Phyrexia to know that Dominaria is fighting back, not that Urza has returned to haunt them."

"I'm sorry. I'd had a knife at my throat, there was a sorcerer taking aim at me, and a crowd about to get very unpleasant. I wasn't thinking about consequences."

"I never expect you to."

Ratepe came out of the workroom. They hadn't seen each

other for seventeen hectic days, but when Xantcha kept her greeting restrained, he caught the warning and did likewise until they were alone in the other room.

"Did Urza tell you, we're going to watch the spiders from Efuan Pincar!" He lifted Xantcha off the floor and spun her around.

"He said he was going to leave us there."

Ratepe set her down. "I told him that you'd given me your word that I could go back to my old life. I called it 'the life I had before Mishra awoke within me.' He'd started talking about making big artifact-sentries, just like you'd said. He didn't quite come out and say that he wanted to make room for a new Mishra, too, but I understood that's what he meant."

"I keep thinking about the Weakstone."

Ratepe shook his head. "If Urza paid attention to the Weakstone, he'd have an aching head, but he's less attuned to it now than he was when I got here. He is putting the past behind him. I decided to make it easier for myself. If he leaves me in Pincar City, I'm no worse off than I was a year ago. Better, in fact, since I've learned some artifice." Ratepe tried to sound optimistic and failed.

Xantcha opened the chest where she kept her supply of precious stones and metals. "Wouldn't hurt to be prepared." She handed him a heavy golden chain that could keep a modest man in comfort for life.

"He'll change his mind about you, Xantcha. He's never going to send you away," Ratepe insisted, but he dropped the chain over his head and tucked it discreetly beneath his tunic.

Xantcha hauled out coins as well and a serviceable knife with a hidden compartment in its sheath.

"It's the Festival of Fruits," Ratepe protested, refusing to accept the weapon.

"There's going to be chaos for sure and who-knows-what for us afterward." She took his hand and lightly slapped the knife into it.

"What about a sword, then?" he asked, eyeing her rafter-hung collection.

"I was wrong to have a sword in Medran. Efuan Pincar doesn't have a warrior cult, and your nobility averted its eyes about ten years ago. We'll try to be part of the crowd. Knives are a common man's weapon."

"You're nervous?" Ratepe asked with evident disbelief.

"Cautious. You and Urza, you're acting as if this is going to be some victory celebration. We don't know what's going to happen, not in a whole lot of ways."

"You don't want to go?"

"No. I want to see what happens, and Urza's made up his mind. I haven't survived all this time by being careless, that's all."

"You're nervous about being with me? About taking care of me, 'cause you think I can't take care of myself?"

Xantcha pulled up her pant leg and buckled an emergency stash of gold around her calf. She didn't answer Ratepe's question.

"I know Pincar City," he said petulantly. "It's my home, and I can keep my own nose clean, if I need to. Avohir's mercy, it's the damned Festival of Fruits—seven days of berries! All music and bright colors. Parents bring their children!"

Unimpressed, Xantcha handed him a smaller knife to tuck inside his boot, then closed the chest on her treasures wondering if she'd ever look at Kayla's picture again.

Chapter 23

Urza 'walked them to the royal city shortly before sundown. Knowing that Pincar was crowded with revelers and that the journey would leave Ratepe incapacitated, Urza strode out of the between-worlds near the orchard where Xantcha had battled the Phyrexian priest. Other than birds and insects, there were no witnesses to the trio's arrival. Few signs of the previous year's skirmish remained. Trees still sported scorched and unproductive branches, and there was a gap in the geometric rows where a broken tree had been removed.

Ratepe was stunned and shivering. Urza knelt beside him, healing him with warm, radiant hands and saying nothing about the small fortune in gold hung around his neck.

"You'll be careful getting over the walls," Urza said to Xantcha while Ratepe finished his recovery.

"Of course," she replied, irritable because she was suddenly anxious about entering the city.

Neither of them had asked her if she 'wanted to watch the spiders scream from the plaza of Avohir's great temple, not far from the catacomb where she'd encountered Gix. Xantcha knew she would have lied even if they had. She'd never told Urza about the demon before, and events had moved too swiftly since Narjabul to tell him now. Besides, she hadn't expected to be anxious. If the demon had wanted to find her, he could have found her. Phyrexian demons were many terrible things, but they weren't shapechangers the way Urza was. If Gix hadn't pursued Xantcha to any of the out-of-way places she'd been since their encounter, she didn't expect him to simply appear in the middle of Pincar City's crowded plaza.

"You'll need these," Urza offered her two lumps of milk-white wax.

She hesitated before taking them and asked the question, Why? with her eyes.

"You're vulnerable, and the armor might not be enough protection. Plug your ears first. You'll know when, and you'll have time. Don't fret about it."

He must think the spiders themselves were what made her jumpy, and he might have been right, if it weren't for Gix. "I won't worry," she lied and tucked the wax in the hem of her sleeve. Then she asked the question she'd been avoiding. "Afterward? Should I break the crystal?" She still had the one he'd given her for Narjabul.

"I'll find you."

Xantcha dipped her chin. After three thousand years, it would end without even a good-bye. She could see Kayla frowning in her mind's eye. *The Antiquity Wars* should have prepared her for this.

Urza 'walked away. She and Ratepe waited silently for sundown. Their lives were unraveling, pulled apart between the past and future. Xantcha wanted to hold the present tight. This past year with Ratepe was as close as she had ever come to forgetting that she hadn't been born. She sensed that once the present became the past, regardless of whatever lay in the future, these moments wouldn't be recaptured.

But when Xantcha looked at Ratepe, staring northwest, toward the city of his past and future, she had nothing to say to him until the sky darkened and the first stars had appeared.

"It's time," she said.

They sat together as Xantcha recited her mnemonic and the sphere formed around them.

Country folk who didn't want to pay for a room within the city had pitched tents in the fields and fairgrounds beyond the walls. Between the smoke from their cookfires and a scattering of clouds overhead, Xantcha had no trouble getting the them over the walls and above the southeast quarter of the city. Ratepe said he knew the area and provided directions to a quiet street and the long-abandoned courtyard of a burnt-out house.

"You lived here?" Xantcha asked when the sphere had collapsed.

He pointed at a gaping second-story window. "Last I saw, it was burning. My mother was yelling at my father, telling him to carry me and forget about his precious books."

"Did he?"

"Yes." Ratepe put his arm on a charred door. It opened partway, then struck a fallen roof beam. "We weren't poor. I'd've thought that by now someone would've taken advantage of our misfortune."

Xantcha took his hand, tugging him toward the alley that led back to the street. "Remember how you said everything was smaller since Urza's war? Everything's even smaller in Pincar City."

She and Urza weren't the only ones letting go of their pasts. Xantcha could almost hear Ratepe's disillusionment as they made their way to the wide plaza between the royal palace and Avohir's temple. There were as many empty houses as occupied ones, and those that were inhabited had shuttered windows, despite the summer humidity. Their doors were strapped with iron.

Ratepe didn't see anyone he might have recognized because they didn't see anyone at all. The sounds of the festival came filtered over the rooftops, along with the faint scent of *sleepers*, but the neighborhoods were locked tight.

When they got to the great plaza between Tabarna's palace and Avohir's temple, they understood why, and saw why so many festival-goers had chosen to pitch tents outside the city walls. The crowd was sullen and mean-spirited, looking for fights and, by the sounds of it, finding them with each other. Most of them were men dressed as Ratepe and Xantcha were dressed in the nondescript garments of the countryside. The few women whom Xantcha could see didn't appear to be anyone's wife, mother, daughter, or sister—not quite the family gathering Ratepe had promised.

He didn't said a word when the crowd surged and parted, giving them a glimpse of eight grim-faced men coming through a palace gate, headed for Avohir's temple. The men were uniformed in black-dyed leather and chain mail, except for their sleeveless surcoats, which bore a broad red stripe above the hem. Two of them carried torches that could double as polearms, the other six carried short halberds—wicked weapons with a crescent ax facing one direction and a sharpened gut-hook going the other way. Xantcha knew the kind of damage such weapons could do against a mostly unarmored mob; she hoped she wasn't going to witness it again.

The crowd reformed in the Red-Stripe wake, watchful and not quite silent. Someone muttered fighting words, but not loud enough for Red-Stripe ears. That would come later. Xantcha figured her hopes were futile. Both sides wouldn't be satisfied with anything less than bloodshed.

"I-I don't know what's happened," Ratepe stammered. "*Sleepers?*"

He wanted an affirmative answer, which Xantcha couldn't give. There was oil in the air, the smell faint and mostly coming from the temple or the palace, both still secure within their separate walls. "We happened," Xantcha replied, as grim as the Red-Stripe faces. "We made sure the truth got out, didn't we? These are all your folk, Ratepe, ordinary Efuands, the ones who got caught up with the Red-Stripes and the ones who didn't. Now everybody's got a grudge."

Screaming spiders and Phyrexians would just get in the way.

"I was afraid of what would happen if we just took out the Red-Stripes and the Phyrexians, but this is worse than I imagined it could ever be," Ratepe said. His hand rested momentarily on her shoulder, then fell away.

Closer to the temple, the plaza erupted in shouts and screams. Ratepe succumbed to gawking curiosity as he eased past Xantcha for a better look at the skirmish. She grabbed his arm and rocked him back on his heels.

"Unless you know a better place with food and beds," she snapped, "I say we go to ground in your family's old courtyard." They were traveling light on everything but gold. "This will be calmer come daylight, or the whole city could be in flames," she added.

Without much confidence, Ratepe said that the better inns were on the western side of the plaza. Xantcha, who hadn't eaten since the previous night in Narjabul, was game, though she had to grab Ratepe's arm again to keep him from striking off through the middle of the plaza.

"Forget you ever knew this place, all right? Pay attention to what you see, not what you remember," she advised as they headed north, toward the sea and the palace.

They were on the cobblestones near the Red-Stripe barracks, doing their best not to attract attention, when the temple gongs rang out. This time Xantcha expected the worst and would have bolted for any shadow large enough to contain the sphere if Ratepe hadn't held her back.

"There's a procession every night," he said. "That's what everyone's here for, what they're supposed to be here for. The high priests march the Book around and put it on the dais until midnight."

Xantcha noticed the hulking white-draped platform in the middle of the plaza for the first time. "Every night?" she asked, thinking of tomorrow night when the spiders would scream.

Ratepe nodded.

She nodded, too, seeing to the heart of his requests. "You've been thinking about this from the moment Urza started talking about exposing the *sleepers* with the Glimmer Moon! So, why, exactly, put shatter spiders on the altar?"

"Because the Book won't be there when the altar's destroyed. I figured it would shame the Shratta, whatever's left of them and I wanted the Shratta shamed at the same time the Red-Stripes were exposed. I didn't expect Red-Stripes to be leading the procession."

He cocked his head toward the temple where what he'd described was happening: the same eight armed men they'd seen earlier marched at the head of a short parade whose focal point was an ornately shrouded litter bearing Avohir's holy book. The tome's container was borne on the shoulders of four priests, at least one of whom reeked oil. Xantcha glanced up at the sky.

The Glimmer Moon had risen, but though she knew the habits of the larger moon and its phases, she'd always regarded the smaller moon as a nuisance, sometimes there, sometimes not, never welcome. She didn't know if it rose earlier or later each day and wasn't completely clear on the whole "striking its zenith" moment that Urza was counting on.

"They just carry the Book out to the dais and then carry it back at midnight? A couple thousand paces. You're not hoping for something to happen while they're carrying it, are you?" If Ratepe had wanted to shame the Shratta, she couldn't imagine anything more effective than having a sleeper collapse while the holy book's litter was sitting on his shoulder.

"No," Ratepe replied, but before he could specify which question he'd answered, the nearest palace gate swung open. More armed and armored Red-Stripes emerged.

A sleeper marched in the second octet. He passed so close that Xantcha was sure she knew which of the eight it was: a clean-shaven young man, not apparently much older than Ratepe and not handsome either. His mouth and nose were too big for his face, his eyes too small. When he turned and stared, Xantcha's blood cooled. She forced her head to remain still and her eyes to lose focus. He might not be able to tell she'd been watching him. Xantcha held her breath, too, though that surely was too late. When the octet had passed, she started walking again.

The dais was still unburdened when they reached the western plaza where the guild inns, each a little fortress, stood behind their closed-gate walls. Ratepe handled the negotiations with the guild guards while Xantcha watched the procession go round and round the plaza. The joint guild of barbers and surgeons had a room behind the kitchen for which they wanted an exorbitant amount of copper and silver but not in any of the forms Xantcha or Ratepe carried it. Fortunately—but not, she suspected, coincidentally—there was a money changers' booth butted up against the barber's watchtower.

"Festival robbery," Ratepe said dramatically as he collected the devalued worth of a golden ring. "Tabarna shall hear of this!"

"Avohir, he knows," the money changer replied, pointing to the lead seals dangling from a silk ribbon overhead.

The room behind the kitchen had been let to another traveler. They wound up in a dust-choked garret that Xantcha was sure had been home to a flock of pigeons earlier in the day.

"The food will be good," Ratepe promised once they'd claimed their quarters.

"Don't say another word. You've been wrong about everything else. If you keep quiet now, the meal may at least be edible!" She was jesting, resorting to the rough humor that worked well on the Ohran Ridge and floundered here in the city.

But the food was good. They devoured roast lamb with sweet herbs, a thick grainy paste that tasted of nuts and saffron, honey-glazed bread, and an overflowing jug of the berry wine served only for the Festival of Fruits. It wasn't worth the silver they'd paid for it, but it was good nonetheless, and they hauled the remaining wine up to the top of the stairs when they were finished.

The garret overhung a blind alley, but a bit of acrobatics put them on the roof and gave them one of the better views of the plaza that Pincar had to offer. A breeze stirred the humid air, making it pleasant. In the plaza, Avohir's book remained open on the dais. Red-Stripes stood guard while priests took turns reciting Shratta verses from memory—or so Ratepe said. Their voices didn't reach the top of the guild inn.

The crowd had thinned, and what remained had settled in around ten or fifteen campfires scattered across the cobblestones. Red-Stripes stood guard outside the palace and the temple. Xantcha wondered who held the allegiance of the men who guarded the inns. Not that it mattered overmuch. The sky was open to her sphere if they had to get away in a hurry.

"This is a good place," she decided. "We can see everything that's important, and there's nothing to block the sphere if we need it. We'll watch tomorrow night from here."

They stayed on the roof until the temple gongs sounded again at midnight and the Red-Stripes escorted the huge holy book into Avohir's sanctuary.

"What do they do if it rains?" Xantcha asked as they swung and slipped back to the garret.

If the roof had been pleasant, their rented room was a prison. Leaving the windows open had attracted swarms of buzzing, biting insects without improving the air. The excuse for a bed smelled as if its last occupant had been a corpse, and a summertime corpse at that. Xantcha seriously considered yawning out the sphere, if only for Ratepe's sake. She'd breathed Phyrexian air, the ultimate standard by which foul air should be judged, and survived without a wheeze or cough. Poor Ratepe was sneezing himself inside out and short of breath. In the end they dragged the best of the blankets up to the roof and bedded down beneath the stars.

The day they'd been waiting for began before dawn with more gongs clanging from the temple as the Festival of Fruits started its fourth day. When the city gates opened, the tent encampments disgorged their pilgrims who were, on the whole, far less hardened than the men who'd held sway in the plaza at night. There were children and flower sellers and all the other things Ratepe remembered from his own childhood. He coaxed Xantcha out of the garret for bowls of berries and a second visit to Avohir's great sanctuary.

The line of petitioners waiting for Avohir to dry their tears was prohibitively long and the cloister passage to the priests' quarters and, ultimately, the crypt where she'd confronted Gix was closed off and guarded by the burliest Red-Stripes she'd seen since arriving in the city. They glistened with oily sweat, but they weren't Phyrexian.

"I can't believe they're all gone but that one I scented last night with the litter," Xantcha mused when Ratepe had finished taking her on a brief tour of the sanctuary. "Maybe Gix had pulled the sanctuary *sleepers* back. It doesn't take much practice to be a bully like a Red-Stripe, but a priest has to do things right."

"You put the spiders where they live—"

"I'd feel better if I'd seen that they were still in place."

"We'll find out soon enough," Ratepe replied with the sort of fatalism Xantcha herself usually brought to any discussion.

They were on the temple porch, looking down at the plaza from a different angle and gazing north at an afternoon storm. There was time for one more bowl of berries before the storm swept over the palace. Xantcha was indifferent to sweets, but Ratepe would have eaten himself sick. She saw what they did with Avohir's book when it rained. A team of priests who'd obviously worked together before scrambled to get the great book closed and covered with a bleached sail.

"It's going to get wet and ruined sooner or later," she pointed out as she and Ratepe climbed the five flights of narrow, rickety stairs to the garret.

"Sooner."

"But isn't it too precious to be mistreated like that?"

"It used to be there was a new Book every five years. I think the one they've got is maybe older than that. But it's not any one specific copy of the Book that matters, it's the idea of Avohir's book and the wisdom it contains. When a new Book's brought into the temple, the old one is cut up and passed out. Some people say if you burn a piece of the Book on New Year's Day, you'll have a better year, but some people—my father, for one—kept his scraps in a special box." Ratepe fell silent and stared out the window at the rain.

"Lost?" Xantcha asked.

"We brought it with out of the city. I didn't even think about it after the Shratta." He went back to staring.

"Should I buy a duck?" Xantcha asked, quite serious.

"A duck?"

"Six days after the Festival of Fruits, you'll be nineteen. I made sure I remembered. You said your mother roasted a duck."

"We'll see after tonight."

The festival crowds never recovered from their afternoon soaking. Hundreds of Efuands had returned to their tents beyond the walls, and the rowdy, mean-spirited element took over the plaza long before the midsummer sun was ready to set. Xantcha and Ratepe were spotted standing on the roof, silhouetted by the sun. The innkeeper, a man as burly as the sanctuary Red-Stripes reminded them in no uncertain terms that they'd rented the garret. For an additional two silver bits they rented the roof as well. The innkeeper offered to send up supper and another jug of berry wine.

Xantcha had had her fill of berries. They ate with the other guests in the commons, another leisurely, overpriced meal, then retreated to the roof for the spectacle. The western sky was blazing, and there were two brawls in the plaza, one strictly among the revelers, the other between the revelers and what appeared to be a cornered pair of Red-Stripes. A different, more strident set of gongs was struck, and a phalanx of mounted warriors thundered out of the palace, maces raised and swords drawn.

She couldn't decipher the details of the skirmish from the rooftop, but it wasn't long before three corpses were dragged away and a handful of men, bloodied and staggering, were marched into the palace. One of the prisoners wore an empty sword belt. He wasn't a Red-Stripe; that besieged pair had vanished back into the cadres. By his straight posture and arrogant air, even in defeat, the prisoner looked to be a nobleman, the first of that breed Xantcha had seen since arriving in Pincar City.

The nobleman's appearance crystallized a conclusion that had been lurking in Xantcha's thoughts. "Efuan Pincar has lost its leaders," she suggested to Ratepe. "Wherever I look, whether at the Red-Stripes, the temple, or that mob down there, I don't see anyone taking charge. If there are leaders, they're giving their orders in secret and then watching what happens from a distance, but they're not leading from in front."

Ratepe had an explanation for that absence. "Efuan Pincar's not like Baszerat and Morvern and places like that where every man, woman and child answers to a lord. Our Ancestors left that way behind at the Founding. It's written in Avohir's book. We have a season for making decisions, wintertime, when the harvest's been gathered and there's time to sit and talk—"

"Where's your king? Where's Tabarna? When I came here

twenty years ago, he was visible. If there'd been riots outside his palace, the way there've been last night and tonight, he'd have been out here. If not him, then someone, a high priest, a nobleman, even a merchant. There were men and women who could speak louder than the mob. Look down there. Folk have been killed, and there's no true reaction. There's anger everywhere, but nobody's gathering it and turning it into a weapon."

"Efuands aren't sheep. We think for ourselves." Ratepe countered quickly, a reply that had the sound of an overlearned lesson.

"Well, it's strange, very strange. It's not like anything I've seen before, and that doesn't happen very often. And it's not the way Efuand Pincar was twenty-odd years ago. Your king or someone would be visible. Efuands may not be sheep, Ratepe, but without leaders to stop them, I don't wonder that the Red-Stripes and Shratta were able to cause such trouble for you."

"Are you saying Phyrexians were with the Shratta and the Red-Stripes from the start?"

Ratepe was incredulous, sarcastic, but as soon as Xantcha thought about her answer, she realized, "Yes, I am. I found Gix in Avohir's crypt, but I probably could have found him in the palace just as easily."

"Do you think he's still here?"

"He might be. That passageway I saw wasn't like an ambulator. But Gix was too big to chase me up the stairs. If he's here, he's not going to come walking through the sanctuary doors."

Ratepe said nothing as the sunset aged from amber to lavender. Then, in little more than a whisper, he said, "In the war, Urza and Mishra's war, the Brotherhood of Gix made themselves useful to both sides. They pretended to be neutral. Neither Mishra nor Urza questioned them, but they answered to Gix, didn't they? The Gix in Avohir's temple. The Gix who made you. He controlled the brotherhood, and the brotherhood manipulated the brothers. Avohir's sweet mercy, Gix—the Phyrexians—did control that war. Kayla Bin-Kroog said never to forget the mistakes we made, but she didn't suspect the real rot . . ." His voice trailed off, then returned. "It's happening again, isn't it? Here and everywhere. And nobody's seeing it come."

"Urza has." Xantcha let out a pent-up breath. "Urza's mad in a thousand different ways, but he does remember, and he has learned. He knows to fight this war differently. He knows not to make the old mistakes. I've been listening to him, but I wasn't watching him. Urza lies to himself as much as he lies to you or me, but that hasn't stopped him from doing what has to be done. Until now. I've got to go back, Ratepe, after tonight. I've got to find him and tell him about Gix and about the Thran. There's a part of him that needs to know—deserves to know—everything that I know."

"You won't go alone, will you?"

"Efuan Pincar's going to need true leaders."

"True, but for Efuan Pincar's sake, Urza needs a Mishra that I can trust."

The Glimmer Moon was the evening star this midsummer season, far brighter than the star Ratepe called the Sea-Star and Xantcha called Berulu. It pierced the deepening twilight like a faintly malevolent diamond. Every world that Xantcha remembered where sentient races came together to talk and create societies, folk looked overhead and recited myths about the stars, the moon, and the wanderers.

Gulmany was no exception, but the Glimmer Moon was. It was bright, it wandered, everybody saw it, everybody knew it, and by some unspoken agreement, nobody included it in their myths. Like a loud, uninvited guest, the Glimmer Moon was acknowledged across the island with averted eyes and silence.

Even knowing what an important part it would play this evening, neither Xantcha nor Ratepe could look at it for long, and the pall it cast effectively ended their conversation.

Other, friendlier stars made their nightly appearance. Avohir's gongs clanged to announced the holy book's procession from the sanctuary altar to the white-draped dais. Xantcha found herself breathing in painful gasps, expecting the spiders to scream while the litter was in transit. She clutched Urza's waxen lumps in her fists and had the mnemonic for his armor on the edge of her mind. But the Glimmer Moon didn't strike its zenith in the night's early hours.

She couldn't truly relax after the book was on the dais and the priests had begun to recite whatever passages tradition declared appropriate for the fourth night of the Festival of Fruits. The memory of her one exposure to the spiders kept her nerves jangled. Urza had been steadily increasing the range and power of his tiny artifacts. What if the combination of wax and armor weren't enough? The level part of the roof where they stood was a small square, three paces on a side, twelve in all, which she traced, first to the left, then to the right.

"Stop pacing, please!" Ratepe begged. "You're making me nervous, and you're making me dizzy."

Xantcha couldn't stand still, so she slid over the edge of the roof and into the garret, where the usable pacing area was somewhat smaller. She'd worked up a clinging sweat before thousands of insects got between her ears and her mind. She put the wax plugs into her ears and got Urza's armor out of the cyst within a few heartbeats, but not before she was gasping on the floor.

Ratepe appeared in the garret window just as she'd recovered enough to stand. He grabbed her hand. Xantcha could feel his excitement, but she'd become deaf even to her own voice. They didn't need words, though, to return to the roof where Ratepe's swinging arm showed her where to look for already fallen *sleepers*.

They'd gotten lucky, she thought, observing in sterile silence. Some of the Efuand Red-Stripes must have known there were Phyrexians within their cadres. How else to explain the swiftness with which the standing Red-Stripes distanced themselves from their fallen comrades or, in one instance that unfolded in the torch-lit area in sight of the guild inn's roof, turned their weapons on one of their own?

From the beginning Ratepe had been concerned with the problem of how unaffected folk might interpret the *sleepers'* collapse. The issue seemed to be resolving itself more favorably, if also more violently, than either he or Xantcha dared hope.

She could see men and women whose mouths were moving, and she wished she could ask Ratepe what they were shouting. Probably she could have asked; it was the hearing of the answer that no wish could grant her.

The first of the shatter spiders did its damage as a section of the Red-Stripe barrack collapsed. She could see the destruction from the roof, which was higher than the first of several walls that encircled the palace. The folk in the plaza wouldn't have seen anything, but they might have heard the walls fall, or the inevitable shouts as flames poked through the rubble. Overturned lamps and such finished what the shatter-spiders had begun.

In all, Xantcha thought, it was going very well. She was surprised that Ratepe wasn't visibly jubilant. She tried to ask him with gestures and the old hand code that she and Urza had devised and that, lacking foresight of this moment, she'd failed to teach him. Ratepe pointed toward Avohir's temple, where the shatter-spiders had yet to produce any obvious damage and no priests, sleeper or otherwise, were visible in the pools of torchlight.

Could Gix have ordered a search that had removed her handiwork? The Phyrexian presence in Avohir's temple had been noticeably less tainted with the glistening oil scent when Xantcha had made her second visit to Pincar City and all but absent this past afternoon.

But if the demon had scoured the temple walls, wouldn't he have checked the Red-Stripe barracks, too, or the plaza itself? Were compleat Phyrexians truly lacking in suspicious imagination?

There was a flurry around the dais. The holy readers were no longer reciting, and other priests had joined them, getting in one another's way as they closed the great book and made haste to get the litter poles beneath it. That would explain Ratepe's distress. He didn't want Avohir's book inside the sanctuary when—if—the altar collapsed.

But there was more she should worry about: Red-Stripes cadres had spilled from the barracks and the temple. They began, ruthlessly, to restore order in the swirling crowd. Their only opposition came from those other Red-Stripes who'd turned on the disabled *sleepers* when the spiders began to scream. It seemed that some *sleepers* and Phyrexians hadn't been affected by Urza's artifacts or, even more incredibly, that some Efuands had so embraced Phyrexian aspirations that they pursued them even after the Phyrexians had fallen.

Xantcha grabbed Ratepe's sleeve and made him face her.

"What's happening down there?" she demanded. "Is it over? Can I unplug my ears?"

He shrugged helplessly and, consumed by frustration, Xantcha stuck a finger in one ear.

The spiders hadn't stopped screaming, and breaking the seal that protected her from their power was an instant, terrible mistake. Xantcha lost all awareness and sense of herself until she was on her back. Ratepe knelt over her, pressing his fingers against her ears. One hand was bloody when she felt strong enough to push them both away. Ratepe helped her stand.

The situation had changed in the plaza. Some of the second wave of Red-Stripes had succumbed to the spiders' screaming. They were literally torn apart by the Efuand mob, and gruesome though that was to watch, it was also instructive. The resistant Red-Stripes were more compleat than Xantcha or the already fallen *sleepers*. Beneath their seemingly mortal skins they had bones of metal, wired sinews, and veins that spilled glistening oil onto the cobblestones.

The oil did truly glisten in malevolent shades of green and purple until someone discovered, as Urza had discovered a very long time ago, that glistening oil burned.

A slow-moving question that was not her own passed through Xantcha's mind, and Ratepe's, too—he staggered and might have fallen from the roof, if Xantcha hadn't grabbed him. Across the plaza, most Efuands were not so fortunate, though they had less far to fall. All whom Xantcha could see shook themselves back to their senses and stood up unharmed. None of the Efuands, including Ratepe, could know what had happened, but Xantcha, who knew a demon's touch when she felt it, looked for a strand of ruby red light and found it sweeping through the smoke above the burning oil.

Gix.

Xantcha's hand rose to her throat. She broke the crystal. Ratepe watched her do it; he asked questions she couldn't hear, and she answered with the demon's name.

Avohir's sweet mercy! She read the prayer from Ratepe's lips.

In the plaza, the frantic priests of Avohir had finally slung the litter poles beneath the holy book in position to carry the volume back to the sanctuary. That building had still to show any signs of damage from the shatter-spiders. The sanctuary might not show such damage to observers on the guild-inn roof. They hadn't expected or intended to brirg the great outer walls down, merely the altar and a dormitory cloister behind the sanctuary. And, of course, the spiral stairway down to the crypt.

Xantcha didn't know whether to relax or ratchet her apprehension tighter when the priests successfully navigated through the plaza throng, and Avohir's holy book disappeared into the sanctuary. Ratepe was obviously more anxious, but his lips moved too quickly for her to read his words, even after she'd asked him to slow down and speak distinctly.

Then something happened to make Ratepe put his hands over his ears. All across the plaza, Efuands hitherto unaffected were reacting to a painful noise, but there were no Red-Stripes—no Phyrexians—to take advantage of them. All of them, *sleepers* and compleat, those already dead and those still alive, simply exploded, bursting like sun-ripened corpses. Sound, as Urza had promised, with the power to shake glistening oil until it pulled apart. The Glimmer Moon had struck its zenith. Everything until that moment had been mere forewarning.

Xantcha's whole body tingled from the inside out. If Urza's armor failed, she'd be dead before she knew she was endangered. She tried to imagine the scenes in all the other cities where she and Urza had planted the spiders. Born Dominarians on their knees, as Ratepe was, perhaps spattered with blood that glistened malevolently in the moonlight. All of them wondering if it were their turn to die.

The Red-Stripe barracks collapsed and, through her feet, Xantcha heard the ground wail. A cloud of dust as large as the guild inn billowed through sanctuary doors, a cloud that rose quickly to hide the temple and half the plaza from Xantcha's view. When dust had settled some, she and every Efuand saw that the great dome above the altar and the gong tower—shadows in the night moments earlier—were both missing.

346

From his knees, Ratepe lowered his hands and pounded the roof with his fists. A god who couldn't protect his book or his sanctuary was apt to lose the faith of his worshipers. Xantcha didn't know the depth of Ratepe's faith, but she guessed it had been shaken to its roots.

It was shaken further when an intense red glow filled Avohir's sanctuary, overflowing through the open doors, the windows, and the roof. Xantcha saw the word fire on Ratepe's lips, but the light wasn't fire. It was Gix.

Xantcha broke the chain that had held Urza's pendant around her neck. She held the crystal up in the crimson light. Very clearly, it was broken and, just as clearly, Urza wasn't coming. He hadn't said where he'd go to watch the Glimmer Moon strike its zenith. He could have gone to the Glimmer Moon itself or he could have remained in the Ohran Ridge cottage.

Or Urza's absence could mean that Gix was not the only demon on Dominarian soil and that Urza was already in a desperate brawl. Urza could 'walk anywhere, but even he couldn't be in two places at once.

The red light within Avohir's sanctuary grew brighter, larger. It fluctuated and emitted serpentine flares that faded slowly in the night. The smell of Phyrexia grew steadily stronger. Xantcha imagined Gix burning and battering his way up from the catacombs. She wondered if he had the power to destroy a city and didn't doubt for a heartbeat that the demon would, if he could.

There was nothing Xantcha could do to stop Gix, and until she was sure that the spiders were exhausted, there was nothing she dared do to spirit herself and Ratepe away.

Vast crimson fingers leapt from the roofless sanctuary. They soared into the sky, then arched toward the plaza. Looking up, Xantcha and everyone else saw that the fingers were hollow, filled with darkness and fanged like serpents. The darkness resembled the upright passageway to Phyrexia that she'd seen in the crypt. Xantcha feared they'd all be sucked into the Fourth Sphere. Ratepe put his arms around her, and Xantcha wrapped hers around him. She wanted to feel his warm, mortal flesh with her fingers and wouldn't have cared if the spiders killed her, except that she wouldn't force Ratepe to watch her die.

She saw a ribbon of silvery light emerge from the center of palace. Diving and soaring, the palace light pierced each serpent and drew them all together with a choking knot before dragging them over the north wall and out to sea.

Xantcha shouted, "Urza!" at Ratepe who needed a few more heartbeats before he could shape his lips around the name.

Gix fought back, but as Xantcha had always suspected, Urza was more than a match for a Phyrexian demon . . . or a Thran one. Neither duelist was visible from the plaza or the roof, though they each knew exactly where the other was. They fought with light and fire, with artifacts and creatures that defied naming in any language Xantcha knew. Gix would have lost quickly if the demon had not aimed most of his destruction at the Efuand survivors in the plaza and thereby forced Urza to defend the innocent.

Then Urza loosed two weapons at once: bolts of lightning to counter Gix's last cowardly thrust and a dragon shaped like the one he'd ridden into Phyrexia, but shaped from golden light. Stars shone through the dragon's wings, but its power was anything but illusory. A jet of intense blue fire shot from its mouth as it began a stoop that would take it into Gix's sanctuary lair.

Gix didn't die fighting; nor did he retreat to Phyrexia. Instead he abandoned Pincar City altogether: a relatively small green-gold streak racing to the south, a half-breath ahead of the dragon's flame.

Xantcha expected the dragon to pursue Gix over the horizon, but it continued its stoop into the ruined sanctuary. She braced herself for the physical shock wave of a crash that never came. A heartbeat, and another, and the dragon lifted into flight again, showing first its wings, then its spidery torso, and at last, clasped in a pair of legs, a book that recently had seemed very large and now looked quite small. The dragon beat its translucent wings twice for altitude. Then it stooped again and set Avohir's holy book on the battered dais before climbing back into the sky.

The dragon circled out to sea—Avohir's home according to myth—and the Efuands still standing, including Ratepe, set up a cheer in its wake, but Urza wasn't finished. He brought the dragon back (Xantcha would have sworn he shrank it just a bit, too) for a gentle glide over the palace roofs. Through its bright, shifting light, Xantcha wasn't sure it had picked something up until it was almost overhead and she could see a frail old man getting the ride of his life.

It was a miracle of another sort that Tabarna's heart didn't fail before the dragon set him down beside Avohir's book. The dragon flew straight up after that and disappeared among the stars.

The Efuands who'd cheered the survival of their book, went wild when they saw their king. Xantcha couldn't get Ratepe's attention no matter how hard she pounded his back or how loudly she shouted, "Is it over? Can I release Urza's armor?"

Yes, it's over, Xantcha. Urza's voice spoke to Xantcha's thoughts.

You heard! she replied, releasing the armor and pulling the wax out of her ears. *You came!* The cheers of the crowd, after total silence, were as deafening as the spiders.

Xantcha had trouble hearing Urza when he said, still in her mind, *I've been here all along, keeping my eyes on Gix. I didn't want to frighten you.*

Waste not, want not. How long had Urza known?

Xantcha hadn't kept her thoughts private. Urza pulled the question from her mind and answered it. *Since the priest in the orchard. I went back to all the haunted places. I saw how the Phyrexians had crept into my world again. I found Tabarna in a cell beneath the palace—he was quite mad, but still himself. The Phyrexians needed to trot him out periodically, and they could only do what they did to Mishra because he carried the Weakstone. So I stole Tabarna from them and hid him on another plane.*

That, I confess, was the act that brought Gix here to Pincar City. Since then, everything I've done—everything I've had you do—has been building toward this moment. I healed Tabarna. Madness, you know, sinks deep roots in a man's soul once he's seen sights and thought thoughts no man should see or think. There are some moments he'll never remember again, moments such as I wish I could forget, Xantcha. The Shratta could not be deceived, so they were killed while Tabarna watched. But he'll live another ten years and sire another son or two. I guarantee it.

Xantcha had warned her slave, assume that if you've thought about it Urza knows it. Then she had failed to remember her own advice.

"You've had reason to be suspicious, Xantcha. There's never been anyone who could do for me what I've done for Tabarna."

Urza was on the roof with them, looking very ordinary. He had no trouble getting Ratepe's attention but was unprepared when Ratepe threw himself into a joyous, tearful embrace.

The affection Efuands had for their elderly king—whose speech none of them could hope to hear through their shouting—was nothing Xantcha wanted to understand, though it was also clear that Urza had done exactly what was necessary to insure that the realm would recover from its long battering.

Xantcha stood a bit apart from Ratepe and Urza, giving herself a few moments to consider all that she'd just learned. She stayed apart when Urza extended his hand.

"What happens next?" she demanded thinking deliberately of Gix.

"I go to Koilos."

She folded her arms. "Not alone. Not if you're going after Gix."

Urza frowned, then sighed. "No, I suppose not." He turned to Ratepe. "And you, Brother, I suppose you'll want to come, too."

Chapter 24

The sun just had risen over the Kher Ridge, far to the east of Gulmany island and Efuan Pincar. It would be a summer day with clear air and high clouds that wouldn't come close to raining on these desert-dry stones. Koilos, the Secret Heart, was on the other side of the mountain where Xantcha and Ratepe rested, waiting for Ratepe to recover from the three-step 'walk from Pincar City. Urza was already at the cavern. He'd sworn he wouldn't go looking for Gix until they arrived, unless Gix came looking for him.

Ratepe sat on the ground, chafing his arms and legs against the morning chill and the shock of healing.

"You think he knows everything?"

Xantcha had just finished telling him what had passed between her and Urza on the guild-inn roof not an hour earlier. She was impatient to yawn out the sphere and get into the air, even though she knew there'd be no part for her or Ratepe to play in the coming fight. More than three thousand years ago she'd watched as other demons thrust Gix down a fumarole to punishment that had proved less than eternal. She expected Urza to do a better job and wanted to watch him doing it.

"He's still calling you Mishra."

Ratepe nodded several times. "True enough. But he was something in the sky last night over Pincar City—a little while ago—whenever. I got used to the idea that he was the crazed, foolish man who lived on the other side of the wall. I let myself forget what I knew he was, through the Weakstone. He was the man who came within an hour of destroying the world."

"You weren't the only one," Xantcha confessed. "You ready to finish this?"

"All in a morning's work," Ratepe joked grimly as he stood. "Avohir's mercy, I should be happy. I am happy, but inside, I feel like I felt after I saw my father dead, or when we were falling through that storm over the ocean and we were floating in your sphere. I don't feel a part of anything that's around me. If I ask myself what happens next, there's nothing there, not even a sunrise."

Xantcha replied, "Urza 'walked us under the sun. That's why we missed the sunrise, and I'll try not to drop the sphere through a storm again." She left Ratepe's other observations behind on the ground as the sphere flowed around them and lifted them into the air.

Urza waited not far from the place where Xantcha had read the Thran glyphs. He was taller than any mortal man and clad in his full panoply with robes armored in the colors of sorcery. His hand circled the gnarled wood of a war staff capped with a peculiar blue-gray metal. His eyes were hard and faceted, as if he'd see nothing so puny as flesh, but his voice was strong and vibrant when he greeted them.

"Gix is here, waiting for me."

The scents of Phyrexia were indeed in the air: glistening oil, Fourth Sphere fumes, and the malevolence Xantcha recognized as Gix. She yawned out her armor while Urza laid hands on Ratepe's shoulders. The young Efuand glowed like swamp water once they entered the cavern. Sunlight ended ten paces into the upper, glyph-covered chamber. Urza's war staff emitted a steady light from the edges of its many blades. The light reached to the glyph-covered walls.

"Phyrexian, you say?" Urza asked.

"Close enough. Do you want to read them through my eyes?"

"Not yet. After. I've waited too long to taste vengeance against the Phyrexian who destroyed my brother. It's hard enough to know that Gix is one of the Thran, one of the ones who got away, I don't want to know the rest, not yet. And once I know it, then I'll decide if it's worth remembering. I have much to do, Xantcha. I cannot always embrace the truths that might be written on stone walls. I know that's been hard for you, but it's been even harder for me."

The ultimate confession from the crazed and foolish man who lived on the other side of the wall?

They continued to the rear of the chamber, where Ratepe had spotted a passage. Without torches or powerstone eyes, he had been unable to explore it. The passage sloped steeply downward and was marred by deep gouges in the stone. Xantcha walked on Urza's left, a half-pace behind. Ratepe held a similar place on Urza's right.

"We took everything," Ratepe whispered, softly, but in Koilos a whisper carried like a shout. Urza didn't tell him to be quiet, so Ratepe continued. "The chamber below, where we found the stones, we stripped it bare. We needed the metal. At the end we were so desperate for metal, any metal, that we opened tombs and took the grave goods from our dead and fueled our smelters with their bones."

"So did we," Urza assured him. "So did we."

Xantcha saw light ahead, the harsh, gray light of Phyrexia.

The second chamber of Koilos was as large as the first and empty, except for Gix who stood somewhat behind dead center. Xantcha expected some preliminary taunting and boasting, but neither Urza nor Gix was a young mortal with an itch for glory. They'd come to kill or be killed. All their whys had been buried long ago.

Gix attacked first as they emerged from the passageway. He didn't waste time or effort with side attacks against Xantcha or Ratepe. They weren't innocents with rights to Urza's protection. They'd come of their own free will, and they'd be meat, at best, if Urza failed to win.

The rubine gem in the demon's bulging forehead shone bright. A thumbnail-sized spot of the same color appeared on Urza's breast. Heartbeats later, a boulder, Urza high and Urza wide, bilious green and glassy, stood where Urza had stood between Xantcha and Ratepe. The boulder blew apart an instant later. Fists of stone hammered Xantcha from face to toes and threw her back against the chamber wall. Ratepe was on the floor, covered in a thick layer of dust. Two counterspinning coils of fire and light whirled around the demon until he spread his arms to vanquish them.

An ambulator took shape, closer to Urza than to Gix. The ambulator heaved and rotated upward, sprouting a toothy hole of a mouth and many viscous, reaching arms. An arm came close enough to Xantcha that she judged it prudent to put a little distance between herself and the duel. She scuttled crabwise along the curving chamber wall and was relieved to see Ratepe do the same on the other side.

Urza spoke a word, and the ambulator-creature became a sooty smear. He did nothing at all that Xantcha could see, and yet Gix was slammed against the chamber's far wall. A crystal sarcophagus surrounded the demon. Xantcha thought that might be the end, but purple fumes rose from the crystal, and Urza disappeared as manic wailing filled the barren chamber. Gix shook off the dissolving crystal and clambered to his metallic feet.

Xantcha took heart from the fact that the demon wasn't claiming victory by targeting her or Ratepe. His oddly shaped head swiveled frantically. The rubine light danced over the naked stone, leaving a trail of smoke as Gix sought a target. Twice the demon blew futile craters in the rock, but he was ready when ghostly blue arms seized him from behind. Urza landed on his back in the middle of the chamber. The impact shook jagged stones the size of a man's torso from the ceiling.

Both combatants righted themselves and backed away from each other.

The testing phase was over; the duel began in earnest with flurries of attacks that ebbed and flowed too fast for Xantcha's eyes. The demon was stronger, cleverer, and much more resilient than she'd believed after seeing him flee the dragon in Pincar City. She thought of the excoriation. It had taken a clutch of demons to wrestle Gix into that fumarole. She suspected that he was the only one who'd survived.

Urza succeeded in melting away one of Gix's legs, though that was little more than inconvenience in a battle that wasn't about physical injury. And though Urza seemed to have the advantage more often than not, he couldn't deliver a killing attack. Not that he didn't try a in a hundred different ways from elemental ice to conjured beasts and the ghosts of artifacts he and Mishra had wielded against each other. Gix countered them all, sometimes barely, with an equally bewildering assortment of arcane memories and devices.

Eventually, when it had become apparent that neither flash nor guile was going tilt the balance, Urza and Gix locked themselves in a contest of pure will that manifested itself in an increasingly complex web of blue-white and crimson light. The spindle-shaped web stretched between Urza's eyes and Gix's gem-studded forehead. At its widest, which was also its middle and the middle of the chamber, the web did not descend to the floor. Sparing nothing for effect, the web gave off neither heat nor sound and endured, without really changing, until Xantcha had to breathe again.

How long, she asked herself, could they remain enrapt in each other? Her best answer: for a very long time. She got up on her feet.

"Look at Urza's eyes!" Ratepe shouted from the other side of the chamber.

Xantcha had to walk closer than she considered wise before she found a slit in the web that let her look down the spindle to Urza's face. She didn't see anything strange—nothing stranger than two specks as bright as the sun—but she didn't have Ratepe's rapport with the Weakstone. And, as Ratepe's voice had seemed to have no effect on the duel, she asked, "What am I looking for?"

"You can't see everything changing . . . coming back from the past, or going back to it?"

She started to say that she couldn't see anything changing and swallowed the words. Shadows were growing in the Koilos chamber. Not shadows cast by the web's light, but shadows cast by time, growing more substantial as each moment passed. Metal columns grew along the walls. Great machines, worthy of Phyrexia, loomed up from the floor.

Beneath the widest part of the light-woven spindle a low platform came into being. Mirrors sprang up in a circle behind both Gix and Urza, behind Xantcha and Ratepe, as well. An object similar to Avohir's great book, but made from metal like Urza's staff, grew atop the platform. As Xantcha watched, Phyrexian glyphs formed on the smooth metal leaves.

Xantcha was waiting for those glyphs to become legible when dull-colored metal sprang out of the central platform. The metal shaped itself into four rising prongs, like uplifted hands.

"His eyes, Xantcha! His eyes! They're going back. Gix is dragging them back through time!"

The Weakstone and the Mightstone had pulled out of Urza's skull and were advancing through the spindle.

Gix had said, The Thran are waiting. . . .

And when the powerstones merged into the prongs, Urza would be in the hands of the Thran.

Ratepe shouted, "We can stop them."

"No."

"We can!"

"Not if you're getting influence from the Weakstone. It's Thran. It belongs to Gix. No wonder he was waiting here." Xantcha would have sobbed, if the armor had let her.

"We can stop this, Xantcha. Gix is sending the powerstones into the past. All we have to do is get there first."

Xantcha shook her head—never mind that she couldn't see Ratepe. "That's the Weakstone influencing you," she shouted. "Gix. Phyrexia." Her gut said anything she did would only make things worse, if anything could be worse than watching Urza become a tool of the Phyrexian Thran. She was paralyzed, frightened as she had never been before—except, perhaps, at the very beginning when the vat-priests told the newts Listen, and obey.

"Meet me in the light, Xantcha!"

On the other side of the spindle, Ratepe thrust his hands into the web. From Xantcha's side, looking into the spindle, his flesh had become transparent and his bones gleamed with golden light.

"Now, Xantcha!"

The powerstones had traveled half the distance to the prongs. The etched-metal glyphs were legible, if she could have concentrated and read them. She walked to the right place, the place opposite Ratepe, then hugged herself tightly, tucking her hands beneath her arms, lest she move without thinking.

"I need to be sure!" she shouted.

"Be sure that Gix wants the Weakstone and Mightstone, not you and me. At least we can give him what he doesn't want. It's all we've got to give."

Xantcha reached for the spindle. The light repelled Urza's armor. A good omen or a bad one? For whom? She didn't know and tucked her hands beneath her arms again.

"I can't, Ratepe. I'm Phyrexian. I can't trust myself. I'm always wrong."

The powerstones were three-quarters of the way. The devices beyond the ring of mirrors thrummed to life.

"I'm not! And I'm never wrong about you. Meet me in the light, Xantcha. We're going to end the war."

Xantcha shed her armor and thrust her hands into the spindle. *Begone! Listen and obey. Begone! Do not interfere.*

The demon's anger, roaring through Xantcha's mind could have been deception. Gix should have known that she would, in the end, disobey his command, in which case Gix had outwitted them all and wanted her to reach into the light. But, on the chance that he wasn't quite that imaginative, Xantcha extended her arms to their fullest reach.

Time and space changed around her. She'd left her body behind. To the right, the Weakstone and the Mightstone, two great glowing spheres, rolling toward her, fighting, losing. To the left was the unspeakable, blood-red maw of Gix, calling the stones, sucking them to their doom.

Straight ahead stood Ratepe, son of Mideah, with a radiant smile and outstretched arms.

Their fingers touched.

Gix turned his wrath on her and on Ratepe. It was the last

thing the demon did. Xantcha felt the stones free themselves to destroy the enemy they'd been created to destroy.

As for her and Ratepe, they were together.

Nothing else mattered.

And Rat's face, joyous as they embraced, was a glorious sight to carry into the darkness.

* * * * *

For Urza, the battle had ended suddenly, in a matter of moments and without easy explanation. One moment Mishra and Xantcha had been blocking the light, arms outstretched and reaching toward each other, not him. The next moment—less than a moment—a fireball had filled the lower chamber. Once again his eyes had lifted him out of death's closing fist. His Thran eyes had guarded this cavern for four thousand years before he and his brother found them, and they still preferred to see it in its glory, filled with engines, artifacts and powerstone mirrors.

Or should he say his Phyrexian eyes?

It scarcely mattered. Urza's borrowed eyes preserved him as the fireball raged like a short-lived sun.

The sun-ball consumed itself . . . quickly, Urza thought, though he remembered Argoth and that the time he'd spent completely within the powerstones could not be measured. As his eyes recorded it, there was fire and then the fire was gone, two edges of the cut made by an infinitely sharp knife, without a gap between them.

There'd been no visions, as there had been the other times when the Mightstone and Weakstone had held him in their power. No explanations, however cryptic. Nothing, except a dusty voice that said, *It is over.* He had a sense, much less than a vision, that Mishra had grasped Xantcha's hand just before the explosion consumed them.

In the aftermath silence reigned. A natural silence: Urza wasn't deaf, but there was nothing left to hear. Urza thought light, and it flowed outward from him.

"Xantcha," he called, because he'd been without his brother before.

Her name echoed off the chamber's scorched walls. He was alone.

At the end, she'd chosen Mishra, charming, lively Mishra.

Urza wished them joy, wherever they'd gone. He wished them peace, far away from any Phyrexian or Thran design. They had earned peace, vanquishing their shared enemy: Gix.

The demon had vanished within the powerstone-derived fireball. There was nothing left. Urza's eyes told him that. He could hear them now, faint and smug in his skull.

The truth was written on the upper chamber ceiling. The Thran had fought among themselves, fought as only brothers could fight, with a blindness that transcended hatred. Remembering the battle the Weakstone and Mightstone had shown him the last time he'd come to Koilos, Urza realized he truly did not know which army had escaped to Phyrexia, if, indeed, Xantcha's Ineffable hadn't slipped away to create Phyrexia before that fatal day.

Standing in the Koilos cavern, Urza concluded that he'd have to continue his experiments with time because he'd have to go back himself, not to a moment in his own lifetime, but to the Thran, Gix and all the others. . . .

"Not yet," Urza cautioned himself.

This would be a cunning war. Gix was still extant in the past; Yawgmoth and the other Phyrexians were in the past, the present, and the future, too. The battle—the real and final battle for Dominaria—had, in a sense, just begun. It would be fought in the past and in the future.

And Urza would have no allies, none at all: not Tawnos, not Mishra.

Urza recalled light and moved along the blackened corridor to the surface. No real body. No real need for light, or anything else.

A weight tugged against him.

Xantcha's heart, which the powerstones, his eyes, had preserved.

He wasn't alone.

Urza would never be alone.

Continue the journey into the depths of a reborn and frighteningly hostile world with the two newest titles in the ODYSSEY™ Cycle

As the people of Dominaria struggle to survive in a brutal post-apocalyptic world, an artifact of frightening might is discovered. All those who lust for power, whether wizards, fighters, or kings, are determined to own it at any cost. Little do they know that their actions have consequences— consequences that will determine the fate of the world.

Chainer's Torment
Book II
Scott McGough

January 2002

Judgment™
Book III
Will McDermot

May 2002

Now available:

Odyssey
Book I
Vance Moore

The mysteries of Dominaria are at your fingertips...

The Secrets of Magic
An anthology edited by Jess Lebow

Ancient caches of artifacts await discovery.
The origins of potent spells rest lost between
the pages of archaic tomes. The evolution of
monstrous beasts lies shrouded in mystery.
No one knows how much has been left untold.

Until now.

This new collection of stories from a wide range
of authors delves deep into the long-buried secrets
of the MAGIC: THE GATHERING® world, uncovering
facts never before revealed. Featuring stories by
MAGIC® authors J. Robert King, Scott McGough,
Vance Moore, Philip Athans, Nate Levin, Jim Bishop,
Chris Pramas, Cory J. Herndon, Will McDermott,
and Paul B. Thompson.

March 2002

Legend of the Five Rings

Change is on the wind. . . .

The Four Winds Saga

Prelude
THE STEEL THRONE
Edward Bolme

The Empire teeters on the brink of disaster. To save his beloved realm, the emperor must make the ultimate sacrifice, entering the very realm of death. But in trying to save his people, he opens the door for his worst enemy to seize power.

March 2002

First Scroll
WIND OF HONOR
Ree Soesbee

As the eldest child of the emperor, Tsudao's duty is clear—her life for the Empire, her sword for service, and honor above all. Now more than ever, her courage, her faith, and her integrity will be put to the ultimate test.

August 2002

Second Scroll
WIND OF WAR
Jess Lebow

The forgotten son of the emperor, Akodo Kaneka is the most renowned warrior in all the lands. As the Empire spirals into chaos and the clans bicker among themselves, the forgotten son must find aid among the common people.

December 2002